D0108872

BEHIND
THE
LIE

Also available by Emilya Naymark

Hide in Place

BEHIND THE LIE

A NOVEL

EMILYA NAYMARK

CROOKED LANE

NEW YORK

Copyright © 2022 by Emilya Naymark

Published in the United States by Crooked Lane Books, an imprint of The Quick Brown Fox & Company LLC.

Crooked Lane Books and its logo are trademarks of The Quick Brown Fox & Company LLC.

Library of Congress Catalog-in-Publication data available upon request.

ISBN (hardcover): 978-1-64385-892-0
ISBN (ebook): 978-1-64385-893-7

Cover design by Nicole Lecht

Printed in the United States.

www.crookedlanebooks.com

Crooked Lane Books
34 West 27th St., 10th Floor
New York, NY 10001

First Edition: February 2022

10 9 8 7 6 5 4 3 2 1

For Keith and Ian
Again and always

PROLOGUE

July

OLIVER DUBOIS RAMMED a pickup truck through his front door on a sweaty midnight in July, at the tail end of a massive block party.

It wasn't his truck, and the street was closed to traffic, so the vehicle's emergence out of darkness and slow rumble up Oak Drive scattered neighbors and guests alike into confused groups on candlelit lawns. With a grind of gears, Oliver veered a sharp left and jumped the curb onto the Dubois front walk. The guests, addled by twelve hours' worth of food and alcohol, gawped as the truck butted the front steps as if it were a drunk pausing to gather its thoughts.

Oliver idled for a minute, and the instant a neighbor dropped his Solo cup of sangria and took a step forward, he revved the engine, vaulted the four steps, hesitated, then gunned the truck's snout into the front door, splintering it.

"Whoa, whoa!" the neighbor shouted, and then everyone ran toward the noise, the children weaving in and out between the adults, feet bare on the asphalt and grass.

Oliver didn't listen. The vehicle bucked again under his foot and crashed through the doorway, disappearing inside the astonishingly large new opening.

Locked inside a sedan across the road, Holly Dubois clawed at the fastened door handle, horrified by the sight of her husband destroying their home. The driver gripped her wrist and held tight.

"Let me out," Holly said, in a voice so low and hoarse it hurt.

The driver clutched her wrist tighter. They would have been away by now, blocks if not miles away, if it hadn't been for the police barricades someone had set across the side road to keep the party enclosed. The barricades should not have been there—only the main road was supposed to be blocked. Their car had crept, headlights off, up a dark street parallel to the party, and made the turn that would have taken them to the highway, only to face the blue barriers and, shortly after, the marauding truck.

The driver let go of Holly's wrist and reversed the car. Holly scrambled for the door again, struggled to unbuckle her belt, her shoulder a howl of red pain.

"You know what happens if you leave," the driver said.

Holly clenched her jaw and pressed her fingers against her eyelids, though this did nothing to erase the image of her husband behind the wheel of the truck.

A group ran past them, their voices trailing in the dark, reaching Holly through a crack in the window. "Holy shit, is that Oliver?" and "Don't move him!" and "Call 911" and in the background already: a siren, then another, and another. Then, "Has anyone seen Holly?" followed by, "Who has the kids?" Finally, the police cars and an ambulance, the EMTs spilling out, the crowd parting.

In the sedan, silence.

Some eight hours earlier, the height of the party had seen over four hundred people milling up and down Oak Drive, drinking beer and cocktails, ladling sangria from giant tubs with ice islands. An entire tent had been devoted to food, another to games. The children squealed as they jumped inside bounce houses and on trampolines, and the adults yammered about the weather, sports, and local school intrigues.

Oak Drive was the friendliest block in Sylvan, a small municipality in upstate New York with the winding routes, forests, and horse farms reminiscent of quaint eighteenth-century paintings and the split-levels, colonials, and white-collar politics of suburbia.

The Dubois family, or more specifically, Holly, was the social center of the town. Her clan had lived in Sylvan for three generations, in the very house now sporting a truck-sized hole in its facade.

As the car backed up, with care, its headlights still off, a child wandered away from the noise and lights, his shoulder-length hair backlit.

"Kiki," Holly shouted, loud enough for her son to snap his head in the car's direction, but it was too late. The car was rolling backward, around a corner, doing a K-turn. She rattled the door and lowered the window, aiming to climb out, but the window stopped at a five-inch gap, and she felt her chest contract, as if an iron hoop crushed her ribs. *This is how people have heart attacks and die*, she thought (and under that, *I don't want to die*).

"Let me out," she said, once she could breathe again.

"Fuck you," said her companion.

The breeze changed then, and an acrid odor swept up the streets, making Holly's eyes water, settling grit in her throat.

"My God," someone yelled as they drove past a manicured lawn. "Fire!"

The driver tapped the brakes, letting the car slow, made a sudden left, and took them back toward the block party and the smoke. At the bottom of the hill, hidden from view by a hedge of spruces, bright yellow and red flames snapped into the night air, blackening the siding of Forty-Six Oak Drive.

Dimmed windows, empty driveway.

Empty driveway. With a jolt, Holly realized the blue pickup truck now blanketed with siding and drywall inside her living room belonged here, to the couple who'd moved in six months ago. To the body still sprawled, as far as she knew, in a pool of blood in the den.

A soft sound escaped her associate, a hitched breath. Then more sirens, noise, and shouting, and they were reversing again, a squeal of tires, and off, away.

CHAPTER

1

July: Laney

Laney Bird, momentarily overcome with panic, strained to find her son amid the surging, shouting crowd. Then her training kicked in, partially clearing the fog of day-long drinking, and she steadied, bare feet firm on her lawn, hand brushing against her hip where her gun would have been if she'd been working.

But she wasn't working; she was instead one of the ten hosts of this monstrous party—more of a street fair as far as she was concerned. Who had block parties with four hundred guests? Her neighborhood did, that's who. And things had decidedly turned hairy. She cataloged the dozen or so people dialing 911, the Duboises' wrecked living room, that obscenely incongruous truck inside her best friend's home.

It was no accident she'd been standing on the sidewalk between her house and the Dubois driveway during Oliver's dramatic act of demolition. She'd spent most of the party halfway down the block in the game tent, taking on foosball opponents between swigs of sangria. At some point during those hours, her son had readied an amp and microphones and played a set with his HS jazz band. Later she glimpsed him by their house, speaking with a girl. The light had faded by then and she didn't recognize his friend, but neither did she try. She'd been practicing the Zen of Leaving Her Boy Alone, with varying success, since his last birthday.

Twenty minutes before midnight, before Oliver put an end to the festivities, she gave in to her impulses and texted her son, reminding him of their mutually agreed-upon curfew.

As she looked up from her phone and toward her house, she saw a figure dart away from her garage, cross the street, and melt into the unlit alley beyond. Unease soured the wine in her uncomfortably full stomach, and she poured the rest of her drink onto the lawn before jogging homeward. A quick walk-through showed her home to be dark, empty, cool, and quiet, though tinged with an unfamiliar scent, as if the party had infiltrated her rooms with its smoky, barbecue-perfumed and sunblock-ridden breath. She texted Alfie again, but her son was either ignoring her or busy. By the time the blue pickup shoved itself into her friend's doorway a few minutes later, she was already balanced on the edge between irritation and worry.

The crowd parted for the EMS and police cars, and Laney stepped aside, her stomach cramping with adrenaline. When she heard the fire engines and caught a whiff of burning wood, she gave up any pretense of holding herself together and ran down the hill toward the flames, her shouts adding to the steady roar rising above her normally peaceful neighborhood.

The throng of guests multiplied. Some of the people who'd gone home earlier in the evening came back, crowding either in front of the spectacularly ravaged Dubois house or the more mod-estly ruined Forty-Six Oak. The fire had started in one of the back rooms, put forth enough flames and plumes of noxious smoke to terrify everyone, blackened the yard-facing siding, and was doused before causing serious damage. At least half of Sylvan's firefighters had already been at the party, and they called the engine house within minutes of noticing the fire.

Laney scanned the huddled groups for her son, then texted him once more. It's not that she thought he had anything to do with this fire. Why would she? She didn't think this at all.

And yet. A tightness settled in her chest.

The second ambulance of the night screeched to the curb in front of the still-smoking Forty-Six Oak and two young EMTs jumped out, removed a stretcher, and hurried inside, brushing past the firefighters on the porch. A set of police officers followed. At the other end of the street, the first ambulance bleeped and edged past the emergency vehicles, carrying away Oliver Dubois.

"Hey, Dan!" somebody yelled out behind Laney. Everyone knew everyone here, and now she also recognized the EMT as a nephew or cousin belonging to one of the families on the block. The man waved and disappeared indoors.

A sharp finger tapped Laney's shoulder, and she started, turning to face Alfie, her only progeny and often greatest aggravation. At fifteen, Alfie was tall, nearly six feet, and lanky, with blond curls falling onto his forehead (to hide the acne pinpricks above his brows) and cropped short along the sides and back. His eyes slid past her and toward the house. Though he remained just outside the full glare of streetlights and floodlights and emergency lights, she saw he was blushing, his pale face darker, his cheeks fuller seeming.

"Where were you?" she asked. She hadn't meant to say it like that, with suspicion, but the day was taking its toll and the fire engines were not making her calmer.

He didn't answer right away, studied the soot-streaked siding in front of them. Then he shrugged.

She couldn't help herself—grabbed his right hand and lifted it, squinting at the red-knuckled skin, the torn cuticles. No sign of soot. No odor of kerosene or lighter fluid. Only an angry scratch across his forearm, still beaded with bright blood. But it was summer, and scratches, bug bites, and random bruises afflicted them both. She started to ask about it, but he tugged away.

"Nice," he said. "Good to know where I stand." His eyes met hers for the briefest second, and she felt her own face warm with embarrassment. The past was the past, and she had to trust him. Or pretend to unless presented with evidence. He shook his head, spun on his heel, and marched up the hill toward their home.

At least she hoped he was marching home.

She rolled her shoulders to release the tension gathering there. He had the right to be angry with her, but really, after what happened last year, what could she do with herself? With her dread?

Worse, even if she mastered her own misgivings, the police had a record of him setting fire to the school his freshman year (accidentally, of course; they all knew that) and . . . well. That other fire, the one not at the school—no one ever proved anything. And in any case, it would have been self-defense. She raised her chin. If the police questioned Alfie tonight, at least he was (superficially) clean. She could swear to that.

When Dan the EMT and his partner emerged from the blackened doorway, they were rushing out a gurney and on it a limp figure, belted in sideways, bloodstains seeping through clothes, face obscured by an oxygen mask.

The crowd behind her gasped, and the chatter grew in volume. Laney, who had seen enough in her NYPD past to recognize exactly what was wrong with the victim and lived on this block long enough to identify him even through the bruising and cuts about his head, felt the last remnants of drunkenness vaporize. What the hell happened tonight on her perfect little street?

"Dan, who is that?" someone else called out. "Is he okay?"

The EMT looked up. "Volkin," he said, as they folded the gurney into the ambulance. "Says he lives here. Gunshot wound. Got him right in the butt cheek."

"That's a heck of a lot of blood for a butt shot," yet another neighbor said.

"Is he dead?" the first someone asked, fear and excitement in his voice.

"Not yet," Dan said, slammed the ambulance door and started the siren.

2

July: Laney

B ETWEEN ONE AND five AM, Laney drifted back and forth from the Dubois house to Forty-Six Oak, eavesdropping on the conversations, the conjectures, the hearsay, grasping for an explanation. She also, repeatedly and to no avail, tried Holly's phone. Holly Dubois was not answering.

Around one thirty in the morning, Holly's brother strapped her shell-shocked kids into his SUV while the youngest, Kiki, shrieked loud enough to draw police attention. He shouted that Mommy was taken by a dark-blue car but neither the boy's uncle nor Laney nor the cops were able to extract further details from the child, and he dissolved into a full-on tantrum as his older siblings pressed their hands over their ears and squeezed their eyes shut.

In the past twenty-four hours, Oak Drive had transformed from a peaceful, tidy, tree-lined haven to a bedraggled dump, riotous with garbage, clamorous with chatter. Police tape surrounded the two houses of interest, and cruisers guarded the north and south ends of the street. Cops collected evidence, combed backyards, questioned everyone before letting them leave. A news van, barred from entering the street, lurked by the corner, the reporter poking her microphone at people's faces, her cameraman a shadow behind her.

Those already interviewed by the police stumbled to their cars as the sky lightened to a gentle pink. Another fine, tender July day waited in the wings.

Twice during those early hours Laney spied Alfie sitting on their front steps, arms wrapped tightly around his knees, hair in his eyes. Whenever she attempted an approach, he'd stand and sidle into their dark house, closing the door firmly behind him. And every time he did this, she thought of the figure separating from her garage last night, its quick scurry across the street. Although she'd been too far to see clearly, she was positive it wasn't her son—too short, the strides too shallow, dainty. A friend? A partygoer looking for a bathroom?

She debated texting Alfie and asking but held back. Better to ask in person, after they both slept.

It never ceased to amaze her how a relationship with one's child could be so much like a relationship with a spouse—the same tiptoeing around each other's pain points, the same overblown arguments over trivialities, the same tearful apologies after tempers cooled. Did everyone go through this, or just her and her oddball kid? Holly always seemed to have her offspring in loving hand, indulgent and sweet, raising absolute angels despite her softness.

Speaking of, where in the world was Holly? If there's one thing everyone knew about Holly Dubois, it's that she always put family first. Laney couldn't think of a single good reason Holly would have vanished but envisioned plenty of bad ones.

She raked her short hair, so tired she periodically lost feeling in her face. Still, she walked up the debris-strewn street, retrieving paper plates, Solo cups, and general party refuse, dumping them into garbage cans. What else was she going to do? Go to bed? Unthinkable.

The first hint of heat brushed the lawns, and a filmy vapor thickened the air.

"Hey, Laney." A young cop waved her over, a newish patrolman named Horace something. By now Laney knew everyone on Sylvan's police force at least on a nod-and-handshake basis. Although her own involvement with the SPD hadn't always been innocuous, she'd had the opportunity to work with several of its detectives and patrolmen since landing the job at Boswell Investigative Services.

"Hi, Horace." She waved back.

He leaned against the cruiser that blocked the north end of the street.

"What the flying fuck went on here last night?" he asked.

"I was gonna ask you that, actually."

He shook his head. "I don't know a thing."

"Any idea who shot Step Volkin? Or why?"

Horace gave a convoluted shrug-nod, implying the answer might be yes but he couldn't say more. Except then he said, "And nobody knows where his wife is either."

Laney put her hands on her hips and squinted down the block. So, Vera Volkin and Holly Dubois, both MIA? She didn't like that one bit.

Six months ago, the FOR SALE sign in front of the decrepit house at the bottom of the hill disappeared and a glamorously mysterious duo moved in. The Volkins had arrived in the coldest, stormiest months, when the entire town stayed indoors and burned the bejesus out of its fireplaces and wood-burning stoves. The young couple kept to themselves until sometime in April, when all of a sudden Vera Volkin began showing up at Holly's family Sunday fundays. She often brought small amounts of unusual foods—beet-and-pickle salad, crepes with salmon roe, cranberry mousse—that sat barely eaten on delicate porcelain dishes as Holly's family chowed down on lasagna, wings, and bean dip. The few times Laney—who had a standing invitation to the Dubois household—attempted a conversation with Vera, she found the woman dismissive. Downright rude, even. But Holly seemed to enjoy her company; the company of Step Volkin even more, her face pinking whenever they spoke.

Horace stretched, cracked his neck, yawned (making her yawn), and said, "Did Ed call you?"

That would be Ed Boswell, one of the detectives in Sylvan, more than an acquaintance, not quite a friend.

"Not yet, but I got nothing anyway." Except that person in her garage, who most certainly had nothing to do with the Volkins and possibly everything to do with her son. She yawned again, her eyes tearing. "Listen, I need to get to sleep. I have work this afternoon."

She walked away, thinking the detectives had their hands full. Step Volkin could have been shot by any of over four hundred suspects, including his wife. Or, for that matter, Oliver Dubois. She shook her head. No, of course not Oliver; what was she thinking? Nonetheless, the least Oliver faced were car theft charges for taking the Volkins' truck. If Oliver had been under the influence, he'd probably lose his license, or worse. She assumed he'd been drinking during the party, since everyone was, but she couldn't for the life of her remember how he'd acted. He was simply Oliver—blending into the scenery despite his size, forever overshadowed by his vivacious, affable wife.

It was almost six AM, a Sunday. She figured she'd be able to get maybe five hours' sleep, then go to the hospital and visit Oliver before heading to work. He'd always been kind to her, and if there was anything she could do, pull any strings to help him, she would do it. Although after her divorce she'd drawn a tight circle around herself and Alfie, unable and unwilling to let anybody in, Holly had squeezed through. Cheerful, helpful, generous Holly had become Laney's point of light, her way of looking at the world so much brighter and cleaner than Laney's. Any assistance Oliver needed, Laney would offer. But more than that, she had to understand what happened. Such drama doesn't descend one day from a clear blue sky. What had her friend been hiding? And how could Laney help?

Laney's modest three-bedroom colonial was cool, dim, and quiet, a relief after the chaos outside. The door to Alfie's room stood closed, and she hovered before it in an exhaustion-induced stupor, debating peeking in. To make sure he was home. Safe.

Instead, she pressed her ear to the door and held her breath. After nearly a minute, she was rewarded with a rustling sound from the other side. Home, check. Safe enough, check.

A small part of her relaxed and she breathed out, temporarily mollifying her abiding and unacknowledged fear that one day he'd not be there.

She'd been nearly asleep on her feet for hours and should have crashed instantly, but the image of the person slinking from her garage minutes before Oliver's Drive of Destruction played on repeat against her closed eyelids. No matter how she turned, comfort eluded her. Who was it, and what were they doing in her house? And what did her son know about it?

CHAPTER

3

July: Laney

H ER GUN WAS gone.
Not in its holster, which lay deflated and lonesome inside the gun safe. The empty gun safe. The very, terribly, absolutely empty gun safe. Absurdly, Laney patted her hips and pockets, as if she'd—oh who knows, maybe in her sleep—stuffed a small Glock into her waistband without thinking.

Her bedside table, the top shelf of the living room bookcase, the kitchen counter. She hadn't left her gun on any of those, and why would she? She was paranoid about securing her weapon. Locking it away after work was so ingrained in her muscle memory, she'd go to her safe even if she didn't carry that day.

Heart in throat, she performed one more sweep of the house. Nope.

Despite her intentions, Laney had slept in, startled awake at noon by a medley of garbage truck and hysterical dogs outside her window. Alfie was already elsewhere, the door to his room shut and his bicycle absent from its usual nook behind the shed.

With shaking hands, she texted him, a furious heat suffusing her face.

Where are you?
No response.

Did you get into the gun safe?

This time the three typing dots came up instantly. *NO!*

The muscle under her eye twitched, and she pressed a finger against it.

Typed, *Who was here last night?*

No response.

Come home.

Why?

Because I've had it with tiptoeing around your freakin' secrets. She stared at the unsent message for ten full seconds, then carefully backspaced and deleted it.

She'd have thrown her phone against the wall if she thought it would survive. Instead, she breathed out a series of quick breaths to calm herself and tried to think past the blood yammering in her ears. The safe had a keypad lock, and she certainly never shared the combination with him. No, of course it wasn't him. If he said he didn't do it, he didn't. Someone walked into the house during the party (plenty of opportunity; it's not like she or Alfie kept the doors locked yesterday), hacked the keypad, and stole her gun. That was it.

She sat down on the kitchen chair, her fingers tapping the tabletop like a sprinting spider. That person left her driveway just before midnight, quarter of, and headed away from the party. She had no idea if her bullets, shot out of her gun, were the ones riddling Step Volkin's backside, but the notion barged in and took root. It was possible the perp made it to Forty-Six Oak, shot Step, and fled before the rest of the insanity started, but it would have been tight.

She picked up her phone and began dialing the SPD but stopped at the last digit, her index finger a hair above the surface. Her hand curled into a fist without touching that last number.

As a responsible gun owner, not to mention ex–law enforcement, she had a duty to report a stolen handgun. Her fist fell to her knee, her shoulders slumped; the phone continued to lie on the kitchen table, silent and agreeable. Her actions didn't matter to the phone: Report the burglary? Sure. Say nothing and hope wildly that this had nothing at all, zero, to do with her son or his friends? Well, okeydokey, that's fine too.

She shoved the stupid thing into her bag and grabbed her keys. She had just about time to visit Oliver Dubois before heading to the private investigations agency where she'd been working for the past year.

In the driveway, her hand on her car door's hot handle, she gave in and texted Alfie again. *I need to talk to you.*

The answer, a few seconds later: *????*

She ground her teeth and typed. *Are you okay. Tell me now if—* What? If he shot their neighbor? If he set a house on fire last night? Wouldn't be his first arson. But that was behind them. Completely in the past. *—I need to know anything.*

????

Fine. She exhaled a sharp breath. His confusion felt authentic. If there was one thing she trusted, it was Alfie's utter inability to prevaricate. He'd sew his lips shut with barbed wire before spilling a secret but was incapable of lying about it. She typed, *Never mind for now. I'm off to work. B home late. Catch u before bedtime. BBQ chicken in fridge. Mashed pot. in tupperware. Eat a carrot or apple or something.*

He responded with a rolling-eye emoji followed by a thumbs-up emoji. Followed by a fresh set of question marks.

She'd leave it until she got home and could look at him, judge his emotions properly.

Against hope, she dialed Holly's number, then ended the call when it went to voicemail. Holly was her best friend, but apparently Laney's definition of "best friend" became frozen sometime in elementary school. Why hadn't her friend felt comfortable enough to talk to her? To share her troubles?

True, they were as opposite as two people could be—Holly gracious, sweet, girly, never without a mani-pedi, mascara, or a dab of lip color. She possessed a bubblegum-pink winter coat, for God's sake. Laney, on the other hand, never wore makeup, kept her hair pixie short for convenience, and lived in T-shirts, shorts, and Vans in the summer and button-down shirts, trousers, and leather oxfords in the cooler months, opting for more expensive versions of the same when going to the office or court.

True, Holly had been a touch distant these past months, but who wouldn't be with one brother battling cancer, another in rehab, and money problems on top. Anyway, Laney only suspected money was a problem. It was another topic Holly sidestepped even as she borrowed a bit here, more there, so grotesquely uncomfortable with her requests that Laney never probed, gave her friend what she asked and changed the subject.

As Laney put the car in reverse and released the brake, a thought struck her, and she stopped, parked, and jumped out, leaving the car cockeyed and half in the road.

"Laney, you okay?" a neighbor called out to her. A clutch of them hovered across the street, holding sodas, beer, and water bottles, a wired energy to their limbs, their eyes, keeping watch over an equally jazzed gang of children.

"Yeah! Forgot something!" Laney waved and hurried to her garage, where she crouched and bent her head, studying the dirt and concrete at the foot of the garage door.

The previous owner had planted a rosebush just at the corner of the garage, and during the four-plus years Laney had lived there, she'd let the roses grow wild. This summer the branches erupted in every direction, blocking off a good foot of the driveway. The roses could be easily avoided during the day, but at night, in the dark, perhaps not. She peered at the errant boughs, their thorns clingy and sharp. A fresh splotch darkened the asphalt underneath. Could have been anything—spilled soda, coffee, machine oil. Laney scraped it with a fingernail, detaching a tiny flake of rust-colored dirt. She was familiar enough with dried blood to recognize the stain as most likely that. A quick sniff of its faintly metallic and gamy tang confirmed it.

Driving to the hospital to visit Oliver, she did not think about the fresh scratch across Alfie's forearm last night. Or why he'd be by the garage when they had perfectly fine front and back doors for him to use. Or of the girl he'd been speaking with. She did not think about those things at all. Not for one second.

4

April: Holly

THREE MONTHS BEFORE the block party, before Oliver Dubois drove a stolen truck into his own living room, before somebody shot Step Volkin at Forty-Six Oak Drive, Holly Dubois decided on an early-morning walk. Real early. Four AM early. She had lain awake for hours, her eyes sometimes forced shut to induce sleep but more often open, staring at shifting ceiling shadows and the patterns of bare branches outside her window.

Oliver slept, heavy and soundless, the mattress dipping with his weight. His heft lifted her, so she needed to lie at an angle lest she slide into him. She was used to this, loved it even. Loved him, his quiet bulk, his steady intellect, his way of thinking everything through to the marrow before making a decision and, once making it, never looking back.

A sob uncoiled in her throat, and she clambered out of bed and padded to the bathroom, where she rinsed her face, brushed her teeth, and combed her hair. She'd failed her husband. Failed her entire family, but it was the thought of Oliver's disappointment that kept her from sleeping. Though perhaps she could present the situation to him in such a way that he wouldn't think her unhinged. And yet, wasn't she a grown woman, who'd made (arguably terrible) choices for a good cause? Would he be able to see beyond the results of those choices to the softhearted reasons?

Out of habit she patted a daub of lip gloss onto her lips—she would just as soon leave the house without makeup as go outside naked.

"Buster," she whispered, rubbing the little shih tzu to wake him. After all, walking by herself at four in the morning might be considered wacky. Nobody did that in Sylvan except one or two dedicated runners during their cooldowns, and she wasn't a runner. Walking a dog at four in the morning, however, was perfectly understandable.

Buster made it clear he wanted nothing to do with a walk, giving her a sleepy lick before burrowing into his pink blanket, so she lifted him, threaded him into his sweater, and carried him outside, promising him a special treat for breakfast as a reward. Carrying your dog was also acceptable. Plus, his tiny presence comforted her and kept her hands toasty.

She was going to lose her house.

No way around it. The house that had given shelter to three generations of her family. It warmed them with the outrageous clay-and-metal chimney her grandfather built into the basement, hosted countless fundays, birthdays, and wakes, its banisters smoothed by family hands, its steps worn in the middle by family feet. And now, nearly eighty years after her grandparents laid the foundation, it would go into foreclosure.

Holly hastened down the hill, around the corner, and toward the lake a mile away. The dark hadn't faded yet, but birds were beginning to cheep, and a fog settled on the spruces and pines, swirling along the road, eddying around her as if she were a sailboat.

Buster shivered and tucked his head under her arm.

When Holly's parents downsized and moved into a condo, they sold their house far below market value to their three remaining children. Holly's two younger brothers already had houses of their own and were only too happy when Oliver bought them out. Everything would have been wonderful if that's where it ended.

Except then Holly's brother Adam got lymphoma and stopped working, letting his own mortgage lapse. Her brother Roger got divorced and lost custody of his children, which led to him drunk-driving his car into a tree and breaking his arm, a few ribs, and a clavicle, then becoming addicted to opioids and alcohol, which in turn led to costly rehab. Twice.

What could she do? From the age of eighteen she was the stable one, the one who helped, the one her family came to with troubles, questions, needs. Unlike her parents, she never said no.

At first, she didn't want to bother Oliver. He had his hands full with work, the research he conducted at Calypso Technologies consuming him sixty, seventy hours per week. The bills, their social life, the children were her responsibility. She ran a tight household. She knew how to economize, and a few thousand here or there out of the family savings account couldn't hurt anyone. Hell, she even repurposed old sheets, curtains, and her mother's tablecloths into Halloween costumes for the kids, saving hundreds over the years. By cooking every meal herself, she avoided the expense of fast food and dining out. And her paranormal romance novels were selling moderately better, though she'd calculated she'd need to write about ten this year alone to dig herself out of her current hole. Several times this year she'd been forced to borrow money from friends, being careful to ask for small amounts, pittances to cover the most pressing bills. She couldn't bear the thought of their electricity being cut off and having to see Oliver's or her children's shocked faces. She didn't believe she had it in her to face their anxiety, or worse, disappointment.

Oliver had unknowingly been supporting her two brothers and their families for years. Yes, she had a problem. And not only the debt, or that she'd secretly taken out a first and then a second mortgage against her house, or that she'd forged Oliver's signature to do it.

She stopped and leaned over, light-headed. Buster licked her cheek, and she patted his fluffy head to comfort him.

Even her parents didn't know the extent of her problems. Nobody knew. Except her. And the bank.

Six months earlier she went to a therapist because she suspected her need to help her siblings while cannibalizing her own well-being was pathological, not the full shilling, as her Irish grandmother used to say. But she was unable to discuss herself at all, or at least not that part of herself, and instead analyzed writer's block, which she didn't have, good God no; the words practically birthed themselves whenever she managed a moment at her laptop.

No, she could never bring herself to talk about her family. But really, what was there to scrutinize? She was just overly caring. She loved too much. She couldn't bear to see anybody suffer. Not anymore. Not any more than they had all already suffered. She couldn't stand abandoning any of them.

Light-headed again, she pitched against an oak, its bark rough and wet with fog, and Buster yipped with alarm. Thinking of these things made her ill.

Reaching the lake, she perched on a stump, letting Buster place his paws on her left shoulder, and held him like a baby needing a burp. She even patted his back out of habit.

The moon had set behind the trees, but the lake still held moonlight as if it swallowed the night sky. Water vapor hung like gauze over its calm expanse. As Holly's heart slowed, her mind did as well, and her soul swelled with the furtive rustling of chipmunks and voles, field mice and deer. An owl screeched, a branch swayed and cracked. A freshness swirled down from the mountains beyond, and the sky became a shade less dark.

Holly lowered Buster to sniff the ground, and he shuffled off to a forsythia bush, nosing through leaves and rocks. They'd head home soon. This money thing could be fixed. She'd have to fix it somehow.

Tugging on Buster's leash, she encountered unexpected resistance. She tugged again and squinted in his direction, having a hard time seeing his gray form in the changeling light. As the fog shifted, she saw he was planted at the water's edge, tail and ears upright and an unfamiliar growl deep in his chest.

Now she heard them too—the gulping gasps, the panicked splashes. Not animal. Not bird or fish.

Human.

5

April: Holly

HOLLY RUSHED FORWARD, wishing desperately she'd worn her contacts. Maybe fifty feet out, a hand shoved out of the water, its fingers splayed. The other hand broke the surface and flailed, slapping at the lake. Then it too remained upright, reaching as if to grasp oxygen and siphon it to the starving lungs below.

Her shoes wet, slipping in the silt, Holly stopped, a blinding panic shackling her limbs. Her breathing came harsh and loud.

The hands sank, a slow disappearance of wrists, palms, then the fingertips, until nothing lingered but subtle waves.

She had to move. Why couldn't she move? What was wrong with her legs? Why couldn't she even scream for help, for God's sake? She licked her dry lips, sent a command to her feet—and stayed fixed to the shore. Her chest burned as if she were the one underwater, and she raised a fist and hit herself in the sternum, frantic for a full breath, for her body to reboot. She stumbled and collapsed to her knees on the sharp rocks, tearing her leggings. As she straightened, some tumorous thing in the lake lurched toward her and she fell backward, startled, spitting out a scream that sent Buster into barking hysterics.

A sleek, round shape jerked through the gray-brown-black water, pausing every few seconds to tip sideways and bob. Holly stared at it in electric horror until she realized she was watching someone trudge along the lake bottom. The water was shallow here, and the person must have figured it out as soon as their feet hit mud. With every step, more of the body emerged.

It was a woman, slim shouldered and long haired, staggering one erratic stride at a time, chest deep now, her exhales wild gasps. Ten feet from shore the woman pitched forward, disappearing under the lake with a muffled splash. This time Holly didn't hesitate. Released from paralysis, she sprinted forward as Buster padded back and forth along the shoreline, erupting into a new paroxysm of yaps.

Thigh deep in water, Holly clawed under the surface until she connected with an arm, grabbed the woman, and dragged her onto sand. Was she breathing? She was. She was. She was.

Buster still barked, either in warning, confusion, or to express support, but Holly, possibly for the first time in his short life, ignored him.

She held the woman's hands, rubbing them, blowing on them to warm their icy skin, the flesh corpse-cold. Holly could make out her features now—wide cheekbones and large, bloodless mouth, fastidious eyebrows. Late twenties, dark hair, milk-blue skin. The woman wore sweatpants and a tank top, her bare feet mud coated and torn.

"Abigail?" Holly's voice was so soft that Buster stopped barking and stared at her. "Abigail," she said again, louder, and the woman snapped her eyes open. The eyes were not Abigail's eyes. The woman was not Abigail.

Holly sat back on her heels and passed her hand over her face, as if brushing away cobwebs. Of course it wasn't her sister. She'd been dead for twenty years. Her beautiful face and body gone, forever and ever.

The woman sprang up, nearly knocking Holly in the head. Her eyes were a deep amber, not quite brown, feline, her face speckled with dirt and sand. She opened her mouth and spat a gob of dark water, and for a moment her face crumpled as if she'd cry.

"Are you okay?" Holly reached for her, not quite touching. "Do you need to go to the hospital? What happened?"

The woman shook her head, paled—improbably—even more, and bent over, hands on knees, wet ropes of hair dipping in mud.

"Come on," said Holly. "It's freezing. I'll call for an ambulance." Her phone was already out, though she kept mistyping the passcode.

A vigorous head shake again.

"No hospital at all? You need to go. You could be—"

"No."

"Okay, home. I'll take you home. Where do you live?"

"Oak Drive." The woman's voice was stifled against her thighs.

Holly touched her shoulders and tugged, got her to straighten. "I've never seen you," she said. "And I know everyone."

"I just moved," the woman said. "I'm Vera."

"I'm Holly. What in the world happened? Did you—" Holly didn't know how to finish, because she could not imagine a scenario where a young woman would be nearly drowning in a lake on a cold April morning. In street clothes. "I mean, how—" She gave up and hoped Vera might fill in the blank.

She didn't.

They doddered up the incline to the road, Holly's arm wrapped around Vera's frigid shoulders, both of them beginning to shudder. Buster waited until they reached the macadam, his munchkin face scrunched with distrust, then minced after them, dragging his leash.

"I think—" Holly chattered her teeth for a few seconds. "You need a doctor."

"No," Vera said. She shivered too hard to say more, so she shook her head, though it looked like more shivering.

"You poor thing." Holly squeezed the woman tighter to her and did not ask the other questions swarming her thoughts.

When they arrived at Forty-Six Oak, Vera pointed, drifting in its direction. She rang the doorbell and nearly fell inside when the door opened, saved from collapse by someone's arms. The someone drew her inside and slammed the door.

Holly stood outside that green door, her mind whirling. Should she offer further support? Should she speak to that other someone in case they were more reasonable about saving their partner from hypothermia? Her usual take-charge brain had short-circuited.

Buster rubbed against her sopping-wet leg, and she stirred, lifting him. She staggered back to her warm, crowded house, over-stuffed with three generations' worth of furniture, three children's worth of toys. While her family slept, she poured Buster's break-fast into his bowl, remembered to give him the promised treat, and plodded up the stairs. Lake water and seaweed dripped from her onto the polished hardwood.

In the shower, she kept the water so hot it steamed off her shoulders until the shivering and the chattering stopped. She con-tinued to stand under the shower head, eyes closed. The tears and snot smearing her face were indistinguishable from the condi-tioner she'd lathered into her hair.

It would be wrong to say she hadn't thought of her sister in years. Abigail was always there, under every thought, under every action. But the funeral was the last time Holly had said her sister's name out loud. Until this morning. She never visited her sister's grave. If Abigail afflicted her dreams, Holly didn't know because she made it a habit to never think of her dreams, to forcefully for-get them every morning.

By the time she dressed and administered the day's founda-tion, eyeshadow, mascara, and lipstick, she felt better. And by the time she fed the entire family and sent them off with carefully packed, nutritious lunches, she decided to treat the morning's event like another dream.

She'd forcefully forget it.

CHAPTER

6

July: Laney

LANEY DROVE THE ten miles to Good Samaritan Hospital flipping from AM to FM, but as sensational as last night's events were for Sylvan, they didn't make it to the regional radio. The story did, however, spin on a gleeful loop, courtesy of the local news, in the hospital waiting area.

Visitor pass attached, Laney took the elevator to the second floor, then followed the room numbers until she saw Oliver in his bed. He was alone—surprisingly so, given how many friends and relatives always circled the Dubois household. As a former NYPD detective, Laney had seen a lot of destruction, people doing their worst to each other, to themselves. But the sight of Oliver Dubois, lacerated and stitched, solitary under a sickly fluorescent bulb, was hands down the saddest. She'd brought him a large macchiato and cellophane-wrapped blueberry muffin from the cafeteria but now wondered if she should have opted for something more soothing, a peppermint tea (with a clandestine dash of Bailey's), dark chocolate. Next visit for sure.

Oliver was a large man. Football-player large. He had, in fact, played football in high school before heading to Cornell for his biology bachelor's and graduate degrees.

At six foot four and 220 pounds, he was a foot taller than his wife and almost a hundred pounds heavier. Holly called him her Handsome Potato. It was an apt description, what with his sepia-toned eyes and hair, his blocky, snub-nosed face with its square chin and unexpected dimples.

Today the Handsome Potato was bruised and swollen, his eyes bloodshot, his nose swathed in a splint.

"Jesus, Oliver, what did you do to yourself?" Laney asked.

He flinched at her voice, as if he'd been deep in thought, and nodded, though he wouldn't meet her eyes. A bandage masked his left eyebrow.

"Hey," she said, softening her voice. She dragged a plastic chair closer to his bed and made herself tolerably comfortable, or at least level with his head. After a moment of hesitation, she placed her hand over his. "What happened, Oliver?"

He turned his face toward the wall and removed his hand from under hers.

Beneath the contusions and bandaging, a brutal despair distorted his mouth, lent an animal tension to his shoulders and chest.

With as neutral voice as she could, she asked, "Can you tell me who shot Step Volkin?" She desperately wanted to ask about the fire but wasn't yet ready for that answer.

A muscle twitch in Oliver's cheek was the only response.

"Do you know where Holly is?" Maybe this was safer ground; at least he wouldn't need to confess to a crime. She hoped.

Silence.

A flush of shame surged through her. She'd spent the morning agonizing over her son's secrets and wishing her friend was near so she could unload her worries, never once considering what could lead a man to destroy his own house in such a spectacular manner. Oliver had always been, if not exactly a wallflower (how can you be, occupying that much space?), then a mild, cheerful, obliging man. He was patient with his children, often sharply funny, never pedantic despite his obvious intelligence. A barely acknowledged sting of envy muddled into the shame, and Laney fidgeted, stood, took a step toward the smudged window, then sat again. Even five years on, her divorce was an ache. Not the blinding, breathless anguish it had been at first, yet still painful. The Handsome Potato was fundamentally different from Theo, outwardly good, solid, tender toward Holly.

"How can I help? You know I can help. Holly is my best friend." She paused. "So are you. Just tell me what I can do."

Nothing.

He clearly wanted her gone, was almost holding his breath, his jaw jutting forward, stiff. She sat with him for another few minutes, then gathered her things.

"I'm pretty sure you'll need legal help. Give me a call. I have friends at court." Aside from the accident, she figured he'd be at least a person of interest in both the shooting and the arson. That he wasn't already handcuffed to his bed and no rookie guarded his room meant either the police had a more viable suspect or one of Holly's many cousins pulled strings. The Dubois family didn't need her help, not really. But she offered anyway.

Leaving his room, she nearly collided with Oliver's oldest child, Freddie, the bags under the boy's eyes unsettling in someone so young. Holly's brother Adam, the one with lymphoma, was walking up the hall, pulled ahead by the youngest, Kiki, with the middle child, Hannah, dragging behind.

Adam stopped short when he saw Laney and let the children scramble into the room. She heard Kiki's hoarse little-kid voice chattering at his father, while the older boy and his sister stayed closemouthed. Even as Laney greeted Adam, she listened for Oliver's responses.

After a moment both she and Adam stopped talking, their attention riveted to Oliver's room. Would Oliver not speak to his children? She edged forward and saw, at last, Oliver scoop the six-year-old onto his bed and hold him, at which point his daughter leaned over and tucked her face into his chest. The older boy, eleven, didn't touch his father but gripped the edge of the bed rail.

"Have you heard from Holly?" Laney whispered to Adam.

He shook his head. A year of chemo had left him skeletal and ashen, which, paradoxically, made him look younger, his eyes large and expressive in the delicately boned face. The expression they were communicating now was bewilderment.

"I'm taking Oliver to stay with us." He spread his hands. "I don't even—"

Laney nodded. She didn't even either. "They're letting him go today?" she asked.

"Yeah. He's just bruised, but no concussion. So, yeah."

Fatigue blurred Adam's features. He must have barely slept, what with three extra children in his house and a sister who knows where. Laney pressed his hand. She'd lost both parents to cancer when she was still a teenager. Seeing this man, though she didn't know him well, activated a sorrow she didn't so much acknowledge as feel in her throat, in her heart.

"Whatever I can do," she said.

Adam blinked and breathed in as if to say something, but didn't.

"Are you okay?" she asked.

He pressed his lips. "Yeah. Yes. It's just that she's . . ."

Laney leaned forward, waiting.

"It's just that I don't know what I'll do if . . ." His voice wavered, and she squeezed her fingers around his, hard.

"There's a lot of people working on this, Adam. Trust me. You take care of yourself. They"—she jerked her thumb at Oliver and his children—"need you to be okay. That's your priority."

He nodded, his eyes glancing away from hers. But a subtle change in his posture told her he heard and strengthened.

"I'll let you know whatever I find out," she said, touching him gently on his shoulder. "And you tell me if you need anything."

"Of course."

With that, she made her way to the lobby.

Where she stopped. Eyed the front desk. Made a decision.

"I'm going to visit Step Volkin," she told the receptionist, and asked for his room number.

In the six months the Volkins lived on Oak Drive, Laney spoke to Step exactly never. It's not that he hid himself or worked long hours. Laney had no idea what he did, what either of the Volkins did for a living. Step often came to Holly's family funday Sundays, where he'd plant himself on a window seat with a glass of wine and people-watch, his gray eyes staring, as unblinking as a robot's, recording the jokes and laughter, the surreptitious flirting, the snipes, the gripes, the affection of an extended family. Laney had no feel for who he was or why Holly kept inviting him. She'd assumed Holly was only being her friendly, polite, inclusive self.

Today, Step lay in a hospital bed at the opposite end of the corridor from Oliver Dubois. He looked even worse than Oliver, both cheeks and nose swollen, his lip split and oozing, his body curled sideways and propped by pillows as if he were an infant in danger of rolling over on his face. An IV drip hooked into the top of his hand. Whereas Oliver reminded Laney of a wounded bear, Step seemed smaller, meaner, like a starved coyote.

A nurse entered, glanced at Laney, checked the IV bag.

"Is he all right?" Laney asked.

"Are you a friend?" the nurse countered.

A moment of hesitation, then, "Yes."

Step groaned and shifted, gasped, pressed his lips so tight the skin broke and dribbled dark blood onto his chin. His eyes were half-opened, their gray nearly black now.

Laney wished she'd thought to bring him something, flowers, a balloon. "How are you?" she asked.

" 'Ow you tink?" he asked, and it took her a second to realize it wasn't his accent but the damage to his mouth.

"I think you gave as good as you got," she said. Of course, she was making an assumption, and it was possible that Oliver and Step weren't responsible for each other's smashed heads. But she would bet good cash money they were.

"I woul' 'ave 'illed 'im," Step said, and despite the slurred speech, the certainty in his voice chilled her, put her senses on alert.

"Oh?"

But the nurse had swapped the IV bags, fiddled with knobs, and refolded the blanket over his thin torso, and his eyes closed, his body losing some of its stiffness.

"Did he need surgery?" Laney asked, even though she expected nothing but the most general answer.

"He can tell you all about it tomorrow," the nurse said, and wheeled her cart beyond the curtain to the next patient. "Looks like he might be discharged then."

"Really?" Laney asked the curtain. "Wasn't he shot?"

"Yeth," came Step's muffled voice. "The bith 'ot me."

"Who?" Sharp, wary.

"Yur f'end."

And with that he was gone, out, body limp, a frown distorting his already wretched face.

7

July: Laney

LANEY'S CAR SEAT was scorching to the touch, and she made a mental note to buy a windshield screen for her car, then promptly forgot it as she left the hospital parking lot.

Had Holly shot Step? Ridiculous. As a cop, Laney had witnessed families out of control, husbands beating the shit out of wives, mothers breaking their children's bones, grown children murdering their parents. That and more—heaps of violence and carnage to haunt her sleep for the rest of her life and beyond. But Holly? Gentle, gracious, super-wife Holly? Hell, she made her own Halloween costumes for the entire family. She cooked healthy and delicious meals, every day. She owned more than one apron! What would she possibly have to do with Step? Gloomy, sarcastic, black-clad Step? Married Step?

Laney turned into the Boswell Investigative Services garage. Working for BIS wasn't the same as being an NYPD detective. In some ways, it was better.

BIS was a small, family-owned agency with a core of a dozen steady investigators and bodyguards plus another twenty or so rotating surveillance consultants. Their coverage extended to all of Rockland County and parts of neighboring Orange and Green Counties. Mostly, she split her time between background checks for businesses and landlords, skip traces, and runaway teens. Once in a while there'd be a surveillance case, or, when a client specifically requested female bodyguards, security. The commute was negligible, the work variable enough to keep life interesting and plentiful enough to cover bills, food, and clothes for a teenager who outgrew shoes and jeans every six months.

Tonight was surveillance. A husband, convinced his wife was screwing a bartender from the local brewpub, needed proof, and Laney's assignment was to procure one last video for his divorce case.

She waved hello to the receptionist and slid into her cubicle.

In Laney's experience, women generally shot men they knew intimately—spouses, boyfriends, family members—unlike men, who were more likely to murder strangers when in a murdering kind of mood. Holly and Step? Impossible. And when would she have had the time for an affair? Between the perfect roasts, after polishing the floors, before prepping sausage and peppers for fifty of her closest family? During her daughter's soccer games or her son's track meets? Laney didn't think Holly had time to use the bathroom, much less become embroiled in a sizzling love affair meriting gunfire.

And yet. There was the Handsome Potato, his Wild Ride, and Step Volkin with his slurred accusation.

She fired up her laptop. Cases needed writing and uploading to the agency's secure site, and she had to finish them today.

Other than tonight's surveillance, the next case on her list was for yet another runaway, a boy named Bartholomew Gardner whom everyone called Bubba. Bubba's mother was divorced, ex's whereabouts unknown. According to the paperwork, she'd worked herself to the bone trying to keep roof and soul together for Bubba. She had three jobs—as a kindergarten teacher by day, waiter by night and on weekends, and shifts at a local cheese shop whenever a few hours permitted. In other words, Bubba had lots of free, unsupervised time. He developed bad habits, stopped going to school, became listless and depressed, attempted suicide by hanging, failed, refused to take meds or go to therapy. He ran away, was found, ran away again, was found again, became suicidal again. When he got caught committing an act of vandalism, family court reviewed his history and recommended he be placed in a housing facility called Sunny River, a nonprofit organization in Havencrest, twenty miles north of Sylvan.

His mother, frantic and out of her depth, agreed. Bubba got better. Calmed. The facility had him in group therapy, art therapy, theater therapy, and an on-campus school.

Then, one afternoon last week, two days before his eighteenth birthday, he walked out and did not return.

Sunny River claimed his parents had picked him up and signed him out, which, as his now hysterical mother insisted, had categorically not happened. The case stalled with the local police department because Bubba was now an adult and technically no longer a runaway. He had the right to be wherever he was. His mother felt otherwise, and the case had landed in Laney's queue.

Laney pulled up Bubba's photo and studied it. A thin, moon-faced boy with sandy hair and apathetic eyes stared at her, half-turned as if already walking away.

She had her own reasons for taking on these kinds of cases and was known at the agency for that very inclination. Her track record was better than most, statistically speaking. If pressed, she might have admitted it was because she had skin in the game, understood both the kids and the parents and the muddy waters between.

"So, that was some block party last night," said a quiet voice at her back, and she started, nearly jumping to her feet fists up. It wouldn't do to punch the owner's son, even though the impulse struck her too often for comfort. Jack Boswell was a senior investigator, at twenty-seven the youngest of the Boswell brothers. He'd never worked anywhere but here, known no boss but his father.

"Yeah." Politeness felt beyond her today. Usually, she could chameleon herself into any environment, but Jack provoked deep-seated resentments she barely acknowledged, much less could articulate. She wanted him and his sleek, silver-spooned confidence far away from her and her scuffed desk and coffee-stained chair.

Mostly, Jack dealt with corporate clients: property theft investigations, pre-employment checks, surveillance installations. Taller

than average with a runner's physique, he looked good in a suit,
inspired confidence. Appearance and carriage were half the battle
in the PI business. Act and look like you're an authority and people
on both sides of the law pay attention. Laney, on the other hand,
had her diminutive height and slight stature to battle, but she usually made it work in her favor. Whereas clients respected a man in
a good suit, and that could go one way, they felt relaxed around a
petite woman in comfortable shoes. And that could go all kinds of
useful ways.

She turned to her screen and tried typing, but Jack's unmov-
ing presence behind her was like a hot hand on the back of her
neck.

"What?" She swiveled to face him. When he said nothing, she
added, "Why are you wearing sunglasses?"

The sunglasses made reading his intent impossible, which she
suspected might have been a calculation on his part. What did he
want from her? She had work to do, her brain was scraped raw, and
at this rate she'd barely make it to the cheating wife's house in time.

His shoulders twitched, but he removed his glasses and tilted
his head. A faint but unmistakable bruise darkened the skin under
his left eye. Did everyone get into a fight last night? She started
tidying her notes pile.

After a moment he grabbed a chair, rolled it into her cube, and
sat down. "Listen," he said, his eyes not leaving her. "My father
just spoke to Ed."

That would be his brother, Ed Boswell, the one Boswell who'd
refused to join the family firm and instead became a cop with the
Sylvan PD. Consequently, both the firm and the SPD benefited,
information flowing discreetly from one to the other in a way not
normally seen between law enforcement and private investigators.

He leaned forward, his face so close she smelled peppermint
gum and aftershave. "He's on his way here now," Jack said, and she
had to strain to hear. "They found the gun."

With that he rolled away, snapped his sunglasses back on, and
said, loud enough for the receptionist to look up, "You should be
able to finish the Gomathi case tonight. I believe his wife will act
true to type."

Her back to the office, Laney stared at her laptop. There was only one reason Jack would have shared this information with her, and on the down-low, no less. The gun was hers. Ed knew, told Jack, and Jack was warning her. She tasted salt and realized she'd bitten her lip. She grabbed her phone and typed a text to Jack.

Where?

Two seconds later an answer: *By the lake.* And three seconds after that, *Volkin says Holly shot him. Please tell me your neighbors have surveillance cameras.*

She flipped her phone facedown. What would the security cameras show? A person melting into shadows after leaving her house. What else? Teenagers plotting? A housewife marching in the dark like a gunslinger in a Spaghetti Western, Laney's small Glock by her hip? She suspected if the cameras had caught any of that, she'd know about it by now, and the police would absolutely know about it. Gossip burned through her neighborhood with the speed of light, faster if it concerned one of their own. But just in case, she sent a group text to the nine families who'd hosted the party last night. *Anything interesting on your security cameras?*

Four of the homes did indeed have cameras installed, pointed at the street, their driveways, the lawns between houses.

Unsurprisingly, her neighbors were still glued to their phones, because the four with the security systems answered right away.

Spent all morning looking, and all I saw was party.

Police already asked. Too many people to figure out who's what.

Equipment failed! Crying emoji.

Mine too! Two crying emojis.

Laney lobbed her phone into her bag the moment Ed Boswell stepped out of the elevator. He said hello to his father, acknowledged his brother with a terse jerk of the head, then focused on her.

"Hey, Ed," she said, going for nonchalant cheerfulness.

"Hey, so"—he glanced around, frowned at Jack, tapped his fingers on her cube's wall—"mind going into a conference room?"

If she were to agree right away, he might suspect Jack tipped her off. If she acted weird, ditto. Since she hadn't reported her gun missing, she'd have to pretend she had no idea it was.

What would she have done if he'd asked her three days ago?

"Sure, but quick, Ed. I've gotta finish a bunch of reports, and"—she glanced at her laptop screen—"I have a half hour before I gotta go on a case."

He said nothing, gravely.

"The Harriman Room is open." She led him toward a small meeting room down the hall, as far from the rest of the office as feasible, even though it being Sunday, all the rooms were free.

Ed was as tall as his brother, but wider. Marriage and extended hours behind a desk had thickened his middle and softened his outline. Although only ten years older than Jack, he seemed closer to fifty than his actual thirty-seven, with a loosely fleshed, coarse-skinned face and thinning hair.

"What's up?" she asked, too soon. She should have waited for him to start.

"Tell me about last night," Ed said.

She sat back, forced her shoulders into a relaxed slouch, then shifted and placed an ankle over her knee. One thing she knew for certain was that her own alibi was rock solid. Between the two neighbors' cameras pointed (and filming) in the general direction of her house, plus the dozens of people who most likely already accounted for her very visible presence at the party, she was safe from suspicion. If she weren't, she and Ed would have had this conversation at the precinct. Hours ago.

"Crazy party." She shook her head, rounded her eyes. "I've been trying to reach Holly since last night. Do you know where she is?"

"Laney." The hours of work he must have already put into this were evident in his don't-fuck-with-me tone.

She sat up. "What, Ed? I was playing foosball until Oliver drove Step Volkin's truck into his own house, and I was staring at Oliver's house when the Volkins' house caught on fire."

He stayed silent. Then, "You left the game tent at a quarter to twelve. Fifteen minutes before the crash."

She shrugged. "Maybe, yeah."

"Where did you go?"

"Home."

He raised an eyebrow.

"I had to pee, Ed. I'd been drinking that sangria for hours." It took every ounce of her self-control to stare back, not look away. "Why?" she finally asked.

"Where do you keep your gun, Laney?"

Easy, confident, no clue why he's asking. "In my gun safe."

"Is it there now?"

Confused, concerned. Go slow. "Why?"

He sighed, broke eye contact. "Why would Holly Dubois have your gun? Did you give it to her?"

Quick; reaction must be genuine. "I'm very confused now, Ed. What are you asking me?"

"I'm asking you if you gave Holly your gun."

"No."

"Are you sure?"

"I think I'd know if I gave it to her."

"And it's still in your safe?"

She leaned forward. "Tell me what's happening. I don't understand."

His entire body sagged, and he shook his head. In disappointment? "We found your gun and matched it to the bullets used to shoot Step. What can you tell me about that?"

"What?"

His gaze had an edge to it.

She said, "You're kidding."

He sat forward, said nothing.

She said, "I don't know what happened, but I'm going to find out." This, at least, she managed to imbue with the full force of conviction, and his stare softened. "But I need to get going right now. Okay?"

"Can you come to the station in the morning?" he asked.

"Okay." She nodded, her voice sure, agreeable, soothing. "Of course. Whatever I can do to help. I'll get to the bottom of this."

He glanced at her sharply and stood. "Right," he said.

Back at her desk, she swept her notes into her bag and shut her laptop. She'd done fuck-all, meaning she'd need to work from home tonight to file her reports by Monday morning. And who knew what time she'd be home. She cursed softly and slung her bag over her shoulder. Jack was stiff backed, typing at speed in his glass-enclosed office, his sunglasses giving him the air of a studious vampire. The impulse to thank him for the warning fizzled as she considered his motives, which she decided were impenetrable. Why would he want to help her?

She had ten minutes to get to the Gomathi household if she was going to start her stakeout on time. As she waited for the elevator, she checked her phone. Fifteen messages from the group neighbor text, none of them shedding light on any damn thing.

One message from her son: *staying w friend c u tomorrow.*

The elevator pinged open, but she ignored it, typing, *NO. Come home. We need to talk.*

I'm fine please don't worry. Too crazy on our street now too noisy don't want to be alone now.

She gritted her teeth and pushed the elevator button again. Not being home to comfort him was torture, but she had to do her job and do it properly. The only thing that kept her from driving all over town right this minute looking for Alfie's bicycle was the knowledge that if she lost her employment, they'd be screwed. Her savings would last them a month, tops.

What friend? she typed.

He didn't answer right away, and she was about to do the unthinkable and call him when his message pinged. *Jordan.*

The answer irked her, not least because she thought Alfie's friend Jordan was away at Long Beach Island with his family this week. But maybe she'd gotten the weeks confused.

Just before climbing into her car, she looked up and saw Jack Boswell staring at her from his window. His sunglasses caught the setting sun, igniting orange lights where his eyes should have been.

8

April: Holly

EXCEPT FOR THE meltdown in the shower, Holly spent the hours after the almost-drowning doing the same things she always did. She made the beds and spruced the house, walked Buster again, and sat down to write. She had nearly three hours to herself before the first school bus began rolling the children back home, and the absolute last thing she could tolerate was unfilled time. If she could have volunteered and exercised her way through each and every night to avoid sleeping (dreaming), she would have, gladly.

She wrote an average of three romance novels a year, under different pseudonyms. Ashley DeCoer wrote regency, Saffron Quinn wrote paranormal, and D. R. Fine wrote erotica. The old house offered little in the way of space, but she'd quietly removed shelves from the pantry, painted it a warm, sunny yellow, and manhandled an IKEA desk and chair into the nook. She'd written and released her debut paranormal with no one in her family knowing. Since she only wrote when everyone was at work or school, she managed to keep an entire honking aspect of her life a secret. Which, really, was how she rolled.

When she told Oliver, he was surprised and impressed, but also bemused by her concealment.

"Oh," she said. "You know. It's just for fun. It's not like I manage an entire research department like some people in this household."

He grabbed her and brought her close, bending to kiss her. "Don't be ridiculous," he said. "This is an achievement. I'm proud of you."

A grit of irritation made her wiggle away from him. She felt as if she were twelve, showing her father a good report card and getting a pat on the head.

As far as she knew, he'd read none of her books, though she suspected he tried. It didn't matter. She had her own activities and he had his, and it was unnecessary for those to mingle.

The day she'd helped Vera out of a mud-choked lake, Holly planted herself in her pink chair, closed the pantry door, and opened her latest file. It was a regency, and she began the day's chapter with her main character, a young lady of fine lineage but scant funds, adjusting an old frock to the newest fashion with the use of grosgrain ribbon and silk wallpaper steamed away from her bedroom walls. The young lady accidentally pricked her finger and pursed her lips in frustration. What was she playing at? She was no seamstress. She needed a proper lady's maid and she could barely afford a char, much less a maid or a gown. The lady threw her frock to the dusty floor, stomped on it, unearthed a bottle of sherry from the pantry, downed a glass, another, a third. At which point she had the splendid idea to go for a swim. In a lake. And drown.

Holly snapped her laptop shut. Perhaps she needed to take the day. Too many thoughts bustled in her head, and she hadn't slept enough.

She'd make a stew for dinner. The day had stayed cool, never quite living up to the promise of the April dawn, and a hot stew would be perfect. An hour later she had two pots of it going, and an hour after that, she put on her oven mitts, hefted one of the pots, slipped her feet into her mauve Uggs, and walked down the hill to Forty-Six Oak.

Echoing that morning's act of deliverance, she stood in front of the green-painted door, immobilized, except now she was transferring stew and not a waterlogged woman. The pot was heavy and the handles hot, even through the gloves, so she walked up the steps and rang the doorbell with her elbow. It played, of all things, a few bars of "Great Balls of Fire."

The door opened almost at once, as if the man had been waiting on the other side. His appearance was so unexpected that Holly stepped back and would have lost her balance if he hadn't lunged for her and steadied her arms. He glanced at the heavy pot with confusion.

His fingers on her forearms woke her like a slap. What did she think she was doing here, with a pot of boiling stew fresh off the stove? Who did that? A neighbor might greet newcomers with a plate of brownies or an orchid, not hot potatoes and meat. What if they were vegetarians? Or allergic to onions?

Holly threw her shoulders back and smiled her most welcoming smile. No going back, only forward.

"I wanted to make sure Vera was okay." She paused when the man made no move to invite her in. "After this morning."

This morning did happen, didn't it? She didn't hallucinate a young woman nearly dying in the lake, did she? Her smile wavered; she wasn't sure anymore. Sometimes when she attempted to forcefully forget things, they popped up anyway, and then she had trouble knowing if the memories in her head were real or forcefully forgotten dreams.

The man narrowed his eyes as if trying to hear through her words to something else.

"You are kind," he said, and finally stepped back into the house, holding the door open for her. "Come in."

She entered.

The houses on Oak Drive had been built in the fifties, to more or less the same floor plan. Everyone had a large living/dining area, a cramped kitchen, three bedrooms up a short flight of stairs and a den down a few more. Most people eventually renovated. Forty-Six Oak was exactly the same as when it was built, down to the fact that it had no furniture.

Holly looked around the dim interior with uncertainty. There was no couch or loveseat, no lamp, no dining table or chairs. Not even a TV. Not even a mirror. No boxes anywhere either. In fact, the only visible objects were three candles flickering under some pictures on the wall, and, unnervingly, a doll-sized saucer of what appeared to be milk in a corner by the front door.

"I'm sorry," the man said, and took the pot from her. "I'll put it on the stove, yes? Do you need pot back?"

Now that she could see him better, Holly was struck by his looks. He had an athletic build and an unusual face made up of smooth, oblique planes, like that of a medieval carving. There was something both austere and sensual in the way his spareness contrasted with his sturdy physicality, the crew cut and the hollows in his cheeks meshing with his wide lips and large, gray eyes.

"How is Vera?" she asked.

"She is okay."

They stood in silence as Holly tried, once again, to gather herself.

"I'm Step." His face executed a strange maneuver it took her a few seconds to recognize as a smile. "We only just moved here."

All of a sudden, she wondered if Vera had told him what happened. And who was he? Her husband? Boyfriend? Brother? She had to have told him something. She'd been drenched and filthy. Not for the first time, Holly questioned why the woman had been in the lake in the first place, fully dressed, and at such an early hour. Not to mention whether she'd gotten into the lake of her own volition.

"I'm Holly. Nice to meet you. So. If you need anything." She waited for him to nod or smile or in any way act in the expected manner, but he continued to stand still, watching. "Okay then." She waved at him and turned to go, stopped, turned back. "Can you have her call me when she can?"

Step nodded slowly, not taking his eyes off hers.

She laughed uneasily. "Do you have a pen? Or can I have her phone and I'll put my number in?"

He thought about this, then walked into the kitchen, rummaged in a drawer, and came back with a pen and a menu for the pizza place in town. Holly took the pen and menu, trying not to touch his hands, but even so she sensed the heat of him and angled her face away so he wouldn't see the flush creeping up her neck. It was the way he stared. Who stared like that? It wasn't normal.

The air outside cooled her skin. She'd lost her writing time but decided to make it up that night, after everyone was in bed.

Her house greeted her with an overly warm, charred breath, and she realized she hadn't taken the second stew pot off the flame. That's okay. She still had a half hour before the bus, plenty of time to start a third pot of stew. Her eyes snagged on the stuffed mailbox, and she opened it with stiff hands, flipping through catalogs and bills until she came to the foreclosure letter. It felt alive in her hands, sharp edged, mean. A bully.

You can't ignore a bully. You have to stand up to them. She held the letter to the open flame on the stove top, watching it blacken, flare brightly, then crumple into inky flakes over the white enamel. She understood that this was a completely inappropriate reaction, irrational even, and wondered—with a thought so fleeting she almost missed it—if her dead sister hadn't been guiding her hand.

9

April: Holly

KIKI CAME HOME first, asking in a high, clear voice what that smell was, and Holly said, oh, popcorn, Mommy burnt some popcorn. Freddie and Hannah arrived a half hour later, and she gave them all snacks before starting the bustle of soccer practice, homework, a trip to the library, and stew at seven.

She let Oliver take the bedtime rituals and went for a walk, wanting air and to see if anyone was about. Nobody was. The evening had grown colder, and everyone had tucked themselves behind drawn curtains and blinds. She slowed as she neared Forty-Six Oak and noticed that among other things Vera and that man didn't have, were curtains and blinds. Although she'd been taught to be polite above all, and being polite meant you didn't peek into people's houses, she found it utterly impossible not to.

Tonight, only one of the bedroom windows had a light. Holly hugged her arms around her middle, curved her back against the chill. The sun had set and a blue tint washed over the street—the houses, trees, road blending together as if an artist had smudged the evening canvas with a feathered brush. The curve in the road revealed another side of the house to her. The large windows in the lower den were opened to the night, the lights off, and candles had been placed along the floor and shelves, flickering with the breeze. Unlike the living room she visited that morning, the den contained a beige, linen-encased futon, a set of bookshelves, and a heavy, old-fashioned desk.

Holly stopped. Her heart gave a mighty thump against her rib cage before her brain translated what she was seeing. The young woman, Vera, lay on the futon, her white flesh as matte and uniform as if she'd been dusted with sugar and her nipples like bits of chocolate. She'd arched her neck and flung one forearm over her eyes, her mouth open, dark lipped. One thigh thrown over the futon's back, the other turned out, the foot resting squarely on the floor, inches from a trembling candle.

The man's head bobbed between those white thighs. Vera's fingers twisting through his short dark hair, his tan hand stretched over her belly and groin.

An icy swell flooded through Holly to her toes, only to gush back to her head with a breathless heat. Her mind had emptied and she couldn't move, wasn't even thinking of moving, although anybody, anybody at all could look out their window and see her spying. A violent wind gusted down the hill, and the trees swayed above her head, snapping a branch, startling her. She spun on her heel and walked, then ran home, bursting into her warm, meat-and-potatoes-infused house.

With the door shut behind her, she ran her hand over her face and smoothed her hair. The scene she witnessed didn't shock her (she was blessed with good hearing and excellent eyesight once her contacts were in, and she'd heard all kinds of goings-on in the neighborhood over her thirty-three years), but her own reaction did.

Actually, she couldn't process her response yet. Her entire body seemed in a state of upheaval, running hot and cold, her breathing ragged. She shut her eyes and saw again the man's tightly muscled shoulders, his smooth back. A self-deprecating laugh escaped her, and she massaged her hands over her face, as if erasing the image. She was becoming a dirty old woman.

The house was quiet, only Oliver's baritone audible from the upstairs bedroom where he was reading to the children.

She started to text Laney, because she was bursting with it and she had to tell someone, and it wasn't like she could prance in on

Oliver's story time and tell him right there and then, when a text from an unfamiliar number buzzed her phone.

Thank you for the stew. It was thoughtful. Sorry I was asleep

Holly's face heated all over again. She started a few different texts, but nothing sounded right after what she'd seen. Except the woman didn't know she'd seen. So, her text needed innocence.

Yur welcome, she typed. *How r u?*

Would you like to have coffee tomorrow morning?

Holly nodded at the phone, color high on her cheeks. *Sure*

Great! I'll pick u up at 8:30

Well, at least Vera knew when the last school bus left.

She neatened the kitchen and headed upstairs. Oliver sprawled on the armchair by Kiki's side, his head lolling sideways, a bit of drool darkening his collar. Kiki was curled into a tight, sweaty ball underneath his blankets. On the bunk above, Freddie lay, earbuds embedded, his breathing slow and shallow. She removed the earbuds and powered off his phone, then took a blanket layer off Kiki. Before dimming the lights, she debated waking Oliver, but tucked a throw around him instead and walked out.

Hannah's room was already dark.

After weeks of broken sleep, waking through the night to thoughts of their empty checking account and bloated mortgage, Holly fell into bed half-dazed. Her bedroom, sheets, pillows had recently become adversaries, suffocating. But now she wasn't thinking about the bank or foreclosures. Nor of her sick brothers and their needy families. Not even of the novels waiting to be finished and sent to the publisher.

Her mind frothed with images of that sugar-white body draped against linen, and also the feel of it chilled and slack in her arms by the lake. She twisted to her side. She would not think about the lake.

The young man with the staring eyes wasn't her type. She preferred large men. Not overweight, but big—flesh and brawn over tall bones. She liked Oliver's body. Had always liked him, even when he pursued Abigail and mooned around their house, bringing gifts for her like a dog with its sticks and toys.

Vera's partner was more Abigail's speed. Her sister admired slim, hard-muscled boys, had spent countless nights whispering to Holly of all the things she'd done with them. The four years between Holly and her sister might as well have been a hundred, Holly forever longing to catch up, eternally lagging. Abigail had sex for the first time a year before Holly started her period, and those nightly rehashings were the atmosphere of Holly's coming-of-age, imbuing her dreams and daytime reveries with a feverish, carnal heat.

Holly flipped to her stomach and pressed the heel of her palm against herself, pumping into her hand with a roughness that left her sore when she moaned with release a few minutes later.

She fell asleep at once, as if unplugged, and slept a solid, dreamless eight hours until her alarm buzzed her awake at six.

10

July: Laney

S HADOWING SOMEONE WHO was cheating with a bartender had its perks. Laney chose a seat at the end of the bar and ordered an Irish coffee. The investigator part of her needed the caffeine, and the person-whose-gun-was-just-used-in-a-shooting part of her needed the whiskey.

An hour earlier, the (allegedly) cheating wife had flounced out of her five-thousand-square-foot home and slipped behind the wheel of her Lexus, the husband having already left for an overnight business trip. Laney took a time-stamped picture of the wife and tailed her, keeping a discreet distance.

It wasn't Laney's favorite kind of case, but work was work. When she'd been an undercover, buying drugs, guns, building cases against individuals and gangs, the satisfaction of putting away the bad guys made up for the irregular hours, the danger. Now she often had no idea who the bad guy was. She only knew who paid for her time.

Rani Gomathi's husband was an entrepreneur, twenty years older than his soon-to-be-ex and had the money and determination to collect evidence of his beloved's infidelity. Cheating hardly mattered in New York divorces, but over the past months he'd insisted on that one extra photograph or another video, demanding more and more proof.

She didn't know why he needed proof. His wife all but screamed her infatuation from the rooftops. Why couldn't he simply confront her and agree to call it quits? Instead, he dragged it out like a man with a rotten tooth delaying an extraction.

Her own divorce had been so quick and so final it was less like an illness and more like being shoved out of a plane. At least it propelled her to move on. And she had. She'd quit the NYPD, transplanted to this perfect town in historic Hudson Valley, got a new job. She even made friends. Well, okay, one friend. She'd given thought to dating again. Then took that thought, stabbed it through the heart, and buried it in the backyard.

She stirred her spiked coffee and positioned her video spy pen by her cup. These voyeuristic tools of the trade amused her, and she imagined herself a pulp novel gumshoe when wielding them. The surveillance equipment she'd used as a cop was different, larger, designed to snare an entire organization.

Rani Gomathi tossed her long, black hair over her shoulder, smiled at the bartender, and leaned over the bar. He poured her a glass of white wine and said something that made her laugh. Laney pressed a button, and the pen videoed the wife placing her hand over her boyfriend's, running her index finger over his wrist bone.

At eleven, with at least three more hours to go, Laney finished her drink and decided to wait in her car. She couldn't stop thinking of her stolen gun, of Holly, of her son spending the night with a friend instead of at home because he didn't want to be alone. The thoughts made her antsy. Being antsy got you noticed.

She'd sit in her car and listen to music or an audiobook, try to sort herself out. She was gathering her things when the door swung open, and Jack Boswell walked in. He was dressed in black—T-shirt, jeans, boots—his hair carefully mussed. He was either in costume or this was his real self, and she wasn't sure which irritated her more. She'd told him she was working here tonight, so what was he playing at?

Jack commandeered a stool next to her and placed his credit card on the dark-polished counter.

"Erm," said Laney.

"Thought I'd give you a cover," Jack said. "Otherwise you'd have people thinking you were looking to hook up."

Heat rushed to her head in an instant, stoppering her ears. "Are you joking?" She had to keep her voice down but found it difficult, and a few of the customers gave her curious looks. "I don't need help, Jack. I know how to do my job."

"Blue Moon," he said to the bartender.

A curse caught in her mouth, and she bit it back, spitting his name instead. "Jack." She threw her spy pen and phone into her bag and hopped off her stool.

Despite the bad-boy (or boy-band, depending on your frame of reference) drag, he sat perfectly straight, his shoulders back, spine upright, facing the mirror behind the bar. She could almost hear the tension roiling off him, like a deep-bass beat.

"Holly is officially a suspect in the attempted murder of Step Volkin." He said this so quietly she leaned toward him despite herself.

"And you came here to tell me?" Why would he do that? She was ready to leave. But she didn't.

He said nothing, though his eyes found her in the mirror and held. She placed her phone and pen back on the bar. She would have liked another drink now, but the bartender was busy engulfing his head in a storm of silky, dark mistress hair.

"Other than Volkin's accusation, is there proof?" she asked.

"There are prints all over the gun. Yours, hers, and an unidentified set."

"Well, I guess we can rule out a suicide attempt." She waved to get the bartender's attention, and Jack said, "Yo! Another for the lady, please."

"Fuck's sake! I can order my own drink."

"Clearly not," Jack said, and she nearly clocked him. That's twice in one day she had to restrain herself from punching this man.

"Skip the coffee this time," she said to the bartender.

They remained silent until she got her whiskey.

"Why did you tell me?" Laney asked.

"Thought you should know." He still wouldn't look her way. "What's she been like lately? Notice anything?" His fingers tapped the counter. "Why did she have your gun?"

She drank half her drink in one burning gulp. What was he about? Did his brother send him? Why wouldn't Ed come and see her on his own? Was it because she'd be on her guard with Ed but not with his baby brother?

"Come on." She emptied her glass and stood. "We're too noticeable."

Jack tilted his head at Rani Gomathi and her lover. "Noticeable to whom?"

Laney headed for her car, which was near enough the entrance for a good picture when it would be time for the couple to come out but not so close they'd see her. Though Jack had a point. The way the lovers were going about it, they wouldn't notice a fireworks-spewing, siren-blaring UFO over their heads, much less her.

Jack sprinted to catch up. "Hey. Hey! What's going on?"

She spun on her heel. "Don't invade my space, Jack. And don't work me like I'm some kind of chump. If you or your brother want to ask something specific about Holly Dubois, then come the fuck out and ask me. Don't act like you're having a simple chat about a mutual friend or like you're just tossing around some ideas." To her surprise and horror, she felt her voice waver. Perfect! All she needed was to snivel in front of him.

She bent her face to her bag, pretended to search for her keys, then got a grip and raised her head. She wasn't even sure anymore why she was so angry. It's possible he was only talking it through. Detectives do that with each other. The whiskey surged bitter at the back of her throat, and she swallowed. She didn't need a partner, and she had no interest in playing that role for anyone else.

Jack paled, anger and discomfort fighting it out in his thinned lips, his stubborn jaw. She got into her car, wanting to slam the door, but the town was too quiet now, everyone at home, in bed, getting their last hours of rest before another Monday. The second she tapped the door closed, he rapped the window. She lowered the pane.

"Fun fact, Elaine—I went to school with Holly's brothers, and she's my third cousin. I risked my professional integrity when I gave you the heads-up about the gun. This isn't just another case for me. Or for Ed." His hands tightened over her door, and he looked down, took a breath. Then he let go, stepped back, said,

"They're going to bring Oliver Dubois in tomorrow morning. If you know where Holly is, or anything at all about her actions or mind-set these past months, it would be really helpful if you'd share."

She opened her mouth to spit back a reply, then hesitated. Something in his rant sounded wrong, but she had too many thoughts crashing around her brain to decode it. Maybe the Boswells *were* related to Holly. Everyone was. Maybe they'd even been friends as children. But at this point in her life, she'd been a detective in one form or another for over ten years. Detectives were full of shit. Detectives lied all the time if it meant cracking the shell of a case, getting to the meat. Whose were the unidentified fingerprints? Until she knew how Holly got hold of her gun, she'd say nothing. Her chest tightened, and she looked at her hands, lest he see the anxiety and wariness in her eyes.

He stiffened, his face closing. "I just thought I'd put the situation in perspective for you," he said. "Your friend and neighbor used your gun to shoot a man."

Laney exhaled sharply and threw her head back against her seat. "Allegedly." Her shoulders slumped. "I'll make sure to tell you everything there is to tell. Jesus." After she had a good, long talk with her son. Someone gave Holly her gun. Perhaps someone with plenty of time on his hands over a long, empty summer. Someone who, even at fifteen, couldn't tell friend from foe and did his best for everyone who asked.

God, she was tired. "Go home, Jack. Let me finish up here."

He broke eye contact and rolled his shoulders, checked his phone. Then he walked away without a word.

Regretting the whiskey when it hit her, she riffled through her glove compartment until she found a bottle of 5-hour Energy drink, drained it, and turned on the radio. It was much too late to text Alfie, but she did anyway. Her message was as addled as she felt, wishing him a good night and telling him she'd ground him for a year if he didn't make himself available tomorrow.

She settled on a radio talk show and spent the next two hours listening to calls from people fearing foreclosures and losing their homes.

At one thirty in the morning the bartender emerged, followed by Rani Gomathi, and they walked the ten blocks to his apartment with her arm around his waist and her head on his shoulder. Laney followed on foot, taking time-stamped photographs. Forty minutes later Rani came out, and Laney took a picture of that too.

And twenty minutes after that, Laney was showered and sitting cross-legged in bed, her feet blessedly bare against the cool sheets, her house small and neat around her. She still had hours of paperwork ahead of her.

The mix of energy drink, coffee, and whiskey, plus the whole gun situation, not to mention the attempted-murder situation, made her thinking buzzy, disjointed. The reports took longer than they should have.

After she uploaded the final batch of videos and sent off the last report, she put aside her laptop and stretched out. But her eyes wouldn't close, and her sheets were no longer cool but crumpled and uncomfortable. Her conversation with Jack percolated underneath her consciousness despite her efforts to put it aside. He'd called it "his case." Why? As far as she knew, BIS didn't take on criminal cases and certainly wouldn't handle what happened on Oak Drive last night. She padded to her gun safe, turned on the lights, and aimed her phone at it, using the zoom feature as a magnifying glass.

The safe hadn't been forced. There were no scratches around the door, nothing at all. Whoever opened it had the key code, and she always changed it on the first of every month.

Despite the hour being closer to morning than night and her brain feeling inflamed from overwork, she reopened her laptop and searched for Vera and Step Volkin. Over the next hour, as she logged in to database after database, her eyebrows moved closer and closer together, the results of her search sending a spike of adrenaline-fueled alarm through her overextended nervous system.

11

July: Laney

ALFIE CAME HOME just as Laney finished her morning coffee. She'd promised Ed she'd come to the station and talk, but she never specified when, and she had no intention of going anywhere until she got answers from her son. He looked as shot as she felt—his curls a frizzy halo, his skin dull, and most worrying, broken capillaries under his eyes.

He trudged through the door, head down, and stopped short when he saw her in the kitchen.

"Good morning," Laney said. Neutral. Mild.

"Morning." He said, as cautious as if she were a tiger and he an antelope, and as clearly distrustful of her tone.

She sighed. "Want some coffee?"

He watched her for a few seconds, nodded.

She poured a fresh cup and placed a bowl, spoon, milk, sugar, and a box of cereal on the table, then watched him stir four spoonfuls of sugar into his mug.

"So, how's Jordan?" she asked.

His stirring paused, then started again. *Clink, clink*, went the spoon against the ceramic, until he placed it on the table, sipped the drink. "Okay," he said.

"I thought he was at Long Beach Island this week."

He shrugged.

The effort of keeping her voice calm and collected nearly blinded her, but she breathed through it.

"I'm sorry I had to work last night. Did you sleep okay?" Alfie had always been a creature of habit. From the look of it, sleeping away from home did not agree with him.

"I slept fine." He sipped his coffee, eyes down.

She sighed again. "One more question and you absolutely must answer me, and answer with the truth."

When he lowered his mug, his hand shook slightly. "Okay."

"Did you take my gun?"

And there it was—relief—his shoulders relaxing, his mouth softening. "No. No, of course not. I told you." He looked at her with guileless blue eyes. "Why, who took your gun?"

"Are you sure you don't know that either?" she asked, though a part of her understood him passably well. He had nothing to do with it.

He looked at her like he didn't know if she was joking, searched her face for a clue. "Yes, Mom, I'm sure. I did not take your gun, and I don't know who did." He picked up his coffee and drank deep, almost cheerful gulps. As far as he was concerned, the questioning was concluded.

"Okay." She filled his bowl with cereal and added milk. She was fairly sure he had not eaten well last night either. He tended to be picky. "Did someone visit you the night of the party?"

Ah. The color up in his cheeks now, and his eyes dropped to the cereal bowl. That would be a yes. He mixed sugar into his cereal, added more milk.

She reached for his hand and squeezed hard, startling him to frozen wariness. "Listen. I'm off to go see Ed Boswell, who will ask me many, many questions about who was here, in the house, Saturday night. Because someone took my gun, and if it wasn't you, I need to know—I must know—who was here."

His Adam's apple pumped, but he held the eye contact, his lips pressed together.

She gripped his hand harder. "Tell me I won't be lying if I tell him that nobody but you and a friend were home and that neither one of you touched the safe."

"You won't be lying," he said. Again that sureness in his voice, resonating within her. This was a truth.

She released his hand and sat back. "How did you get the scratch?" The violent, and most likely infected, welt across his forearm, hidden now because as soon as she pointed, he snapped his arm down to his lap, under the table.

His eyes narrowed against incipient tears; he said nothing. Okay, at least she had truthful answers to the two most crucial questions. The rest she'd worry out of him eventually.

She rubbed her face, got to her feet, left the kitchen, gathered her laptop case, bag, shoes, came back, retrieved a banana from the counter and placed it in front of his cereal bowl.

"Eat your breakfast," she said. "I'll be home for dinner. And please put some bacitracin on that cut, will you?"

The Sylvan PD was walking distance, but she drove, parking five minutes after she left her house.

Today Ed Boswell's hair gleamed with product, and his shirt was freshly ironed and accented with a cheerful marigold tie. But the bags under his eyes belied the effort, and Laney wondered, not for the first time, why he chose law enforcement over the family business. In this line of work, people often joined the force either because it's what their fathers did or to become someone completely different from their fathers. In her case, it was the former; in Ed's case, it was sideways.

"So." He shuffled through his papers and tapped his pen on his desk. Without looking up, he said, "Do you have any idea why Holly would shoot Step Volkin? And, by the way, how do you think Holly got hold of your gun?"

Laney had ruminated on the second question all morning. "I guess I must have left the safe unlocked." A sheepish shrug. "I try to be very careful, but . . . I looked at the lock, and it doesn't appear to have been forced."

"Could anybody have gotten hold of your combination?"

She considered this, but it seemed improbable. "I don't write it down. I memorize it and change it once a month. Maybe if some-one stood behind me—" Wait. A memory darted to the forefront,

Holly visiting her a few days before the party. Laney had just come home.

Ed raised an eyebrow. "Yes?"

Holly had come over briefly, went home, came back. Laney got a call and locked the safe before answering. The entire time Laney fussed with the safe, Holly was across the room, looking out of the window.

"I don't know." She tried to relax her shoulders and face. "I don't know how it happened." The only other person who could have looked over her shoulder was Alfie, but she believed him when he insisted he had nothing to do with it. Would Ed?

Ed lowered his pen and fixed her with a humorless gaze. "When was the last time you had your gun on you?"

"Last Thursday. I worked a surveillance case." Another shrug. "I like to have it with me. Old habits."

"Gotcha."

She waited.

He said nothing.

She waited.

He didn't move.

She could wait all day. But damn, did she want to leave. A trickle of sweat rolled down her back, and she fidgeted.

"How's Alfie doing?" Ed asked.

She stretched her face into a wide smile. "Awesome, Ed. How are your kids?" Just two friends shooting the breeze.

"One's at a STEM camp, the other one is volunteering at a shelter for the summer."

Laney tried to stretch her lips even wider, but she didn't think her mouth worked that way. "That's just—fantastic." She stood. "Okay, well, I got work, so."

"How's Holly been these last months?"

She sat back down. Safer ground now. She cared about Holly. And Holly was an easier subject than her son. "You know. Busy. But good. She was always good. Worried about her brothers. You know about them, right?"

He nodded slowly. "Yeah. I know Adam and Roger."

Of course. They were all third cousins. She stood again. "Listen, I don't really know much else. She was worried about them, and then the rest of the time she was just Holly."

"Did she ever confide in you about money problems?"

Well, there were the loans. Did that qualify as confiding? Holly did the very opposite of confide. She had requested, absolutely red with embarrassment, almost crying and giggling with nerves. Laney had rarely seen anybody over the age of six so transparently distressed and had written her friend a check right away, if only to end the misery. That Holly paid her back, every bit, surely meant there weren't money problems so much as cash flow issues.

Laney shook her head. "She borrowed a little over the winter, but she didn't confide in me. She paid me back, and I didn't ask. I figured she'd tell me if she needed to. Why? What are you thinking?"

He sat forward and knit his fingers together, not taking his eyes off her.

She guessed he wanted her to say something specific, but she couldn't for the life of her understand what. "Ed? What's up?"

He looked away. "You tell me if anything comes to mind," he said.

"Yes. Yes, of course I will. I gotta go to the office now." As she opened the door, she added, God knew why, "I'll tell your dad you said hi."

Which, of course, she didn't do, instead speed-walking past her boss's room and settling into her cube.

Sometimes life made sense only when she was investigating. There was a gloriously abstract aspect to analyzing strangers. She could use her brains without tripping over emotions at every breath. Take, for example, one of her most recent cases—a teenage runaway it took her all of three hours to locate. The girl's parents would have known where to find her, too, if fear and preconceived notions hadn't blinded them. The girl left clues all over her social media like glitter yarn, leading Laney through the internet's labyrinth to the geometry teacher living in a condo three towns over. He'd told his neighbors the girl was his niece.

What was she not seeing clearly in her own life? Past experience indicated heaps.

Take the Volkins, for example. She'd been utterly unaware of their existence until sometime in April, when the couple began hovering around Holly. At first, Laney thought Vera another cousin or niece, the resemblance to Holly was so striking. Both women were slim and fine boned, with dark, glossy hair, delicate features, and good skin. Then she noticed the telltale signs— the hollow cheeks, the eyes in turn glassy and bored or furtive. Vera was another one of Holly's charity cases. Someone she found somewhere and was trying to rehabilitate with the power of love. Vera seemed harmless, if annoying, drawing the eye of every male (and occasional female) in the room, knowingly so, without once making an effort to charm anybody other than Holly.

But then again, Laney herself had been one of Holly's charity cases once. She would not begrudge a lost soul the benefit of Holly's friendship. She remembered being new to the neighborhood, still raw from her divorce, unable to trust a single soul. Holly's casual kindness warmed her, made her feel like an ordinary woman going through an unfortunate but normal crisis rather than the epic failure she imagined herself to be.

She logged into a database and continued the search she'd started last night. The Volkins had immigrated to the United States in 2007 after winning visas in a lottery. Vera's hometown was Kiev. Step was from Saint Petersburg, but they arrived together. They were both in their mid-twenties now, a two-year difference between them. It meant they would have been fourteen and sixteen when they flew to the United States, alone, without their families, which should have made them unaccompanied minors but somehow didn't. She found no records of them classified as such, nothing on whether they received public assistance. No school records. They arrived and seemingly vanished from all systems, went off grid, surfacing four years later when a marriage certificate showed them married at New York City Hall. In 2017, they became naturalized citizens.

Other than that, nothing—no social media, no phone numbers, no addresses, no LinkedIn profiles. She'd seen her share of shady characters, but those two were downright bizarre. And the oddest thing of all was them washing up in Sylvan, the least interesting town in the Hudson Valley (which, to be fair, is exactly how its residents liked it).

She sensed a presence behind her and she twitched, turning and closing her laptop in the same movement.

Jack stood there, backlit in a dark suit, angular and spiky haired.

"Are you creeping up on me?" she asked.

He stepped forward and now really loomed over her, much too tall, and she jumped to her feet. It didn't do her much good.

"What?" she asked.

"I wanted to apologize," he said.

"Will you sit?" She pointed at a chair. "There's an imbalance of power here that's making it hard for me to hear you."

His face didn't soften, but he looked down, grabbed the chair, and sat, rolling it just to the edge of her cube. After a moment, she also sat.

"I shouldn't have gone to the pub yesterday. It was your case. I'm sorry." He sounded half-strangled as he spoke, as if the words were too big for his throat and choked him on exit.

"So why did you?" She wasn't mad anymore, but that sense that he hadn't been transparent with her last night returned.

Impossibly, his posture became even more wooden, though he raised his eyes. "Let me make it up to you," he said. "Let me buy you dinner tonight."

She almost laughed at how unexpected and cheerless the invitation was but caught herself. "That's okay," she said, once she sorted her emotions. "Really. I accept the apology."

He smacked his knee with his palm and stood, pushing the chair away into the neighboring cube. "I had a case near the pub and thought I'd see how you were doing." Shrug, too sharp to be casual. "Ended up backfiring." Chin up, shoulders tensed. "So, dinner? Yes?"

"Jack." What the hell? Who asks a person to dinner like this? Like a cyborg with a neck spasm? "I have to go home and feed my kid. But, ah, thank you. For the apology. And the offer."

His eyes slipped past her again, and he nodded. "Rain check?" he asked.

"I don't really go out, Jack," she said, and although he was already turning away, he snapped his face toward her, eyes flaring with the first unrestrained emotion she'd seen from him all day.

"You've been here almost a year, and every time I try to help or be nice, you get all—" He shook his head. "I'm not your enemy."

She snorted. "I know you're not my enemy. I've had enemies. All of them are dead now."

In the ensuing silence they stared at each other, and she wondered if she'd just got herself fired. Imbalance of power indeed.

The corner of his mouth quirked. "I'm sure they are." He looked at his father behind his glass wall, tapped his fingers on a cube divider. "Let's have lunch tomorrow, then. I need to talk to you about a case. A working lunch. Okay?"

And now she felt like an idiot. Of course, he was only being professional, making up for a lapse in judgment. Warmth crept up her cheeks. What in the hell compelled her to think the invitation was romantic? Was she losing her mind? She was older than him, with a kid. She was his subordinate. Besides, she now remembered he had a framed photo of a cheery blonde on his desk. She twitched with embarrassment but maintained eye contact.

"Sure," she said. "If you put it that way."

He nodded and headed for the elevator.

"I like sushi!" she called after him. Because if it was going to be a working lunch, she might as well enjoy it.

The next few hours found her doing her best to focus on her two skip trace cases, while thinking about Alfie, her missing gun, Holly, and Jack and his mysterious case only once every ten minutes or so.

CHAPTER

12

July: Laney

Laney had nothing in the house for dinner, unless a couple of eggs and a handful of wrinkled grapes could be master-cheffed into a meal for two. She doubted it. Left to his own devices, Alfie would eat a bowl of pretzels and call it a night. Come to think of it, they were probably out of pretzels. She couldn't seem to stay on top of the groceries.

Too drained to even contemplate cooking, she stopped at Nuncio's on the way home and ordered lasagna, baked ziti, salad, and garlic knots. While she waited, she texted Jack.

I never asked—what happened with Oliver coming in for questioning?

Now you want to talk to me.

Never mind. She bit the inside of her mouth. Served her right for opening herself up.

Silence. Silence. Silence.

Then a ping from Jack. *Not much happened.*

?

He answered the basic questions, and for the rest he got a lawyer.

Why did he get a lawyer? Step Volkin hadn't accused Oliver. So, either Jack wasn't telling her everything, or Oliver was lawyering up preemptively.

Exactly.

For stealing the truck? Crashing into his own house?

He replied with a shrug emoji.

She clenched her teeth. *Is he in trouble?*

Silence.

Then, the three answering dots, and finally, *Is he?*

She rolled her eyes and shoved her phone back into her bag. Jack was privy to Ed's criminal investigation, of course, officially and unofficially. Despite the very obvious coolness between the brothers, their cases always came first. Neither one would hurt the other's success. Her heart rate quickened, and she momentarily forgot her growling stomach. Jack was actively investigating the Dubois family. But for what? Whatever he was looking into must have happened before the block party.

She paid for the food and pulled open Nuncio's door, the bag bulky in her hand, only to stop short. Her son stood in the doorway, his face paling at the sight of her. A young girl, walking up behind him, bumped into his back.

"Ow, why are you stopping?" the girl asked.

Alfie didn't move, the three of them standing in a row through the doorway.

Laney spoke first. "I picked up dinner."

The girl peered around Alfie's side. She was shorter than he but older, not a teen. A rowdy mass of blond curls framed her lean face. She poked him with a small, slightly grimy finger. "Is that your mom?" She stared at Laney and smiled, revealing a chipped canine tooth. "I'm Mona."

Laney noted the smudged mascara, the too-large clothes, the grainy skin. "Nice to meet you, Mona," she said.

None of them moved, still standing in the doorway, the girl angling around Alfie's back to stare at Laney.

"Err," said Alfie. He hadn't stuttered in over a year, but now his face contorted, his lips tightened, and right away Laney said, "It's okay. Come home. Both of you. There's plenty for everyone."

He shook his head.

"Great!" said Mona. She grabbed his upper arm and grinned. "We'll meet you there!"

Yet nobody moved—Alfie a stopper between them, not letting one leave nor the other enter.

Laney cleared her throat. "Okay, well." She gestured toward the parking lot. "Let's go. Right?"

Mona split off and cantered into early-evening light. Alfie, blushing so furiously Laney worried he might have a stroke, said, "Wu-wu-wu—"

Laney interrupted again, as she often did, even though it didn't help, possibly made the stutter worse, "Oh, come on. I want to meet your friend." She stuttered herself on that *friend* but hoped he hadn't noticed. "Come." She stepped forward, which made him step back, and then she was heading toward her car and he was disappearing into the girl's dented dark-green Ford.

Laney drove the four miles home with the windows open, leaving a heady waft of garlic and dough in her wake. She felt she'd seen Mona before, though she couldn't remember where. The girl was pretty, sure, with dark-blue eyes and a lively, expressive face, but that aura of aged street urchin unsettled Laney.

Alfie came home, alone, just as she was spooning ziti onto three plates.

"Oh," Laney said. "Where's Mona?"

He grunted, toed off his sneakers.

Conversations with Alfie were often tortuous, an aftereffect of the stutter he'd all but lost and the resulting reticence he had trouble releasing even with her. Maybe nowadays, especially with her.

She set the ziti on the kitchen table, poured half the salad into a plastic bowl, and gestured for him to sit.

They ate in silence for a while.

"So, who is she?" Laney asked.

Alfie shoveled a golf-ball-sized mound of pasta into his mouth.

Laney sipped her beer. "A teacher? She looks like a teacher." Something told her Mona wasn't a teacher.

Alfie stopped chewing and kept his eyes on his plate.

Laney pushed away her food. "Hey, I don't know what planetary disturbances are causing everyone around me to act batty, but I've had just about enough of it." She put both elbows on the table and rested her chin in her hands. "So, out with it. What's up?"

Her son swallowed loudly and continued staring at his plate.

"Right," she said. "Now you're making me worried. Just nod or shake your head. Are you okay?"

He scraped back his chair, stood, and walked out of the kitchen, up the stairs, and into his room. Laney heard his doorknob lock.

She considered his half-eaten dinner, her own barely touched plate. "Shit," she said, and followed him. After a quiet knock, she said, "Just tell me you're okay. In general. Do I need to worry?"

A footstep, a chair being moved, a thump that meant he'd placed his saxophone case on his bed, the quiet click of latches being undone. At last, his voice. "Don't worry. I'm okay."

She stood at the door until he began practicing. Realizing she'd get nothing more from him, she returned to the kitchen, finished her ale, poured another, and dispatched her ziti, in that order.

When Laney was eighteen, her brother had killed himself. Their parents had already passed by then, their respective cancers claiming them a few months apart. She'd become an adult, fell in love, married, and had Alfie while still in a state of mourning. Not that she'd ever spoken about her feelings. No, self-examination led to bad thoughts, made life unbearable. Look what self-examination and feelings did to her brother. If someone had asked Laney why she didn't push Alfie harder, why she watched him so closely while giving him so much space, she'd have had a hard time verbalizing the feelings she'd spent her entire life suppressing. But if she could, she'd say she was petrified the darkness that had taken her brother was in her son. That she'd passed it to him. If he needed space, she gave it to him. If he did poorly on a test, she didn't scold, instead gently suggesting he study harder (good thing he was conscientious about schoolwork). His silences, moodiness, sadness scared her witless. She had no idea if his behavior was normal for a teenage boy. She hadn't been like him, that's for sure. She'd been a tomboy—always outdoors, skateboards, the beach—her whole life.

Alfie saw a therapist at school once a week, and she was grateful for that. But it was summer now and he hadn't been in a month.

Although she wanted to be the kind of parent he could come to with problems, she was clearly failing, though not for lack of trying. Alfie was unlike anyone she'd ever known. Sometimes, in her more disheartened moments, she imagined he was a changeling, or an alien. But then he'd flip his head and she'd see his father in the shape of his eyes, her own father and brother in the dimpled chin. It wasn't so much that Alfie saw the best in everyone; it was that he accepted everyone exactly as they were, and was monumentally incapable of recognizing dangerous behavior. A year ago, he'd turned that pure gaze onto a person who meant him harm, terrible harm. He'd come out of that situation alive, though with a bullet hole in his arm and nearly frostbitten toes. Even so, she was never sure he blamed the man who shot him, or even disliked him. She suspected her son understood him.

Laney took out her phone. She wanted to give her son privacy, but . . . surely she could guard him without crowding him too much.

She scrolled through Alfie's Instagram feed, bypassed screenshots of his favorite web comics, paused over a photograph taken at the town's lake, smoky fog over silver water, and stopped cold at a picture that looked abstract at first but on second glance revealed itself to be a naked back. Messy blond hair swept across in a diagonal swoop, and faint scrapes glowed like red hashtags across milky skin. The caption under the picture read *@mona.mad.malice*. Laney tapped on the name and immediately fought the urge to shut her eyes. Staring back at her was Alfie, image after image, smiling, laughing, blushing, in a T-shirt, without a T-shirt, sleeping, and mixed in, selfies of @mona.mad.malice with him, alone, with clutches of other girls, a few with other boys. In many of the pictures she wore a uniform shirt, green with a half-moon orange logo and blue lettering, like a camp counselor. Mona did not go for artistic filters, sticking to straightforward documentation.

Laney pulled at her bottom lip. So, her fifteen-year-old son had a girlfriend. A girlfriend who appeared older than fifteen. She was about to exit when she scrolled to an image of Mona's flip-flopped feet, the blue toenail polish harmonizing with cobalt lake water, emerald trees all around, and a slim figure like a pearly cutout in the background. Laney's fingers were slick with sweat, and she had to wipe them on her shorts to zoom into the picture. As she brought the phone close, she remembered where she'd seen Mona, because there, silhouetted against frenzied vegetation, stood Vera Volkin.

Her fingers started tapping a text to Holly when she caught herself. Did her friend know Mona? What the flaming hell scary nonsense was her son getting himself into? She almost marched to his room again but stopped. It would be pointless. He was on alert against her. A suffocating anxiety threatened to overwhelm her, but fury fought it out and won.

Laney grabbed a pair of blue nitrile gloves from a drawer, a tote from her closet, and slipped on her sandals. It was dark, and the neighborhood vibrated with activity—children calling to each other, running and circling in formation like birds, parents in groups, discussing the only thing on everyone's minds, the same thing that was on Laney's mind.

The Dubois house stood dark and broken, police tape over its door. As Laney walked down the hill, Alfie's sax solo drifted out of his bedroom window, a song from a midcentury big band.

Forty-Six Oak was also dark, also police taped. She knew from an earlier text with a neighbor that Crime Scene had examined the house, cut the second bullet out of the drywall behind Step's body, photographed, dusted, bagged, and carted away the computers. Laney shook out the gloves and pulled them on. Whatever bizarre adult quadrangle detonated Saturday night concerned her directly now, the gun being the least of her problems. She needed to get ahead of whatever freight train her son was unwittingly inviting his way, and understanding the Volkins was her first stop.

CHAPTER

13

April: Holly

HOLLY CHECKED HER bank balance, then her credit card balance, then her other credit card balance. Bad news on top of bad news. She was now four months behind on the mortgage payment, which somehow felt both not too awful and insurmountable. Her only choices at this point were asking her myriad friends and family for money or losing her home. She texted Roger, the addict brother, and asked, again, when he might pay her back. No pressure, she added (as always). Whenever you can. She scrolled through her mail for responses to the job applications she'd been sending out. Nothing there either. Although she had a liberal arts degree from a local SUNY college, she married and fell pregnant before graduation, and Oliver never had trouble supporting them. Her homemaker role suited her, and she rolled along without a moment of angst until her brothers' lives began to sink. She couldn't stand by and let them drown. Not when she could, with negligible effort, help.

She simply did not know how she got so behind on everything.

When the knock came, Holly pretended to herself she'd forgotten the breakfast date with her new neighbor and opened the door with a polite but quizzical smile. Her pretense disintegrated in an instant, the other woman's solid presence bringing back last night's every sensation.

"Are you still up for breakfast?" Vera asked, and Holly nodded, fighting to compose herself.

Vera was underdressed for the bright, cool day. She wore a chocolate suede skirt over bare legs, ribbed sweater made from thin, silky material, and red leather slip-ons. She'd parted her long hair in the middle, letting it fall nearly to her waist.

Holly grabbed her jacket and came out, working hard (and completely failing) to erase the memory of this woman's white flesh gilded with candlelight, pliant.

"Let's walk?" Vera asked. In this town, people either drove the mile to the store, church, or gym or they jogged, but they seldom walked for the joy of it, other than perhaps to a neighbor's, and only if the neighbor lived less than three houses away. In fact, one of Holly's cousins used to strap her daughter into her SUV, back out of her driveway, back into her friend's driveway directly across the road, and release the child for a playdate.

"I'd love to," said Holly.

Holly rarely felt tongue-tied, but a silence gripped her as she fell into step with the woman. When she was ten and Abigail fourteen, they'd walk this way to the ice cream shop, the conversation flowing in one direction toward the younger girl—instructions on makeup and hair removal (not that she needed it yet), gossip on who was a slut and who was a snob, and music, always music.

At the top of the hill, with the town stretching green and weekday-still below them, Holly reached and pressed Vera's shoulder, wanting to touch the smallness of her bones. No denying it, this woman had something, more than something, of Abigail to her—the hair, the careless elegance, even the bags under her eyes, the unhealthy hollows under her cheeks. This moment, the touching, teetered on awkward, but Vera angled herself into Holly and tucked her arm around her waist as if they'd been friends for decades and not hours. It seemed to Holly that an odd and secret understanding vibrated between them.

With a great heave of self-control, Holly had successfully avoided dwelling on the circumstances of their meeting. But the woman's closeness made this denial impossible.

"Are you all right?" Holly asked.

"I'm all right."

"I mean—"

Vera broke away and ran across the street, then beckoned for Holly to follow.

So, that topic was off-limits. Understandable. Except now Holly thought of nothing else.

At the coffee shop, Holly ordered an espresso and a blueberry muffin and Vera had mint tea and a single boiled egg, from which she separated out the yolk, disposing it into a napkin. The young woman checked something on her phone, tapped a few keys, placed her phone screen down on the table between them.

"I want to thank you," Vera said. "For everything yesterday."

"Oh, honey." Holly blinked. She had almost called her Abigail. Funny how her sister was never Abby or Gail but always Abigail, to everyone. It was the way she held herself. Holly used to speculate whether the boys she fucked hollered *Abigail!* as they convulsed inside her.

And then she couldn't help herself. "But what in the world were you doing in the lake? It's too cold yet. No wonder you—" What? Got a cramp? Fell into the deep end in your clothes? Once again heat suffused her face and neck. She broke off a hunk of muffin and crammed it in her mouth. It was grainy, the sugar rocklike, and she had to spit it into a tissue.

Now they both had food balled up in napkins, mirror images of each other.

Holly pushed her cup and plate to the side and leaned forward. "You can tell me what happened." Did she sound ghoulish? But she needed to know. She needed to frame yesterday morning's episode in some way that made sense. "Maybe I can help."

Vera's face twitched, as if a bird flew overhead, cast a momentary shadow. "Nobody can help," she said.

"Why on earth not?"

Again that quick shadow, a darkening of skin as if the blood underneath gushed and ebbed. Vera looked at her hands and softly, nearly in a whisper, said, "I was attacked."

"What?" Holly wasn't sure she heard right. She had been there. There'd been no struggle sounds, only that gasping and splashing that even now threw her thoughts into turmoil. What was this woman talking about?

Vera nodded. "They put me in a boat and then shoved me out. They know I don't swim."

Holly frowned. She hadn't seen or heard a boat. But then again, she'd sat distanced from the shore until Buster made her aware. Plus, fog swallows sound, corrupts it.

Another, more disturbing thought intruded. "Who? Who put you in the boat?" Were there murderous criminals prowling Sylvan even as the two of them sat with their uneaten breakfasts?

Vera sipped her tea, eyes never leaving Holly's. "They're not after anybody else. They wanted to prove a point."

"What? What point?"

"That they are stronger than me. That they can do whatever they want."

Holly looked closer at the woman's overly thin face. Why hadn't she noticed? Vera was obviously strung out. She should have been frustrated, annoyed, angry. Here was someone dragging crime, drugs, God knew what else into Holly's tidy world.

Except who was she kidding. Her world wasn't tidy, and her brother struggled with addiction, no less so than this woman across from her. She wanted to help her, just like she wanted to help every sorry, lonely, needful soul she'd ever met.

"Look." This was a frame she understood. She knew all about solving this sort of problem. "I get that it's hard. Tell me everything and I'll help. I have friends and cousins who are cops. One of my cousins is a lawyer. There's a good rehab not far from here. You tell me what you need."

Vera's eyes softened, but she shook her head. "I don't need rehab, Holly. I need you."

14

April: Holly

H OLLY HALF SMILED, waving her hand at Vera as if shooing away a fly. "Well, I don't know what I can do for you by myself. I'll try." The need to sort this woman out, to help, pulled at her.

Vera lowered her eyes, her skin blooming the faintest rose. "The men will be back." She met Holly's gaze again with evident difficulty, reached for her hand and squeezed. Her fingers were cold and small, with neat, buffed nails.

"Who are they? What are you involved with?" Holly returned the squeeze. This intimacy so soon should have felt forced, but it didn't. It felt just right.

Vera eyed the server hovering ten feet away. When she spoke, she kept her voice low and Holly had to lean far over, turning her head so the woman's lips were only inches from Holly's ear. She smelled of mint and lemon.

"They asked me to bring them something. But I couldn't. I told them I didn't have what they wanted. But then they . . . you know . . . threw me out of a boat."

Holly waited for more. Sat back. Spread her hands.

"Hon, I have no idea what you just told me." She raised her cup and found it empty, lowered it, gulped water from a glass instead. "Are you"—she gestured vaguely— "are you"—there was no way to be polite about this—"is this a drug thing?"

Vera remained placid except for a tiny quiver of her lips. "In a way," she said carefully.

Holly took a deep breath. "Okay. I can help. My brother is suffering as well, and I got him into rehab." Never mind that it didn't take and he had to go twice. She was fairly certain the second time didn't take either. But he'd always been needy, dissatisfied with life. A person had to be ready to quit. Was this woman ready? "Is it what you want?"

A slight shake of her head. "No. What I want is for you to get something for me."

"Oh. Well, I'm sorry, but I don't see why you think I have any of that. I don't . . . we live a very clean life. I'm not sure why . . . why . . ."

Vera touched Holly's shoulder, a gentle tap as if to quiet the words and thoughts together. "Not that. I need you to get me a sample of what your husband is working on."

Holly's heartbeat quickened. Whether the sensation surging through her was disappointment or unease, she had to get away from this conversation. She dug her wallet out of her bag and said, "I'm sorry for any misunderstanding. I'm going to go."

As she paid the bill and left a tip, her heart hammered faster and faster. Oliver led a research team at a pharmaceutical branch of Calypso Technologies, a company started by a stratospherically rich person whose name she could never remember. She listened to her husband speak of his research often, never once paying attention. Chemistry, biology—none of it held the magic for her it did for Oliver, and she suspected he understood that she pretended to be interested.

Because isn't that what you do when you're married?

Three blocks from home, Vera caught up with her, her stride so calm and purposeful it was obvious she had lagged behind to give Holly time to think. But there was nothing to think about.

"I can't help you," Holly said.

"You're mistaken there," Vera said. "Not only can you, but you will be happy to."

Holly stopped and turned. "Please, don't," she said. "I didn't understand. I thought you were . . ."

"I know what you thought."

"Don't follow me." She began walking again, and Vera followed.

"We will pay you," Vera said.

Holly kept walking.

Vera named a number.

Holly froze, her blood whooshing to her head, white noise in her ears.

"What?" Weakly.

"Your second mortgage, your credit card bills. Oliver need never know."

"How . . . ?"

Vera raised an eyebrow and crossed her arms. She said, "All you need to do is visit your husband where he works and walk out with a few vials. I'll tell you what to do."

"I can't do that," Holly said, but somewhere underneath, not even that deep, an understanding wriggled to life. She could, in theory, do that.

Vera must have seen something of that reflected in her eyes, or her voice, because her face gentled and she put her arm around Holly's waist. "Why don't you come and visit Step and me for a bit," she said. "Your kids won't be home for hours. You have time."

After that they walked in dueling silences, Holly's pensive, Vera's cheerful. Holly hesitated before her own home, Vera waiting with seeming indifference. This was nuts. Holly pulled away and marched toward her front walk but stopped. Would it hurt to hear them out? She didn't have to do anything they asked. She could leave, say no, go to the police. In fact (she turned around), she had the power here.

She continued to Forty-Six Oak as if in a cloud, her mind buzzing.

"Tea?" Vera asked, and Holly nodded, though she didn't want it.

The living room was as empty as last time, its air cool, redolent with a faint scent of something herbal, crisp. There was nowhere to sit.

"You know," Holly called out toward the kitchen, "I think I may have an extra couch in the crawl space. After my parents moved out of the house, they left furniture, but, erm . . . we redecorated, so . . ." She just couldn't help herself. She wondered if under the circumstances she sounded deranged. Or deluded.

Vera emerged from the kitchen and gestured at the stairs to the den. Holly was sure she was blushing again as she followed her hostess and perched on that linen-covered futon. The man, Step, had observed their descent, a laptop near his elbow, then closed it when they entered. The memory of his bare shoulders moving in the candlelight still flustered her (would probably vex her forever). She found looking at him intolerable and angled her body away, which required a convoluted maneuver, since he sat directly in front of her. She had an uncomfortable idea that he was reading her. It was how he stared with those large, gray, unblinking eyes of his.

"You've met Step," Vera said. "My husband."

Holly smiled in the vague direction of the husband without looking at him. What kind of name was that, anyway?

"Are you okay?" Vera asked. "Tea needs another minute or two."

"I'm fine," Holly said. "I'm—" She wished to be out of there and back home. And simultaneously she wished to stay, hear their proposition, relax into the cushions.

"So," Vera began.

Holly cleared her throat and interrupted. "Step—is that short for something?" She glanced at him and immediately away, as if she'd come too close to a hot current.

"Stepan," he said. "Stepan Alexeyevich Volkin. But that's a mouthful. Even I don't want to spend time saying all of that." His voice held a tinge of amusement, and that flustered Holly further. She could not settle on a role for herself within this trio. She told herself she was the one with power and they needed her. But, disconcertingly, it felt the opposite.

Vera said, "Your husband. As you can see, we're not asking for the moon. Three vials."

"Six. And a file," Step said, startling Holly.

"Right, and a file," Vera agreed.

"But you don't need me," said Holly. "Anybody can visit Oliver."

Vera smiled. "I wouldn't say anybody. He trusts you. You showing up would surprise precisely nobody."

"But if I took the vials, everyone would know right away. I'm not a magician. I can't hypnotize people into not seeing me take them."

"Well, of course not. That's silly," Vera scoffed and exchanged a glance with Step. Step didn't smile, but his face rounded, as if he'd relaxed his jaw muscles. "We'll give you look-alike vials. You take the ones we need, replace with the look-alikes."

"But . . ."

"Holly," Step said, his voice not soft anymore but ringing. Something happened to the light in the room, as if it dimmed, while simultaneously bringing the details of his face into greater focus: the faint shadow along his jaw, a tiny cut where he'd shaved. "We will show you what to do. We will practice. You'll be safe. And afterward, no more money worries. You keep your house. You pay off bills. You take family on nice vacation." Although the words sounded soothing, positive, his delivery was strange, commanding, as if he were issuing orders, not requests. He was not trying to convince her anymore.

Vera edged toward Holly and took her hand. "The money is a bonus, Holly. It's just something to show our gratitude." She moved even closer and wrapped Holly in a warm, scented embrace. "You're good," Vera said. "A good person. We watched you. You want everyone around you to be happy." She moved back and tucked a strand of Holly's hair out of her face. "Doing this for us, you'll make many people happy."

What was it that Oliver had been working on? She couldn't remember. He'd been on the same project for years, five at least. A dementia cure? Or was it wrinkles? She twisted her fingers, first in one direction, then another. "What exactly is it that you need?" she asked.

Vera recited a list of long names containing many syllables.

Holly frowned. She might not have recognized the compounds, but she knew of Oliver's aggravations. "But it's not ready. Not a bit of it has been properly tested. I remember him being frustrated that getting permission to start testing was taking so long."

"Exactly!" Vera said. "The drugs he's created can help people now. Right now. Today. They can save lives and greatly improve the quality of those lives."

"But they haven't been tested!" Holly repeated.

"That doesn't matter," Vera said.

Holly opened her mouth, and Step interrupted, his voice touching something in her so she had to fight the urge to agree to whatever he asked right then and there. He said, "Think of it this way. If you were dying of cancer, *dying*, and someone said, here's a pill and this pill might save you or it might kill you, would you take it? For that chance to live?"

She didn't have to think. The answer was obvious, the question rhetorical. Still, she said, "I'd take it." Furthermore, she'd give it to anyone who asked. Anyone who was already doomed.

"This is the same," Vera said. "We'll do our own tests, and we will synthesize the compounds based on what you get for us. People destined to die won't die. Because of you."

She remembered Oliver tackling something to do with longevity, but Vera's summary seemed extreme. Everyone died. Oliver was developing a postponement, nothing else.

Step rose abruptly, and Vera twitched, her hand jerking against Holly's hip. "She'll do it." She rubbed Holly's arm, though her embrace was no longer warm or comforting. "Won't you?"

Holly shook her head and disentangled her limbs from the woman's hold. How strange it all was—the empty rooms, the couple, their knowledge of her life, their offer. Dreamlike.

Once, years ago, her world had lost meaning. A psychotic break, her doctor said. She'd clawed her way out of that murky chasm because people needed her, waited for her, and she was always a responsible girl. She'd lived her life carefully since then. If the shadows called to her, she fought them off. Hence her extreme overscheduling, her need for constant contact with friends and family.

And yet, the one aspect of her "break" she'd kept to herself was her happiness within that chasm. Was it happening again?

Had the worries over her brothers and the financial stress driven her mental once more, so she dreamed while awake?

She'd go home. She'd resume her hamster-wheel life. And she'd research a little. Of course she'd never betray Oliver. Not ever.

But.

Before leaving their house, she looked back. "Oliver will lose his job." She noted that she sounded as if she'd agreed and was only clarifying a point. Would doing what they asked really, truly be a betrayal? It wasn't Oliver's company. He was only an employee. Wasn't it his goal to bestow these cures for whatever-it-was on people who needed them?

Step, who had trailed her to the door, slipped ahead and put his arm across the doorway. "Not if you let us show you how and practice. Nobody will ever know it was you."

She debated ducking under his arm. In the hallway's dimness he appeared taller, stronger. She was close enough to smell him—a carnal scent reminding her all over again of his nude body, his splayed fingers over Vera's belly. "Okay," she said. Her mouth had gone dry, and the word came out weak, a whisper. He lowered his hand and stepped aside, brushing against her.

Stupid, she said to herself. *Stupid, stupid, stupid*—a *stupid* for each step it took her to walk home. Her living room was a mess, the kitchen needed tidying. She hadn't worked on her novel in two days. But she was now overwhelmingly hungry. She hadn't been able to eat peacefully in months, not since the first foreclosure letter arrived.

Her stomach growling, she cooked a tuna avocado melt, then fried an egg and put that on top. She sat at her kitchen table, the kids' notebooks and drawings shifted to the side, Kiki's toy train acting the paperweight, and devoured the first proper meal she'd had in a long time, washing it down with a large glass of iced tea. Buster hopped onto her lap and followed her fork intently with his large eyes until she fed him a crust. She shouldn't have been feeding him from the table, but a divine carelessness overtook her, and she let him lick her plate to his heart's content.

By the time he finished, the first bus arrived, and she waited for Kiki to tumble out and into her arms. She prepared a bowl of noodles for him, and then Freddie and Hannah were home, asking for their snacks. Next came baseball practice and an early scout meeting, followed by the rush home, where she emptied a box of pasta into boiling water, dumped a can of plum tomatoes into a skillet and added Italian sausage, then a pinch of oregano from her windowsill herb garden.

Oliver Dubois came home that night to a fragrant home, sleepy children, and an opened bottle of wine.

"Tell me about your day," said his wife. "I want to hear all about it."

Because finally understanding what your spouse did for a living was a good idea under any circumstances.

It absolutely was.

15

July: Laney

LANEY WAS PREPARED to play with the Volkins' locks, but their patio door stood slightly ajar, its latch bent and jagged. The thin glass vibrated under her hands as she slid it open. She'd walked into the epicenter of Saturday night's devastation—the den, where the fire had started, where Step had been found. An acrid odor still clung to the walls. She pictured Step lying on his side, gasping with pain, his face ashen as blood poured out of the gunshot wound. It wasn't so much an exercise in ghoulishness as a desire to visualize and understand the events.

Her flashlight illuminated dark, blotchy stains on the scuffed parquet, sooty streaks near the ceiling. She crouched by the corner, where a square of wall had been cut out by Crime Scene investigators. According to neighborhood gossip, one of the bullets had been extracted out of Step's body at the hospital; the second one had slammed into the wall roughly two feet off the ground. Carefully, Laney lowered herself to the hardwood and flipped to her stomach, placing her thighs over the darkest stain. She looked at the cut wall, back at herself, and raised her hips two feet off the floor. She then stood quickly and brushed crud off her legs. She should have worn sweatpants, not shorts and flip-flops.

But at least she now knew something she hadn't known before. Step had not been standing, nor lying flat on the floor, when he'd been shot. It was almost as if he'd been kneeling, or on his hands and knees, his head toward the wall. She supposed it was possible Holly shot him. Step had no reason to lie about it—or rather, no reason known to Laney. Holly must have been in the den's doorway, Step facing away from her. On his knees.

Laney frowned. Even if she believed Step Volkin, the scene painting itself before her eyes made no sense. She couldn't reconcile it with her affable, delicate friend who could barely make herself utter a curse word without stuttering or blushing.

Upstairs, the house was astonishingly empty, as if the couple had never quite committed to inhabiting it. Between her flashlight and the ambient streetlight streaming through the windows, the living room lay bare, featureless except for the small paintings dotting the walls. They were five- or six-inch-wide rectangles of wood, shellacked to a deep gloss, and religious in nature. Somber saints with halos like crescent moons stared at her with pained expressions, the style reminding her of the artwork she'd seen when she worked that Russian racketeering case in Brighton Beach. Laney couldn't decide what was creepiest: the massive bloodstains in the den, the empty living room, or all those tiny holy men watching (judging?) her intrusion.

The kitchen was more lived-in. The Volkins clearly spent time there, evidenced by a small bundle of bills and flyers spilling from a counter, glasses and a bowl in the sink, a faint rank smell indicating a full garbage bin. She shined her light at the cabinets. Thick golden oak, plain white knobs, the varnish rubbed off around the handles and edges. She dragged a chair toward the cabinets, then climbed on top. The Volkins might not have enjoyed decorating or even buying furniture, but they ate like normal humans. The cupboards were stacked neatly with sugar and tea packets, a box of oatmeal, a jar of sour cherry preserves and one of black currant, one of peanut butter, boxes of mac and cheese, rice, a bottle of honey, a package of crackers.

Laney removed everything to the counter and swept her flashlight over the interior.

Nothing. Empty. Cobwebs.

She turned and sat on the counter, her feet on the chair seat. She pointed the light down and swung it along the floor and into corners. Other than dust, grime, and footprints, the floor was unremarkable. Nothing on the fridge except for a promotional magnet holding the trash collection schedule in place.

She jumped down and looked under the cabinets. Dust, a paper clip, a pebble. As she leafed through the pile of letters and junk mail, a scrap of paper slipped out and fluttered to the floor. The scrap looked like a label from a pill bottle, or half of a label anyway. She smoothed it against her knee, then turned on her phone's magnifier. A part of a bar code, a name. *Calypso* something or other. It struck a memory. She shoved the pile of junk mail into her bag to go through at her leisure later. If Crime Scene had left them, the papers were probably useless, but then again, maybe not.

Just as she put her foot on the stairs leading to the bedrooms, a loud knock startled her, and she flipped off her flashlight.

"Who's in there?"

Laney recognized the voice. It belonged to one of the older men on the block, a Mr. Pasado who lived directly across the street. He must have noticed her light bouncing around in the dark.

"I know you're there! I've called the police!"

Dammit.

He peered through the front windows, moonlight reflecting off his bald patch. "Who is that?"

Laney crept down the stairs to the den and dashed through the patio door, not bothering to shut it all the way. She speed-walked through the Volkins' backyard, into the rhododendrons separating their property from the next, then edged her way out onto the street, shaking leaves from her hair. A dog's aggrieved barking made her jump, and she cursed under her breath and shushed at the animal, which only outraged him more. As the dog's owner yelled at him from inside his house, Laney walked away, forcing a relaxed slump to her shoulders. If anyone noticed her, they'd see a diminutive woman in shorts and flip-flops taking a casual stroll. Nothing suspicious.

At least she was now at a right angle to Mr. Pasado, with a house and a half separating them and no chance of him seeing her. She might have been able to explain her presence somehow, but she didn't have the strength to try. The police cruiser arrived at the Volkins' a few minutes later, the car door slamming as the patrolman got out. Though she couldn't hear the cop's end of the conversation, Mr. Pasado's indignation rang out loud and clear. By the time she looped around and approached her house from the other end, a clutch of neighbors had gathered down the block, and her phone began pinging and buzzing in her pocket.

With a dragging reluctance, she slipped out her phone and saw the neighborhood group texts lighting up her screen, one excited bubble after another.

Someone broke into the Volkins house
Who?
What?
Tracy you drunk again?
Stop hahah no I'm serious, Pasado called the police
What?

Laney turned her phone off and opened her door.

Home was quiet, Alfie still in his room, no longer playing. She knocked on his door and he answered, his face accessible, his eyes searching hers for affirmation that all was well.

"You doing okay?" she asked.

"I'm okay." He chewed his lower lip. "Are you?"

Softening, she brushed his fingers lightly with her hand. "Yes, honey. I'm fine. I'm going to see Oliver Dubois, okay?"

He nodded.

"You're sure you okay?"

He nodded.

"Will you talk to me if you're not?"

He nodded again. And that's the best she was going to get.

16

July: Laney

Holly's son Freddie was sitting on the front steps of his uncle's house when Laney parked and walked to the front door. She'd called ahead, and Adam said yeah, sure, whatever. The strain and flatness in his voice were palpable, and she wondered how he was handling having his brother-in-law, three surplus children, and Holly's dog in his house. He'd only this past winter finished yet another round of chemo; Laney remembered how cautiously optimistic Holly had been.

Freddie hunched over his knees, his sleek-haired head turned sideways, toward a tree. Laney was so used to seeing children's faces illuminated by a screen that her first thought was something happened to his phone. But as she got closer, she saw the desolation in his features, and her throat tightened in empathy. Of all Holly's progeny, Freddie was most like his mother in both looks and temperament—an easygoing, gentle boy. At eleven, he was still small, none of his father's stature apparent.

She sat next to him on the steps. "Hey," she said.

"Hey." He sounded smothered, exhausted.

She put her arm around his shoulders and squeezed. "I'm gonna go talk to your dad."

"All right."

"Afterwards, I'm in the mood for ice cream. How about you? You want to come with me and get a cone at Shake-n-Twist?"

He shook his head.

She sighed. "Hang in there. It will work out."

His head snapped around to face her. "Have you heard from her?"

"No." The trust in his eyes terrified her. "I just know your mom. She will come back to you, even if"—she had to look away—"even if. She will come back. She loves you too much not to."

And with that, she stood and walked into the house, her face hot with shame. She hoped she hadn't lied to Holly's son in the worst way possible.

Adam and his wife were murmuring in the kitchen while their children and the other two Dubois kids sprawled in the den watching a movie. Buster tottered into the kitchen, gave Laney's ankle an exploratory lick, and disappeared again into the den.

Revealing nothing she knew or suspected, Laney asked after Adam and his family, then excused herself. Oliver was ensconced in a back bedroom, a long hallway separating him from the rest of the first-floor living space. Framed photographs lined the hallway on both sides, and she paused to study them—partly to center her thoughts, partly wondering if something in those pictures might give her, as an outsider, a view into her friend's mind. Most of them were from when Holly and her brothers were children, professionally taken photographs often involving matching sweaters. She inspected a couple before she realized there were four children instead of three. School-age Holly, in a pink dress and purple leggings, Adam and Roger with their wide grins and neat haircuts, and another girl. The most startling thing about this girl was how much she and Holly looked alike, as if it were the same child but a few years apart. The pictures showed the siblings progressing in age, lengthening, thinning, Holly with pink highlights and short hair, the older girl in a low-cut top and glitter on her eyelids. The last picture was of the three siblings Laney knew, taken years later. She doubled back and peered at the next-to-last photo. Something about that older girl disturbed her, and Laney had to look away before the thought crystallized. She reminded her, not a little, of Vera.

This girl could only be Holly's sister, but Laney'd never heard her friend or any of the family mention one, the implication being the sister was either a lost soul or dead. Knowing Holly's generous nature, which precluded the kind of estrangement some families practiced, Laney had the uncomfortable feeling it was the latter. Well, she'd never discussed her brother with Holly either, so . . . she guessed they were even in the keep-major-life-events-secret category.

Standing before the door to Oliver's room, Laney took a deep breath and knocked, then turned the doorknob and went in without waiting.

His bruises seemed worse than yesterday morning, the redness turned black, the swelling around his eyes and nose raw, painful looking.

"Hey, Oliver," Laney said.

He sat slumped in an armchair, turned toward the window, illuminated by the streetlight and a small lamp on top of a dresser. His shoulder twitched at her voice, but he remained silent.

The only other place to sit was the bed, so she leaned against the window frame and folded her arms around her middle.

"How are you doing?" she asked.

When he said nothing, she tugged back the curtain and peered at the quiet street. The window was half-open, the evening air fresh, with a tentative dampness promising rain.

"How did Holly get hold of my gun?"

No response.

"What was she doing with Vera?"

Again, that shoulder twitch, followed by Oliver's mouth clenching so tight she heard his teeth grind, an eerie noise that went straight to her gut.

Mulish silence was an acceptable result of interrogation, though not the best. You learned from what the other person didn't say, from their reactions to your words.

"Why did you fight with him?"

Oliver was, if not twice Step's size, then a good third larger. If he'd wanted to hurt Step, he could have sat on him and achieved a more permanent result than a badly aimed gunshot. So why did Holly feel the need to shoot? No matter which scenarios Laney played out, none were logical, and that tormented her. Sure, people behaved illogically when viewed from a cool outside perspective, but once you understood them, their behavior always made sense. Jealousy, revenge, self-defense. None of it explained why Holly stole Laney's gun and shot a man her husband could have knocked out with one well-aimed punch. Had clearly been in the middle of knocking out.

But it wasn't just that. After ten years with the NYPD, Laney could spot a man who liked to throw his weight around, who wouldn't hesitate to hurt a person if they thought the person threatened them. Oliver didn't strike her as that type. Which meant he'd fought Step for some other reason.

She began pacing, her hands behind her back. "You know, I looked up Vera and Step. Or I started to. I still have more to check." She always did better if she could bounce her thoughts off another person. For a while now, that person had been Holly. "They're weird, Oliver. There's something about their documents that makes no sense. I wondered if they were forged or hacked, but I can't find any evidence right now." She stopped and looked at him. He'd slouched more since she walked into the room, as if his inner structures were softly collapsing on themselves, forcing his big, bruised head downward. "Your record is clean. You're an upstanding citizen, a good neighbor, a scientist. What did Step do to you?"

A noise outside, a rustle, and she looked out the window. Freddie had left the front stoop and moved to the pavement, stood in the road.

"Won't you talk to me?" Laney asked Oliver, sounding much more plaintive than she wanted to.

On the street, Freddie took another step forward. A car crested the hill and gunned it toward the boy, its lights engulfing him. Laney momentarily froze in place, then jerked the window up all the way and screamed Freddie's name. There was a screech and a curse, and the car careened away, Freddie small and untouched in its wake. Laney dashed out of the room and ran through the house and outside, where she grabbed the boy and pressed him to herself. What had he been thinking? What the hell had this child been thinking?

Behind her, Adam and his wife had run out as well and hovered on the front walk. She knelt and guided Freddie's chin up so she could look into his eyes. Once again, the desolation she saw made her hands tremble.

"Freddie? Did you see that car? Why did you do that?"

"What happened?" asked Adam.

The boy's face crumpled. "I don't know," he whispered.

"Jesus, Mary, and Joseph," Laney said, stood and held the boy close again. She pressed her palm to her chest to slow her heart. "You know what." She turned to Adam. "Let me take Freddie home with me. I think he needs to see his friends. He can spend time in the neighborhood tomorrow, and Alfie likes him. We'll play Monopoly or something. He's not looking too good tonight." She faced the boy. "Would you like that?"

He nodded into her side.

"Yes, that might be a good idea," Adam's wife said. "It's not very fun here right now."

"Okay, let me say good-bye to Oliver, and we'll go."

In the dismal back room, Oliver raised his eyes at her. Even through the insult done to his face, his feelings were exposed—sadness. Deep, horrifying, bone-crushing sadness. Wherever Holly was, whatever Holly had done, it was very quickly demolishing the people she loved.

Oliver said, "If that's what Freddie wants, you can take him."

She touched his shoulder. "Okay. It's okay," she said.

About to leave, she dug the label she'd found in the Volkins' kitchen from her pocket. "Do you know what this might be from?" Since he'd already faced away from her and wouldn't take the piece of paper, she put it on his arm, so that a sliver of yellow lamplight fell on it.

He peered, then lifted the scrap to his eyes. His mouth twisted with disgust.

"You recognize this? What is it?"

Without looking at her, he put the scrap in his mouth and swallowed.

"Damn, Oliver," she said, all patience dissolved. "Just for one second, stop being deranged, will you? I know something awful happened. But for heaven's sake, don't lose your mind!" Her voice rose, and she nearly screamed the last word. She glanced at the door, expecting Adam or his wife to barge in. She couldn't wait to leave this house and its unbearable tension. "All you have to do is ask, and I'll do anything to help," she said in a softer tone. "Holly saved me when I knew nobody. I owe her." But it wasn't that either. She would have done anything for Holly many times over. To repay not just one kindness, but many. Years' worth. "I'm on your side. Believe me."

Oliver lowered his head into his hands.

She brought Freddie home that night and made popcorn, dished out ice cream, asked Alfie to play whatever game Freddie wanted on the Xbox. She passed her fridge back and forth, back and forth through the evening, getting iced tea, whipped cream, chocolate chips. Opening and closing the door.

And only in a moment of contemplation, as she stood in the kitchen listening to the booms and thwacks thundering from the den where the boys played, did her eyes land on the business card held by a magnet on the fridge door. Oliver's business card. The card she'd seen daily for years and had therefore ceased to see. Oliver was the lead scientist at Calypso Technologies. As far as she knew, he worked in a research department specializing in . . . she had no idea. She wasn't even sure Holly knew.

She took the card down and stared at it. Why was a vial label from a Calypso Technologies laboratory stuck under the Volkins' mail pile?

17

April: Holly

THE MORNING AFTER she'd drunk-questioned Oliver about the experimental drugs he was keeping from the world, Holly had a headache. Okay, she was hungover, her eyes bleary against the crisp April light, her mouth dry, her stomach sensitive. She stood at the corner, waiting for the school bus. Kiki, usually garrulous and energetic, clung to her icy hand with an anxious determination, declining to interact with the four moms and six children at the bus stop. Scents of lilac and blooming magnolias spiked the air, making good on the promise of a hot spring, summer around the bend. Bake sales, dance recitals, soccer, track, church, birthday parties, the minutiae of their days burbled between them, and Holly laughed, shared recipes, and made plans for a girls' night this Saturday. Or next, or the one after that, or wait, maybe May would be better for everyone. Buster ran around off-leash, yapped at the children, and flopped onto his back every few minutes, inviting a belly rub. The entire scene was so clean, so wholesome, it could have been an insurance commercial, or perhaps an ad for a healthy adult breakfast cereal.

She could do this on autopilot. Her words were as familiar as prayer or a beloved song lyric, and though her thoughts raged, her mouth never betrayed her.

After the bus left, the women went their separate ways with a wave and a smile, knowing they'd be back at the same corner in six hours.

Six hours.

Holly closed her door on the fragrant day and faced her kitchen. It needed tidying—a wine bottle soured on the counter, dirty dishes curdled on the island, in the sink, on the table. A splotch of something dark and gritty stained the floor.

She'd gotten tipsy last night. Blotto. Soused. A second bottle of Chardonnay languished under the bushes out front, and she'd have to fish it out. Later; she'd find it later. At some point after dinner, she'd dropped her bowl of raspberry sorbet onto the kitchen's hardwood.

"Leave it," Oliver had said, grabbing her around the waist as she tried to clean it and pulling her up, close, kneading her as if he hadn't touched her in weeks. She was as diligent about their sex life as she was about her children's sports schedules. Once a week was date night, ironclad. Often, an additional morning or evening quickie completed the arrangement. It kept the marriage loving, devoted.

Hadn't it?

"You're frisky tonight," Oliver breathed into her ear, and she giggled.

"You're the one pawing me. Let me just get this bowl off the floor."

"Come here."

He lifted her blouse, and she hissed, "The kids are still awake."

"Barely." His mouth sticky on her neck, her breasts, his hands pressing, rubbing, pulling her body as if he wanted to cover himself with her skin, her flesh.

They crept (stumbled) to their bedroom, Holly shushing his every noise and him scoffing at her shushes. Thank goodness the children were indeed asleep, because Holly didn't know what had gotten into Oliver. He tumbled her onto the bed and out of her clothes, his tongue everywhere except her mouth because he'd pressed his hand against it, even though she stopped making noises the moment the bedroom door closed.

Whether spurred by the wine or by the lilac-scented night, he pushed into her with a teenager's desperation, a fist tangled in her hair, his chin digging into her shoulder. He was crushing her chest. She struggled to twist sideways, unsuccessfully, and then dug her fingers into his rib cage, sobering him into lifting himself to his elbows.

She started to tell him to slow down, but he cut her off with a kiss—hard, biting, breathless, and so desirous that her body responded despite her, not just unfurling but inviting him, greedy and wanton.

After, she lay on her back, her hair feathered up and out on the pillow, his heavy head on her breast.

"I guess I should serve wine with dinner more often," she said.

He said nothing, and she moved to slip away when he mumbled something into her skin.

"What?" she asked.

"You should grow your hair," he slurred, and it sounded more like *you shu go yr har.*

"Even longer?" She hadn't allowed herself the luxury of a salon in over a year, doing her own trims every three months.

"Mmm . . . like the first time I saw you." He rolled onto his back and bunched a pillow under his neck. His eyes were closed.

A cold heave of disbelief sloshed inside Holly. "What?" She'd had a pixie cut the first time he saw her, bangs with pink stripes dyed into them.

"You looked like you were glowing. The sun was behind you." He stroked her shoulder with an imprecise finger, poking her collarbone. Holly had to strain to decipher his next sentence. "You were wearing a Bowie T-shirt. Red and white. My beautiful girl."

She shoved his hand away, but it didn't matter. He was asleep.

That T-shirt had belonged to Abigail, and of course it was Abigail who had hair to her waist. Holly sat on the edge of the bed and did not cry as her husband snored softly behind her.

The Handsome Potato. That's what Abigail dubbed Oliver, and the name stuck, attaching itself to him so that even his parents sometimes referred to him that way. Twenty years later, Abigail's sharpness still cut.

Holly washed and dressed in pink yoga pants and a long-sleeved Henley, padded barefoot down the stairs, and carried the second Chardonnay bottle outside, not bothering with a glass. She perched on her front steps and watched the neighborhood unwind and dim as one by one the windows grew dark.

Before the wine seized them earlier in the night, she'd extracted quite a bit of information from the Handsome Potato.

The longevity drugs he'd been developing were strong, and possibly life changing, in every way. He even hinted his team might get a Nobel Prize for their work someday.

"But why can't you test it yet, if it's that good?" she had asked.

"Well, for one, fifty percent of all our rats die within a week of being injected. The other fifty percent thrive and party, but those odds aren't good enough for human trials."

On her porch at midnight, thighs still trembling, Holly glugged the rest of the wine and burped delicately into her fist. Fifty percent were awful odds. She'd tell Vera and her freaky husband tomorrow that the drugs were basically poison. Fifty percent poison.

That settled it. Nothing more to ponder. She staggered to her feet, accidentally knocking the empty bottle into the azaleas. Oh, well. Too dark to search for it now. She burped again and opened the heavy oak door her grandfather had cut and then carved himself, its leaf-and-branch design so familiar she knew each curl by feel. Once upstairs, she leaned against the doorframe to her bedroom and watched the Handsome Potato as he sprawled on the queen-sized bed. He snored, for all she knew dreaming of a dead girl.

When she tired of her own thoughts, she shuffled toward the bed and folded herself into the narrow space available to her. She'd considered sleeping on the living room couch, then decided against it because she hated for anyone to know of her unhappiness. Especially Oliver. They'd both had plenty misery in their lives. And there would be more coming.

In the morning Oliver grabbed the Tupperware she'd prepared for his lunch, patted the children, kissed the top of her head as if she were another child, and left for work, his face peaceful and free of concern. The world was a sweet place for Oliver Dubois.

She fed and sent off the older kids, waited with Kiki, and gossiped with the neighborhood moms, only to find herself once again alone in a silent, beloved, familiar, messy home.

She had six hours.

The house needed cleaning, but what was the point? It would be someone else's house soon.

Holly's phone pinged, and a text fluttered to the top of the screen. *Let's talk. Want to come over?*

18

April: Holly

VERA OPENED HER door and smiled at Holly with such accep-
tance and warmth, Holly couldn't help but smile back, the
morning's resentments fading. Vera wore a white sundress with
blood-red piping along the neckline, waist, and hem. She looked
crisp and unsullied, like a sugar cookie.

"Aren't you cold?" Holly asked. It wasn't sundress weather,
barely in the upper fifties.

"Not at all! I'm hardy." An even wider smile. "Come in, come in.
I have tea all ready." She closed the door behind Holly and leaned
into her for a quick, lemon-scented hug. "I'm so glad you're here."

If someone asked her three months ago how she'd feel about
committing an act of corporate espionage against her own husband,
Holly would have said, "Never. That's wrong. Just plain wrong."
Followed by, "Who would do such a thing? And why?" She still felt
this way (mostly), especially with the whole "fifty percent of rats die
horrible deaths" thing. She was here only to explain her position
and back out politely. No need to hurt anyone's feelings.

"I have an hour," Holly said. "Then I have to go home."

Step, busy viewing something on a laptop, raised his eyes at
her, his stare so direct she looked away at once, cursing herself
for being wimpy. Ballsy people never looked away. Ballsy people

outstared each other. She'd need to grow some balls if she was going to face her future with any kind of grace.

"There's chamomile, Earl Grey, oolong. Which would you like?" Vera extended a beautifully lacquered box filled with fragrant sachets.

"Oh, gosh." Holly's laugh sounded brittle even to her. "I'm not sure! Now, wine is a different story. Also, chocolate." She cleared her throat. "But I don't mean now. It's too early for wine." The thought sent a headachy spike pulsing behind her eyes.

Vera grinned and turned to Step, and he, as if receiving a telepathic command, pushed away from his desk and disappeared into the basement, coming out a minute later with a dusky bottle of Cabernet Sauvignon and three stemless glasses.

"Oh, you'll like that one," Vera said.

"No, I can't, really." But somehow a glass was in her hand, and she was lifting it to her mouth, and oh.

The wine was exceptional, with notes of black cherry, dried tobacco, and cloves, settling perfectly in Holly's belly, clearing her head, spiriting away the last queasy notes of last night's overindulgence.

"Listen." She swirled her glass gently, watching the dark liquid. "I can't help you. The drugs aren't safe. Very much not safe. It won't be right."

Vera sipped her wine and nodded, her eyes wide and agreeable. "We know that."

"You do?" Of course they did. Of course. They knew everything. "So . . . why do you want them?"

Step, who hadn't touched his glass, lifted his chin. "We know how to make them safe." He looked aside for a second, then back at her. "We believe we understand where the problem is. But we need the actual compounds in order to synthesize more and tweak them. We have an entire testing laboratory set and ready, just waiting. On their own, it will take Calypso Technologies fifteen years, easy, before a single person benefits from their invention."

He stood and walked toward a postcard-sized wooden painting hanging on a wall and studied it, then turned his back on it. "Besides, the guy who owns Calypso Technologies, it's all only for him. He's the one who thinks he should live forever. If any crumbs spill over to the rest of humanity, that's like extra credit. It's not important to him. All that money, all that research, all those bright minds, all to create something so a single man can live to a hundred and forty."

"Two hundred," Vera said.

Step frowned at her, slid his eyes back to Holly. "We can give this to everyone. We can fix it, test it, and begin production for the entire world within two years."

Holly's glass was empty, and she poured more of the delicious Cabernet. "Sweetie," she said, the word popping up out of nowhere, out of a crazy box in her head, forcing a blush to bloom on her neck and cheeks. "Look. I won't do it. If you know so much about it, you can re-create the drugs yourselves, right? Why do you need me to go and steal and—"

Step named a number, and Holly closed her mouth. Then drank her wine in a long, thirsty series of gulps.

"That," Step said, "and you'll be our Prometheus. Bring the fire of life to humankind. Why should the gods be the only ones to have it?"

Vera leaned over and poured the last of the wine into Holly's glass.

"Promethesesu . . . Prometh . . . Premethesis." Holly shook her head to unstick her tongue. "He didn't end well, did he?" She looked at Vera, who shrugged. "Didn't he have his liver eaten by an eagle?"

Step sat next to her and placed a heavy hand on her knee. "You will pay off your mortgage and we can discuss paying off the credit card bills. Life-prolonging, precious medication will be available to everyone, not just the billionaires." His index finger nudged her chin to face him. This time, she found she could maintain eye contact. The wine had given her balls. Wineballs.

"Tell you what," Step said. "How about I read your cards?" His voice changed, became lighter, more playful. He'd tilted into her space, and she didn't move back.

"Oh, what a great idea," Vera said. "You don't know, but Step is part Romany." She nodded. "He's been reading fortunes since he was a child."

Holly laughed. Something about a tween Step arranging tarot cards struck her as ridiculous, but the laugh died on her lips, the sound escaping her more like a surprised caw than a laugh. He'd already risen, reached and extracted a pack of playing cards from a shelf.

Vera had drifted away and now floated back with a glass of cool, mint-flavored water, which Holly guzzled as if she were dying from thirst. Which she felt she nearly was.

"Here," Step said. "Cut the cards."

Holly did.

"Again. And once more."

He contemplated the deck in his palm, closed his eyes, covered it with his other palm. His sallow face grew smooth, relaxed, except for a tautness around his mouth. He opened his eyes and positioned the first card in one move. Not tarot, regular playing cards.

"The first three are your past. The queen of diamonds. A young woman, flirty, chatty. Like a bright light in your life."

Something happened in the room then; the light dimmed when he spoke. The edges of her vision darkened, and his face came into razor-sharp focus. Holly's chest tightened and her breathing grew shallower. She didn't want him to do this.

"Second card, nine of spades. An accident or misfortune."

"Stop," Holly said, but it was too late, because the third card descended, tapping the table with a heartless slap.

"Ace of spades." He looked up, and again she held his stare, didn't turn away. "Death. The young woman died in an accident."

Holly gasped and rose to her feet. "I need to go," she said, but Vera clasped her wrist.

"You've thought it was your fault all this time," Step said. "It was an accident." He held up the nine of clubs. "Fate is a motherfucker."

"Sit down, Holly." Vera tugged her arm, bringing her back onto the futon, squished between them.

Unbelievably, Step was laying down another card, starting a second row.

"Stop, stop. Please." Holly lifted her empty water glass, put it back down again.

Step swept the cards into the deck and tucked them away into his shirt pocket.

They sat in silence until Holly said, "That's some party trick."

"Is not trick." Step's accent thick now, his pupils blown so large his eyes seemed nearly black with a thin gray rim around them. "Holly. Stop feeling responsible for things that are not your fault. Fix the ones that are your fault. And give a gift to everyone else. Do this for us."

She was unsteady on her feet when she walked out of their house and had to stop halfway up the hill. The day was cool and still bright, trees blooming and breathing pollen onto cars, bicycles, lawns. Onto her face. She blinked against the grit.

Step had gotten only part of the story right. What happened with Abigail was Holly's fault, and the only comfort she had was that nobody but her realized it. Her phone pinged, and she gazed at it as if in slow motion, the text taking long seconds to assemble meaning inside her mind.

Her friend and next-door neighbor, Laney, wanted to know if she was up for an evening drink on the patio. *I think I'm going to turn in early hon*, Holly texted.

Laney responded with a hug emoji, a thumbs-up emoji, and a *later*, followed by a two-glasses-clinking emoji.

Holly had four hours left before the first bus started bringing the children home. Her overstuffed mailbox upchucked another foreclosure letter, a past-due credit card bill, the gas-and-electric bill, and the water bill. She incarcerated the bills inside the ancient bread tin she'd inherited from her grandmother and shook out a garbage bag. An hour later, the house looked better—dishes put away, counters and sink cleared and wiped, the floor Swiffered.

Yes, Abigail had been her fault. The foreclosure was her fault. She was out of money and her brothers were nowhere near done needing more. Needing her. And Oliver had thought he was fucking Abigail last night. How many other times had he thought this? Was that his default fantasy? Teenage Abigail with her mermaid-long hair, her dark-red lips, every time he held Holly?

Wine—last night's, this morning's—breathed from her pores. She felt sticky, sick, her eyes grainy. This was no way to live.

She stripped and showered, then dressed in pomegranate jeans and a cream-colored turtleneck. She troweled on foundation, eyebrow pencil, mascara, and mulberry lipstick. When she rang the "Great Balls of Fire" doorbell of Forty-Six Oak for the second time that day, she felt clean, clear, and decided.

19

April: Holly

"AGAIN," SAID STEP, a week later.

"The white storage cabinet on the second shelf. Six vials," Holly said. Step had shown her a detailed plan of Oliver's laboratory, and the room she'd previously dismissed as boring and messy suddenly acquired sense and structure.

"And the cameras?"

She counted off on her fingers. "One, to the left of the door, capturing the entire room. Two, on top of the cabinets by the sink. Three, on the other side, by the window."

Step nodded. Vera sipped her tea, her eyes squinched like a purring cat's.

"Where is the laptop usually?" Step asked for the fifth time.

"Also by the window, on Oliver's desk."

This part would be the trickiest, because she needed to attach a thumb drive to the laptop and copy a file from the network without being captured by the camera directly above her head.

"Password?" Step asked.

"I can get it."

Step's eyes narrowed with approval, his lips twisting at the corners. It was the closest to a smile she'd ever seen on him, and it made her unreasonably gratified. But then again, she was a people pleaser, and he'd been a tough customer.

"I should get back," she said. The excitement percolating through her seemed unwarranted, downright wicked. A part of her stood to the side and observed her behavior in shock, if not abject terror, while another part—the one that was speaking and walking and laughing—was mental with energy and glee. She'd be able to make mortgage payments! Multiple ones! She'd pay a chunk of a credit card bill!

"What's so funny?" Vera asked with indulgence, running a finger lightly along Holly's arm. Apparently Holly had giggled again, her hand against her mouth to stifle the hilarity boiling up inside.

Holly coughed and forced herself to be serious. She was rehearsing a crime. This was somber business. Not to be taken lightly. But all she had to do was meet Vera's amused glance, and she snorted, which caused Vera to snort, and they both doubled over with laughter.

She laughed because what else was she going to do? Hide? Run away? She couldn't afford to. Holly might have been bad with her family's money (she had reasons, though; didn't the reasons count?), but she wasn't a gullible idiot. She had demanded the Volkins prove they could deliver on their promise, and sure enough, they wire-transferred a hefty sum (though not alarmingly hefty) into her checking account as she watched. Down payment, Vera had said. The rest to come after Holly completed her mission.

She disentangled herself from the other woman and smoothed her hair.

"Now I'm really going," she said. And then a thought struck her, as if aimed into her brain by an exterior entity. "Are you both around tonight?"

Vera flicked her eyes toward Step, then back at her. "Yes," she said, drawing the word out with a soft question at the end.

"Come do something with me."

"What?" This from Step, cautious, his shoulders hunching, then pushing back as if he reminded himself to relax. He cocked his head. The chain around his neck had loosened, and she saw it was a religious medal, a saint dangling over his shirt. She couldn't unsee it now—the agonized glossy brown head of the martyr with its rolling eyes raised to the heavens, the halo like a gold sickle topping his tousled hair. What in the world possessed her to ask them about tonight? For a second, she wondered if the impulse had been transmitted by Step's saint or by her own angel. (Not that she truly believed in such things, not anymore. Not much.)

"So, I volunteer at a soup kitchen once a month. I'd like you both to come and help. When it gets warmer, more people come for the food, and we need more volunteers."

"A soup kitchen?" Vera asked.

"For what?" asked Step.

"For people who might be food insecure."

"Food insecure?" Vera looked at Step, but his eyes remained on Holly.

"You know, people who maybe can't always afford a hot, home-cooked meal. Or, for some reason, can't cook for themselves. We cook for them."

"So, like what, homeless people?" Vera asked.

"No, not necessarily." She looked back and forth between these two—sleek, young, healthy. What did they know of poverty or homelessness? And really, what did she know? Well, she knew something. She knew what it meant to leave home, to sleep in the woods, bathe in a lake, eat food strangers left for her. She knew something of being not right in the head. But, as Oliver liked to say whenever she remembered that time, who was right in the head anyway?

"What are you thinking right now?" Step asked.

"Oh, leave her be," Vera said.

Holly shook her head. She never spoke of the aftermath of her sister's death. Never. "Don't worry about it," she said. "I shouldn't have asked you to come."

The ensuing silence felt like agreement, like judgment.

"I don't think you would be happy if we went with you," Step said after a while, his voice quiet, and Vera glared at him.

Holly nodded as if Step's response was normal. She would not ponder why he thought that, and she would not ask. She was pretty good at not pondering uncomfortable things. A master.

She got home with heaps of time to walk Buster and prep a quickie dinner for the family. She was still super-wife-and-mother Holly Dubois. Her mind was not breaking. She was completely, totally, absolutely A-OK.

20

July: Laney

T HE DAY AFTER Laney met her son's girlfriend for the first time, she met her again.

Laney came home later than usual, having stopped at the grocery store. Work had been hectic, some client emergency chasing Jack and his father out of the office and consigning her to incoming queries on top of her own cases. The mysterious lunch with Jack never materialized, which fact, when she had time to mull it over, left her emptier than a missed meal should have. The buffalo chicken wrap she bought from the deli and ate at her desk did little to relieve this feeling, but by then she was too busy to pay it much mind.

Alfie was home; she could hear sounds coming from his room. The sun hadn't set yet, but tarried, low and red, glaring through the trees, and the light inside her house was like champagne.

She flicked on the kitchen light, extracted a tray of chicken from a shopping bag, sprinkled it with rosemary, salt, and lemon juice, and stuck it under the broiler. She'd steam broccoli, slice tomatoes, and that would be dinner enough. If Alfie wanted more, he could make toast.

She was rinsing tomatoes and considering Holly's nature (wanton housewife? would-be murderess? none of it computed) when a creak on the stairs warned her Alfie was sneaking. No way would she let him leave now, not when dinner was almost done. She was about to tell him that when she turned and saw it wasn't Alfie.

No, the person who froze before her frown, one bare foot hovering over a stair, hair disheveled, was Mona. Her top was inside out. And she was definitely in her twenties.

Laney placed her knife on the counter and her palms on her hips.

"Hi, Mrs. Bird," Mona said, going for the nothing-whatsoever-is-going-on-at-all smile and failing.

"Mona, right?"

"Yes." She paused again, giving Laney an in.

"Stay for dinner, won't you?"

"Oh," Mona's hand floated to her shoulder, where she felt a seam, which made her look down, which made her realize her shirt was inside out. As her face flooded with color, she said, "Sorry, I need to leave."

Laney took three plates from a cabinet and plunked them on the kitchen table. "I think you should stay."

Alfie was now halfway down the stairs, and his dark-blue eyes flicked between the two women with worried uncertainty.

"No, really. I should go." Mona found her sandals in the mudroom by the front door.

Laney stomped toward the mudroom. Her emotion was rising, making it harder for her to plan ahead or weigh her words.

"Mom," Alfie said behind her, and she could hear concern and warning in his tone, but she ignored it.

"How old are you, Mona?" she asked.

"Excuse me?" Mona asked.

"Where do you work?" Laney asked. "Because you don't look like you're a high school student. Are you? A student?"

"Mom, stop."

Mona laughed, a nervous, high-pitched titter. "It's been nice to see you again, Mrs. Bird," she said, and opened the front door.

Laney said, "You do know Alfie is fifteen, right?"

Mona stepped outside, then turned back. "Mrs. Bird, I care for Alfie very much. And he cares for me."

"Stop with the Mrs. Bird, will you? I'm not old enough to be *your* mother, for God's sake." She pointed at Alfie, his eyes wide and dark. "He's a child."

"Stop it," Alfie said. He said this quietly, but the words carried, and Laney lowered her arm.

Mona looked at him over Laney's shoulder, then ran down the front walk toward her little green car. How did Laney not see that car when she came home?

Laney closed the door, marched into the kitchen, and removed the blackened chicken remains from the broiler, turned off the stove with a loud, irritated click.

"Dinner," she said.

"I'm not hungry," Alfie said, still in that quiet voice.

"Are you having sex with her?" Laney blurted. Even though the answer was in that inside-out top, in his blanched cheeks and lips, in his fury-narrowed eyes.

He didn't answer, instead walking slowly, as if exercising great self-control, to his room.

She threw her oven mitt to the floor and sank to a chair. Absent-mindedly, she typed a message to Holly and hit send, then moaned and raked her fingers through her short hair. She needed someone to talk to!

Are you busy? she typed to the next person in her recent-texts list.

No, came the reply within seconds.

Care for a drink and a bowl of pretzels on my patio? she texted.

This time the answering text was started and stopped three times before the final version came through. *K*

Thirty minutes later, the sun gone, citronella candles lit on every flat surface on her patio, Laney extended a cold beer to Jack Boswell.

"So." He accepted the glass and settled on a wicker chair.

She'd so rarely seen him out of his suits that the sight of him in cargo shorts, T-shirt, and running shoes was disconcerting, intimate, as if she'd glimpsed him in his bedroom.

He said, "Did you have an epiphany about Holly?"

She gawked at him for a moment, regrouping. Of course; he assumed she'd called him to discuss their most pressing noncase.

"Only that I miss her more than ever." She took a sip of her drink. "I really needed her tonight, and, you know. Gone."

He squinted at her. "Why, what happened?"

"You don't have kids, right?"

A half grin curled his lip. "No, not yet. Maybe never." He shrugged. "I'm not like Ed. I don't feel his need to be a family man."

"Yeah. Well." Why did she call him, anyway? Was she really that desperate for a friend? For the past four years Holly had served that role, filling in the emptiness left after Laney's divorce. But no, that wasn't right. Theo had been such an absent husband that it wasn't him Holly replaced. Laney drank a hefty portion of her beer. She wasn't used to introspection, and the way her thoughts were heading, she was giving herself a headache.

The sound of the front door slamming startled her, and she jumped to her feet, then ran to the edge of the patio. Alfie was speed-walking up the hill, his T-shirt a spectral blotch winking between tree branches.

"Hey!" Laney jogged after him. "Where are you going? Stop right now!"

He did, only to glance at her and say, "I'll come back tonight," his tone such a complex mix of pleading, accusation, and guilt that her mouth clamped shut.

She watched him disappear around the bend and walked back to the patio where Jack sat, quiet and still, his face neutral.

"Jack, I'm sorry. I need to go." Where? After her son? She suspected Alife would refuse to come home with her. Never mind that she had no idea where he went.

"What's going on, Laney?"

She puffed out a quick breath. "I wish I knew." She looked at him but couldn't maintain eye contact.

He put his glass next to hers and said, "I see. Why don't you tell me what your kid did that got you in a twist, and I'll straighten him out." He cracked his knuckles. "I'll show him what's what." He tapped a fist into his chest. "Man to man."

She grinned, surprised he could do this, change the tone of the evening in one sentence. "Stop it."

"Okay, but what did he do? Smoke weed? Get drunk at a party?"

Her expression this time must have been a deal less cheerful, because he sat up straighter, all softness erased from his face. "I'm sorry," he said. "That was obtuse." Of course Ed would have shared Alfie's history with his brother. Smoking weed and drinking was exactly what Alfie had been doing a year ago. Except not at a party but with an older man, a vengeful ghost from Laney's past.

"It's fine," she said. "It's his girlfriend."

He kept quiet this time and raised his glass for another sip.

"I believe she's in her twenties."

He swallowed, his glass frozen in midair.

"He's fifteen. I think they're having sex. Or something close to it."

He lowered his glass. Said nothing.

She said, "That's a misdemeanor at least. She can get a year in prison."

He looked at his hands.

"What?" she asked.

"It's a misdemeanor," he said. "If you report it." He met her eyes. "Are you going to report it?"

"He's a child," she said. "It's a crime, whether or not I report it."

He said nothing.

"Are you quiet because he's a boy and she's a woman? If the genders were reversed, would you be more disturbed?"

He blinked at his shoes. "Perhaps," he said.

"Do you really think he's more equipped to handle this than a fifteen-year-old girl would be?"

"I don't know him," Jack said.

"All you need to know is he's two years shy of the age of consent."

Jack sat back and raised his eyes again. "Do you think he's going to be happy if you put his girlfriend in jail?"

She stood and began pacing. "I can't let it continue," she said after a few laps around the patio.

"Then tell him that," he said.

"What would you do?" she asked. "I mean, if you were him and your mother told you to stop dating a girl?"

"Is she hot?" he asked.

She stopped and stared at him in disbelief.

"I'm joking," he said. "I think it's weird to date someone that young, no matter which way the genders go. But to answer your question—if my mother told me at fifteen to stop dating an older woman, I'd say okay, then sneak around anyway."

That was pretty much what Laney supposed would happen as well.

She sat back down, the cushion under her sighing unhappily. "So what do I do?"

"What's this woman's name?"

"Mona."

"Just Mona? No last name or anything?"

"Shit."

"That's her problem right there. Shit's a shitty name."

Laney cocked an eyebrow.

He said, "Tell you what. You put your investigator cap on and investigate that last name for me, and then Mona and I will have a chat. How's that?"

"What are you going to say to her?"

"Oh, I'm sure I'll think of something. But that will leave you out of it and your kid won't walk around treating you like yellow snow."

She finished her beer and brought two more for them. "Am I wrong not to report her right now? She's breaking the law." But more crucially, she knew Alfie was deeply involved, had felt it in her bones when she saw his face tonight.

He shrugged. "I guess that's up to you."

"Fuck."

He popped a handful of pretzels into his mouth and chewed. Then said, "So, Ed told me an interesting call came in last night."

Whatever slight level of relaxation she'd achieved vanished, and the muscles along her back tightened.

"Oh yeah?" She drank more beer, now warm and unpleasant.

"Yeah." His posture was at ease, but his face seemed sharper, attentive. "Someone broke into the Volkins' house." He let that hang between them. "You know anything about that?"

She shrugged, which was terrible, an admission, but she didn't trust her voice. She shouldn't have been drinking. Once again she regretted her impulse to invite him over, to confide in him. She should be stronger than that.

He sat forward, his elbows on the glass patio table. "Laney, did you go inside the Volkins' house last night?"

Her resolve weakened. Couldn't she trust him? How badly could a man wearing silly electric-blue running shoes hurt her? She wanted to tell him, to share her thoughts, to talk it through. Who else would understand? He had the training and the mindset for investigations.

Her jaw clenched shut. What did she know about him, after all? Only that he was a privileged and beloved son, an investigator with his own cases and a primal duty to his family.

"Tell me something," she said. "What case did you want to discuss with me over lunch?"

He studied her face, his own giving away nothing. "You know what? It's all good. I think I got it."

And just like that the night's mood curdled, the air around them growing heavy with moisture, pressing on Laney's chest, on her eyes.

"I'll be off, then." He got to his feet and brushed pretzel crumbs off his shorts. "Get me Mona's name, and I'll take care of it."

"Yeah, yes." She stood to walk him to his car, her limbs exhausted, her mind even more so. She didn't want to think about anything anymore; it was too tiring.

Once indoors, she started a pot of coffee and set her laptop on the kitchen table. Despite the citronella candles, she'd managed to get bitten at least a couple dozen times. She spent the next few hours writing and uploading reports, sipping lukewarm coffee, and scratching herself bloody.

When Alfie came home, he hesitated at the kitchen doorway.

She closed her laptop and rubbed her eyes. "I'm worried about you," she said, picking up their conversation as if there hadn't been a five- or six-hour interval. "You're so young."

He lowered his gaze, his shoulders hunching.

"I'm only asking you to slow down, okay? There's no rush, is there?"

As always, it seemed her words traveled to him through molasses, a minute or two passing before he nodded.

"Good night," she said.

"Good night," he said. Then, something he hadn't said in a long time, "I love you," and it sounded like a peace offering and a plea.

CHAPTER

21

April: Holly

A week later Holly walked down the hill to the Volkins',
not noticing the hot sun or the flagrant blooming of every
single flowering shrub and tree. She managed to wave hello and
exchange niceties with two neighbors and even offered to make
her famous chocolate-peppermint cake for a child's birthday party
the coming weekend, all on autopilot, while underneath her mind
skittered from thought to terrified thought.

Only when the door to Forty-Six Oak opened did the day
clarify itself for her. Today was the day. Before today, she was
law-abiding, decent. Still was. Still would be until sometime this
afternoon, when she would go into her husband's place of work
and steal from him.

Vera looked at her critically, then squeezed her arm.

"You look good," Vera said, but she sounded tense, and looked
tense, making Holly regret the decision to come here for a last-
minute rehearsal.

"Come out back," Step called from the patio.

He'd arranged his laptop on a wrought-iron table and parked
himself in a wooden chair, a glass of Scotch by his hand. And
when he got to his feet and walked toward the two women, Holly
realized it wasn't his first glass of the morning. Nor his second.

"You look like a champ," he said to Holly, but it came out more like *chimp*.

Vera rolled her eyes. "Are you ready? Do you have password?"

Whenever those two got drunk or emotional, their accents became gloppy, as if their mouths and brains had to work overtime to expel words.

Holly nodded. A few days ago, as Oliver tried to work from home, she stood with her hands caressing his shoulders, rubbing, kissing his neck, behind his ears, the top of his head. Delighted, he stopped typing and kissed her, but she nudged him away. "Sorry. I shouldn't distract you. You need to work." She withdrew, and he seized her around the waist and pulled her back, burying his face in her middle. She pushed his hands off with a wink.

"Work," she said.

"You're no fun," he mumbled into her hip. But he let go and turned to his laptop, because he did have work, and he had a deadline, and he was the most scrupulous person she knew. As he entered his password, she caught the keyboard strokes and memorized them—a trick she'd learned from a sorority sister back in college. It was always easier if the password used a word or phrase, though she could also absorb random letters and numbers. Focus and mnemonics, that's all it took. Oliver's password surprised her with its clarity—*FortressOfSolitude1985*. She felt as if two icy fingers pinched her heart. Would it really be so simple?

Oliver glanced at her.

"What's wrong?" he asked.

"Nothing," she said quickly. "I'm tired."

"Well, go to sleep early tonight," he said, his attention on his screen.

Holly did not go to sleep early that night. She did not sleep at all, and instead watched television, texted her many friends until even they told her to wrap it up for the night, and eventually went for a long walk with Buster, which still did not tire her enough.

Consequently, today, in the Volkins' backyard, with the sun shining and feeding all the green, she was twitchy and wrung out, ready for everything to both start and be already over.

They ran through the rehearsal a few times, but an incipient headache dulled her performance, and after forty minutes Step gestured at Vera. She disappeared, reappearing five minutes later with a cup of tea, a small plate of biscotti, and two orange pills.

"Let's sit," Vera said. "We always sit before leaving to make sure we didn't forget anything. Here." She pushed the pills into Holly's hand.

"I have to go soon," Holly said.

"Half hour. Then you go. Drink." Vera's eyelid twitched, and she squinted against the tic.

Holly took the pills and drank her tea, dipped a corner of the cookie into the warm liquid and nibbled at it. Within minutes her headache vanished and her mind cleared. What would happen if she stayed here? Didn't drive to Calypso Technologies? Didn't commit a felony? The sun shifted through the trees, and a bright ray illuminated the medal around Step's neck.

"That is the most beautiful thing I've ever seen," Holly said, wondering why she was so calm. So remote. Whatever they gave her to eat and drink just now was magic. Why couldn't she have that every day of her life?

She reached an index finger to touch the medal but pulled back when she noticed Step's body tense. Normal Holly would have been mortified, but soon-to-be-criminal Holly didn't care, acted contrite only to be polite. Also, what in heaven's name was in those pills?

"Family heirloom," Step said. He looked at his fingers, then met her eyes, and she didn't flinch, flush, or lower her head. She met his stare and held it.

He said, "My family died in an accident when I was ten. This medal belonged to my father, and he . . . and then it was mine."

Having been raised Catholic and since drifted, Holly had an ingrained faith in saints, one she would have dismissed outright if questioned. "Who is it?" she asked, meaning, *What does he protect?*

Step turned away, shaking his head. "Saint Rakh," he said. "Are you Catholic?"

She nearly said the usual—Catholic lite, Easter Sunday and Christmas, blah, blah—but she didn't. "Yes," she said.

"Saint Dismas, then," he said.

Vera cleared her throat, her eyes questioning. "Step," she said, a warning in the tone.

"It's time to go," Step said.

Holly had texted Oliver earlier, asked if he'd like to meet for lunch. Thank God he was only too happy to agree, didn't question her reasons. Although she'd paid the most pressing bills with the money Vera had given her, she needed more. Much more.

"Hey," Step said, and placed a firm hand on her bare shoulder, sending a shiver through her as if his hand wasn't flesh but ice. Because of the day's heat, she wore a spaghetti-strapped dress, dark blue with a slim skirt. "Don't worry. You'll be fine."

Vera gave her a sharp squeeze, which might have been meant as a hug. She said, "By this evening you'll have the money to pay off much of what you owe." And then, as if reading Holly's mind, "Remember, it's not Oliver from whom you're taking this. It's from a multibillionaire who won't miss it at all. Not in the grand scheme of things."

Holly buried her forehead in Vera's neck. It's what she used to do with Abigail. "And what will you have by this evening?" she asked.

Vera pulled away and looked into Holly's eyes. "Again with the second-guessing?" A note of annoyance.

Step caught Holly's hand and placed something small inside, folded her fingers around it. "Come on," he said. "Oliver's waiting."

She opened her hand, and the Saint Dismas medal rested on her palm.

"For good luck," Step said. "Bring it back when you have everything." He smiled, the alcohol giving him a blurred sheen, but under that he'd grown ashen, ghastly even, as if he were half-dead.

"I'll take good care of it," she said, because she sensed the medal meant something deep to him, and because Vera looked near ready to snatch it out of her fingers.

She tucked the medal into her sizable handbag and walked around toward her car, the heat dry and clean against her skin. She found it impossible to admit she'd do something awful in less than an hour, but that's where her actions brought her, and that's what she would do. What was the alternative? Lose the house? Live in a tent? Even her extended family couldn't save her. She got herself into this trouble; she'd get herself out.

She would do this one thing, and nobody would be the wiser. Her family could continue as always.

The sixteen-mile drive to Oliver's research facility took almost forty minutes, during which he texted twice, checking on her.

Traffic, she texted, followed by, *Accident*. In truth, she drove too slowly, enraging her fellow drivers to the boiling point. One man lowered his window and banged the trunk of her car with his fist as he finally passed her.

I'm coming out in a sec, Oliver texted when she arrived and parked.

Need to pee, she texted back.

Okay, come up.

The man who started Calypso Technologies was obsessed with aging. As in, he had gone on record, multiple times, stating that he planned to live forever. Or at least past his two hundredth birthday. His research facility pursued this goal on multiple fronts—everything from severe diet modifications to gene therapy to whole-brain emulation and figuring out a way to download human consciousness. One way or another, this man would live, even if it meant his mind floated in a box while his body rotted.

Oliver's specialty was biomedical compounds. He led experiments that (at least according to the Volkins) had zeroed in on a series of drugs that could, when taken as a precisely targeted cocktail, eradicate dementia, increase cellular life span, decrease the degeneration of DNA strands, and improve the youthfulness and elasticity of skin. The only drawback was these methods were years away from clinical trials, much less from public consumption.

"Except you will change that," Vera had told Holly. "Our Prometheus."

"Oh, please," Holly had said, with her typical dismissal of any praise.

Vera shrugged. "Even if you don't believe it or understand it, it is so."

It is so, Holly said to herself as she walked into the dim coolness of the lobby, asked the security guard how he was, if his psoriasis was better, signed herself in, and stuck a visitor label to her dress.

Oliver was locking the lab door as she stepped out of the elevator.

"Hey, hon." He leaned down and kissed her, pressing her close briefly. Her heart thrummed at his obvious pleasure to see her. He was a good man. Had always been good. The best.

Being the director gave him a few privileges. For example, he had his own glass-encased office inside the lab. And his own bathroom connected to that office. She paused, uncertain if she should ask him to unlock the office, decided an extra few minutes to gather herself wouldn't hurt and sidled into the public ladies' room. She stood alone in the pristine, echoing white bathroom. A couple of deep breaths, a dab of cool water on the back of her neck. She undid the clasp on her bag and touched the Saint Dismas icon. Who was Saint Dismas, anyway? She'd need to Google him. The name sounded familiar, but religion classes were decades ago, and she'd spent most of them whispering back and forth with girlfriends.

She left the restroom looking pensive and coughed demurely into her hand.

"Hon," she said, "the toilet is overflowing."

"What?" He seemed ready to march in there himself.

"Could you let me in to use the special, fancy-schmancy director bathroom?" She smiled and touched his hand, caressed his wrist.

He returned the smile as he always did, his stalwart features blobbing together, and let her in, following, flicking the lights back on.

He was checking his phone when she exited the private bathroom and wrapped her arm around his.

"Better?" he asked.

She kissed him on the side of the jaw, because even on her toes and in heels it was as far as she reached, and they walked out toward the elevator. As the doors pinged open and he stepped inside, she slapped her thigh and said, "Shoot!"

"What?" He pressed his palm against the closing doors and they slid back, vibrating against his hand.

"I left my purse in the lab."

He made a sound between a groan and a sigh. "Do you need it?" he asked. "Lunch is on me."

"No, I don't feel right without it. Give me the key card and I'll run in and grab it. You go on and get us a table. I'll meet you there."

He frowned.

"Sound good?" she asked, with the widest, craziest, cheer-fullest grin she could muster.

He glanced down, then back at her, and handed her his card.

His sepia-toned eyes seemed sad for a second, deadly serious. Then the elevator doors closed between them, and she was alone in an empty hallway with a key card in her cold fingers.

She keyed herself in, flipped on the lights, and locked the door from the inside. Her head held high, she forced a calm, sweet expression on her face, and rushed toward the inner bathroom, locking that door as well. After that, it was a quick matter to remove Step's RFID scanner and copy the key card onto a blank. Her next actions were unrehearsed, but she performed them swiftly, her mouth grim, her hair in her eyes.

Once back in the lab, she found the first five vials without a problem, in a cabinet in his office, neatly labeled. The sixth proved a challenge. Neither his desk nor the cabinets contained it, and she had come out into the main lab when she heard footsteps outside, voices. Lunch hour had ended, and the other scientists and assistants were about to return. In desperation, she scanned the cabinets and counters, and there, inside a glass case just by the window, lay a set of vials, the one she needed closest to the door. The very locked door.

The voices outside murmured on, a male and a female, discussing something urgent.

Whatever those orange pills had done for her was wearing off, and her palms itched, slick with sweat inside her vinyl gloves. Where in God's effin' name would Oliver keep his effin' keys to this effin' cabinet?

Somebody leaned against the door, and she whimpered, but clamped her mouth closed and stomped her foot. Where? Where would her logical, steady, diligent husband keep his keys?

The doorknob turned, the voices grew louder, and the door stayed shut. Then the voices quieted.

Holding her breath, she dashed into his tiny office and opened one desk drawer after another. A bundle of keys lay tangled in a green slinky in the bottom drawer. She snatched them, ran to the cabinet, and, miraculously, opened it.

She now had all six vials, but she wasn't finished. Senses at painful alert, she listened, and heard nothing more from the hallway. Whoever had been there either left or was taking a moment to commune with their phones. She didn't care, had no time to care.

Her last assignment—the laptop. She opened it and keyed in the password with one hand while attaching a thumb drive with the other, opened the drive, installed the executable file it contained, withdrew the drive, logged off, closed the lid, and rushed to the door, only to stop short, double back to the bathroom, and grab her handbag.

On her way out, she remembered to turn off the lights, and so when she stepped into the hallway, the couple entwined in a passionate embrace sprang apart and stared at her as if she were a ghost, emerging haggard and clammy from a charcoal-shaded chamber.

The three stared at each other, mouths open, two red faces and one bloodless, until she broke the excruciating moment by nodding at them and nearly sprinting to the staircase. She'd met both of them before, along with their respective spouses and children, at a company picnic a year ago.

Alone on the stairs, she removed the baseball cap, gloves and gray sweatshirt she'd worn in the lab and shoved them into her bag.

As she sat in the cozy restaurant with her husband, picked at her salad and guzzled her Chardonnay, she briefed him on the children's teachers and sports and the results of dentist visits. Her mouth moved and familiar, comforting words spilled out. She inhabited a doubled world. In one, she was the delicate, mild homemaker, a writer of romance novels, a mother of three. In the other, she was a criminal, sitting on top of stolen compounds worth tens, maybe hundreds of millions. She was a spy who betrayed her own husband. And she wasn't completely clear on how she felt about any of it.

22

July: Laney

As much as Laney wanted to put all her resources into find-ing Holly, not to mention ferreting out everything she could about the mystery female in her son's life, she had a job she both needed and enjoyed. With the runaways, it felt like a calling. Plus, she had always been a meticulous detective. It was a matter of pride to resolve her cases to her clients' satisfaction.

The day after confronting Mona, Laney had an appointment with Bubba Gardner's mother. Before the meeting, she performed checks and made phone calls. In many ways she was old-school and liked to keep a list of her cases and her notes in a real note-book, written with a real pen. Whenever she closed a case, she drew a green highlighter over the entry in her notebook, and a notebook full of green made her happy.

She interviewed the mother in one of BSI's tiny conference rooms, taking copious notes, bringing cups of coffee and water to the distraught Mrs. Gardner. When the other woman, unable to speak further, placed her hands over her eyes, Laney got out of her chair, walked around the narrow table, and pressed her shoulder.

"I promise you," Laney said, "I will do whatever it takes to find Bubba."

The woman took a shuddering breath and dabbed her eyes, and Laney let go, went back to her chair.

"But what I need to know is," Mrs. Gardner said, "what happened?"

"I will find out," Laney said. "You have my word."

The woman waved Laney's word away. "No, I mean"—she snuffled and blew her nose—"I mean, what happened to my son? Why did he—" She gestured in the air, swirling her hands. "He used to be such a good boy." Her eyes, large, swimming, raw, stared at Laney as if she truly expected an answer.

"I don't know," Laney said. "I have everything I need for now. I will contact you later today with my findings and will continue to send you a report daily until"—she forced a smile—"we find out what happened." Because saying *until we bring him back* would be too hopeful and, given Bubba's history, unrealistic.

Except for the receptionist, she had the office to herself, everyone in court, with clients, or in the field, and thank God for that. She'd come into the office dreading seeing Jack and was relieved when his desk remained empty.

As she organized her notes, something about the Gardner case tugged at her mind. She'd seen the name Sunny River before but couldn't remember where. Or maybe it was the logo that looked familiar. The Sunny River logo depicted a ray-spiked sun, like a cross section of an orange, and a serpentine blue ribbon beneath. She peered closer at that logo. She had definitely seen it before.

A Google search brought up a website showing cozy white cottages nestled within an oak grove, violets and petunias in window boxes, cobalt-blue shutters on windows. There were pictures of teens raking and planting vegetable beds, adolescents painting at easels, groups of them in circles talking, faces earnest and clear-eyed. It was a funny kind of place for a youth home, but that's how things went in the Hudson Valley. Old mansions became high schools, three-hundred-year-old barns turned into village halls. The main cottage, originally a parsonage, had been privatized and expanded in the nineteenth century before being taken over by the town and transformed into a school and then, in the eighties, a community center. According to the local news reports, the facility had had its share of problems recently: a girl had torched another with a homemade flamethrower; a boy walked out of a group therapy session, left the building, walked five miles undeterred, and threw himself into the nearby Garnerville Reservoir.

Laney looked at the clock and figured if she left within the hour, she'd have time to go to Sunny River, check it out, maybe speak with someone. After deliberation, she decided against calling ahead. It was better to assess the situation in person first. A place that allowed a suicidal teenager to leave with unauthorized adults would just as soon invite a congregation of ravenous alligators through its front doors as agree to speak with an investigator.

But there was one thing she absolutely needed to do before setting out, and she promised herself she'd spend only forty-five minutes on it. Her fingers hovered over her phone.

Alfie was still her child. Still so young. It wasn't so much that he believed everyone was good, but that good and bad were equally human qualities, and therefore acceptable. Alfie was a terrible judge of character. She had to admit, though, he might have inherited that from her.

Whatever was happening between him and that . . . that . . . grown woman wasn't okay. Her fingers tapped her phone. She checked his Twitter account and Instagram. Within seconds she had clicked through to Mona's profile and was reviewing posts, her face growing darker with every minute. She soon located the real person behind the handle, sort of. Mona Powell grew up in western Pennsylvania (as evidenced by comments under a #ThrowbackThursday photo of adolescent Mona looking vague and distant as a sibling tugged at her black shirt), one of eight children (more comments). She was twenty-three (part of her profile info) and did not seem to have a job. Laney checked Tracers, TLO, and IRB but could find no high school or college data. Mona did not have a LinkedIn profile.

But it was only when Laney found Mona's mother's Twitter page and followed it with the fake profile she used when she needed to do her investigations anonymously that a fuller picture emerged. Mona was a negative, a missing space in holiday posts, a name excised from lists. Going back years, Laney found a post asking for the whereabouts of seventeen-year-old Mona, and her throat tightened. It had been slightly more than a year since a very similar plea posted on her own—Laney's—Facebook page, begging strangers to help find her son.

She closed her laptop and sat back in her chair. What the heck was twenty-three-year-old loser runaway Mona doing with her fifteen-year-old high school sophomore? She opened the laptop again and started a message to Mona's mother, then stopped. There was more to this. This girl was involved with the Volkins, and Laney had a stronger-than-ever inkling she had something to do with the shooting and with taking Laney's gun. True, Alfie swore she hadn't done it, but that only meant he wasn't aware of her doing it.

She closed the laptop for the second time. She needed to get this woman away from her son, preferably in a manner that wouldn't throw a grenade into their tiny family. Then she needed to figure out how Mona fit into what's been going on with the Volkins and Holly. Because it was all one ugly, thorny ball of mess.

Laney wrote Mona's full name and her social media handles onto a sheet of paper, tucked it into a folder, and left the folder on Jack's desk. She was about to walk out of the office when she doubled back, grabbed a Post-it, and wrote, *She's a wrecking ball. If you fix this, I owe you big time*, and placed it on top of the folder. Halfway to the stairs, she paused, came back again, and added, in a smaller script, *But if you can't fix it in two days, I'm calling the police and Alfie can hate me until the day I die.*

As she took the elevator to the garage, she wondered why Jack had volunteered to help her. Did he want something from her in exchange? That he might want to help because he could and he liked her and understood her dilemma flitted through her mind, but she swatted the thought. Then she swatted it harder and stepped on it until there was nothing left but a faint feeling of longing, as if she'd glimpsed a childhood friend's face in a crowd, not to see it again.

She'd go to Sunny River and be a good investigator. She'd do the due diligence to find Bubba. And sure enough, if she opened her mind, she'd remember where she'd seen the Sunny River name and logo.

23

June: Holly

SIX WEEKS AFTER Holly first stole from her husband, she turned up the air conditioner in her car and took a deep breath. Held it. Let it out slowly. On her lap lay the paperwork for a smaller, refinanced mortgage. She'd paid off nearly half the previous one, and the new payments promised to be easy. A snap. Something she'd be able to pay in her sleep. The house her grandfather built was hers once more, and nobody but the bank and Vera and Step Volkin knew there had been a moment when it almost wasn't. True, she had to forge Oliver's signature again, but it was for a good cause. Everything she did was for a good cause.

Yet her skin crawled.

Was she getting a summer cold? She placed her palm against her forehead—feverish, achy. Her phone buzzed inside her purse, and she ignored it.

She had walked into the bank an hour ago holding a briefcase stuffed with cash.

"Are you kidding me?" she had asked Step when he handed her the briefcase. She'd gawked at the bills, neatly bundled hundreds and twenties. They weren't crisp notes but softened with age, creased, greasy even. A few had markings on them, words written in pink or black marker.

"If anybody asks, you were going through the junk in the attic and discovered the money stuffed into coffee cans and chocolate boxes," Step said. "I read about just that thing happening to someone in Iowa. Their grandmother hid over two hundred thousand dollars all over the house."

And that's exactly what she said to the teller, who, after calling over her manager, smiled and put the bills through a counter.

"It's your lucky day," the teller told her, her tone a mingling of awe and envy.

But which day was the lucky one? The day she pulled a drowning Vera from the lake? The day the Volkins recruited her? The day she walked into her husband's office and committed a crime for which she could go to federal prison for years? She'd researched it. Up to ten years plus fines.

Holly rubbed her hurting belly. It had been hurting ever since she stole the vials and launched a program into Calypso Technologies' servers that would allow someone to remotely access its system undetected.

She forcefully refused to think about what she had done to Oliver. How it would look if the feds came knocking. She'd take the entire blame, of course. Take every lie detector test out there and swear on her own and her children's lives that he had nothing to do with it. Only her. She was the bad actor.

Her phone buzzed again, and this time she opened her eyes and looked at it. Three messages—a girlfriend asking if they were still on for lunch the next day, her brother Adam asking if she'd take his kids overnight so he could recuperate from his latest procedure, and Vera. Asking Holly to stop by. Now.

The act of putting the car in gear and driving to the Volkins' was a relief. A part of her was happy to keep going, plunge ahead, see where the next stage in this insanity might lead. What did they want with her now? She was almost eager to find out, the way you might feel after a biopsy—get an answer and end the horrible anticipation.

"Here, try this." Vera extended a martini glass to Holly. It was only noon, a Thursday, and she had yet to start dinner, but she took the glass and drank obediently.

"Espresso martini," Vera said. "Good, right?"

Holly nodded. Yes, the drink was delicious, an iced espresso with a kick. Her stomach burned, but she drank more of the cocktail anyway.

"So," Step said. "You got us some very good stuff. Excellent."

"But we need more," Vera said. Interrupted him, her eyes dark and glistening.

Holly shook her head, slowly, even though she'd suspected something along these lines. She was theirs now. They could destroy her life in an instant. "We agreed on six vials."

"And a file," said Vera.

"We're done," Holly said.

Step placed a printout in front of her, the vial labels zoomed up large. "Can you get these for us?"

She finished her drink and gave the glass back to Vera. "I think they might begin noticing the stuff disappearing," she said. Although they hadn't noticed. At least Oliver had said nothing. But then again, he'd been quiet the past few days. Her heart skipped, then beat faster. *Had* he been quieter? Had he been looking at her funny?

"You're good," Vera said. "We're monitoring their communications. Nobody's worried."

"I won't," Holly said. She aimed her aching body toward their door.

Step blocked her. Not menacing. No, his face was weirdly calm, his eyes tender, even. She swerved around him, and he blocked her again, his hand warm on her freezing arm.

"Holly," he said. "Don't go yet."

"Step, really. Where is your mind?" Vera stood behind Holly, hair tickling her skin. "Forgive him. He was raised by wolves."

Step inhaled sharply and let his breath out in a soft laugh.

"Let me go," Holly said. "I did what you asked."

"And we're asking again." This from Step, who, instead of backing away, moved even closer. "You'll get paid again. Hmm? Wouldn't that be nice?"

Holly shut her eyes, which was the only way to get away from his staring eyeballs other than shoving him aside. And she couldn't do that. She wasn't violent. Even now she couldn't be rude. "I don't want to," she said.

Vera wrapped her arms around Holly's waist. "But you're so good at it," she said.

Did they intend to fuck her into submission? What the . . . ?

"I can't think," she said, because that was true. She couldn't. Not a single, sensible thought.

"Say yes," Vera said.

Step said, "You can pay off more of that mortgage. Adam's medical bills are still piling. There's a new holistic treatment I read about. What was that called?"

"Yes!" Vera wriggled against Holly. "Yes, I remember. Great results. But expensive."

"Just do what you did before. Easy as pie."

"We'll help."

Holly flicked her eyes open. "And if I don't?"

Vera shrugged behind her, a shift of arms, a change of pressure. "We'll turn you in."

Step nodded. "Also easy as pie."

"I'll turn you both in."

They laughed. Vera said, "Hard to turn us in if we're gone. Come on. You're not really that dumb. We have video of you in the lab."

She felt light-headed. "Can the two of you give me some space here?"

And just like that, they withdrew. She returned to the den and stared at the printout Step had placed there.

Then she picked it up, folded it, and slipped it into her purse.

"Another martini?" Vera asked.

"Okay," Holly answered.

They sat on the couch, Holly limp, her head thrown back onto the cushions, her stomach throbbing with pain. She welcomed the pain, sipped more of the second martini, knowing it would make things worse.

Vera curled her knees to her chest and placed her head on Holly's shoulder. Step relaxed as well, his limbs slack for a change, unlike his usual springiness. His thigh rolled against Holly's, jean against thin cotton, heat and muscle against skin stimulated to goose bumps.

Vera's cool fingers traced the line of Holly's jaw, her neck. "You're so lucky," Vera said.

Holly's eyes remained closed, and she swallowed. "How am I lucky?" she asked.

"You've had such a good, safe American life. Mother, father, brothers. Everyone loves you. A childhood in this beautiful place. Your family would give you anything you asked."

Holly opened her eyes, then placed her hand over Vera's and pushed it away. "Safe?" She turned her head and met Vera's feline gaze. "Whoever told you I had a safe childhood?"

Vera folded her hand around Holly's, wouldn't let herself be pushed away. "Didn't you?" she asked.

The familiar lump returned to Holly's throat and her breathing quickened, grew shallower. If she didn't watch it, she'd get light-headed, maybe throw up. It happened sometimes when she thought of Abigail. "I had a sister, once," Holly said. "She died. I was twelve and she was sixteen."

Step and Vera were watching her now, their attention like an electric wire, keeping her from the usual sobbing that accompanied this revelation. She continued, "She drowned." Step's freaky card trick had hinted at this, but saying it out loud overwhelmed her, and all she heard for a minute was the pounding of her blood in her ears.

Both of them placed their hands on her as if to soothe, Vera's on her cheeks, her shoulders, her arms, and Step's steady hand on her thigh, her knee. "Shh," Vera said. "Don't cry. Abigail was meant to die. Don't you see? Her death brought you to us. And now you are bringing life to millions of people."

Holly held her breath, and a trembling started in her core so that her teeth chattered.

"It's fate," Step said, his hand traveling up toward her abdomen, stopping just short of her breast. He pressed down and the trembling subsided, her muscles unwinding under that steady pressure despite her thoughts. "You are a better person than your sister was. You have a purpose."

Holly tried to sit up, but the couple flanking her were like vines, pinning her into the cushions with their earnest hands, their faces inches from her skin. To her shame, her body softened, blooming under their touch, her breath quickening for another reason now.

"I need to leave," she whispered.

Step's hand slipped under her skirt, and she gasped, bit her lips. "Stop," she said.

They stopped their hands' roaming but didn't remove themselves from her, their bodies flush against hers. And she wanted to stay. Oh, how she wanted to stay. She wanted to let herself liquefy, to give over control, to let them touch her, kiss her, take her to whatever end or purpose they wanted.

Extricating herself from their fingers and bodies felt the hardest thing she ever had to do, but she did it, standing up on legs unsteady with fear and want.

They watched her, amber eyes and gray, knowing and aloof, calculating.

"I never told you my sister's name was Abigail," Holly said. She faced them, already stepping backward.

"No," Vera said. "You didn't."

"How did you know?" Holly asked.

Step laughed. "Do you really need to ask that question? You know all information is there for the taking." He grew serious, leaned forward, elbows on knees. "There is nothing about your life we don't know," he said.

Another suspicion grew inside Holly's thoughts, but she pressed her mouth shut, still unsure.

"Bring us this next set of compounds, and you'll get your money. You'll be able to pay off a chunk of what you still owe," Step said. "Or whatever you need it for."

She climbed the stairs to the hallway, opened the door, but didn't walk out yet. She said, "And then? Will we be done then?"

Vera, who had followed her, smiled, tapped an index finger against her hip. "Of course," she said.

24

June: Holly

THE FIRST SCHOOL bus was rounding the corner when Holly reached her home, and Kiki tumbled out, running toward her on sturdy legs. He chattered on and on as she took his hand and led him into the house, settled him at the kitchen table, gave him a bowl of Cheerios and apple slices on a plate. She hadn't touched her novel in a month and a half, ignored her publisher's emails, had chauffeured her children to sports and religion on autopilot, made cooing noises at them if they lost, or fell, or argued with friends.

She'd been absent from what she thought of as her real life, instead living a chimera where she never quite believed whether what she'd just done or experienced truly happened.

That evening, after soccer (Hannah), baseball (Freddie), and a visit to the pet store to look at the fish (Kiki, but really all four of them), she herded them home, threw a sirloin on the grill with a couple of Jersey tomatoes, and scrubbed potatoes for baking.

The family ate outside on their deck as the sun descended and a coolness grazed their bare arms, making them shiver in their T-shirts and shorts. Well, the kids ate. Oliver pushed his steak from one end of his plate to another, and Holly stopped even pretending to eat.

After the children scampered off to play indoors, Holly and Oliver remained. She squinted at the melting sun, a red smudge between the trees. Oliver, who had spent dinner looking at everything but her, turned his head and studied his wife.

"Are you feeling okay, Hol?" he asked. He was one of the few who called her that, and rarely. Her heart ached at the tenderness in his voice.

"I'm fine," she said, still facing the trees. "How are you?" She took a breath and met his eyes, squared her shoulders. "How was your day?"

"Oh, you know." He shrugged.

She noticed his untouched plate. "You didn't like the steak?" she asked.

"Wasn't hungry."

Their children's voices ebbed and soared, and then a door slammed, and a few new childish voices added to the din. Their kids' friends had come over.

Oliver said, "How's your book coming along?"

Holly wiped her mouth with her napkin, pushed back her chair, and approached her husband. They'd kept the lights off to minimize insects, and now they were both shadows within shadows, their skin a subtle gray in the gloaming. She nudged his knee with hers, and he shifted his chair at a right angle to the table so she could straddle him. Even with her ass on his lap, she had to tilt her head to offer her lips, and he paused, his arms inert, his head stubbornly unbent. But she moved against him, slipping her palms under his shirt and up his sides, where his skin was most sensitive, and he shuddered, wrapped his arms around her and lowered his head, the kiss between them sharp with teeth and quickly breathless.

Three children plus guest children make for a challenging dilemma, but over the years Holly and Oliver had developed coping strategies so ingrained they seemed choreographed. Quietly, kicking off their shoes, they crept to the tree fort built far enough from the house that no window light, nor streetlight, nor moonlight reached it, and slid through the opening. They kept their clothes on, mostly, and they moved against each other with a needy desperation born of suspicion, distrust, and supplication.

They were back in the house before any of the kids noted their absence, silence descending on them again.

Once the children were asleep, Oliver sat outside and smoked. Holly caught the unfamiliar scent as she came downstairs with the laundry basket and stopped, blood pumping through her veins with such force she grew dizzy. The last time Oliver smoked was in high school; his coach told him quit the death sticks or quit the team.

Her entire being, every cell, pulled her toward the deck door, toward this man who had watched over her during the worst year of her life, who had always been there for her, who waited until she was old enough and then scooped her up within his love, cocooning her. But she didn't go to him. She couldn't.

Instead, she put the laundry on the cold wood floor, ran to the bathroom, locked the door, and threw up yellow bile and brown espresso martini into the porcelain bowl.

25

July: Laney

THE AFTERNOON HAD grown hotter and muggier, and Laney's ancient Toyota barely kept up with the air conditioning. She drove along the winding driveway onto Sunny River's grounds and parked under an extravagant willow, happy for the shade. The air here, though heavy, had a whiff of freshness to it, either due to the density of surrounding trees or the expansive garden erupting turbulently behind the buildings.

The cottages were more decrepit than the website suggested— the paint dull and peeling, grass overgrown, moss on the roof shingles. The property languished at the end of a mile-long downtown, most shops closed, FOR RENT signs, sidewalks cracked and uneven, the only action near a barbershop and a deli, and that action being three men smoking and chatting idly in the afternoon's blaze.

With her phone, Laney snapped pictures of the shaggy grounds and structures. Walking around to the back of the main building, she saw a young woman sitting on a set of concrete steps, smoking. She wore skinny jeans with a loose green top and flip-flops. A lanyard ID tangled with a thin gold chain around her neck.

"Hello," Laney said.

"Can I help you?" The woman held her cigarette suspended, caught midtoke. Early twenties, chipped green-apple nail polish, dark circles under her eyes.

"I was interested in some of your outpatient programs," Laney said. "My name is Elaine." She extended her hand.

The woman hesitated, but it takes restraint to refuse someone's hand; most people will shake out of habit. She did, enveloping Laney's fingers in a quick, damp embrace. "Jo," she said. "Is it for you?"

"No," Laney said, and in a moment of inspiration cut with guilt, "For my son."

Jo took a deep drag of her cigarette. "How old is he?"

"Fifteen."

"Oh." Jo shrugged. "We have some programs, sure. Go inside and I'll give you brochures when I'm off my break." She tapped ash into a shrub. "The kids can be a handful, but they're great, really." She squinted at Laney. "To be fair, though? I wouldn't put my kid here."

Laney sat next to her. "Oh?" she asked.

"There's no money. I'm being honest. And frankly, if you want to go and tell them I said this, I don't care. I'm thinking of quitting anyway." She ground out the stub and turned so she was looking directly at Laney. "We're understaffed. We can't do even a third for these kids what we should be doing."

Laney waited, but the girl grew gloomy and stayed quiet.

"Do you work with teens?" Laney asked.

"I'm the administrative assistant." Jo shook another cigarette out of the box and lit it. "You're not looking for a program for your kid," she said.

"No? Why, what am I doing?"

"You're either with a newspaper or you're a cop. Parents don't come here to check us out unless their kid is ordered here by court."

Laney smiled. She had underestimated this girl. Lesson learned. Chipped nail polish did not mean sloppy mind. "Why would a newspaper or a cop be interested in Sunny River?"

"Which are you?"

Laney handed her business card to the woman. "Investigator. Bubba Gardner's mother is my client."

Jo shook her head.

Gently, almost in a whisper, Laney asked, "Do you know what happened to him?"

The girl continued smoking in silence as her cheeks and forehead grew splotchy and her nose dripped. She drew the back of her hand over it, then used the hem of her top to wipe her eyes and face. Laney handed her a packet of tissues she always carried in her bag for exactly these kinds of situations. Making someone feel understood went a long way toward getting them to share.

Jo looked as though she'd break her teeth if she clamped her mouth any tighter.

"Jo? What's going on here?"

The back door opened, nearly missing Laney's shoulder, and a woman peered out from the darkened hallway. Her eyes settled on Laney, then took in Jo's reddened face.

"What's up?" the woman asked.

Jo shrugged, switching to sullen mode. "Just taking my break."

The woman checked her phone. "Five more minutes, then you need to go in." Next, directed at Laney, "Unauthorized personnel are not allowed back here."

Laney rose to her feet. "Of course." She smiled. "I'll be going."

Unauthorized, bullshit. The back courtyard had no fence, no signs. It was no more unauthorized than the front.

She walked to her car, her neck crawling with the knowledge she was being watched. Sure enough, once she'd buckled in and faced the front door again, she saw the older woman in the doorway, her arms folded across her chest, her face neutral.

Laney waved, and the woman lowered her arms and walked back inside, closing the door behind her.

Once home, Laney documented the meager notes for her outing to Sunny River and logged into Facebook. But there were more than a dozen profiles with Jo's name, and who knew if the girl would respond to her from behind the safe wall of social media. Her only other option being a second visit, Laney dialed the Sunny River number and asked to speak with Jo.

Silence on the other end, as of someone holding their breath.

"Jo? Is that you?"

"Yes." The tone cautious, giving nothing away.

"Look," Laney said. "Bubba has a mother who loves him. If there's something you can tell me, it would mean everything—" Her voice broke, surprising her. Dammit. Sometimes it was possible to be too close to a case, and these runaway teens ripped her soul to shreds. "I know you can help. Please help us."

The woman hung up.

Laney tossed her phone on the table. Fine. She'd have to do her due diligence some other way. Surveillance. Maybe find a different employee. Maybe speak to another kid.

She was grilling hamburgers for dinner when her phone pinged with a message from an unknown number.

I couldn't talk before. I can't give you names, but it's not just Bubba, the text said.

Laney wiped her hands on her shorts and sat down. *What can you tell me?*

14 girls disappeared since Jan.

Laney stared at her phone, her hand uncertain over the keyboard.

The next text came in before she decided what to say. *Disappeared like they walked down the road and hopped on the bus to the city to meet up with their pimps.*

Laney's eyebrows climbed to her hairline. What the hell?

The three incoming dots waved for a full five minutes before a long text pinged into view. *They told us not to talk to anybody about it but fuck it. Everyone here—all the nurses and therapists, everyone is great. We all just want to help these children. But the bosses don't give a fuck. They only care about the money and they count everything, every tampon, every french fry, every dose. The kids don't get their meds if the cash flow slows for the month.*

Laney pulled on her lower lip, trying to sort this out. One case at a time, though. *And Bubba?* she asked.

The burgers began to smoke, and she scampered to flip them onto a plate. It's a good thing Alfie liked his meat well done.

By then another text waited for her. *Many of these kids don't have anyone who cares. The stories they tell will keep you from sleeping for years if you let them get to you. I was so happy when Bubba's parents came and took him. He said they were moving to Florida.*

Laney didn't have to think long for her next question. *Jo, what did they look like?*

The dots took a while this time as well. *Young. I thought really young to have a teenager, but some people start early and have good genes. She was pretty. You know, long dark hair. I couldn't tell you what he looked like, except he had short hair and creepy eyes. I gave Bubba a hug before he left.*

Another pause.

Then, *I really thought he would be happy.* Crying emoji, angry emoji, curse word emoji. Followed by, *What a fuckshow.*

Laney tapped her fingers on the table. Typed, *What do you think is going on at Sunny River?*

Nothing.

Jo?

Nothing.

Do you think they're trafficking the kids?

Sure sounds like it now, don't it?

Laney typed, *It's not your fault. You're a smart girl, Jo. You did good to message me. Can I call you? If I have any more questions?*

Nothing. Then, *Are you going to call the police?*

Yes, I have to if what you're saying is true. If you're talking about prostitution, of course. But I'm not sure if the police can do anything.

Laney sighed. What most people didn't know was that teenagers walked away and disappeared all the time. It wasn't a crime. The cases would go to a missing persons file, and that would be that. If the girls at Sunny River were being sex-trafficked, that was different, but even so, finding them might be impossible.

You wouldn't have any pictures of the people who took Bubba, would you?

It was unlikely she might, but the question was worth asking.

Jo didn't answer, and Laney, her mind at split attention, assembled a dinner even she had trouble choking down. Alfie, quiet and as cautious around her as she was around him, ate it dutifully and volunteered to clean up afterward.

26

June: Holly

Amazingly, the routines of everyday life lurched along as spring dissolved into flamboyant summer. Holly rose every morning at six, walked and fed Buster, roused her children, made sure the youngest dressed appropriately for school, fed them, nestled lunch boxes into their backpacks, waited at the corner for the bus, waved them off. Then it was tidying up the house, an errand or two, a couple hours of unproductive staring at her manuscript, back to the corner for the bus.

The massive block party was five days away, and there were still tents to procure and bounce houses to rent.

Holly hadn't seen the Volkins in a couple of weeks. Her brother Adam seemed better, the warmer weather and sunnier days having improved his temperament, given him energy. Her brother Roger was staying sober. She was paying her bills, and a little extra money in the bank was a comfort. She could put the past few months behind her, learn how to be herself again.

And yet the tension she'd lived with for so long lingered. It hadn't lifted but only shifted slightly so that she could breathe and eat, though not yet sleep. That was something, wasn't it?

The morning she found the letter in her mailbox, she understood her life was never returning to what it had been.

Hours later, as Laney was getting ready for bed, her phone lit up with a text. The photograph filling her screen sent blood roaring in her ears. Vera Volkin with her arm around Bubba, standing next to Step's blue pickup truck, Step at the wheel, and to the side, smiling widely at the boy, Mona Powell.

Realization hit her hard, a punch to the stomach, as she recognized that the green camp counselor shirt Mona wore was not a camp uniform but that of Sunny River, because right there, over her right breast, was the half-moon orange sun with the blue logotype above it. And along with the recognition came a memory. She opened her closet, reached for the tote she'd taken to the Volkins' house the other night, and dumped the contents onto the floor. There. The youth home's brochures, three of them, damp from humidity, their ink already wearing away.

The envelope contained a printout of three more compounds and a deadline—the Monday after the block party. Relief scraped away her silly belief in the possibility of salvation. It was freeing to face her new, forever reality without striving for false reassurance.

Feeling reckless, Holly grabbed a red crayon from the kitchen table and scrawled a *NO* on the paper, put it back into the envelope, and walked it down the hill. She slipped it into the Volkins' mailbox with relish. A dare.

She understood now that she would never work for them again. Not for money. Not even to save herself. She couldn't. She couldn't. She just couldn't. The guilt alone burned her from the inside. If she'd gotten away with the theft, well, the guilt would lessen with time. But with every fresh visit to the lab, the risk of capture multiplied. Her heart couldn't survive that anxiety day in and day out.

The texts began an hour later and continued to erupt from her phone for hours until she turned it off. She took her daughter along when Buster needed a walk so she'd never be outside alone. The next morning, she dawdled at the bus stop chatting, then texted Laney to see if she wanted a coffee. But no, her friend was at work (surveillance for an insurance claim, she texted), rain check for the afternoon or evening at the latest.

No sooner had Holly locked her front door than the doorbell rang. She opened her pantry/writing space and sat down, shutting the latch. The doorbell rang again, and the texts began. Let me in, let me in, you're being an idiot, nothing good will come of this behavior.

Holly put her head on her desk and pressed her palms against her ears. Then she sat up, got to her feet, opened the pantry door, walked to her front door, and opened that.

Vera stood there, smooth and clean, a pleasant smile on her neat face and eyes hidden behind sunglasses. She walked in, nearly knocking Holly off-balance. Before Holly could say a word, Vera shoved the door closed with her foot and said, "We'll make sure you go to prison."

Holly said, "I—"

"We'll poison your brothers and children. We'll leave you and Oliver alive so you can live with this knowledge. In prison. He'll never work as a scientist again. In prison."

Holly sat down. The living room wavered before her eyes and her stomach heaved, sending bile into her throat. She pressed her fist over her mouth and shut her eyes.

After a moment, Vera sat next to her. "What's all this?" she asked. "Why the rebellion all of a sudden?" She pried Holly's hand away from her mouth and stroked her fingers. "I was going to tell you later, but we're leaving next week. The work is nearly done. Endure for a little longer, okay?"

Holly nodded. She had no choice.

"Look at me," Vera said, and when Holly didn't, she tapped Holly's chin to turn her head. "Good. Now, don't annoy us, okay?"

Holly nodded again.

The next morning, as the school bus disappeared around the corner, Holly said her good-byes to the other moms, declined an invitation to lunch, and retreated to her front porch. The kids had roasted marshmallows at a neighbor's open fire pit the night before and had run through the house with chocolaty, marshmallow-coated fingers, leaving thick smudges of it on walls and couch cushions. But instead of pulling out a bucket and a bottle of Mr. Clean, Holly perched on her front steps and turned her attention to the unassuming house at the bottom of the hill where Step Volkin's blue pickup truck stood under the pines.

That was so typical of them, to park like that, where sap would drip onto the paint and solidify. Who did that? Holly wondered, not for the first time, if she could ask Laney Bird to cast her investigative eye on the strange Volkins, but then, as always, dismissed the idea. What if Laney found something that tied Holly to them? Would she be duty bound to report her? Laney was a straight arrow, one of the most honest people Holly had ever met. What was it like to be so genuine? Holly didn't know. In her entire adult life, she'd never tried it.

She waited as Step and then Vera left their house, locked their door, and slid into Vera's gray Honda. They backed out and sped around the bend, heading away from town.

After a few minutes she stood, brushed the dirt from her behind, and walked toward their house. A neighbor rounded the corner walking her labradoodle, and Holly stopped to chat, because that was the normal thing to do, and she'd act normal if it killed her.

Then she strolled to the small house under the pines, looked around to make sure nobody else was walking dogs or jogging or taking a morning constitutional, and slunk to the backyard. The back door was locked, as were the basement windows, the den windows, and the patio sliding door. Holly leaned against the stucco foundation and shut her eyes, centered herself. Abigail used to sneak out of their house all the time, even though their father locked it up tight every evening. Holly glanced at the second floor and her heart fluttered. One of the bedroom windows gaped partially open.

Great. All she needed was a ladder. But the Volkins, who still had no living room furniture, could hardly be expected to have a ladder lying about. After a cursory check of the shed and the house perimeter, Holly confirmed that no, they did not have one. She'd have to get hers and somehow carry it down the street without piquing anyone's curiosity.

But they lived in a friendly place, where everyone borrowed something from someone daily. Towels, wheelbarrows, shovels, even toasters and blenders made their way from house to house, depending on need and forgetfulness, so there was nothing unusual about the sight of one neighbor carrying a twenty-foot ladder to the property of another.

She was just being neighborly.

By the time she brought the ladder around back, leaned it against the siding, climbed it, punched the screen from the window, and slithered her way inside, she'd worked up a sweat and her stomach started its acidic burn, but to her knowledge absolutely no one had noticed her.

Vera and Step might not care about furniture in the rest of their house, but their bedroom was obviously their (surprisingly gaudy) haven. Four-poster bed, red silk sheets, tufted pillows, gilt mirrors on the walls, plus a mirror on the ceiling, white-and-gold-lacquered chest of drawers and wardrobe, silk rugs, and a stuffed polar bear head roaring between the windows.

Holly hesitated, wondering if she was seeing the real Vera right now in her red-silk glory, or if this was Step. As in every other room, a small candle flickered before an icon. Although the temptation to open that wardrobe or riffle through the dresser tugged at her (what secrets might she unearth?), Holly crept out of the bedroom and down the stairs to the den. Step's laptop was cool to the touch, the den's icon spying over her shoulder. Although she understood this to be weird, she moved to block the saint's eyes from seeing what her hands were doing. Which was opening the laptop and entering Step's password.

One thing she'd picked up from her friendship with Laney Bird was that using people's preconceptions could be helpful. Step of the unsettling eyes, Step who scrutinized her and found her flimsy, weak, easy to sway, may have been correct, but he was also patronizing. When he had opened his laptop to show Holly the layout of Oliver's lab and to load the malware onto the thumb drive, he'd logged in carelessly, Holly's presence behind him no more threatening than a moth's. She needed only to follow his precise fingers' dance over the keyboard, and the password revealed itself to her.

She knelt before the desk and began opening every folder in the system. She started with the obvious ones—Pictures, Documents, Music, Videos, Desktop—then moved to the more obscure, but although she was far from computer illiterate, she understood nothing of the file types she saw, and clicking on them led her down a rabbit hole of empty folders and restricted data.

A glance at the time showed her she'd been at this for over an hour. Wherever Vera and Step had gone, they were likely coming back soon, and she needed to hurry. If Step had anything on his laptop worth finding, she better find it now.

She sat back on her heels and closed her eyes. She fancied the icon watching her, and she opened her eyes and turned toward it. The glossy saint, shrouded in a dark robe, his face angled at three-quarters, seemed thoughtful, saddened by the sight of the world's sins spread beneath him.

And although this was an Orthodox saint and Holly wasn't completely sure which one, she squared her shoulders, clasped her hands in front of her chest, and said, "If they're doing something bad, please help me stop them." She ruminated on this statement, then added, "I don't care if they're doing something bad to me. It's not about me. In general. If they're no good, help me." The candle continued to flicker under the painted rectangle of wood, the saint remained silent, and Holly, who never managed more than three to four hours' sleep a day, felt a touch on her forehead—which might have been a cobweb, or a hallucination, or her sister's ghost. If it was Step's patron saint, he wasn't much good at being a patron. She nodded at the icon. Saints answered to a higher power first, their constituents second, and from this point on, she decided to let other forces guide her actions.

She turned back to the laptop and entered a file search for each of the compounds she'd stolen.

The fourth query popped up a folder. Drilling down through the files inside, Holly came across a folder of videos.

She clicked on one.

As she watched, her face grew paler and paler. When the video ended, she was crying, her eyes swollen, her nose running. She plugged her own thumb drive into the USB port, copied the video folder, closed everything she'd opened on the desktop, logged off, closed the laptop, and moved it carefully to its previous position.

She then blew her nose, climbed the stairs, padded through the garish red bedroom, climbed out the window, replaced the screen, lowered the pane, slid down the ladder, and carried it to her house.

No one paid any attention to her, although her face betrayed her and she had a bleeding scrape on her upper arm where the ladder had snagged her as she folded it.

That night the neighborhood met for a last planning session before the block party, the exception being Oliver, who stayed home. Those who hadn't yet paid their share brought checks, decisions were made as to whose lawn would host the sound system and whose the porta-potties. Someone brought a case of Bud, and someone else mixed a bottle full of Kamikaze shots and passed it around. Holly made chocolate chip macadamia cookies, and Laney contributed a giant bag of potato chips. The planning committee went into the wee hours, the warm night scented with citronella candles and dog roses.

Holly smiled and nodded, gathered her children and put them to bed, avoided her husband, came back out with more cookies, listened, agreed to everything.

And all the while a completely separate plan crystallized inside her heart.

27

July: Laney

L ANEY DIDN'T SLEEP. The moment the picture of Mona Powell wearing Sunny River's uniform while standing next to Bubba Gardner and the Volkins appeared on her screen, she marched to Alfie's room. He lay curled in his bed, the covers over his head, even though the air was stuffy and overly warm. She'd have to wait until morning before ripping his head off for once again putting himself directly in disaster's path.

Probably for the best he was asleep. She needed time to compose herself.

Except she found that impossible. When at three in the morning she was still awake, her mind ticking off all the ways she kept failing at parenting, she threw off her blanket and padded to the kitchen. The Scotch she poured went down warm and hit hot, and she took another swig before collapsing into bed and finally disconnecting.

She woke with the sun, feeling if not refreshed, then more focused. By the time Alfie was dressed, she had eggs and cereal on the table and two cups of coffee.

The few hours of sleep gave her the strength to wait until he finished his eggs and had taken a bite from a slice of toast before she said, "You're not going to see that woman ever again."

He stopped chewing, his eyes rounding and his skin going white.

"I won't allow it," Laney said. "She's mixed up in something very bad." She handed Alfie a napkin, and he spit his mouthful of bread into it. "And she's too old for you." It was really quite impressive how calm she was.

Everything about him tightened. His mouth, his shoulders, his fists. For all his difficulties expressing himself verbally, her son was a monumentally transparent human being, and she would have pitied him for the turmoil raging across his features if she didn't believe that for once she had to put her foot down.

A thought struck her, and she leaned forward. "How did you meet her?"

A worrisome defiance struggled to life in his eyes. "At Holly's on a Sunday. She invited her." He crossed his arms, as if to say *so there.*

"Listen to me. She's tied up with the Volkins, with that man who was shot." (Whom Holly allegedly shot. With Laney's gun.) "Shot with my gun."

He stood up, and she did too, hands on her hips. "Sit."

He made a move to step around her, and she grabbed his wrist. "You sit, and you listen, and you tell me what you know."

He didn't sit, but he didn't take his hand away either, so she said, "Mona Powell is eight years older than you, which makes her legally a sex offender. She can serve time for this and be put on a sex offender list for the rest of her life."

He wasn't looking at her, instead staring over her head at the front door. She continued. "I have a case about a runaway, and I believe she's involved with it." And then, because he twitched when she said *runaway,* "What do you know about it?" She tugged at him and he looked down, meeting her eyes. "You know, don't you? You know what Mona is involved with?"

Twisting his arm free, he walked around her and paused in the hallway. He said, "She's done with them. I've been helping her get free of them. You don't know anything, and you don't understand anything." He might have made it out the door too, but she was quick and got there before him.

"You're not leaving."

"Let me out."

"Alfie."

"Let me the fuck out!"

"Language!"

And with this he grunted, swerved, and ran toward the back door, and she couldn't chase him anymore, not without harming him or herself in the process. The door slammed so hard she heard something break, either the jamb or the pin.

When her heartbeat settled and her eyesight was no longer blurred with furious tears, she stomped into her room, donned a clean blouse and slacks, and left for work.

Because she couldn't afford not to.

28

July: Holly

THE DAY OF the block party couldn't have been more perfect—hot and clear, with a wholesome cerulean sky and fresh, delicate breezes that wafted alternately the scents of jasmine and petunias and charcoal barbecue. Children squealed and jumped inside a blue-and-yellow bouncy house, more children squealed and jumped on a trampoline, and still more children simply squealed and jumped.

The ten core families at the center of the party closed off the road and set out picnic tables and chairs, coolers, bowls of chips and grapes, watermelon triangles, blocks of cheese, plates of crackers. Three grills churned out hamburgers and sausages, roast vegetables, corn, and steaks. A communal table creaked under the weight of aluminum trays heaped with pasta dishes, salads, and desserts.

By early evening close to four hundred guests milled up and down the street, and the high school jazz band, invited by Alfie Bird, was setting up on someone's driveway.

Vera and Step, young, smooth, and crisp, were visiting each neighbor's table, charming and flirting their way through the already-drunk husbands, the more-than-half-drunk wives, the gangly, spotted teenagers. They looked and behaved like movie stars, sunglasses even as the light waned, not a hair awry, not a drop of sweat.

Holly watched a teenage girl elbow her friend when Step walked past. "I think they're vampires," she heard the girl say, and her friend, who'd been texting, smirked and said, "He's a VILF," to which the first girl answered, "Aren't they all?"

As the sun cast the sky mauve, the shadows deepened and then swallowed the back patios and driveways. The band broke into a wobbly rendition of "Old Town Road," and Holly, thinned by months of disquiet, crept once again to the house at the bottom of the hill. She was not concerned with leaving tracks this time and had brought, among other things, a sturdy steak knife. Her lifelong experience with the neighborhood homes taught her the locks on the original-to-the-house patio sliding doors were flimsy, a simple latch barely covered by a strip of aluminum. The Volkins' latch gave way to her steak knife like an old tooth to hard candy, and she was in, sliding it shut behind her.

Forty-Six Oak was dim, illuminated by a few candles and ambient light filtering from the street. The closed windows blocked most of the party sounds, giving the rooms a smothered quality, padded with a thick but strangely active silence. The candles made the air feel sentient, their flickering like the breath of the saints on the walls. Holly shivered in her thin cotton blouse and skirt. The taupe clutch in her hand was heavy, weighing her arm down, and she pressed it to her middle, her fingers feeling the solid metal within.

Old Holly, before-everything-went-to-hell Holly, would have been mortified at the mere thought of stealing her friend's gun. But this Holly hadn't hesitated. Two days ago, Laney came home while Holly was outside with Buster. They'd drifted into conversation, which turned into an invitation to chitchat over a bottle of pinot grigio on Laney's patio. Within the first fifteen minutes the women wandered into Laney's garage, then into her living room as Laney kicked off her oxfords and crouched before the gun safe in her closet. A call from work caught her attention, and she unbent, heading to the kitchen to take notes from someone on the other end.

Holly, being the person who tidied after everyone else, moved to shut the closet door, and saw that Laney hadn't locked the safe completely. It had swung open, just a bit.

There were envelopes inside the gun case. Cash. A wedding ring catching the white light from the window. And the gun. Smaller than Holly had expected. Duller. She reached for it without planning and twined her fingers around its cool hardness. Then lifted it to the light. Then put it into the pocket of her over-sized pink cotton cardigan. Then closed the safe's door, making sure it clicked, shut the closet, and joined Laney in the kitchen where, having finished the call, her friend was cutting a hunk of cheddar into cubes.

"Let me just take Buster home, hon," Holly said. "I'll be right back."

She hadn't planned on stealing the gun, but there it was, hitting her thigh as she walked into her house. Not sure what else to do with it, she tucked it into her writing desk. Maybe stealing was like sex or driving a car. The first time was always awkward and scary, but then it became routine. Once you steal your husband's pharmaceutical secrets, what's a friend's gun? Except underneath, she was shivering, her entire body pulsing with adrenaline and anxiety. No, she hadn't planned on taking it, but she was glad to have it. And she'd return it after the block party. She only needed it just in case. Just for show.

Two days ago. Two days to plan and sweat and not sleep.

The Volkins were leaving Sylvan. Except for demanding she steal the last batch this coming Monday, they were done with her.

And whereas a month ago this news would have lifted a massive weight off her chest, now it only increased her misery. Somehow, when Step Volkin told her they were going to improve on the drugs and test them, she'd not thought how. Now she knew how. She'd seen the results of those tests. She could no longer pretend she hadn't. As if sensing her intentions, they'd not left their house after the Tuesday she'd sneaked into their den. Holly watched and waited, but as Saturday dawned, she realized her only option was to choose a moment during the party when she knew they'd be out on the street.

Once inside their empty house, Holly went directly to the laptop downstairs and entered the password. She understood her role in the horrors she'd watched on Step's hard drive. And if she had to go down for that, she would.

But maybe she didn't have to. More importantly, maybe she could find out where they had established their lab and send this information to the authorities. And then the testing would stop. The victims rescued. Healed. She wasn't sure what authorities, exactly. Or how she could do this anonymously. But she'd figure it out.

Her mind hyperalert, she searched through the laptop in a preplanned, organized fashion, even as her ears listened for every footstep and her eyes darted at every movement. For days she'd forced herself, over and over, to watch the videos she'd saved to her thumb drive, avoiding the nightmares playing out center stage, trying to spot something that would tell her where they were filmed. But the rooms she saw were blank, the lighting clinical, the windows nonexistent or, if present, blind with drawn shades.

Ten minutes, twenty ticked by, and she was no closer to having what she needed. Where were the videos taken? Who were the young wretches on those tables, strapped to those chairs?

After years of indifference to her husband's work, Holly had finally made herself memorize the names of the compounds she'd stolen as well as their properties, their intended uses, their current failure rates, and more pointedly, their side effects.

She heard the door open, followed by Vera's soft chuckle and a drunken thump as a body pressed against the entryway wall. Holly rose to her feet soundlessly, held her breath, took a step away from the laptop, toward the patio.

Silence. She stopped and listened. She imagined the couple upstairs, doing . . . what? She crept toward the patio door and pulled, hoping to leave before they realized she'd been there. The door stuck. Panicking, she pulled harder. The door ignored her.

When Step flipped the lights on, they all popped into view: Holly clutching the doorframe, eyes wide and nearly black with dilated pupils; Vera with her hands on her hips, her jaw clenched, her perfect hair a gloss over her shoulders; Step, dark browed and fuming, patches of red on his cheekbones.

"An uninvited guest," Vera said. "How very unwelcome you are." She inched forward.

Holly let her arms fall to her sides and forced a smile. "It seemed quiet and peaceful here," she said, her voice quavering despite all effort. "I hope you don't mind." She dropped her shoulders, which had hunched defensively of their own volition.

"We mind," Step said.

Vera walked to the desk and placed her hand on the laptop lid. "Whatcha been looking at?" she asked.

Holly shrugged, a sharply nervous gesture. "Nothing. It's just so crazy at my house right now, I thought I'd hide here for a bit. I thought I'd wait for you."

And now they were both flanking her, Vera with her arm around Holly's waist, Step a tall and hostile presence behind her, locking her in.

"I'll go now," Holly said.

Step moved against her, his flesh hot, his breath boozy, the smell suddenly reminding Holly of her father in the years immediately following Abigail's death. He placed his palm over her throat and pressed so that she had to arch her neck, her face angled up now, meeting his stare. His mouth twisted into a grin, but a twitchy nerve in his cheek revealed a harsher emotion.

"What are you fantasizing now, hmm?" Vera asked. "That you can fuck us?" She slipped her hand between Holly's legs, the fingers slim and insistent. "That you can report us?"

Sandwiched between them, Holly's body quivered, and Vera smirked, her interpretation of the quiver both an insult and not wrong. Holly tried to twist away, but they held her, and now Step drew his palm along her throat, into her blouse, cupped her breast.

"I think she wants to fuck us," Vera said over Holly's head.

"Been a long time, hasn't it?" Step said into her ear.

"Let me go," Holly said, and pulled sideways, away from them.

"I think she doesn't know what she wants," Vera said, and released her hold. "I think she came here looking for a way to get over on us. I think she's obsessed with us."

Holly tried tugging the patio door again, but it stayed shut, the broken latch having snagged on the jamb.

"You're like a child," Vera said, her voice ringing loud, no longer slurring, no longer kittenish. "You imagine what you want, and you believe it's the truth. I'm getting so tired of explaining the truth to you. Aren't you getting tired of it?"

Step nodded. "I'm sick to death of her."

Vera flopped onto the futon, threw her head back, the line of her perfect throat a precise curve. "What you did is punishable by a five-hundred-thousand-dollar fine and fifteen years in prison. If you try to turn us in, we'll disappear. But first we'll make sure that your children and your brothers are injected with a concentrated dose of what we're researching." She shrugged. "You won't be able to stop it. They might survive. Most do. Or they won't. I mean, we'll make sure they get a huge dose." She turned toward Step. "What else? Oh, right. Oliver will lose his job, go to prison, blah, blah, blah, you lose your house, et cetera, et cetera. For God's sake, why do you need me to go over this again and again?"

Holly pulled on the door once more, putting her back into it this time. No luck.

"You'll be how old when you get out? Fifty? Older?"

"Ancient," Step agreed. He reached for Holly and gripped her wrist, hard, squeezing until she stopped squirming and stood still, afraid any movement would break her bones. "So, go ahead," he continued. "Report us. We'll be gone before you hang up the phone. All the evidence is on you."

Holly jerked and broke free, but she had to walk past them if she wanted to leave. She hesitated, and in the hesitation, her natural need to fix the world took over.

"I won't report anything," she said. "I don't want to go to prison any more than you do."

"Oh, don't worry about us. We're good," Step said.

Vera said nothing, her fawn-colored eyes on Holly.

"I just—" Holly hung her head. Even now she didn't want to play games, she didn't want to lie. Not really. "I just don't want those people to suffer. The test subjects." She lifted her eyes. It was true; that was at the heart of her pain, right there. "Can't we stop the tests?"

Vera's smooth forehead crinkled in confusion. "Stop what? The test trials? But how would we know the dosage amounts or the side effects without the trials?" She glanced at Step as if seeking an answer from him.

"Yes," Holly said. "Stop the trials. Wait until more work is done."

"Hmm." Vera pressed her lips into a soft smile. "She's such a baby, isn't she?"

"Naïve," Step said.

Holly edged toward the stairs. "I need to get back," she said.

But Step moved directly in front, a solid obstacle between her and the exit. "Give me your phone," Step said at the same time Vera drifted off the couch and opened the laptop.

"Why do you want my phone?"

"Just checking," Step said. "For pictures taken off the laptop, for example. A message sent that shouldn't have been. A recording of our current conversation."

Vera's fingers tapped keys, her face illuminated with a cool glow. She slammed the lid closed and straightened, nodded at Step. He shot his hand out, grabbed Holly's arm, twisted her so she lost her footing, ripped her clutch out of her hand and opened it one-handed. The pause in his momentum as he took in what was inside nearly sent Holly into a paroxysm of excuses, but he snapped his eyes at her, and she froze, all pretense torn away, ready for anything.

"Ver," he said, his tone different than usual, low and cautious.

Vera took Holly's clutch from him, her face hardening the moment her hand touched the bottom. She withdrew Holly's phone and handed it to Step.

He entered her passcode, which both surprised Holly and didn't. Clearly, she wasn't the only one with party tricks up her sleeve. She broke away from him, but he snatched her again, pulled her near.

And it was while Step scrolled through her phone with one hand while gripping her biceps with the other that the upstairs door crashed open and heavy footsteps thudded in the otherwise hushed home.

She recognized the tread right away, her insides twisting with a new anxiety even as Oliver barreled into the den.

A wet stain darkened his shoulder and chest; his hair was disheveled, his eyes red rimmed and dark. But he wasn't as drunk as he acted, his unsteadiness deliberate.

He glared at Step's hold on Holly, at the way her body touched the other man's, and then he shifted his eyes to Holly's.

It had been weeks, months since the last time she'd looked, really looked, into her husband's face. He was haggard, skinnier, aged, his handsomeness grown craggy, his mouth a thin, down-turned line. With a shock, she understood he knew what she'd done, or at least some of it, of her complicity. The last time she'd seen such pain in his features was twenty years ago, on a pebbly beach by a lake, one dead girl, and one barely alive at his feet.

"Come home now," he said in a voice that was raspy and low, an unkind voice.

She tugged her arm, trying to break free of Step's hold, but he yanked harder, and brought her flush against him.

"Do you want to go home?" Step asked. "I don't believe you do. I believe you like it here with us." He indicated Oliver with his head. "Tell him. Tell him what you do for us."

"Step," Vera said, a warning.

"Get your fucking hands off my wife!" Oliver roared, and slammed into both of them. Step's legs buckled, and he smashed to his knees, taking Holly with him, tearing something in her shoulder, making her cry out. And still Step held on, a malicious slant to his mouth.

Oliver, with his footballer arms, reached around the other man and pulled, wrenching them apart at last, sending Holly sprawling before she scuttled out of the way and to her feet, her shoulder a flaring agony. The two men flailed at each other, Oliver gaining control and straddling the younger man, his fist rearing back before bashing into Step's straining face.

"Oliver!" The sharpness of her voice did nothing to slow her husband.

His fist rose and fell with a fierce and sickening rhythm until Step growled, lifted his hips, and unseated him, then scrambled atop his chest and punched his nose in quick, violent jabs. Oliver gurgled and gasped, weakening, and Step wrapped his fingers around his opponent's throat and squeezed, his own face growing dark red as Oliver's turned blue.

Holly screamed and began pulling at Step's shoulders, to no avail. "Stop, please stop!"

An elbow sent her sprawling sideways as Vera grabbed Step's arm and clawed at him. She was spitting words at him, thick, sibilant syllables that meant nothing to Holly and had no effect on Step. Vera jabbed her fingers into her husband's eyes, but all he did was lower his head and squeeze Oliver's neck harder. With a sharp smack at his shoulders, Vera shoved off and spun toward the stairs as Holly began to scream.

Oliver's legs lay lifeless.

The gunshots were so loud she heard nothing for a second or two, and her heartbeat accelerated so much she saw black. The shock of it had stopped her yelling, and she sat on the floor, her skirt and blouse spattered with blood.

Step's hands were no longer wrapped around Oliver's neck, because he was curled on his side on the floor next to Holly, his hip and thigh so drenched in blood it looked like someone had emptied a tub of ketchup on him. His face was colorless, contorted, and of the four of them, he was making the least noise.

Oliver gasped and sat up, all bloodshot eyes and gore down his chin.

Vera held the gun, then lowered her arm, letting it dangle by her hip.

Unsurprisingly, none of them called 911.

Oliver placed a palm over his eyes as if wanting to shut out the world, his chest rising and falling raggedly, no longer because he couldn't breathe but because he was crying. Sobbing, the sounds so unfamiliar it took Holly a few moments to recognize what they were.

Holly wanted, with all her might, to kneel over him, to kiss him, to tell him how terribly, terribly sorry she was, but the sheer inadequacy of an apology immobilized her.

Vera bent, retched, then stood straight and pointed the gun at Holly. Her skin was shiny and smooth, stretched taut. Her eyes had narrowed. Holly saw no bitterness in her mouth's set but a sternness, a grim determination.

"Get up." Vera wiped her mouth with her other hand.

"You shot Step," Holly said. Had Vera meant to shoot Oliver? Was she, Holly, almost responsible for her husband's death?

"Fuck you," Vera said. Her eyes whipped to Oliver. "Oliver, stop blubbering. You're fucking fine."

He lowered his hand and locked eyes with her.

Vera said, "Fuck you and your fucking morals. Fuck you and your insane wife. Fuck the both of you up the ass with a poker." She paused, her breathing short and harsh. "This is how it's going to go. Holly is coming with me."

Holly shook her head, and Vera walked up to her and slapped her. "Shut up." She turned back to Oliver. "She's coming with me, because it's the only way I can trust you to keep your mouth shut."

For the first time since she shot Step, her eyes turned toward him, and she paled even more. He was staring at her out of a ravaged, broken face, still not making a sound, even his breathing so quick and shallow as to be barely noticeable.

She jutted her chin and refocused on Oliver. "You say anything about what you know, and she dies. No questions. We'll know the second you betray us."

"Please," Holly said.

Vera slapped her again. "Shut up."

As Holly put a foot on the bottom stair, Oliver staggered upright and lunged for Vera's gun hand. Vera flung her arm in an arc, the gun connecting with his temple, felling him to the floor in a mute heap.

Holly yelped, but Vera gestured for her to stay still.

Oliver propped himself into a partial sitting position and looked at Holly. Blood trickled down his forehead and into his eye and he wiped it, smearing it over his cheek.

Words dried in Holly's mouth, and all she could do was wish for a break in the fabric of reality, something to take her out of this unbearable pain and guilt. Then something did break; she became blank, perceiving the room around her and the burning discomfort in her shoulder as if from above. A part of her sighed with ease; she'd found her way to the quiet place that had held her after Abigail's death. It was a familiar place, not a bad place. Even the man who stared at her with such misery was the same.

Vera punched Holly's limp shoulder, saying go, go, run up the stairs and out the door and into the car. Holly went. It was easy. All she wanted now was tranquility, a lack of demand.

And through everything the night remained balmy, star flecked, though surely there should have been a hailstorm, a tornado, a cyclone. How could nothing be different? The party was still going, with karaoke beginning in one of the driveways, somebody mangling an Amy Winehouse tune, somebody else laughing into a microphone.

"What will you do with me?" Holly asked.

She wasn't scared. She'd faced death before and had made her peace with it. She had known, years ago in the lake, that she'd never be afraid of dying again.

"Not up to me, bitch."

29

Laney

L ANEY SLAMMED HER car door, then immediately regretted it. It wasn't like her to slam doors and stomp around in a fit of pique. She used to have control over her emotions. There was a time she could joke around with drug dealers even as they tried to grab her ass or threatened her. But her fight with Alfie this morning had exhausted her reserves. Add a missed lunch and her mood was execrable. Hangry, lonely, and irritated to a dangerous edge, Laney walked slowly (because dammit, she did have that kind of control) to her front door, retrieved the mail, and waved at a neighbor before stepping inside.

A wall-shuddering *thwump-thwump-thwump* EDM beat came from above, which meant Alfie was doing something on his laptop, either laying down his own tracks or listening to others. But at least he was home and alone. Anyway, she presumed he was alone, due to the absence of a little green car in front of her house.

A quick inventory of her kitchen drove her back outside and reaching for her phone. Her only options for dinner were cans of soup and eggs. She could not understand why she constantly failed to keep up with groceries and cooking. Other single moms did it. Why was it so beyond her? During her marriage, her ex took care of the food—that had been the arrangement. She worked while he stayed home to paint his unsettling paintings between tackling the meals. As it turned out, this was a subpar arrangement for all except Laney, who missed every sign of both Theo's and Alfie's unhappiness until her marriage imploded in what seemed to her one evening.

Welp, no use dwelling. She'd have to gather herself and devise a better system, but today she was calling in vindaloo.

While waiting for the delivery, she sat on her front steps, the heat having abated and the early evening turning tender over her skin. A glorious golden light shimmered in the leaves as the sun lowered, and she squinted down the block, her eyes skimming past the still-broken Dubois house and following the curve of the hill to the bottom where Forty-Six Oak huddled in piney shadows. Its windows glowed in the dusk.

Laney sat up. Someone was home at Forty-Six Oak—the first time since the block party.

She pulled two twenties out of her wallet, dashed into her house and up the stairs to Alfie's room. In a momentary lull between the thwumps, she knocked and yelled, "Indian delivery will be here in ten. Money is on the counter. I'll be right back."

She didn't wait for him to open the door but heard him do so as she left, followed by a quizzical, "Mom?"

The Volkins' door chime, when she rang it, played a few bars of "Great Balls of Fire." In the ensuing silence, she had to resist the temptation to press her ear to the door. There, a shuffling, slow but nearing.

A twitch at the side window told her someone was appraising her, and then the door opened, smoothly and quietly, leading into a warm darkness. She stepped through, her eyes adjusting, and faced Step.

He seemed aged, his skin colorless, rough, and his hair unkempt, dark and tufty. He moved with difficulty, and she took hold of his arm, propping him up. She had questions and she didn't want him keeling over before she asked them.

"You're home," she said.

The house was even emptier, if possible, than last time. Gone were the icons and the candles. Even the smidge she could glimpse of the kitchen was bare, the doors open, the drawers pulled out.

"What do you want?" he asked.

"I saw the lights on. I need to talk to you."

He placed a palm against a wall and leaned sideways, closing his eyes as if fighting a fainting spell.

His almost violent solitariness unsettled her. She'd marched here armed with queries and accusations but now hesitated. He was connected to her friend's disappearance, his own wife's disappearance, and that of a teenage boy. And yet here he stood, thin, trembling, diminished. Pitiful.

He breathed in sharply and said, "I need rest."

"Let me help you," she said. "Do you want to go upstairs?" In any case, he would be more likely to talk if she showed him kindness. Most people would.

He listed further toward the wall and nodded. Placing her arm around his waist, she was surprised by his emaciation, his flesh firm but meager, the hardness of bone palpable. He broke out in an unhealthy sweat as she guided him up the stairs and into a bedroom purged of all furnishings save a pile of blankets and a sleeping bag on the floor. She stopped, shocked that a man in his condition would live like this.

Even though he allowed her help with a gloomy tolerance, a softening around his eyes and mouth indicated he appreciated being off his feet. He turned on his side, curling stiffly into a fetal position.

"Step," she said. "What the hell is going on? What happened to all your furniture?" Shit. He was leaving. Someone had come and removed the little they had.

He grimaced. "I change my mind. I want you to leave."

"Where is Holly? I know you've been taking kids from Sunny River." Or at least one kid. "Where is Bubba Gardner?"

He took a deep breath, releasing it slowly, deflating as he did so. In the dim warmth of the bedroom, his pallor lessened, and his eyes, when he opened them again, sharpened. The clever arrogance she'd noticed in his first weeks in Sylvan struck her again. His gaze was intelligent and probing, distrustful.

"I ask you to leave and you don't leave. I tell you I need rest, and here you are. Still talking. Look, this is what happened. Your friend came on to me. Multiple times. I turned her down. She became mad. She came here uninvited and shot me. Later, in the hospital, I found out Vera is gone. Crazy lady is gone too. My truck is smashed." He stared at her, gray eyes too light in the room's mutable twilight. "I will only rest here for a few days. Then I leave."

She lowered herself to the floor next to him and crossed her legs. She wasn't going anywhere. "Where is Bubba Gardner? I know you took him. That's a crime."

He contemplated her from his decrepit nest.

She sighed. She'd call Ed Boswell when she got home and tell him of her suspicions, but Bubba's being eighteen muddled any urgency.

He tried to settle deeper into his blankets but gasped and blanched again. "You're as crazy as your friend."

He looked so miserable that she reached and adjusted the covers, helping him into a position that seemed more comfortable. She was always good at getting people to trust her, but she couldn't get her mind to the right place now. This was too personal. Her son was in the mix.

To regroup, she stood and went to the kitchen, where she found a plastic cup at the back of the unplugged fridge. After rinsing it and filling it with cool water, she returned to the bedroom and helped Step drink. When water dribbled down his chin, she wiped it with a corner of the blanket.

As he relaxed a touch more, she asked, "How did you and Vera meet?" Couples, especially those who clearly still loved each other, adored revisiting their origins. And she needed to know who they were. Any knowledge was leverage.

Although his face softened, a flash of longing skewed his features. She would have mistaken it for pain if it weren't for the reddening of his lids. "We met," he said. "We met when we were young. Children." He tapped his fingers on the blanket. "She's smart. Smarter than me. Sometimes. Very single-minded."

"Oh?" Laney tried not to sound interested. "What is she single-minded about?"

He licked his lips and drank another deep draft of water, emptying his cup. "She likes life," he said at last. "She likes to live."

"Don't we all?"

He shook his head. "Absolutely not. Most people hate their lives. They hate themselves. Most people have no idea how to live."

"That's not true," she said.

"It is," he answered. "Vera is the only person I've ever known who loves life in all it's disgusting, animal, breathing, eating, fucking glory. She even loves pain."

"Lots of people love pain. It's called BDSM."

He ignored her. "She cherishes all parts of life. She once had a bad tooth removed without anesthesia. She told me later that she floated to the ceiling, above the pain, and listened to herself scream."

Laney frowned. "Did she do this on purpose?" What sort of person would do that to themselves?

"She did it because her tooth was bad, and we lived in Russia."

"Dentists are sadists in Russia?"

"No money for anesthetic."

A shudder ran through Laney. Vera had been a young teen when she left Russia. Younger than Alfie. Involuntarily she imagined Alfie having a tooth removed while he screamed and screamed, and she had to clamp down on that image real fast.

Step shifted and winced.

Laney said, "Where is she now?"

He lowered his eyes, which had a weird effect, as if a light had been dimmed in his face. "She is where she wants to be," he said quietly. "And you need to leave."

"I'll go in a minute." She took his empty cup into the bathroom, filled it with cold water, and brought it back, placing it within easy reach. "Step, where is Bubba Gardner?"

His eyes remained closed, but his jaw tightened. She could see his pulse quicken in the hollow of his neck, a sudden flutter. "Never heard of him," he said after a moment.

"I know you went to the Sunny River Youth Home, and I know you took away a boy named Bubba Gardner. I have proof."

He didn't move.

"What went wrong, Step? Hmm?" She stood and brushed the dust off her legs. "I'll leave my card right here." She slid her card onto the floor. "Oh, and Step, listen to me carefully. If you or your wife or Mona fucking Powell come near my son, I'll kill you. No hesitation."

A spasm went through him, and he writhed briefly before settling into the filthy blanket.

"I'll bring food for you later," she said, because although she meant the threat, she was not a monster.

"You don't need to."

"No, I don't. Nobody needs to do anything for anybody. But it would be a sad world if nobody did."

She let herself out, but she didn't go home. Instead, she did what she hadn't had a chance to the last time, which was stroll to the side of the house where the Volkins' trash can stood nestled between their garage and an overzealous rhododendron. The block party had taken place four days after the scheduled garbage pickup and three days before the next. Which meant the garbage had never been put out, seeing as the lady of the house vanished and the man had been in the hospital.

If she was lucky, there'd be four days' worth of trash in the can. If she was very lucky, there'd be more. She dragged the can into the backyard and tilted it onto the flagstone patio.

The trash was weird.

30

Laney

W HAT DOES MOST people's garbage consist of? Packaging,
rotten food, direct mail, broken things.

The Volkins' garbage consisted almost exclusively of packing
material. Laney had never seen so much Bubble Wrap, Styrofoam
peanuts, padded envelopes, corrugated cardboard. For such an
empty house, they sure had a lot of stuff delivered. The rancid stench coming from the pile told her they weren't complete
androids and did, in fact, eat—although the food liquefying at the
bottom of the trash can was unrecognizable and could have been
anything from beefburgers to bananas. Whatever it had been
once, was now black, oily, and lumpy.

But as she'd learned, time and again, some people's trash is an
investigator's gold, and she painstakingly overturned every packing peanut and envelope, trying to breathe through her mouth
the whole time. Her tenacity was rewarded when she found a ball
of thin papers, which, after she carefully peeled them apart and
smoothed on the stones, proved to be receipts.

She kept the receipts, then scooped the slime-coated garbage back
into the can and tucked it into its regular space under the rhododendron.

Once home, she ladled half of the now tepid rice and vindaloo
delivered in her absence into bowls, then called Alfie for dinner.

They sat in their compact kitchen with its overhead fluorescent, windows open and a warm cross breeze wafting the scents of evening jasmine and weed.

"Gerald is smoking again," Laney said, meaning the neighbor behind their house.

Alfie shrugged without looking at her and speared a lump of meat.

"So, about this morning," she said, and stopped because he'd put down his fork and raised his eyes in defiance. "Don't storm out on me ever again. Got it? If you're old enough to date a grown-ass woman, you're old enough to listen to what I have to say."

He sat back, his lips pressed tight, crossed his arms over his chest.

"Mona is involved in bad things, and I don't want"—she had to stop there and gather herself—"anything bad to happen to you."

"Mom, you don't understand anything. She's not working with them anymore."

Laney leaned forward. "Working with whom doing what?"

He breathed out in exasperation. Lowered his eyes. "I can't tell you."

"Why? What will happen if you tell?"

"Nothing!"

"Then tell me."

"I promised."

"Alfie." She reached and put her hand around his fist, but he jerked his arm away. "Alfie, I won't be mad. And I won't do anything to make anything worse. I promise. Tell me."

He shoved away from the table, his eyes as large with suppressed tears as when he was small.

"Alfie! Alfie, listen, stop, stop, will you? Tell me, is she helping traffic kids? Is she doing that?"

But he was up the stairs and in his room, and there went the lock. *Click.*

She sat back down and pushed her bowl away, then put her arms on the table and let her head sink into her arms. She'd spent so many years suppressing every thought of her ex that when her mind and soul brought him to the surface, she felt ill, light-headed, ready to puke. How would Theo have handled this situation? Would he have fared any better after being Alfie's primary caretaker for his first ten years? Who was she kidding. Theo would have been three sheets to the wind by this time of evening, and his way of dealing with Alfie, as she eventually found out, was to make sure he was fed and watered and leave it at that.

Even though she was blindingly exhausted, she took the containers of remaining vindaloo and rice, grabbed a plastic fork and napkins, and walked down the hill. She rang the bell and set the cartons on the front steps, then retreated to her house, where she stripped, put on a T-shirt and pajama shorts, and got into bed. Sleep overcame her by nine, a deep, solid, dreamless sleep in which her brain mercifully unplugged from every thought and worry.

The morning found her feeling sharper and more determined. She washed her hands, put a vinyl cloth onto the kitchen table, and used tweezers to lay out the receipts she'd fished out of the Volkins' garbage. The day Bubba was photographed with Step, Vera, and Mona at Sunny River, the Volkins had visited a convenience store up the highway, filled their car, and bought doughnuts, candy, and soda.

She Googled the convenience store and found it was five miles north of Sunny River.

She emailed her boss, told him she was following a lead, and left a twenty on the table for Alfie with a note asking him to do their laundry. About to leave, she stopped, turned around, and fired up their rickety printer. Then she printed the Bubba photograph from her phone, wrote the date it was taken on the top, and placed it next to the note. Alfie believed Mona had stopped doing whatever she was doing for the Volkins, yet the photograph was taken only last week, four days before the block party. Alfie was gullible. He was quixotic. And although everybody had to learn the world's harsh realities in their own way, Mona would no longer be part of his learning curve. No more than she already had been.

Then Laney got into her car and aimed for Sunny River.

In her year of working for Boswell Investigative Services, she'd befriended the managers of four convenience stores and two gas stations. She'd quit law enforcement and had no leverage when requesting surveillance footage, but as a licensed investigator and a (sometimes strategically) chatty person, she often contrived to get a copy of the footage anyway. Most people wanted to help when it came to runaways and bad actors in general, and roughly fifty percent of the time, Laney got the files.

The gas station she headed for now was a long shot. She'd never needed to work with them before, and the Volkins' visit was over a week ago. The chances anyone would remember them were slim to none. But if that gas station was the only place they visited on the day Bubba Gardner disappeared from a youth home known for losing teens, she'd visit it too. And that was that.

She passed the exit that would have taken her to Sunny River and kept going for another eight minutes, then pulled into the convenience store's parking lot. Waiting for the people ahead of her to buy their soda, lottery tickets, and gas, she scoped out two security cameras—one for the inside, one for the outside of the store.

The man behind the counter rang up her iced tea and Slim Jim and she smiled, made eye contact.

"Hot day," she said.

He was young, early twenties, with short black hair and a smudge of beard on plump cheeks. "You're not kidding," he said.

"So, you must see some nutty things working here," she said. "I used to work in a gas station mart when I was in school. Holy shit, I can't even tell you." She'd never worked in a gas station mart.

He grinned. "You worked in a gas station?" He shook his head.

"One day," she said, "I came out to wash this guy's windshield—my boss was a real stickler; we all had to take turns washing windshields—and the driver is sitting there, holding his wallet to pay for the gas, while his girlfriend went to town on his joystick. If you know what I mean." She chuckled, tapped her fingers on the counter. That was a story one of her friends told her once, so at least it was true.

"What?" he laughed. "That's crazy, but I have something that comes close. Just the other day I came out to pump someone's gas and there's six old people in a car, a nice car, an SUV, and they're all naked. Like, jiggly, old-man boobs, old-lady boobs, just, you know. Hanging out. All happy. They smiled at me and gave me a tip." He covered his eyes with his hand as if trying to erase the image.

She grinned. "At least they were happy, right?"

In the following moment of reflective silence, she slid a printed photo of Bubba toward him. "I can tell you're an observant guy. I like that. I like that a lot. It's a very useful thing to be." She looked at the photo and smoothed the edges, as if caressing Bubba's face. "I'm a private investigator looking for this boy. We think he might have been kidnapped last Tuesday. You wouldn't remember him coming in, would you?"

The young man scrunched his eyes and bent toward the photo. While he did that, she pulled up the picture of Vera with Bubba on her phone.

"How about her? Maybe he was with her?"

The man's face changed, and he pointed at Vera, then picked up the photo of Bubba. "You know what? This woman actually comes here a lot. Her and a guy. Like they live around here or something."

Laney's heart did a tap dance against her ribs, and it was all she could do to keep her face straight. "Oh?" she asked. "How often do they come?"

He shrugged. "Maybe once a week. Like I said, I think they live around here. She's got nice hair. He never says anything, but her I remember." He brought the picture of Bubba to the window. "You know, I think yes, I think they had this kid with them the last time they stopped here." He gave the picture back to Laney. "They always have a kid with them, so I can't be positive."

Laney's eyebrows shot up. "What? What do you mean?"

"I kind of thought they were doing some kind of Big Brother Big Sister thing. Like they were volunteering their time. I mean, the kids always look out of it."

"Out of it?"

"Yeah, like they're, I don't know. Like they're high. Like they never say anything and they always want sweets."

As Laney digested this not-quite-unexpected development, she wondered if all the kids the Volkins had with them were from Sunny River, and decided she'd go back and try learning more about who went missing and when.

But more to the point, where were they taking these kids?

"Were they all boys? The kids?"

"No. Mostly, though, but no. A few girls." He grew serious. "So you think they kidnapped them all?"

Laney pursed her lips. "I don't know what I think right now." She glanced at the cameras. "Would it be possible to get a copy of the surveillance footage from those cameras? How long do you keep it?"

"About a month, usually. I need to call my boss, though."

"Sure, of course. Please do. But maybe you could call him right away? I'm really worried for this boy now. I'm worried that—" That they were being sold? Killed? What? What? What was being done with these teenagers? Her eyes widened, and although she'd been more than half pretending with this young man until now, she was completely herself, a mother of a teen, an ex-cop who had seen her share of horror perpetrated on other people. "That he's in very bad trouble."

The young man nodded and took out his phone, but a new batch of customers came in and Laney had to wait.

"I left a message," he told her when he got the chance to call. "He usually gets back to me within an hour. You can wait if you want."

"Sure," she said. "Thank you." She stepped outside and found a perch in the shade, where the heat, though heavy, was less oppressive. Cracked open her tea. As she waited, she performed a methodical overview of businesses in a forty-mile radius. The forty miles was a guess, a starting point. She opened her spiral notebook and started a list. The good news was that this far into upstate New York, there were vast stretches of not much. Every small town and village had its main street with a bagel shop, café, diner, bar, gas station. There were mom-and-pop businesses, hair salons and barbershops, supermarkets and libraries. Motels.

She didn't know if the Volkins went someplace public or if there was a private residence where they took the teens. But if Sunny River was the first point and this gas station mart was the second, the third must be somewhere near, and possibly off the same highway. If they took this trip once a week, it would probably not be a long one. After a half hour she took a break to scroll

the Twitter and Facebook accounts of surrounding police depart-
ments, focusing on the 911 calls if the department listed them. She
didn't expect much to come up, and her expectations bore out. In
the past month there were traffic accidents, fires, a woman fainting in a grocery store, a child lost and then found a few hours later.
There were more animal attacks than even traffic accidents—
coyotes, foxes, four rabid dogs, chicken-killing raccoons, and not
one, not two, but three separate bear intrusions.

She wasn't sure what she thought she'd see. Maybe something
unusual, but she figured it would stand out if she saw it. She had a
photograph showing Bubba with Step and Vera Volkin on the day
he disappeared from the group home. She had a receipt showing
that at least one of the Volkins had stopped at this gas station that
day, though it proved nothing, not really. She had a gas station
attendant who had been too overcome by Vera's attributes to pay
attention to anybody else she might have had with her. She had a
starting point. But that was all she had.

Her stomach grumbled, and she put away her phone and ate
her Slim Jim, which was going to have to be it for now. She'd buy
a sandwich later, after she heard about the security footage.

Resuming her search, she began flipping backward in time—
posts from two months ago, three, six, a year—but before she
could focus properly, the door opened and the young man gestured for her to come in.

"My boss says we can download the files for you, but we need
our IT guy. And since we have to call him in to do that, it will
be a hundred dollars." He seemed uncomfortable passing this on,
as if he felt his boss was trying to make an extra buck from a sad
circumstance.

She smiled with encouragement. This was excellent news, and
she had a budget. "That's great," she said. "Here's my card. Do you
think you can get the guy to do this today? Or maybe tomorrow?
I'm sure you understand in cases like this, we shouldn't waste any
time." Then, to reassure him, "The fee is acceptable. I'll have a
check for you when I come by. Okay?"

The man nodded, took her card, and turned to the next customer who walked in.

The noonday heat was suffocating when she got back into her car, but there was something she needed to do before returning to the office. The police department overseeing Sunny River's village was a small one, located in a distressed downtown with half the storefronts sporting FOR RENT signs. The young desk officer drooped, bleary with heat, and when Laney mentioned Sunny River, he frowned and sighed, then asked her to wait.

She only had the time to look at a chair before a detective hustled out of a side room and brought her into his office.

She showed him the photo of Bubba with the Volkins and Mona Powell, shared her suspicions about Mona, kept both Alfie and the Dubois family out of the story, and ended by saying she believed there might be a sort of safe house where these kids were being taken. Then she admitted it was conjecture and she had no proof of anything.

After listening carefully, the detective said, "How do you know these people?"

Yes, that was the tricky part, wasn't it. "Vera and Step Volkin live on my block. I know them socially."

"Huh, you don't say!"

"Yeah, life is weird."

"And how did you make this connection between them and the disappearances?"

Even trickier. Admit to sorting through her neighbors' garbage? Breaking into their house? Maybe skip that. "When I visited Sunny River, I spoke to a social worker who works with the kids. When I asked her if she had a photo of the people who claimed to be Bubba Gardner's parents, she showed me a pic of Step and Vera." Laney shrugged. "Small world, right?"

The detective frowned but nodded slowly. "And Mona Powell? How do you know of her connection?"

Laney tried to keep the agitation from her voice. "She used to hang around Vera. I looked at Mona's social media, the public posts. There were pictures of her with Vera." She saw a question forming on the detective's face and preempted it. "Vera Volkin is gone. She left last Saturday evening."

His eyebrows climbed.

"The police are looking for her in connection with another incident. A shooting."

He lowered his pen and sat back. "Well," he said. "This is probably more information than we've gotten about any of the kids to date." He folded his hands in front of him. "Mrs. Bird. I'll be honest, that place has been an absolute shit show—excuse my French—for years. Kids disappear from it all the time. Oh, they report it, but what can we do? The facility has no security. The kids come from terrible situations, just terrible, terrible stuff. A few I know personally have mental illness, but the county psychiatric hospital is even worse, so we're keeping them at Sunny River as long as we can." He sighed. "We'll follow up these leads, of course. And I'll get in touch with Sylvan PD about Vera Volkin."

Laney stood and extended her hand.

The detective took her hand and held it, tight. "Six months ago, a fourteen-year-old girl at Sunny River made a flamethrower out of hair spray and torched a fifteen-year-old girl. A month later three boys beat up an orderly so badly he lost an eye and spent a month in the hospital. Now, I'm not saying wherever they're going is better, but . . ." He let go and sat back down. "We'll look into it."

"Right," Laney said. "Okay then."

Walking into the dusty parking lot, she realized she was no longer hungry but rather craving a drink. Even so, on her way to BSI's office, she stopped to pick up sandwiches for her coworkers, something they took turns doing once a week for the sake of team spirit. She bought roast beef and Asiago for the boss, Mediterranean vegetables with hummus for the receptionist, turkey, ham, and provolone for Jack, and an iced tea for herself, into which she emptied a travel-sized bottle of Tito's. A few bags of chips, pickles, and four cookies rounded out her donation to the company lunch table and earned her happy smiles and a pat on the shoulder from the boss. Jack seemed surprised when she handed him his pickle-juice-stained paper bag, but he took it and put it aside.

"Thanks. Listen." He glanced out of his office to make sure no one was near and gestured for her to sit. She did. "I got your note," he said. "About Mona."

Laney shook her head. "Never mind," she said. "It's handled. I handled it."

"Oh." He frowned.

She shrugged. "I told Alfie he had to stop."

Jack studied her face, sat back, placed an ankle on a knee. "Yeah? How did that go?"

"About how you might think."

"What happened?"

Laney shook her head again. "Never mind. It's done."

"No, I mean, what changed your mind? Why did you confront him? Why now?" He put both feet on the floor.

"I think—" She closed her mouth. Jack knew her circumstances too well for her to tell him only part of the story. She'd have to confess to her suspicions of Mona's involvement with the disappearing kids, and by association, Alfie's involvement, spare as she hoped it was. And anyway, what was she doing with this man? Did she really think he'd be her friend? Her partner? No, she'd had enough partners to last her a lifetime. She'd been solving cases on her own for over a year, and there was no reason for that to end.

Getting to her feet, she felt her face heat. After what happened five years ago, she'd rather walk barefoot on hot coals than trust anyone with her child or her investigations ever again.

"I think it's personal, Jack," she finally said, and walked to her cube, where she unwrapped her cookie and shoved a huge chunk into her mouth, following that with a healthy glug from her tea bottle.

She almost choked when Jack sat down on a chair next to her.

He waited until she swallowed and gulped more vodka-tea before speaking. "What's going on?"

"Nothing is going on. I'm working on the Gardner case. I have a lead, so—" She gestured at her laptop.

He didn't move. "What's the lead?"

She wiped her mouth and said, "It's not very clear in my mind yet. I'm still working it through."

Jack nodded. "Got it." He raised an eyebrow. "Is your lead connected to the girl that was found a half hour ago up in Stony Point?"

A half hour ago she'd been at the deli ordering sandwiches. She had no idea what he was talking about.

He said, "I guess not."

"Why, who is she?"

"Her name is Alyssa Vallebuono. She's fifteen."

Laney blinked. She didn't like where this was headed.

"She disappeared from Sunny River three months ago. A man out fishing with his son found her by the hiking trail over there, by the water." He handed her his phone.

The girl in the picture lay on her side, knees drawn up. The skin on her face, neck, and arms was flaming red and peeling, boiling off her flesh. It took Laney a second to realize that the girl's top had been white when she'd put it on and not the rich carmine shown in the picture.

She gave him his phone back.

"She's at Good Sam now, but my guess is some kind of chemical burn." He leaned toward her, his eyes neutral. "Any ideas?"

Dammit, dammit, and dammit again. The image of the girl raged through her, vivid, painful. What did her son know about this? Was it possible he knew? No, no. No.

"Okay then," she said, "Mona Powell is connected to Bubba Gardner's disappearance. And possibly more disappearances." She raked her fingers through her hair. "She works there. Or worked. At least until last week."

He grew serious. "That's your lead?"

Laney nodded.

"Shit, Laney, what are you saying? Are you saying that your teenage son's adult girlfriend was involved in the disappearances of at least one and maybe more teenagers, one of whom was just discovered with her skin melted off her body?"

"All I know is that she worked at Sunny River and—"

He stood up and walked toward his office, then turned on his heel and came back. This time he didn't sit. "Why didn't you bring this to us as soon as you found out? You should have texted me at least. I spoke with her! I could have—"

"You did what?"

He glared at her. "What you asked me to do. I had a talk with Mona."

Goddamn her impulses the other night. She should know better than involve strangers in her life. Or her son's life. "And?"

"I think she'll leave your son alone. But that's beside the point now, isn't it?"

"Where is she?"

"I had her, Laney. I could have gotten her to say a lot. I could have taken her to the precinct if you told me about this."

He was right. By keeping this to herself, she'd cost them time and an opportunity. She rubbed her eyes. "I didn't know you were going to see her."

"You asked me to."

"To be fair, I didn't. You volunteered."

"Laney."

"Okay, fine. Fine. Where is she?"

He frowned. "If she's still there." Looked at his phone. "I have court in an hour. Call Ed and have him meet you there."

He punched something into his phone. Her phone pinged right away. It was an address for a motel room near Main Street in Sylvan. The place rented by the day, week, or month and had been an ongoing point of stress for the local administration.

"I know where this is," she said. "I'm going now."

"And you'll call me as soon as you're done speaking with her."

Laney was already closing her laptop and shoving it into its case. "Yes."

"Laney."

She paused.

His hands on his hips, his head angled away from her, he asked, "What else are you not telling me? What do you know about this?"

Heading for the door, she said, "Jack, I've told you everything."

"What do you know about Holly working for the Volkins?"

Laney stopped. Working for them? She turned to look at him. "What are you talking about?"

He said nothing, waited for her to say anything else. When she didn't, he shrugged and returned to his office.

31

Holly

HOLLY'S SHOULDER WAS a flaming, throbbing knot of pain. She shifted to the left, tried leaning sideways to ease the pressure, but her mobility was limited by the seat, the tight space, the belt.

Vera drove in silence, her thinned lips the only indication of her feelings.

"I'm in a lot of pain," Holly said.

"I'm sure Step is as well," Vera said.

Holly stared at her in disbelief.

"Fuck you," Vera said.

"Fuck you too," Holly countered immediately.

Neither one of them raised their voices. They might as well have been discussing the merits of the local pizzeria (a little too much sauce, not enough crust).

Holly endured until the next exit before speaking. "Why did you—"

"Shut up!" Vera slammed on the brakes, jolting Holly forward against the seat belt and forcing an agonized yelp out of her as her eyes clapped shut. Horns blared behind them, and Vera stepped on the gas again, pressing them into their seats as they accelerated, to the braying of more horns.

"I'm sorry," Holly repeated, and when she opened her eyes, she thought for a second, for just one moment, that Abigail was sitting next to her, her face contorted with anger.

"I don't care," Vera said. "It's a pointless thing to say."

Holly fidgeted and dropped her head against the seat. This woman shot her own husband to save Oliver. Why? "I didn't know Oliver would come."

"Pfft."

Holly had never actually heard anybody say that—*pfft*— though she'd read it in novels.

"Vera?"

Silence.

"Why did you save Oliver?"

Vera rolled her eyes, a gesture so juvenile Holly once again had the eerie feeling she was sharing a car with her sister.

"I didn't save Oliver from dying. I saved Step from becoming a killer." She pressed her lips tight. "You really fucked it all up, you know that."

Holly nodded. She did know that, though she thought they probably had different understandings of what exactly got fucked up.

"Where are we going?" Holly asked.

"Oh for crying out loud, can't you keep quiet?" Vera shook her head. "We're going someplace where maybe you can be useful. Just listen to yourself! Oh, boo-hoo, I'm about to lose my house. Oh, boo-hoo, I can't pay off my druggie brother's rehab. Oh, boo-hoo, my husband is boring!"

Holly sat up straight. "I never said Oliver was boring."

"Might as well have."

"Now you listen to me. You don't get to say a thing to me about my family! Do you understand?" She was angry, and being angry felt better than being sorry. She leaned into it. "I mean, really! Fuck you and the beast from hell you rode in on! You and your Step! I mean, why do you think you're better than me? You're fucked up. You're doing something awful to other people and you think you're something hot, and you're just a piece of fucked-up, cold-bitch-hearted, insane Eurotrash!" Her voice rose painfully at the end, sending her into a coughing fit.

"Well, Holly, tell me what you really think."

Holly crumpled into a limp heap, her range of movement constrained, her shoulder an ache ranging from blinding hot to almost tolerable. "I think I made a mistake," she said.

Vera jabbed the heel of her hand into Holly's nose, so fiercely that blood spurted down Holly's pastel blouse.

The next two hours passed in silence, Holly sniffling blood and watching the road. According to the few signs here and there, they were heading for the Catskills.

"Vera?"

"What."

"Where are you really from?"

Vera checked her mirrors and switched lanes, remained quiet. Then she said, "From Kiev. But first from Moscow. The outskirts. There's a neighborhood that's called the Devil's Land, if you translate it. That's where I grew up. In an apartment block."

"You didn't like it there?"

This was met with a snort. "No, Holly, I did not like it there. My mother died when I was eight, father when I was nine. They sent me to an orphanage." She grimaced. "I set fire to the orphanage before I left."

"Are you serious?" Frowning, Holly studied Vera's profile again, the clean lines of it. She knew almost nothing about Russia, but she had a feeling its orphanages were not great places to be.

"When I was in the orphanage, a man saw me and took me." She cut a cool glance at Holly, then refocused on the road. "Not what you think. This man, he was like Fagin, you know? From Oliver Twist?"

Holly nodded. She knew Oliver Twist.

"Then he brought Step in, and we became friends."

A tiny flare of understanding sputtered inside Holly. "You were both orphans?" Of course, that made sense. They were so close and Step always so possessive of Vera.

"You lived with that man?" And then again, a young, attractive girl, growing up without a mother to protect her, with strangers. Surely she'd been sexualized.

Vera shrugged. "I lived with that man. Step did too. Many of us did. He was okay. He taught us."

"But did he . . . did he make you . . ."

"What? Prostitute myself? I did what I wanted."

By now they were going through dark woods, the unlit road a serpentine spool into the forested depths. The odors of pines and fresh night air wafted through the partially open window, a whiff of wood smoke. Somebody had lit a campfire.

It would have been a peaceful and beautiful drive if it wasn't for the fact that Holly was a hostage with a punched-in face, her husband most likely instigating divorce proceedings. And oh yes, let's not forget the man who tried to kill him and now had a bullet in his ass. Or the drugs she stole. Or the corporate secrets she copied and gave away.

"We're here," Vera said, pulling onto a gravelly shore, the car's headlights illuminating a black lake, a motorboat, and across the water's expanse, a dark house like a cutout in the charcoal sky.

32

Laney

UNSURPRISINGLY, MONA POWELL no longer dwelled at the address Jack had texted Laney. Not only that, but the door to her efficiency room gaped open, and when Laney knocked and then poked her head inside, she saw a maelstrom of clothes, unmade bed, fast-food wrappers, and soda bottles, but no Mona. Most telling, the bathroom, though grimy, was empty. No toothbrush, no makeup, not even a shampoo bottle.

The single narrow closet stood equally stripped, only a lone scarf dripping from the rod.

Laney's phone vibrated, and she stepped outside to answer, steeling herself when she saw it was Bubba Gardner's mother.

"Is it him?" Mrs. Gardner asked. "I heard they found someone at Stony Point. Is it him?"

Laney, recognizing the agony of not knowing, of guilt, put as much reassurance and calm into her voice as possible before saying, "No, no. Not him."

"Are you sure? How can you be sure? I heard . . . I heard . . ." But what Bubba's mother had heard was buried in her sobs.

"It's a young girl," Laney said, and winced at the memory of that blistered face, those emaciated arms, so red. "It's not him. Listen. Are you hearing me?"

The sounds on the other end quieted. Then a wail. "Where is he?"

"I will find him," Laney said. "I will find him. I promise. Okay? I promise."

Of course, she knew better than to make such promises, but dammit.

She saw a police car pulling into the parking lot as she drove away but didn't stop. She'd been much, much too easy on Alfie until now, but no more. Her stomach hurt from thinking how close to tragedy he'd been walking. Again.

Would it always be like this? Was it just her luck to be blessed with a child prone to associating with all the wrong people? She slapped her steering wheel in frustration.

Once home, she realized she was, yet again, out of proper dinner food, so she made a giant omelet, throwing in a can of mushrooms and topping it with sliced cheese.

Alfie, when she called him down, was subdued and wan, his eyes red rimmed.

She waited until he finished eating, both of them clanking their forks against their plates in a tense silence.

"We need to talk," she said.

He glanced at her, then at the window, and made as if to rise, but she said, "Don't even think of leaving."

He settled back.

"You're going to tell me what Mona did for the Volkins."

He shook his head and bit his bottom lip.

"Alfie."

"I promised." This in a hoarse whisper.

She pulled up the picture of Alyssa Vallebuono's blistered face on her phone and placed it between them on the table. He stared at it, blood draining from his cheeks.

"This girl." Laney pointed at her phone. "This girl lived at Sunny River, and she disappeared. What do you know about it?"

"Nothing." Still a whisper.

"Did Mona get this girl to leave? Who did she leave with?"

Alfie shook his head, but this time his face crumpled, the heels of his palms against his eyes, his mouth twisting with the effort to get a grip.

She let him breathe through it until he steadied. Then, "That case I was telling you about, the runaway. The boy is eighteen. He stayed at that place, and I know for a fact that the day he disappeared, he left with Vera and Step Volkin, and Mona Powell was there with him. Now before we find him looking like this"—she jabbed at her phone again—"you tell me everything you know. Everything."

He wiped his eyes with his hands. "She was going to stop," he said. "She told me she wanted away from them and asked me to help her. I was helping her."

"How the heck were you doing that?"

He squirmed under her glare. "I brought her food."

She raised her eyebrows. "Food? From here?"

He nodded.

Well, that explained why there was never anything to eat in the house.

"And I gave her money."

"What?"

"From my savings account."

Laney tried very, very hard to keep from jumping to her feet and screaming. He had, the last time she checked, over five thousand dollars in his account, a combination of infrequent gifts from his father and the money she unwaveringly deposited every month for when he'd need a car. But she'd deal with that later. After all, it was his money and she'd shown him how to use the bank card. Neglecting to check the e-statements for the past couple of months was on her.

"Look." She got up and set her hands over his shoulders from behind—not quite a hug and not quite a throttle, but something that tried to be both and neither. "Do you know where they take the kids? Do you know where Mona lived before she moved into the motel?"

He shrugged. "She talked about a lake house upstate."

Her fingers squeezed harder, and he fidgeted, but she didn't let go. "Where?"

"I don't know. I don't remember her saying any town names."

She stood over him for another few minutes, but he was done; she sensed he'd told her everything. It was in the way the tension left his muscles, as if after a spasm.

Although she'd promised herself to be strict with him (what was he doing consorting with criminals? how could he not recognize when people were bad?), she leaned down and hugged him, a proper hug, with his head cradled against her shoulder.

"Alfie. I understand why you did it. You have a good soul. But you know that not everyone does, right? Not everyone is good." She tightened her grip. "You scare me, baby."

"Mona is good," he said, and he sounded so sad, so broken-hearted, that she found herself patting him. "Everyone is good," he continued. "But not everyone has the option to act on it. I wanted to give her that."

Laney stepped away, letting him go in a sweep of her hand. "Honey," she said, "you'll never make a good cop."

He snorted. "I never want to be a cop." Then grimaced apologetically. "No offense."

She began clearing the table. "None taken."

Afterward, when he'd vanished back into his room, she texted Jack.

There's a house on a lake upstate, she wrote. *I think the kids are taken there.*

The response came five minutes later. *Where?*

I'd tell you if I knew. Rolling-eye emoji, mad emoji. She stared at her phone for a few seconds before typing, *I mean it. I'll tell you everything I know once I know.*

There was no answer.

And in any case, she was already lying.

33

Laney

AFTER DINNER LANEY made herself a cup of coffee, spiked it with a healthy dose of Kahlúa, and took her laptop to her patio.

Finding the right house on a lake in upstate New York might be like finding a needle in a haystack, but she hoped she could at least narrow the search. If the girl they found today was indeed a victim of whatever transpired at the lake house, then it couldn't be too far upstate. Stony Point was only a few towns over from Sylvan. She drew an arbitrary eighty-mile circle around Sunny River and continued the search she'd started at the gas station, scrolling methodically through the police department and village social media accounts for every town within the circle.

An hour later she noticed something curious. Gebble, a small town located roughly thirty-four miles north of Sunny River and abutting a state park's lake, generated a fair amount of complaints regarding a motel called Rainwood. There were reports of vagrancy, dereliction, an unpleasant dog. The place was apparently a massive eyesore, and the locals constantly demanded their police department do something about it. The complaints dated back several years, but roughly eight months earlier they'd stopped.

Laney scrolled back and forth, but either the owners of the Rainwood had gotten on top of the situation or someone else had. She Googled the property. The resulting pictures and stories ran the gamut: a spiffy, mod vacation haven in the sixties, gay destination and party scene in the seventies, sad and dilapidated in the nineties and aughts. The motel clung to life through the sheer will and haphazard care of its elderly owners—a set of twins on the north side of eighty.

But although the complaints and 911 calls fizzled in November of last year, an interesting buzz commenced on Yelp and Tripadvisor. Starting in February, visitors to Gebble began posting odd reviews of the town, mentioning mysterious lights near the lake after dark, strange black vehicles, shady characters wandering the streets at night. One poster, an @heather-mom-of-three, who had stayed at the Rainwood with her children, claimed someone tried to break into her room. When she called the office, there had been a kerfuffle (her word) outside her door, and she swore she heard the person being dragged away. Since nobody was hurt (by which she presumably meant her or her children), she didn't call the police. But she gave the motel one star and claimed she'd have given it negative five if that was allowed.

Was this motel connected to the teen disappearances from Sunny River and therefore connected to her case and, possibly, to Holly? It was near seven in the evening, the light still golden against the slats of her deck. She stared at the last text she sent Jack and considered telling him what she'd found, but in the end, what *had* she found? A flea-bitten motel near a lake. No proof, nothing tying it to anything. Only a hunch. She'd visit on her own first, take a look-see.

By the time she parked in the motel's gravel driveway an hour and a half later, twilight cast everything in blue, the dense forest at the edge of the property like a dark animal, bleeding shadow onto the unkempt lawn. She walked around the perimeter, taking pictures on her phone of the things that looked odd or just plain unsavory: the decrepit shed with eight state-of-the-art locks on the door, the sopping-wet blankets and bed covers hanging off the peeling wrought-iron railings, the parking lot with its forty spaces and three cars, the dead potted plants on the balconies. As she was scoping out the office, a black van pulled into the lot.

A man wearing a suit, white shirt, and dark tie jumped out and crunched his way toward one of the rooms. He stopped short when his eyes connected with Laney's. Although the fading light made it hard to pick out his features, she figured he was in his early thirties, with short hair and sideburns and a bulky, muscled physique.

She smiled, took a step forward.

His eyes flicked toward the room, then toward his van, as if calculating distance against speed.

"Hey, neighbor," Laney said. "Just getting some air."

He turned on his heel, marched back to his van, slammed the door, and peeled out of the lot in a spray of gravel.

She took a picture of the license plate.

He'd been heading toward room number three, so that was where she went too, phone up and filming. The thick curtains were drawn tight, but a splash of lemony light spilled under the door. She knocked.

A second later the light blinked out, and no amount of knocking induced whoever was keeping very, very quiet inside to open up.

It was full dark when she pulled open the cheap aluminum door to the office and stepped into a dank, dim room with a flaking counter and an old-fashioned desk bell, which let out a tinny *plink-a-link* when she tapped it. The man who wobbled in from the back was tall and heavy and carried a small oxygen tank in a sling around his neck, the cannula snaking up his green polo shirt to burrow inside his mustache.

He stared at her expectantly, his expression neither welcoming nor off-putting.

"Hello, sir," Laney said. "How're you doing this evening?" When in doubt, treat people with extra respect. It can never backfire, even if the other person is suspicious.

The man raised an eyebrow, waited.

She looked around at the pressboard paneling, the water damage on the ceiling and vinyl floor.

"This place has quite a history, I bet," she said.

"No soliciting," the manager said.

"Sir, I'm not selling anything." She took out her card and placed it on the counter. "I'm an investigator. I'm investigating the disappearance of"—and here something twisted inside her mind and the words she said were not the words she intended—"Vera Volkin." She pulled up the picture of Vera on her phone. "Have you seen her?"

The man's eyes darkened, the pupils dilating, but he remained silent, turned away, and fiddled with his oxygen tank. Then, "I've never seen that person."

Laney nodded. "Right. Okay. What about this boy?" She showed him the photo of Bubba.

This time there was no physical reaction. The manager didn't even look at the photo, instead said, "What makes you think they're here? I've never seen them."

"Does anyone else work here I can ask? I can come back."

"No."

They stared at each other for a half minute, Laney wondering why, exactly, was she there, other than the weird Yelp reviews.

She smiled and tapped her finger on her card. "Well, thank you for your time, sir. Please call me if you have anything you'd like to share."

With that, she walked outside but didn't get into her car yet. The door to room number three stood partly open, voices murmuring within. The black van was back, parked in a different spot, closest to the trees. If she'd still been a cop, she'd have had no issue knocking, identifying herself as police and asking to come in. She would have had a partner watching her back, and a radio, if not a body cam to record the interaction.

But being a civilian, albeit trained in investigation and surveillance, she had none of those things. She crept toward the unlatched door and listened. Somebody, a woman, was crying—stifled, gluggy sobs, and a man's voice droned rhythmically over the crying, insisting on something, though with a singular lack of inflection.

Well, that by itself could be any number of things. Laney had no cause to call the local police or go in or do anything other than walk away. Still, though, she stayed and retrieved her camera from her bag, set it to video, and began recording. She might be able to pick something out later. She did this for ten minutes or so until the door slammed shut, at which point she turned her attention to that wrecked shed with its heavy locks.

It was the oddest thing. Although the shed seemed original to the property and hadn't been maintained, its pine slats gray and splitting, the roof sagging and furred with moss, the locks were new. Not only that, the door had an alarm system. When she heard a latch click behind her, she sauntered (quickly) toward her car, feeling both foolish and bemused.

The man in the suit had exited room number three and was striding with purpose toward the shed. Laney shot a video of the man unlocking every one of those heavy-duty locks, then enter the code into the alarm system, heft open the rickety door, and close it behind him.

Room number three was shut and dark once again.

The shed looked to be no bigger than one hundred square feet. She'd seen meth labs in spaces that small, but really, if this motel hosted a meth lab, why not commandeer a room?

An owl hooted and something scurried over her foot, making her jump. A large, cat-sized animal shimmied past her and toward the dumpster at the far end of the parking lot. When it crossed a streetlight's white cone, she realized it was a rat—the biggest rat she'd ever seen, and that's saying something, considering the places she'd worked in the past. By now she was beginning to question why anybody would stay in this place and wondering if she should make notes of the three other cars in the lot before leaving.

The humidity still saturated the dark air; she felt coated in an oily film, though that might have been a psychological side effect of having entered the motel's office. The owl hooted again, a distant thunderclap vibrated the sky, and a smell of ozone and dust rose from the earth.

The shed door opened.

The man walked out, this time carrying a suitcase so heavy he listed slightly to the side as he heaved it over the threshold, where he paused to lock and arm everything again.

She waited until he lugged the ungainly thing to his van, struggled to lift it into the back, and drove off. And even then, she was reluctant to go home. Something was definitely happening here, but unless she could tie it in with Bubba or the Volkins or witness an actual crime, she was stuck.

It wasn't until she stopped at a gas station on her way home that she zoomed in on the videos and photos she'd taken. In one of them, she could clearly see the space inside the shed as the man opened its door, illuminated faintly by streetlight and a red bulb. She zoomed as far as possible, a wash of excitement rolling through her. Although the photograph was grainy, dark, and difficult to discern, she was quite sure it revealed that the shed was not a dwelling but an entrance, containing but one thing—a staircase.

34

Holly

THE FIRST NIGHT in the house was the worst because Vera incarcerated her in a tiny room, something Holly suspected was literally a walk-in closet. The closet was bare, not even a blanket, no window, no light. Once the door closed, darkness and silence swallowed her, the pain in her shoulder and a nasty headache her only stimulation.

She was hungry and very thirsty, but she was afraid to ask for anything, afraid even to knock on the door. She'd never been very good with the dark. Outside, yes, the night didn't scare her. But this sensory deprivation chamber was something different.

Holly had spent twenty years filling her life to the brim—children, friends, family, dinners and lunches, volunteering at the schools and pet shelters, scouting, coaching, and when even that left an open hour here and there, she began writing her romance novels, because they were fun and gave her an excuse to Google-travel and daydream.

When her brothers' needs started to consume her savings and then her house, she doubled up on her extracurriculars, never for a moment wanting to be alone with her thoughts and fears. And when the Volkins stepped into her life, she fell into the mystery and intrigue they offered with eyes wide open.

Now she felt along the wall until she found a corner and slid to the hardwood floor, each shoulder against a wall and her head pressing into the joint. No matter how wide she opened her eyes, she saw nothing. The only mercy was that she was so dehydrated she didn't need a toilet.

After a while—she didn't know how long—she heard voices. She had trouble focusing on them, her heartbeat a suffocating, arrhythmic thrum, reverberating in her ears, making her gasp for air. But as the minutes wore on, her heart slowed, and her breathing normalized. Her muscles softened their rigid hold and she slid lower along the wall, letting her legs stretch forward. Her shoulder throbbed, but she was getting used to it.

The first intelligible word she heard was "tea," followed by the phrase "we sent it on."

She pressed her ear to the wall and moved around until the voices became more distinct. One of them was definitely Vera's, her precise, confident tones as familiar as the odor of old wood surrounding Holly. This place smelled like every lake house in her life—a touch of water damage, a touch of mold, a cool dampness—not unpleasant, but deeply unsettling for the memories it stirred.

Despite her efforts, she gathered little sense from the phrases and words leaching through the walls. Later, maybe after she dozed, or after her mind went for a stroll and came back, she heard someone else, a lower voice, closer. It moaned. It coughed. It cried for a while, a childish, hiccupping whimpering. Then it began to sing. A slow, quiet tune, wordless mostly, the person remembering only the refrain. Holly recognized the song, something Freddie, her oldest, might have listened to on his tablet months ago.

Holly slid further to the floor, curled in on herself, and clasped her hands under her chin. First, she prayed for Oliver to be okay. Then for her children to be spared. Thinking of them hurt her heart so much she almost cried out from the overwhelming helplessness and guilt. After that, after her breathing stabilized again, she prayed for Step to be alive, because even though she was the one who brought the gun, she hadn't meant to use it. She hadn't meant for anyone to die. She couldn't be responsible for that as well. Last, she prayed for the sad soul in the room next door to be released. She did not at any point pray for forgiveness because she didn't believe she deserved it.

In the morning, when the door opened and a shaft of knife-sharp light poured over her, she shuddered and squinted but stayed put, terrified.

"Well, get up," Vera said. "What are you waiting for?"

Holly stumbled out of the closet and followed Vera to a bathroom. Washing helped her mind focus, though it did nothing to boost her strength.

Vera waited for her at a desk, the old oak scratched and rubbed pale in places, her fingers poised over a laptop. Her hair was long and glossy, her skin smooth, the whites of her eyes bright, her lips full and red—everything perfect, as if she hadn't shot her own husband the night before and fled a crime scene. Holly stood at the doorway, uncertain of what she was expected to do. What she'd be allowed to do.

"How is Step?" she asked at last.

"Not good," Vera spat out, without looking at her. "He'll be better."

"I'm sorry," Holly said, for the umpteenth time.

"Oh, fuck you, Holly." Vera stopped typing and looked at her. "You're like a child. You think if you say you're sorry, then what you did will not have happened."

Holly walked further into the room. It was an old room, with wood wainscoting and yellow walls, kilims on the hardwood floor, heavy curtains—yellow with red poppies all over—on the tall windows.

Vera pointed at a wingback chair. "Go on, eat." A plate and a cup sat on a round side table next to the chair. Holly lowered herself carefully, favoring her sore shoulder, and lifted the cup to her lips. Tea, lukewarm but strong. She drained the entire thing in a few greedy gulps. The sandwich, grilled cheese, also tepid, went down quick, and she felt more alert, slightly more energized as she finished.

Only then did she realize Vera had been observing her the whole time, her body as taut as a cat watching birds at a feeder.

Holly rose to her feet, wondering what would happen if she walked out. The room vibrated around her. She gripped the back of the chair to keep from falling, nausea rising up her gorge.

Vera smiled. "There you go," she said sweetly. "On your way."

Holly found she could walk, but the nausea now flowered into a sickly heat, a furnace burning in her gut. She needed air. She reeled out of the room and followed a dark hallway to another door, but that one was locked. She doubled back, along a different corridor, found a door that definitely led outside, and it opened.

The heat and sun made her almost shrink into the house, but she forced herself forward, her sandaled feet sinking into the dry lawn. A lake glittered fifty feet below and she stalked toward it, her arms outstretched as if she were blind, which she nearly felt she was. She walked over the damp sand and into the water, the cool shock of it refreshing enough so the terrible heat inside her subsided somewhat. Creeping toward a weeping willow, she crouched under its hanging branches, her arms wrapped tightly around her middle.

"They're going to kill you," a voice said.

She gasped because she hadn't heard that voice in over twenty years and she wasn't sure how she could now. When she turned her head, there was Abigail, half in the lake, her wet hair shimmering in the sunlight and fanning around her hips.

CHAPTER

35

Holly

THE SUMMER HOLLY Dubois, née Spencer, was twelve, much like every summer before that going back before she was born, even before her parents were born, the entire Spencer clan relocated to Ellenville, a lakeside community in the Catskills. They swept the spiders from the family vacation home and shoved a bed or mattress into every room, pantry, or hallway to fit the ever-growing tribe. The younger members, including Holly and Abigail, camped on the lawn in tents. The mothers stayed the summer with the children, and the fathers came and went with the weekends.

Abigail, sixteen that summer, had lobbied to stay in Sylvan but was overruled, and she had made a chaotic, strawberry-body-spray-scented nest for herself in their tent. She spent the mornings sleeping, the afternoons napping on the lake shore with an occasional dip into warm, seaweed-clogged water, and the nights elsewhere. She'd climb into the tent at three, four in the morning, accidentally kicking Holly awake to roll into her mess of sleeping bag, sheets, pillows, and discarded clothes. Holly would turn on her side and look at her sister's sharp cheekbones, her full lips, the mascara smudged and grainy around her closed eyes. Her sister smelled of smoke and beer, cologne, a tang of sweat.

"Where were you?" Holly whispered, night after night, and Abigail would smile, flip onto her back and tell her. Some nights it was David, their third cousin, the one with exotic features and eyes the color of lake water. Other nights it was Phillip, the property caretaker, a twentysomething who spoke with a thick Portuguese accent. And once in a while, Oliver Dubois, whose small family had come to stay in the neighboring house and who, though the same age as Abigail and therefore not very interesting, possessed an impressive footballer physique and was obviously, and embarrassingly, smitten with her. That's when she dubbed him the Handsome Potato, his features superhero-blocky even then, despite the soft layer of baby fat rounding his cheeks and plumping his lips. Holly had giggled, but the nickname stuck, sometimes diminutized to HP.

"Check this out," Abigail said one night, two weeks into the summer. She crawled in carefully, gingerly, and Holly wondered if she'd hurt herself, but then realized Abigail was only drunk. "You've never had this," she said, and extended her hand, palm up, toward Holly.

Holly propped herself on an elbow but saw nothing in the dark. She pulled her flashlight from under her pillow and flicked it on, casting a wavering yellow cone of light onto her sister's fingers. On her index finger lay a tiny square of paper, and although Holly had never seen it before, she knew right away what it was from Abigail's descriptions.

"Want it?" Abigail asked.

"No," Holly said. "I'm tired."

"I saw angels tonight," Abigail said. "In the water. They glowed like Christmas decorations, and then they walked out of the lake. They shimmered."

Holly closed her eyes and tried to imagine this. "That sounds beautiful," she said.

Abigail sighed. "It was." She turned onto her side and curled her bare knees to her chest. "Life is so beautiful."

Holly wanted to tell her she loved her, as if wishing to pull her sister back from the angels. Instead, she reached across the two-foot divide between their air mattresses and touched Abigail's damp face. "Good night," she said.

But Abigail was already dreaming, either in sleep or still tripping.

For twenty years after that night, Holly questioned how different the next day would have been if she'd taken that puny acid tab from her sister's finger. If she'd stuck out her little-girl tongue and licked it into her body or spit it out. If she'd gone through Abigail's stash and removed the rest of the tabs, the joint. If her sister had woken at noon and not placed that damn tab in her mouth and then wandered down to the crowded beach looking for angels.

If she hadn't waded into the sun-warmed water and floated on her back, long hair trailing, snagging on seaweed, fish nipping at her heels and the tender spots behind her knees. If she hadn't drifted to the deep center of the lake, surrounded by splashing children and families in rowboats, only to open her eyes to the blinding sun and try to stand up, and sink twenty feet to the silty bottom.

Holly, who had been munching a PB and J sandwich, carefully trying to keep sand out of her mouth, looked up, as if jabbed in the belly, to see her sister's arms sticking straight out of the water and a young boy rowing calmly past. She jumped to her feet, wasting time being unsure, even (God help her) feeling self-conscious in her panic, then ran, the lake a shock against her hot skin, and swam.

The lake was crowded, choked with children, their mothers, grandmothers, beach balls, floaties, an obstacle course of rubber and flesh, and not a single one of them noticed the dying girl in their midst. By the time Holly reached her, Abigail's arms were no longer above the water, and she had to dive to grab her, a waxen, open-eyed Ophelia, limp and heavy. Finally, a young man, someone who'd made it his habit to watch Abigail, realized what had happened, plucked her out of Holly's embrace, and brought her out, spreading her on the pebbly beach like a grass doll, her hair covering her face.

A woman pushed Holly out of the way, and she stumbled and fell onto the sand. She understood, sluggishly, that the woman was her mother, and her mother was screaming.

Oh, Holly thought, *Mom is screaming. I never heard her scream. Someone else is screaming. Who is it?* She looked to the left, to the right, oh so slowly, and felt her throat ache, grow raw. She was screaming. It was her. She and her mother were screaming together as the young man—whom she now recognized as Oliver Dubois—and then EMTs performed CPR on Abigail's airless, lake-clogged body.

She had no memory of the next days. None. As if she'd screamed herself hoarse on that beach and been unplugged, like a toy, and then turned back on after the funeral—strangely, still on the shore.

It was late evening, the beach deserted, all the families cooking supper or driving to town for a movie or pizza. Holly walked into the water up to her calves and then trudged around the entire lake's perimeter, all three miles of it, her bare feet dragging through silt. It took her four hours to do the walk, after which she rested. When the moon rose, she did the walk again.

She walked through the night, every night, sleeping on the beach during the day. Her brothers walked with her some nights, her cousins others. Her parents were inconsolable, refused to look at her. Whenever she found herself in the same house as them, let alone the same room, she wanted to scrape broken glass through her wrists. But she couldn't do that to them, so she went to the lake instead.

Three weeks after Abigail drowned, Oliver Dubois came to the beach and walked with her.

Eventually he was the only one left, keeping her company after her brothers and cousins and mother returned to Sylvan. Her father took time from work and stayed with her, and then he too went home when he saw that Oliver and Oliver's family were looking after her.

She left the beach only to shower and change her clothes, but she slept there, wrapped in a sleeping bag even when it rained. Oliver brought her muffins in the morning, sandwiches for lunch, pizza or a grilled chicken drumstick for dinner. He continued to walk with her. Listened when she told him of the angels Abigail saw. Held her when she sobbed so hard she thought she couldn't possibly survive such an inner wrenching.

Four years later they had sex for the first time—in his car. It hurt, and she wondered if that's how it had been for Abigail with him and if that was why he'd only been the occasional one, third in line after David and Phillip. But the sex got better, and then it got very good indeed, and Oliver proposed, which seemed only natural. Everyone expected it.

She said she needed to finish college first, and he said of course, I'll be here. She went away planning to experiment, with other boys, maybe girls. She promised herself she'd do whatever she wanted, and she did, none of it sticking, none of it touching her.

They married her first year back from university. He started a job as a junior lab technician while baby Freddie already grew and swam inside her.

Sometimes she thought she'd been a duckling, imprinting on the first man who cared for her. But no. That wasn't it. Oliver had loved Abigail, had known Abigail. He grieved for her, walking that lake with Holly every night, holding her hand, transferring his love one step at a time.

Over the years, her crushing grief and guilt softened to an occasional melancholy. But really, with three children, four nieces and nephews, aging parents, two needful brothers, and an army of raucous cousins, who had time for melancholy?

She was fine until Vera Volkin fell into a half-frozen lake on a fog-laced April morning and looked at her with her sister's knowing eyes.

Okay, she had not been fine. She'd been about to lose her family home and was so far in the hole with her credit cards she could see no way out. But she had not been losing her mind. Not the way she was now.

Now she was burning from the inside out, Abigail no longer within her but out, asking, demanding, tormenting, and promising; and Holly no longer two girls, as when Oliver looked at her, but one. And a thieving, spying, lying, treacherous one at that.

36

Laney

L ANEY HAD TO return to the Rainwood and see what was going on in that shed.

First, she texted Alfie.

How are you doing?

He began responding right away. He really was a good son. Never snarky, never selfish. Never demanding, either. He'd gotten involved with that woman because he wanted to help her. That said something about his character.

I'm fine, he texted.

She wanted to call him and hear his voice, but that was one thing no normal teenager in this day and age appreciated, so she controlled herself. *I love you, baby*, she typed.

Okay, he responded after a longer pause. *Where are you?*

Following up on a lead, she texted. *I'll be home late.*

Second, she called Gebble PD and asked to speak with the detective in charge of the complaints about the motel. He wasn't in, so she spoke to another detective. It took a few tries, but she managed to convince him she wasn't a nutjob, that she really was following a case, that she had reason to believe children were being trafficked there. She described the suspicious van, the crying, that outhouse locked up tighter than a you-know-what, and the staircase that obviously led somewhere deeply objectionable.

Third, she called Jack Boswell. When he didn't pick up, she texted him an abbreviated version. If she was right and the Volkins were taking kids to this place, she wanted Jack to know. And although she wouldn't have been able to explain it, she wanted Jack to look at her with respect and not with the cool distrust of the past few days. Not that she needed his respect. She didn't need a thing from anyone. But she'd promised him she'd share, and that's exactly what she was doing. Nothing else. Not at all. She was being true to her word.

At the Rainwood, Laney parked at the far end of the lot, under a copse of half-dead birches overgrown with thorn-studded vines. The air this near the lake had a heavy, earthy odor of rotting leaves and stagnant water.

Renting a room with an unobstructed, close view of the shed, Laney closed the door and reminded herself that she'd been in worse places during her time with the NYPD. Thank goodness the room's windows opened, or she'd have had to do her surveillance from her car. The room reeked of mold and cigarettes, with an undertone of old sweat. Indescribable stains on the bed, chair, and walls gave Laney pause, until she told herself she needed only a few hours. Just long enough to observe that shed. She was pretty sure she wouldn't pick up a flesh-eating disease from the chairs, and she'd be certain to strip and wash her clothes on the hottest setting once she got home.

She removed one of her cameras from her bag and trained it on the outbuilding. If anything was going to happen there tonight, she'd photograph it. If anybody walked in or out, she'd document it.

All of this was conjecture; she knew that. But something about this place, about that shed and its stairs, wasn't clean, and not in the same way this room wasn't clean. If the Volkins took those teenagers anywhere, she'd bet cash money on the Rainwood. And if she had to sit here for a week to find out, she would.

As it turned out, she had to wait only two hours. Unfortunately, most of those hours she spent asleep. She had positioned herself by the window, a bottle of water at her elbow, her eyes trained on the shed and the visible portion of the parking lot and lawn. Twenty minutes later she was deeply, thoroughly, mind-stoppingly asleep, her forehead planted on the grimy windowsill, her mouth open, drool a long, thin, silvery thread connecting her to the gritty floor.

Only when the noise level outside reached the mall-on-Black-Friday point and the knocking on her door could no longer be ignored did she grunt, sit up, swallow her drool, cough it back out, and jump to her feet.

She opened the door and clicked on the light while still dazed, only half sure of where she was or her purpose.

"Police," said a middle-aged woman in a patrol uniform.

"Hi," Laney said.

The woman peeked around her into the room. "Are you alone, ma'am?"

"Yes."

Somebody outside was crying.

The policewoman's attention focused on the camera, and she glared at Laney.

"I'm a private investigator," Laney said, to forestall the questions she saw brewing on the officer's face. "Hold on, I'll get my ID. I was on the job in the city." Being a fellow cop, even retired, carried weight in some situations, and Laney always played that card if she got the chance.

"What are you doing here?" the cop asked.

Laney pointed outside, where at least four patrol cars and a chief's SUV rotated red and blue lights and roughly two dozen men and women, ranging from early to advanced middle age, milled on the lawn in various states of undress. Dog collars, thick leather wrist cuffs, chains, PVC dresses with cutouts for breasts and bottoms, at least two leather hoods complete with face masks.

A man wearing nothing but a leather thong was demanding to see the warrant, indignation dressing him in authority.

"I . . ." Laney began, and paused. She was what? None of those people were teenage runaways, at least not anymore, if they ever had been. None of them was Step or Vera Volkin. Or Holly, for that matter. "I was investigating a case," she said. "A runaway boy. I thought he may have been taken to this motel." She handed her card to the policewoman, who took it with a look of distinct distrust. "What is this?" Laney asked, gesturing at the lawn. "It looks like a seventies swingers' disco. With whips."

The policewoman's shoulders relaxed, and she smirked. "The things I've seen tonight." She shook her head. "I will never unsee them."

Laney edged her way outside to the cement walkway. Police officers lugged cases of beer and liquor up the steps in the shed. "Are you telling me there's a literal BDSM dungeon down there?"

The cop guffawed and immediately placed her hand over her mouth. "That lady over there?" She indicated a woman wearing thigh-high PVC stiletto-heeled boots, a tool belt weighted with coiled whips, and other things Laney couldn't make out (and didn't care to). "She's the middle-school principal."

"Wow," Laney said. "You'd think she'd want to take a break from ordering people around."

This time the cop laughed harder, a bright-red flush suffusing her plump cheeks. "Lord," she said. "This just takes the cake."

"So, let me get this straight," Laney said. "What are they doing that's illegal? Is it prostitution?"

"God, no. Well, I don't know, but no. They're running an unlicensed sex club, selling liquor without a license, operating a space without a certificate of occupancy. You name a building code violation, they broke it."

Laney glanced at the motel office with its lopsided portico, guessing the underground club wasn't the only spot on this property playing fast and loose with building codes. "But you didn't find anybody underage?"

The cop shook her head, her eyes growing serious and guarded again.

"What about Russians? Any Russians in the group?"

"Okay." The woman straightened to her full height. "I'm going to ask you to stick around and not leave. I don't know what you think you were recording over there, but you need to wait until the detectives speak with you. Right?"

"Yes," Laney said. "Yes, of course."

She pulled a chair out of that noxious room and positioned herself with a good view of the proceedings. When she couldn't keep the befuddling mix of disappointment and amusement to herself any longer, she pulled out her phone, intending to text Jack, only to find four missed calls and a voicemail from him and a text and voicemail from Alfie.

She opened Alfie's text first. *I'm going to sleep now*, it said. *Good night.* This was her child's equivalent of *I'm not quite as mad at you as I was, and I believe I will be less mad soon*, and it made her day better just to see it.

Alfie's voicemail, recorded an hour ago, jolted her upright, and she lurched into the room, gathering her things before she even finished listening. Her car waited far enough from the hoopla that the cops didn't see her leave. If the Gebble PD gave her grief for leaving, they were welcome to do so. She'd deal with them later.

As she made the turn onto the highway, she played the voicemail again.

"Mom! Someone broke into the house!" There was more, but she couldn't make out the words, no matter how often she replayed it, because her son was crying, and someone was screaming.

37

Laney

LANEY SCREECHED DOWN her street and parked against the curb, since two police cruisers crammed her driveway. Alfie stood across the street, two of her neighbors flanking him, staring at her house. She glanced at the smashed bay window and the gaping front door, then ran to her son and wrapped him in her arms.

"I'm sorry. Are you okay? Are you hurt?" The words poured out of her without pause, and she stood back and inspected him. Her son towered over her, wrinkled T-shirt and shorts, blond hair a chaotic tangle, face blotchy and tearstained. His distress brought her to her senses. He couldn't see her like this. What was she thinking? He was standing up, and he wasn't bleeding; therefore, the next step was to model composure whether or not she felt it.

"I'm okay," he said.

"Did they hurt you?"

"He. One person. No, Mom. No. He left when I came down the stairs."

Her eyesight dimmed for a second at the thought of her son alone in a house with a violent intruder.

"You confronted him?"

Alfie shook his head. "He heard me and left."

"Did you see him?"

The boy's jaw hardened. He nodded. "Step Volkin."

"You told the cops?"

He nodded again.

She turned to the women on each side of him and thanked them for watching over him, then marched toward the cruisers and their oscillating lights.

Ed Boswell stood by her front door, writing something in his notepad. The Crime Scene team had turned on all the lights, inside and out, and Ed's face appeared washed-out and tired in the glare.

"Laney," he said, putting away his pen.

She bit back an apology—she had been working a case; it's not like she'd been gallivanting in nightclubs. Her son was old enough to be on his own. Nothing to apologize for. Nothing.

She said, "Did you get the motherfucker?"

"We're looking," Ed said. "Alfie said he heard him go down the street and then he heard a car. We've sent out an alert."

She peered through the broken shards of her front window at the living room. Whatever few pictures she'd had on the wall— Alfie in his Boy Scout uniform, an old photograph of her long-dead parents and brother together on a trip to Florida—were lying in pieces on the floor. Her television smashed in. Her standing lamp a crushed heap.

"Can I go in?" she asked.

The Crime Scene cops were still puttering through her posses-sions, dusting, taping, photographing. Ed studied the room, said, "Yeah. Why don't we go in and you tell us if it looks like he took anything?"

But nothing was taken. Step inflicted an impressive amount of damage in mere minutes. Anything that could have been knocked off a surface, stomped, or torn was. She was careful to walk around the objects likely to hold evidence and strode into the den, then the kitchen. The den was mostly intact, only a desk overturned, its papers spilled. The kitchen seemed okay as well, except for the dishes and glasses shattered on the tiles and the bread loaf in the center of the counter, as if Step had considered making toast before being chased away. The container of vindaloo she'd given him sat upended on the table, the gravy splattered in a dark-brown spew over the wood, the chairs, the floor. It off-gassed a rancid yet fruity odor, and Laney walked to the windows above the counter and slid them open. Her neighbors' voices floated in from across the street, punctuated with an occasional reassurance from Alfie that he was all right.

"At first glance, he didn't take anything," she said to Ed, who'd followed her into the kitchen.

"Laney?"

She chewed on her lip. "Yeah?"

"Why did Volkin do this to you?"

A grim defeat gripped her, and she sighed, lowering her face and pressing her fingers against her eyes. She then lifted her head and looked at Alfie's silhouette outside before turning toward Ed. "If I were to guess, because I confronted him and told him I knew all the details of his trafficking ring. And I told him I'd kill him if he touched Alfie." Not to mention that Alfie had most certainly warned Mona, and she in turn warned the man she'd sworn to Alfie she no longer obeyed. And that man accepted Laney's threat and gave it back a hundredfold.

Ed glanced behind them at the techs moving toward the kitchen and led Laney outside to the driveway.

"I'm not going to explain that you telling Volkin you'd kill him is Menacing. He could have had you arrested. I have to assume you knew that."

"Obviously, he decided to handle it himself." She rolled her shoulders. "But yeah. I know."

"Next. Trafficking ring?"

"I don't have proof of any of it. I thought I had something and that's where I was earlier, but"—she threw her hands up in frustration—"I discovered something else. Illegal, but unrelated."

Ed opened his mouth, and she interrupted. "I didn't bring it to you because I had nothing, just guesses. I still have nothing. But if this was his reaction to our trafficking conversation, then maybe I have something." Her eyes settled on her broken front window. "Volkin understands the law, I think. If caught for this, he gets charged with trespassing and burglary, both a first offense for him." She nodded at the question in Ed's face. "I researched him. He's clean. At least legally. I don't think he'll let anyone get him now. But if he does, he can claim intoxication. He can say Alfie invited him in. He can say all kinds of things and get away with this."

Ed put his hand on her shoulder and finally got a word in. "Nobody's getting away with this."

A crunch of gravel behind her, a voice. "Are you okay?" Jack Boswell. He'd left messages for her while she slept in that god-damn motel room—where are you, what's going on, Alfie's fine, don't worry, call me, call me, call me.

She hadn't allowed herself to hear the concern in his voice, only reacted to the urgency of the words, her foot pressing harder and harder on the accelerator as she drove home.

"Hey," she said. "Yeah. Yeah, I'm okay."

He stood next to his brother, younger, in better shape, but with an air of defiance to Ed's steady confidence. "I spoke with Gebble PD," he said.

Ed didn't look at him, but his head cocked sideways, listening.

Laney flashed back to the parade of corseted, vinyl-encased middle-aged flesh. She would have laughed if she weren't standing in front of her violated house. As it was, she only shook her head and grimaced. "Don't," she said.

"It was a good lead," Jack said. "That motel definitely looked suspicious enough."

"Stop." The harsh note in her voice startled all three of them, and she had to take a deep breath to let go of at least some of the fury she directed at herself. "Don't patronize me, Jack. I knew Step was unhinged, and I suspected when Mona left, she would go to him or to Vera. I threatened him. And then I left my child unprotected."

Ed said, "Laney"—but she put her hand up, and he stopped— "all right, I won't tell you it wasn't your fault. But if you believe there is trafficking going on, and you know who's doing it, then—"

"You know what? I'm putting a cork in it for now." She glanced at Alfie, still standing across the street. "I'm taking my detective hat off for the night."

"Yes, of course." Ed started to say something else, but she turned away, though not before she saw Jack gesture to his brother, calling him over.

Putting on a mask of assurance and calm, she walked over to her son. Immediately one of the neighbors, a young woman named Corinne, offered them her guest bedroom.

"You can't stay there," Corinne said. "Come stay with us."

"That's very kind of you."

Laney was about to accept when Alfie said, "That's okay." And before she could object, he added, "I have a piece of plywood left over from that Boy Scout project. We can put it up over the window."

Laney opened her mouth, and he interrupted again. "I have a bolt lock we can put on the door. Until tomorrow."

Laney and the two neighbor women stared at him for a few seconds until Laney turned to Corinne and said, "He's right. It's not too much damage, and we will have a lot of cleanup for tomorrow. But oh my gosh, thank you for offering. And I can't even begin to thank you for being here for Alfie when—" What? When his mother wasn't there? "Really, though. Thank you."

And before anybody changed their minds or objected, she spun around and walked toward her front door, Alfie's heavy step directly behind her.

Crime Scene left after putting their equipment and evidence bags in their van, and within a half hour Laney and Alfie were alone, their house a bright chaos around them.

True to his word, and despite the exhausted bruises under his eyes, her son lugged a four-by-six sheet of plywood from their garage to the broken front window, and they nailed it to the frame. The plywood didn't cover the entire window, but enough of it that any future invaders would need to be cat sized to succeed. Even so, Laney found a blue plastic tarp and duct tape in the basement, blanketing the remaining opening.

By four AM they finished, climbed the stairs and collapsed into their beds without talking. Sleep claimed Laney quickly but incompletely, and she dozed, fitfully aware of the lightening sky, the stirring birds, the soft sobs on the other side of her wall, but not so conscious she could react.

When she finally woke, it was full light and hot. Something must have happened to her air conditioning; she couldn't feel its hum in the walls. She threw open the windows in her room and padded into the bathroom. At least Step had left the upstairs part of the house undisturbed. She took a cool shower, brushed her teeth, and felt ready to face whatever came. Which was when she finally awoke properly, remembered the sounds coming from Alfie's room and crossed the hall to his firmly shut door.

She knocked, got no answer, knocked again, gently turned the doorknob, and cracked the door open. Alfie lay curled on his side, his face so peaky it was gray and his eyes nearly swollen shut with tears. He was awake.

After fifteen years of raising this person, she knew better than to show him affection or pity when he barely held himself together. The only thing that worked was being cool and business-like, attentive but not coddling. Every problem had a solution, she used to say, and if she went soft along with him, he'd never see beyond his own overwhelming emotion.

"Why are you crying?" she asked, as calmly and quietly as she could, even though every cell in her body screamed for her to touch him and tell him everything would be fine. Instead, she opened his windows to the morning and sat on his chair.

Alfie broke down in another bout of sobbing with a force that terrified her. And still she didn't reach out but sat with an outward show of tranquility, her limbs at rest, her eyes steady on him. She counted to a hundred, said, "Tell me."

As the weeping slowed, he wiped his face with his shirt and said, "Mona broke up with me."

Laney expected another onslaught of tears, but he kept it together, eyes averted yet not shrinking away when she finally reached out and held his feverish hand.

"It hurts so bad," he whispered.

She said nothing. They stayed like that for a long while as his breathing eased and slowed and his limbs slackened. She let go of his hand and stood. Let him rest while he could. She understood very well how searing a breakup could be.

As she went downstairs and fished out a garbage bag, she reminded herself that Mona was, at least in a legal sense, a child molester. Laney always suspected that love, like everything else, would be harder for Alfie than for other kids. He was different, and although anybody meeting him for the first time nowadays would hardly notice anything strange about him, she knew better. She suspected he walked through life acting a role, watching others' behaviors and trying them on for size. And she understood the pull Mona had on her son. He probably never had to act with her.

She picked up a dustpan and broom and started with the broken glass in the living room. There had only ever been three people who accepted her son exactly as he was: her, the man who'd tried to kill him a year ago, and this grown woman who brought danger and anarchy into their lives. Would Alfie always attract broken souls? And what did that make her?

The tightness in her chest hurt.

She was abysmally tired, that was all. Yesterday had been one of those days that lasted a week, and she'd slept badly. She was tying off a bag and reaching for a second one when the stairs creaked and she turned to see Alfie on the steps, his eyes taking in the destruction.

"How're you doing?" Laney asked, and without waiting for a reply, said, "I'm okay here. You can go rest some more."

"I'm fine." He wandered to where she stood and took the full garbage bag. "I'll take this outside, and then I'll help."

"Alfie, wait. Tell me again what happened. Tell me everything you remember."

He frowned and shifted the garbage bag to his other hand. "I was in bed. I had my window open because it was hot. I think the AC died. I heard his footsteps first, from way down the block. It was so quiet except for that. And then he tried the door. Like he was messing with the doorknob for a while."

Laney pictured that scraping sound, the only audible thing in the midnight silence, her son alone. "How long was he messing with the doorknob?" she asked, commendably businesslike.

Alfie shrugged. "A while. Ten minutes. I wasn't sure. I thought maybe it was a raccoon outside."

"A raccoon on the doorknob?"

"I guess that's when he broke the window." His voice trembled, but he gathered himself. "I called 911 and waited. That was it. I heard him tearing things apart down here, and I didn't know what to do."

She nodded. "You did the right thing."

"Then I heard the sirens, and he walked out. That's when I saw who it was."

She took his hand, but he snatched it away. "I'm sorry I wasn't here," she said.

"It's fine." He picked his way to the back door, carrying the garbage bag above the overturned chairs. "Did you find that boy you were looking for?"

Bending to lift the lamp, she shook her head, even though he wasn't looking at her. "No, honey. I got nothing last night."

He came back a minute later as she righted the coffee table.

"Alfie? Did you call Mona after I left?"

His eyes reddened again, and he wiped his nose with the back of his hand.

"I'm sorry," he said, a whisper.

She let him be, rearranged a cushion.

"I asked her about the boy," Alfie said. His voice grew thick and so sad, Laney had to fight to keep from crying herself. "She wouldn't tell me anything."

They labored in silence for a while after that.

"Did he take anything?" Alfie asked as he returned a candle to its shelf.

"Not sure," she said. "At first glance, no. It seems he just wanted to break our stuff."

"Mom?"

While gently extracting the photos from the broken frames, she stopped and shifted her body so she faced him directly.

"Yes?"

"Is it . . . I mean, is it . . ."

"Yes?"

"Why did he do this? Was it because—"

The hesitancy in his tone told her he suspected the destruction was Mona related. But the other thing it told her was that he didn't want his suspicion confirmed.

"I don't know, honey. Here, grab a bag."

Laney moved the couch to sweep the glass out from under it, finding fragments of a ceramic bowl and a G.I. Joe action figure from Alfie's younger days. Her house was filled with junk, the detritus of a busy life.

"Well, at least we get to clean, finally," Laney said.

"There's a crow in the kitchen," Alfie said.

"What?"

"I shit you not." He hovered in the kitchen doorway, and she could only see around the edges of him, so she nudged him, and sure enough, a big black crow had flown in through a window and was striding back and forth on the counter, pecking green grapes from a plastic bowl, tugging a piece of sliced bread from an untied bag.

Laney dug the heels of her hands into her eyes and rubbed. She was going on three hours of sleep, tops, and Alfie possibly on less than that. The presence of a giant black bird in her house was so surreal she couldn't absorb it. And what do you do with a bird that big? Shoo it?

Just then a second one poked its way through the window, followed by a third.

She folded her hands over her chest. "Well, that's just dandy, isn't it," she said.

"I've never seen a crow that close before," Alfie said.

"That's because they're meant to be somewhere above our heads, living their birdy lives."

"I guess they like grapes."

"Hey!" Laney shouted, and waved her arms at the birds.

They ignored her.

She was heading to the basement to grab a mop (maybe they wouldn't ignore a mop handle) when she realized Alfie was no longer standing next to her. He had buckled to the couch—which he had put back in its place—his head in his hands.

Laney sat next to him and touched his arm.

"Everything is just so weird," Alfie said into his palms.

"Yeah." She patted his back. "I think I'll feel better if you stay with a friend for a day or two. What about Jordan? Is it okay if I call his parents and ask?"

Alfie was still for a moment, and when he lifted his head, his skin was a nervous red. "Jordan is in Long Beach Island."

Irritation and resignation mingled in her chest. "So, I take it you didn't stay with him the other night," she said. But she'd suspected this, hadn't she? At least he was coming clean now.

"I'm sorry," he said.

She leaned away from him. What would a better parent do? Yell at him? She figured he'd been punished enough, the ramifications of his actions surrounding them. Well, at least some of his actions.

"Alfie, don't lie to me. Just. Don't. I'll do anything to protect you, and I only want you to be safe. Don't you know that?"

His eyes grew large and watery. "I know," he said.

"So I need you to go stay with someone. How about Ben?"

"But what if Step comes back?"

"I'll be fine. Better if I don't have to worry about you."

A startled caw came from the kitchen.

"You don't have to worry about me anyway."

She cocked her head. "Really?"

Despite everything, he appeared better, color in his cheeks, an increased energy in his eyes, in his muscles.

"I won't leave you," he said.

"Okay, well, we'll talk about it." She got up. "I'm going to try to get those creepy crows out of our house now."

But when she came out of the basement, mop held upward like a torch, she saw a fight would not be necessary.

All three birds were dead, spread out on the counter and the floor, their round, black eyes wide and staring, hunks of bread dropped uneaten from their beaks.

38

Laney

IT TOOK LANEY less than twenty minutes to scrape all food from the fridge into bags, then jettison whatever chips or bread remained, the open canister of iced tea mix, the cookies, the crackers. Everything but canned goods went into the trash. Alfie helped, both of them in rubber gloves. When done, she made him hold open a trash bag as she swept the dead birds inside.

And after that, she told him in no uncertain terms that he had to stay with a friend or else.

"Or else what?" he asked.

"Or else nothing. Stay with a friend or stay with a friend. Those are your two options. But once you're there, don't leave. Stay and answer your phone if I call."

He started to say something, but she interrupted.

"At least until I fix the window and the door." She put her hand on his shoulder, and this time he didn't pull away. "And until I can douse the entire kitchen with bleach. If I can't get it all finished today, I'll book a hotel room. But I don't want you alone right now while I'm running around, and I don't want you in this house, period. Please?"

He didn't answer for a few minutes, studying the heaps of bulging trash bags on their patio. "Okay. I'll call Ben."

She'd delivered Alfie to his friend's house, returned home, and just arranged for a guy to come and look at her window when Ed Boswell rang.

He said, "Do you have time to talk? I want to hear what you found out about the Volkins directly from you, not filtered through my brother."

Laney nodded at her phone and sat on her front steps. It was already hot, sticky, and her house, even from the outside, felt wrong. Understandably violated, yes, but also treacherous, untrustworthy.

Ed said, "And as an FYI, your neighbor across the road has a security camera mounted on his house. We're looking now to see if it caught anything."

"Good thing you called, Ed. I was going to stop by the station."

"Are you okay? How's the window? I can send my nephew to help. He's in construction."

"Oh, right. Thanks. I already called someone. He said he might be able to do the window and the door today or tomorrow. He might have the glass at his shop."

"Okay, good, good. Glad to hear that. I should have the information from the security camera in an hour or so. Come by as soon as you're able."

For the next forty minutes, Laney lugged some of the garbage bags to her curb and removed the remaining canned goods from the kitchen cabinets, stacking them in boxes in the basement. She'd have to buy massive amounts of industrial-strength cleaner to disinfect the counter tops and cabinets from whatever happened to those birds—poison? bird flu? What the hell kind of acid trip was happening in her life? But that could wait.

Quick shower, change of clothes and she entered the Sylvan PD an hour and fifteen minutes after Ed's call. He guided her to the small office he shared with two other detectives and pointed at a wooden chair facing his old desk. The blessed air conditioning helped clear her mind after the breathtakingly suffocating heat.

"So." Ed put his elbows on his desk and twined his fingers. "Jack filled me in on what was going on at Sunny River. What you believe was going on." His face, serious until now, dimpled with amusement. "He also informed me of last night's raid at the, what was it"—he checked his notes—"Rainwood Motel. What else should I know?"

When she finished rolling her eyes, she explained her suspicions, her conversation with the Sunny River social worker, Jo, and the photographs placing the Volkins and Bubba Gardner together on the day he disappeared.

"Have you heard from the gas station?" he asked.

"Not yet."

"Okay, I'll call them and let them know this might be part of a criminal investigation. Now, you said you thought Volkin vandalized your house in retribution? Because you spoke to someone who worked for him?"

She sat back and crossed her arms over her chest. "There was a young woman who worked at Sunny River. I believe she befriended some of the youths and aided their being trafficked away from the home."

Ed raised an eyebrow, waiting. Then said, "And her name is?"

Obviously, Jack hadn't told Ed everything, and she felt a warm swirl of gratitude for his discretion. "Mona Powell. Someone else spoke to her for me. It was made clear to her I was the one who uncovered her connection to the Volkins and her involvement in whatever was happening with those kids." She dropped her arms and leaned forward, gripping the edge of his desk. She saw the question bubbling up in him and intercepted. "But Ed, there's something else. Something happened this morning."

"What's up, Laney? What else?"

"I think Step Volkin tried to poison me. Alfie and me both. I mean, I'm not completely sure."

"What?"

"Listen. When we were cleaning up, these birds flew in through the window and started eating the bread and grapes on the counter. And they died."

"The birds?"

"No, Ed, the grapes died. Yes, the birds! And you know what? I keep everything in the fridge, including bread and fruit."

"And Alfie?"

She threw her hands in the air. "I don't keep Alfie in the fridge. Ed, listen to what I'm saying. I think Step Volkin broke into the house and made a mess in the living room to distract from the fact that he poured poison on my food."

Ed sat back and stared at her. "Because the birds died?"

"Yes."

"Where's the food now? And the birds?"

"In trash bags outside my house."

He held up a finger, then pointed at her, indicating she stay put, and walked out. After a few minutes he came back and took his seat again. "We'll check on that," he said.

She chewed her bottom lip. "Could have been just sick birds, though, and I overreacted."

"Could have been." He raised his eyes at the large wall clock and said, "Also, your neighbor's security camera had nothing."

She would have been surprised if it had caught Step. Last night was dark.

"Laney, I mean it had been powered down. Remotely."

She stared at Ed for a second, trying to parse this new bit of information, but fatigue caught up with her, her brain both sleep and food deprived. "What are you saying?"

"I'm saying that someone, not your neighbor, logged into his security panel and disabled the camera."

"You mean like hacked?"

"Something like that."

Laney slumped. "I need a coffee," she said.

"The same thing happened to the neighbor on your left. The house to your right has no alarms, so we couldn't check." He stood. "I'll get you that coffee."

"Step is good with computers," she said.

He sat back down. "How do you know?"

She dug into her memories, something slipping, flitting away every time she went for it. "Holly, I think. She used to talk about them. Mostly about Vera, but she talked about Step too." Laney placed her elbow on the desk and rested her chin in her hand. "Did Step tell you that Holly was in love with him?"

He shrugged. "I think he told that to everyone within hearing distance. Do you believe him?"

Did she? She remembered Holly at one of her many parties, making cosmo shots (Teeny Tinis, she'd called them) and laughing with Vera, the two of them standing so close they looked conjoined, and Step leaning against the wall, glowering. "I don't think so. I don't believe anything he says. I think something happened between all three of them, but I don't think it was between Holly and Step."

And there it was again, her words surprising her. But of course, she needed only to remember the intense way Holly had looked at Vera, as if her new friend was fascinating instead of vacuous.

"What?"

"I don't know, Ed, I just don't know. Holly was, I don't know. Obsessed with that girl." She rose to her feet and paced to the other desk, then back.

He tapped his pen, dark eyes thoughtful, watching her.

She plopped into the chair, her legs tired. Her entire being was tired. "You don't believe me?"

"I think there's a lot of shit happening between all of you and I don't know any of it." He rolled his shoulders. "Oliver Dubois drives into his living room the same night his wife disappears with Vera Volkin. Same night, Holly allegedly shoots Step Volkin in his house. Still the same night, someone sets fire to the Volkins' house. According to Step, Holly was obsessed with him, and according to you, Holly was obsessed with his wife. And for some reason you still didn't explain, Volkin has some kind of murderous designs on you." He sighed. "You sure are all living a much more exciting life than I am."

"You're right about stuff happening we don't know." Her nerves were too raw. Everything was poking right through the surface. "I should have paid more attention. I knew something wasn't right with Holly."

He leaned back. "Let's back up a few minutes. You said someone spoke to"—he glanced down at his notepad—"Mona Powell for you. Who was that?"

She chewed her lip. "Jack did."

"Excuse me?"

"I asked Jack to do it because—" Her voice wavered, and she had to stop, gather herself. "Because she was spending a lot of time with Alfie. I didn't want to be the bad guy in Alfie's eyes. So I asked Jack."

Ed put his pen on his desk, looked at it, then back at her. "So, Jack knew of her involvement with the missing teens when he spoke with her."

Laney sighed, shook her head. "No. Not then. Ed, I'm afraid it was Alfie who told her." She couldn't look at him anymore and shielded her eyes with her hand. "Jack told Mona to leave Alfie alone, and then Alfie called her and told her I found out she was involved. That she was getting the kids out of the group home and to the Volkins somehow. I believe that she then told Step, and he—" She could no longer speak.

Ed said, "Wow."

They sat in silence. Then he picked up his pen and scribbled more notes.

When done, he said, "I'm going to let that percolate for a bit. Let's circle back to Holly. How much did you know of her finances?"

That was the second time he'd asked the question. "Not much," she said. "We almost never spoke about money. I mean, she'd asked me for a few loans last winter, but she paid me back. She didn't seem to want to discuss the details, and I didn't want to make things uncomfortable for her." When he remained quiet, she prodded. "Why? What's up with her finances?"

There was that steady gaze from him, studying her. "I thought I'd ask."

Just then the two other detectives who shared the office walked in, carrying with them a garlicky whiff of pizza. It was nearly lunchtime, and although Laney hadn't eaten since dinner the night before and she was starving now, the smell made her queasy.

She glanced at her phone. "Okay, well. A guy is coming to measure my windows, and I should go."

Ed rose again and walked her to the door. "Keep me posted," he said. "On anything."

"Will you do the same?" He didn't have to. She was a civilian, and there was no reason for him to tell her anything. But she hoped their friendship might weigh in on her side.

"If I can," he said. "And of course I will if it concerns the missing-boy case."

"Fair enough."

"Laney?"

"Yeah?"

"Is there anything else I need to know about Alfie?"

She shook her head.

He regarded his shoes. "There are some people in this world who attract energy." He looked up. "You know what I mean? In spite of themselves. Sometimes it's good energy, and sometimes it isn't."

She hoped he didn't see the flush creeping up her neck as she said good-bye. He wasn't wrong. Alfie was just the right combination of curious and gullible that gave her agita. He'd always marched to the beat of his own drum. There definitely was something about her beautiful, strange boy that drew attention, and not always the right kind.

On the way home she stopped at a hardware store and picked up three gallons of bleach, disinfectant, a pail, sponges, and thick rubber gloves, then swung by the diner and ordered a tuna triple decker with bacon to go. She was so hungry that she unwrapped it and fished out the bacon strips while still driving. The idea of eating inside her house repulsed her, and her patio, still pocked with bulging garbage bags, wasn't much more inviting. She parked in her driveway, opened the windows, and slowly, methodically worked her way through the triple decker, pickle, coleslaw, and potato salad, washing the lot down with a large iced coffee.

Fortified, she sighed, texted Alfie to ask how he was doing, and brought in the cleaning supplies. She was swabbing her kitchen counter with Lysol when the window guy arrived to measure her window and writing him a check for a deposit when her phone pinged with an incoming text.

I need to talk to you, said the text, and it took her a few seconds to realize that it wasn't from Alfie as she'd expected, but Jack Boswell.

The second text came soon after. *It's about Holly.*

Everyone wanted to discuss Holly with her today. Like she had answers.

What about Holly?

Mind if I swing by? I'm in the neighborhood.

She was about to reply she'd be back to work tomorrow and needed the day to take care of her damaged home when his car crested the hill and coasted to a stop at her front walk.

He waited for the repairman to leave before getting out of his car and walking over to where she waited by the rosebush.

"Are you okay?" he asked.

She shrugged. "I'm beginning to believe Alfie's theory that we're all living in a simulation."

He frowned.

"The Matrix?" she said.

He frowned again and shrugged.

She said, "Never mind. The house feels weird now, but it's fixable."

Five neighborhood children rolled past on skateboards, chatting idly, their voices high-pitched and easy.

Jack said, "You know that surveillance case I've been working for the past three months?"

"I thought you had a few surveillance cases."

"There was only the one big one. Pharmaceutical espionage. The company contacted me because they suspected their lead scientist was stealing and selling samples of experimental compounds."

A jolt of energy shot through her. Was he talking about Oliver?

He said, "Your reaction tells me you know who I mean. So, I've been keeping an eye on things. I put in surveillance equipment. At first, I was convinced it was Oliver, and all I had to do was catch him on video." Jack broke eye contact, his face darkening. "I should have recused myself from the case. I told my dad I shouldn't take it, but he wanted me to. Our family and the Dubois family have known each other for a hundred years, easy." He glanced at her again, held her gaze. "I did something I wouldn't have ever done for any other suspect. I went to him and spoke to him. It was clear to me he was innocent. I just knew. So, I asked him if he'd mind me putting up cameras in the lab to catch the spy, and he refused to let me. He put up a fight, a real one. Like he almost gave me a black eye." He grimaced at the memory. "In the end, I set up the cameras one night after he locked up anyway."

Jack shifted and leaned against the garage door so his shoulder was inches from Laney's. His body seemed both coiled with tension and tired, as if he was expending massive energy to hold himself upright. "The surveillance footage was erased. I thought I'd lost it all, but remember Arty?"

She nodded. Arty was ex-NYPD, a computer forensics expert the firm contracted on occasion.

"I gave the cameras to him, and he's been tweaking them this way and that way for weeks. The other day he was able to rescue a bit of footage." Jack turned his face toward Laney, and she looked up at him. She still didn't understand why he was sharing this information with her.

He said, "Turns out Oliver was right. He had nothing to do with it."

Laney's throat tightened, and she swallowed. The caffeine she'd drunk made everything hyperclear—the sound of his voice reverberating in her stomach, the day's heat a weight against her chest.

He nodded at the question in her eyes. "It was Holly."

"What do you mean, Jack?" The conversation she'd had with Ed Boswell returned to her. Her neighbors' security cameras hacked, the questions concerning Holly's finances. Oliver taking the vial label she showed him and eating it. "Are you seriously telling me Holly stole her husband's work and sold it?"

"Sure looks like it on video."

She pushed away from the garage and walked toward her car, then turned back. "Why?" The question came out weak. She suspected why, though she still refused to accept it.

"I don't know yet," he said, looked at his meager shadow. "I know she's your friend."

"She is," Laney said, decisively. "It's those people—that—the Volkins. They bewitched her. It's like they cast some kind of spell on her."

Jack nodded. "Interesting."

"What? What do you mean?"

"That's exactly what Oliver said."

Laney stopped her pacing. "You told Oliver?"

"Jesus, Laney. Of course I told him. I ruled him out as a suspect. Holly is family, but he's my friend." And now she could see he was himself nearly in tears. "How could she . . . he loves her. Really loves her. This is . . . he'll never be the same, you know. Never."

"But—" She had no clue what to say. At all.

"The only thing Oliver did was try to save his wife. Ever. That's the only thing he ever, ever, ever did."

She squinted against the sun's glare. "What do you mean by that? There were other times when he saved her?"

He was silent a moment. "She never told you?"

"For God's sake, just spit it out! What didn't Holly tell me?"

"She had a sister once. There was an accident. I was too young at the time, so I don't remember much about it, but the whole family was devastated. Her sister drowned, and Holly almost did. Oliver pulled her out of the water. Nobody talks about it, though."

"And?"

"And? And that's it. That's the story. He'll do anything for her. Including covering up for her."

The heat, the lack of sleep, caught up with Laney all at once, and she swayed, needing to reach for the wall. He was next to her in an instant, his hand around her waist, his warm body against her arm, pressing her close, supporting her. "Hey, hey," he said. "What's going on? Are you okay?"

She nodded, and the movement made her head spin. "It's the heat," she said. On top of everything else, a vicious set of cramps attacked her. Perfect timing.

"I'll help you in," he said, and she raised her palm. She didn't need his help. The weakness passed, and she gestured for him to follow her to the back, where afternoon shade offered a respite from the sun. She sat gratefully on her patio chair. He eyed the bulging garbage bags and sat down across from her.

The facts, as presented to her piecemeal by the Boswell brothers, told a story she suspected neither one of them saw fully. Holly

Dubois, facing financial difficulty—and let's be honest, who wasn't nowadays—had turned to corporate espionage to make ends meet. Her husband found out and protected her anyway. Laney wasn't sure if he benefited from the espionage himself, but his behavior since the block party told her the answer was not straightforward.

Throw in the disappearances from Sunny River and the teenage girl still fighting for her life at Good Sam hospital, and Laney found it hard to believe that one couple, albeit extremely strange, could be responsible for not one, not two, but three criminal endeavors. And yet, every string in this baffling knot led to them.

"What's on your mind?" he asked.

"What was Oliver Dubois working on?"

"Hmm?"

"Well, that's important to know, right? What was the thing that got stolen?"

"Something to do with longevity. It wasn't even approved for test trials yet. Very experimental stuff."

She propped her feet on an opposing chair and hugged her knees.

"Let me ask you something. If you stole experimental drugs that weren't safe for test trials, what would you do?"

"I'd test the drugs."

"On?"

"Rats?"

"Hmm . . ."

"What?"

"And if you wanted to go beyond the rats?"

He grew still. "People?"

"What kind of people?"

He made a face. "People who won't be missed."

"Or not missed too much. Runaways. Drug addicts. Homeless. People without families to care for them. The mentally ill."

"Sunny River," he said.

"Sunny River."

"Fuck," he said.

"Yeah. The girl with the chemical burns."

His jaw hardened. "And Holly did it. She's responsible."

"How positive are you? Do you have fingerprints? Is it really, really her? Can you see her face?"

"She wore gloves," he said. "And a cap with a visor. But it's her hair and her build. I'm still waiting to hear, but the evidence is more than likely going to be turned over to the FBI. There's suspicion that the drugs and the files she downloaded were sold to another country. That makes it a federal crime. What? Laney? What's going on? What are you thinking?"

"I don't know yet." But she did.

"Tell me."

"What's going to happen to Oliver?" She was pacing again, the crime's knotted threads unraveling before her.

"Hard to say. These cases can be very hard to prove. Look, I don't want anything to happen to him either."

She stopped in front of him, hands on hips. "You came here to tell me these things or to ask me something?"

His answer came, slow but deliberate, as he watched her closely. "I wanted to see your reaction. For a while I thought you knew and were protecting her."

"And now?"

He sighed. "Now I know better."

But maybe he didn't. She asked herself if she would have protected Holly if she had known, and the answer was murkier than she would have liked. No, not murky at all. She would have done, would do, everything feasible to help her friend. Morality, she'd found, was a mutable concept. Friendships, less so.

And right on top of that thought, another one. Jack was her friend too. Certainly more than a colleague. Someone who had, repeatedly, been there for her when she needed help. She clenched her jaw at the realization, a subtle panic fluttering in her throat.

"Jack, I have a lot of work to do here. I'll see you tomorrow."

"I'll help."

"No."

She couldn't have him there, didn't want him. Didn't want his help, or his clever eyes, or his warm hand steadying her. They stared at each other until she won and he walked away.

She waited until he got into his car, slammed the door, and drove up the hill. Then she waited some more. Then she went into her house, threw cold water on her face, took an ibuprofen, changed her clothes, and grabbed her handbag.

Maybe she didn't yet know where Holly was, or Bubba Gardner, or Mona, or Step. But she had a very good idea who might.

39

Laney

Y EARS AFTER LANEY'S parents died and she'd moved away from the house where she grew up, she began to have a recurring dream.

In the dream, she was in that childhood home, doing nothing much—watching TV or leafing through a magazine, staring out the living room window.

The only room she never entered in this dream was her parents' bedroom, because her parents were there, asleep. No matter the time of day in the dream, they were in that bedroom, sleeping.

Because of this, the house had a dispirited Sunday afternoon feel to it, so quiet she could hear the clocks tick.

When she entered the house where Oliver Dubois and his children were temporarily staying, Laney paused, uneasy, because the aura here was the same.

Despite three adults and five children, the house was Sunday-afternoon quiet, the air inside both charged and heavy so that even the youngest boy sprawled on a loveseat, listless, a Lego boat half-built on the floor next to his foot. She felt the misery in the house like a vacuum, and its tendrils spiraled from the room in the back.

Oliver's brother- and sister-in-law did not escort Laney down the long corridor but pointed and turned away in silence. Once again she walked through the hallway, surrounded by photographs of Holly and her siblings. She paused and looked at the next to last one, where the older sister stared at the camera with faraway eyes. Jack had said that the sister and Holly were both drowning, and Oliver had saved Holly. She suspected much lay in the unsaid part of that sentence. A young girl died that day. How culpable did Oliver feel, and how far would he go to atone?

Laney knocked and went in without waiting for an answer.

Oliver sat in the same chair he'd been in the last time she visited, his bulky form rigid against the window's bright light.

"Hey," she said.

He nodded at her without looking.

"How are you doing?" she asked.

He turned toward her slowly, his bruised eyes baleful and bloodshot.

"I'm doing great, Laney." His tone was caustic enough to boil paint. "What brings you here?"

She perched on the edge of the bed. His clothes were rumpled and stained under the arms. Even his russet hair appeared duller, powdery.

"Holly brings me here," she said.

He continued staring at her, his expression shifting to a hard anger.

Before she could show him what she had on her phone, he smirked and said, "You think you're her friend? She pities you. Don't you know that?"

Laney blinked, the words dying in her mouth. She broke eye contact and took a moment to remind herself why she was there.

She said, "I don't care what you or she think of me." She pulled the photos on her phone, stood, and held the screen before him.

"This girl was found yesterday." She zoomed in. "The doctors think she might survive, but it won't be pretty." She flicked to the next picture. "See that? I'm told that's a chemical burn. And this. And this. No, you don't get to look away." She moved the phone so it was before him again. "You know why I'm here?" She held up a finger. "One, I know you recognize what's happening to this poor child. Hey! Don't look away! She's only sixteen, Oliver." She held up a second finger. "Two, I know Holly has been trying to contact you."

His eyes snapped toward her in surprise.

Laney put the phone back in her pocket. "I just need to know where she is. There are more kids, Oliver. More who are having this done to them. I believe wherever Holly is, they are." She folded her arms across her chest. "So tell me where she is."

He squished his eyes closed, his face a twisted grimace. Then he rose to his feet and reached for the top drawer in the dresser by the bed. Out of this drawer he retrieved a phone, entered his passcode, opened an app, and placed it on the bed.

"I put a tracker on her phone three months ago. Based on everything you've said just now, I'm assuming you know why I would have done that."

She picked up his phone and stared at a dot on a map. Holly.

He said, "How did you know she tried to contact me?"

Laney fished her own phone out of her pocket. "I didn't know for sure. But I believe you're the steadiest thing in her life right now. And that's saying a lot."

The skin on his forehead and cheeks glistened with a sickly sheen. He'd broken out in a fresh sweat. "She did text me a few times. I erased the texts." He closed his eyes. "I wanted to block her but didn't have the stomach."

Laney entered the dot's coordinates into her phone, then looked at Oliver. "I still don't really understand what happened between you. But whatever Holly got herself involved with is hurting people." She shook her head. "I won't believe that she did whatever she did knowingly. That's not her."

He said nothing but moved a step toward the window, then toward the bed, then toward the chair, as if his internal anguish made it impossible to stand still or speak. The psychic bleakness she sensed when she'd entered the house clogged this room, and although she would have liked to comfort him, she couldn't, had no words. She walked out, said good-bye to Holly's brother and the children, left the house, opened her car door. Only then did she hear his heavy limp behind her.

"Are you going to her now?" he asked.

She nodded.

He walked around to the passenger side door and opened it. "I'm coming with you."

His broken face, with its swellings and cuts, looked rotten, and he moved with difficulty. Whatever beating he'd gotten from Step Volkin was catching up to him from the inside. Laney swept the papers and folder she had on the passenger seat to the back and said, "Okay."

Even with the seat pushed out all the way, his great big legs bent uncomfortably and his elbow invaded her space. Yet she was, in her heart, glad of the company. Partly because she was apprehensive of what she'd find on the other end of the journey, and partly because Holly's marriage had always seemed wonderful to Laney. She would have had trouble putting this into words, but she wanted to bear witness to a love that could survive such levels of betrayal.

And in any case, she was confident she could worm a confession out of Oliver. She had an hour-and-a-half drive ahead of her. She could do it.

40

Holly

H OLLY'S SKIN BUZZED. The sun was a hot compress, the shade like crawling mites, the grass like knives, and her sister's smooth hand on her forearm like water, like cooling balm, like a stick of menthol ChapStick smeared all over.

"I'm so sorry," Holly said, which lately seemed to be the only sentence she could say. She wasn't scared, though in the back of her mind thoughts whimpered about ghosts and/or insanity being a terrible fate.

Abigail leaned her wet head on Holly's shoulder, drenching her thin top. "It's true that you could have tried harder to save me."

Holly pressed her fingers against her eyelids, blocking out the world. "I did try," she said.

"Oh, whatever. I don't hate you."

"Okay," Holly whispered. "I'll take it." She lowered her hands, opened her eyes. Abigail was still there, her swimsuit soggy, her young body speckled with leaves and dirt. There were twigs in her hair. "Am I seeing you because I'm about to die?" In the silent next minutes, she traced a letter on her sister's small hand. "Or am I dead? Did they kill me?"

Abigail sat up and *tsk*ed, tossing her hair over her shoulder. "Oh, come on," she said. "Of course you're still alive, dummy.

Jeez. They just fed you full of whatchamacallits." She cocked her head at Holly. "I'm going to guess acid."

Holly, who'd never so much as touched a joint, never mind hallucinogens, wondered at this diagnosis. "Is that what it felt like for you?" she asked. Why would anyone choose to feel so out of control?

"Kind of. Maybe. I don't know." She lay on the grass, a shaft of sunlight white across her face. "The more interesting question is, why did she give it to you?"

Another thought fought its way through the scurriers at the back and emerged, poking blindly forward. "Are you really me speaking to myself?"

Her sister smiled. "Now that would be a trip, wouldn't it? Make sure to remember everything I say. You'll want to report it to your therapist later." She laughed and flipped to her stomach, kicked one leg at the knee, flexing a tender, white foot, the red nail polish glinting like poppy petals. "If I were you, I'd leave this place." She turned on her side, propped her head on her hand. "Why haven't you? They're not shackling you or handcuffing you. Don't tell me you're a scaredy cat. You always were such a timid kid. Kind of cute sometimes, but I never understood why you were."

Holly grabbed onto a willow branch and pulled herself to her feet. The world spun. She squinched her eyes, waited it out. When she opened her eyes, the grass by her feet was wet and dented but bare of sister or ghost.

She was alone.

She walked along the shore, nothing new to her—just like old times—over lawn and sand. Twice she had to wade into the water to go around fallen trees and rocks. She soon came back to where she started, and her suspicion was confirmed. The lake house stood on an island, and the only way out was to swim or row. The motorboat, the only one she could see, bobbed across the water off the mainland.

"Come on, Holly." The voice startled her, and she jumped, yelping helplessly.

How did Vera sneak up behind her? She hadn't heard a thing.

"It's not time to go home yet," Vera said, leading her toward the house.

"When can I go home?"

"Soon. Never. In a year." Vera laughed softly, pushed her into the hallway, guided her up the stairs and to a tiny room, more of a cell, with a twin bed wedged against a wall and nothing else. It was an improvement over the closet, so Holly didn't fight. She was tired anyway, crazy tired, barely able to stand upright.

"There you go." Vera helped her sit, then lie down. From a pocket she removed a syringe and jabbed Holly's inner arm, depressing the plunger so quickly Holly hardly had time to react.

"What are you doing to me?" Holly asked, even as a knifelike cold raced from the point of injection to her hand, up her arm, across the shoulders, south to her heart and belly and sex, up to her head.

Vera smiled, perfect lips stretching over perfect teeth, her eyes the palest, crystal blue.

"Why are your eyes that color?" Holly asked. Weren't they brown just yesterday? She was sure they were brown, amber, like Abigail's.

"What color did you think they were?"

"Brown," Holly said, slurring. "Like toffee candy."

"Mmm, sounds good. But no, dear. My eyes were always blue." She snapped her fingers. "But you know what? I wore contacts. Just for you." She ran her hand over her hair. "I'm going to let this boring color grow out too. You know I'm a blonde, right? Natural." She winked.

"Abigail," Holly said, "what do you mean? You're a brunette. Just like me."

Vera snorted. "Good one." Patted Holly's cheek. "Night night."

And suddenly it was night, though surely it had been morning only a few hours ago.

Holly awoke with the moonrise, its weak light painfully blinding to her sensitive eyes. Abigail was waiting for her, sitting wetly at the foot of the bed.

"Is it you?" Holly asked.

"Who do you think I am?"

"Are you Vera?"

"No, dummy. The bitch is gone out. Come on, get up. I need to show you something."

Swinging her legs over the edge of the bed, Holly got up, feet on the icy floor. She felt grainy, hungry, ill. She needed the toilet.

"Okay, fine, go pee. I'll wait."

So it wasn't Vera after all. If the girl staring at her with large, dark eyes was a figment of her imagination, she certainly would know what was happening inside her body. The bathroom was down a long hallway, and Holly passed five doors—shut, darkness and silence behind them.

"Are we good now?" Abigail asked at her elbow as she washed her hands.

"Am I going to make any sense of this, ever?" Holly asked.

Her sister sighed. "Perhaps. But you need to work on your getaway plan."

They walked back into the hallway. "Why do you think they're drugging me?" Holly asked. "I don't understand."

"I have an idea."

"What?"

"Jeez, you're not twelve anymore, Hol. Use your noggin once in a while." Abigail stepped up to one of the closed doors and turned the knob. The door opened, and she went in.

Holly paused for only a moment before following.

There were six hospital beds in the room, two rows of three. Each bed contained a person. Each person was laced through and through with needles, tubes, wiring. Fluorescents lit each bed, barely illuminating the machines working on behalf of the bodies.

An alarm beeped to her left, and she recoiled, grabbed for the door. The person in the leftmost bed sat up, his eyes wide and staring. He was skeletal, clearly undernourished, and now the others sat up too, all of them turning their waxy faces toward her as if they were sunflowers and she the sun.

Somebody was running up the stairs, and Abigail grabbed her wrist, pulled her out of the room and down the hall to the narrow door of her cell. She managed to jump inside and shut the door just as whoever had been summoned by the alarm made it to the landing. And only then, as she slid along the door to the floor, her hands pressed tight against her mouth to muffle her labored breathing, did she realize that all the people in those beds were very young—not one of them older than fifteen or sixteen.

41

Laney

LANEY KEPT THE car quiet as she drove—no radio, no chatter. She wanted no distractions for Oliver. She wanted him deeply immersed in his thoughts. About a half hour in, she asked, "What did her text say?"

His shoulders hunched higher.

"Why didn't you tell anyone you knew where she was? Is she safe?"

He grunted.

She rolled down the window, and the heat barreled into the car, stuffing it with oppressive mugginess. Oliver endured for a few minutes, then turned to her. "Do you mind?" he asked, pointing to the windows.

"If you tell me what the hell happened."

His legs twitched, as if he'd had to fight the impulse to jump out of a car plunging forward at seventy miles per hour.

She said, "It's not just between you and Holly anymore. Whatever is going on affects other people. Badly. I'm not calling the cops yet, because all this"—she waved at the road—"is conjecture. I have no idea what's at the other end. But I'm telling you right now that the moment I get a hairy feeling about wherever we're going, I'm calling the police. So if there's anything you might

want me to know beforehand, tell me." She sensed his bemuse-
ment and elaborated. "How involved are you?"

He wiped his face with his hand, and she rolled up the windows, kicked the AC down a few degrees.

"That's a very interesting question," he said, as the car began
to cool. "How involved am I. I guess if you're going to give it
a long overview, I've been involved with Holly for twenty years.
That's one way to look at it."

A quick glance told her he was red-faced, bitter mouthed.
"And the short overview?" she prodded.

The silence hung between them, as heavy in its way as the
humid air had been a few minutes ago.

"The short overview is that I lost my job. Fired. For stealing company trade secrets." He shrugged slowly. "There's no solid
proof I took anything."

So what had he been doing? Pretending to go to work every day?
Laney quashed the impulse to drown him with questions and put
on her investigator hat. One question at a time. "Did you take it?"

He snorted. "No, Laney. I did not suddenly wake up one
morning and decide to undo ten years of research and career
advancement by stealing my own formulas."

"So . . ."

"Holly stole. From me. She stole from me."

His voice was so flat, so low, so desperately hurt that Laney
was overwhelmed with the urge to pull over and hug him. But
that would have been weird, so she kept driving, swallowing past
the empathetic lump in her throat. She kept her mouth clamped
shut because he was opening up now, and she would not jeopar-
dize that.

He said, "They came to me first, you know. The Volkins. Vera
tried to seduce me. Like in some bad eighties spy movie. They
offered me stupid money for my research."

Laney switched lanes and exited onto a smaller rural highway.
The Thruway's noise receded, and foliage, lush and heavy, surrounded them left and right.

"Why didn't you accept?" But what she was really asking was
why did Holly accept when he hadn't. She didn't think money

swayed everyone, but she'd had plenty of bitter experience to understand it swayed many. Given enough in the balance, it swayed most. What was the difference in the balance sheet between Holly and Oliver?

"Why would I? It's my work. My research. I have a good salary. What they were offering me came with a lengthy prison sentence if I got caught. I laughed them off and forgot about them until a month later fucking Vera shows up at our house for dinner." He leaned his temple against the window. "I thought she was going to keep trying to get to me, and all along she was already in with Holly. I was absolutely convinced she was only there because of me."

The car passed through a tunnel and emerged on the other side hugging a cliff, the trees along the road sparse and the sunlight strobing against their eyes so that Laney had to squint and decelerate.

"Believe it or not, I only realized what had happened when Holly came to visit me that first time. I could see right away something was up. And then after, when I came back to the lab, I saw she'd taken some of the samples I'd locked away." He shifted and dropped his head back, stared at the ceiling inches above him. "I wanted her to tell me, but I couldn't ask her. I thought if she was going to ruin me, then let it be." He pressed his fingertips into his eyelids. When he spoke next, his voice was rougher, harder. "I failed her once. I said to myself, maybe this is payback. Or a test. Every day she acted like nothing happened. Every day I willed her to come to me of her own accord. The more time passed, the less I cared about my work. About anything."

"Jesus, Oliver. You should have confronted her if you knew. For fuck's sake."

He nodded. "Have you ever been betrayed?"

The question was a twist to her guts, her face warming in answer. "Yes." Too many times.

"And did you ever confront the person?"

She shook her head. "Never got the chance."

He cut his eyes at her without turning his head. "Right. Well, I tried to cover her tracks. After the first time, whenever she came,

I made sure to leave fakes lying around. They beat me the first time, but all the rest of the stuff she took was nothing. Saline with some vitamins thrown in."

Laney turned onto a one-lane road, taking them away from the cliff's edge and into the woods.

"When did they fire you?"

"Last week. Apparently, somebody saw her come out of the lab the first time she visited. They said she looked shifty. And then the vials were missing. It was bad. Of course, I swore up and down it wasn't me. Or her. I nearly came to blows with a guy over it. But yeah. They let me go."

Last week was when Jack Boswell resurrected the hacked surveillance footage. Laney slowed even further, the road becoming rugged, more serpentine. She wanted to say something soothing, but nothing came to mind.

"But why did Holly do it?" she finally asked.

Still limp against the seat, Oliver turned his face toward her. "Because she thought I didn't love her enough."

"What? Nobody does that because they're not loved enough!"

"I didn't say she wasn't loved enough. I said because she thought I didn't." He sighed. "If she'd been happy with me, she'd never have done this to me. Not for anything. Or anyone." He shifted and looked at the wall of green outside. "If she'd loved me or trusted me enough, she would have come to me for money. If it was about money."

Laney wanted to bring up the financial troubles but then changed her mind. What did she know, anyway? When did anybody ever love her enough to hide her trespasses? And why were they talking love all of a sudden? She ground her teeth in irritation. What did that have to do with anything?

"So why did she shoot Volkin?"

Oliver snorted. "She didn't."

"What?" Laney stole a look at him but had to concentrate on the curving road ahead. "Why is Step telling everyone she did?"

With a note that sounded a lot like satisfaction, Oliver said, "Because it's no fun admitting your own wife shot you in the ass."

"What?"

"Yeah. Vera shot him."

"Well, why the hell didn't you tell the police that, Oliver? I mean, what the fuck?"

"Because, Laney, I had a lot on my mind. Okay? I didn't really feel like chatting with anyone. Is that fucking okay with you?"

"Jesus, no, Oliver. Not really. Not really okay. Were you ever going to tell the cops it was Vera?"

"Yes!" The word resonated inside her small car, and she gripped the steering wheel harder.

"Okay. All right. Why? Why did she shoot him?"

He folded his arms over his chest and glowered at the windshield.

"Oliver?"

"Because Volkin was going to kill me. He came close."

They drove in silence for a mile, and then Laney said, "Jesus." She glanced at him again. "Who set the fire? I'm afraid to ask, but now that we're talking and all."

"I did."

She nodded. At least this made some kind of sense. "And you drove into your own house because?"

He lowered his head and pressed his palm against his brows. "I don't know, Laney. I think I went crazy that night. I wanted to destroy everything. I wanted to—" His voice wavered, and he clamped his mouth shut.

"Okay. I know."

"You know?" Acidic again.

"I was a cop in the city, remember? Listen, the things people do when they're pushed beyond endurance. I mean. I get it. I've seen it."

He snorted again. "Well. Anyway. Anyway, Vera shot him. If it makes any difference, I don't think she meant to kill him. I'm not even sure she meant to hurt him, really. It was the only way she could get him off me." He leaned his temple against the glass. "Don't think I haven't entertained the thought that she saved my life."

Laney made another turn and emerged into a clearing, then slammed on the brakes. She was less than twenty feet from water's edge, a green lake spreading before them like polished malachite, reflecting a sallow sky. And in the middle of this lake an island, like an illustration from a children's book. Except the emerald mound before them was scored with treads and the ancient house standing in the center of it was peeling and bent, the roof overgrown with vines and the doors splintered.

Laney threw open her door, stepping out into air that buzzed with insects and shimmered with vapor. There was an overturned gurney on the island's lawn, a wheelchair half in the water, bobbing gently in the waves. It looked absolutely, thoroughly abandoned.

A heat of disappointment burned through her, and she turned, ready to get back into her car, when, amplified by water and the humidity hanging like a scrim over the lake, she heard the creak of a door hinge and the slap of foot on stone step.

42

Holly

HOLLY JERKED TO her feet and lunged to the window, gripping the splintered sill to keep from falling. She was weak and so tired she'd passed beyond any normal concept of tired and into a kind of disembodiment. Alone again—no ghost or hallucination to keep her company—she tried to open the window, but it was locked or painted shut and wouldn't budge.

The motorboat sat on the island's lawn now, and a man had climbed (fallen) out of it, was limping up the lawn toward the house with a crutch. A smaller figure stumbled out of the boat, also fell into the water, righted herself and ran ahead of him, then doubled back to help, but he shook her off. In that instant, as he angled his face and the porch light blazed awake, Holly recognized Step and recoiled, moving away from the window. Her first thought was to hide until she understood that of course he knew she was there and hiding meant nothing.

Slowly, she crept back to the window and looked down. He stood before the porch stairs, his entire body bent in on itself, swaying. His grunt as he placed a foot on the first riser and dragged himself to the next carried all the way to her window. And despite everything, despite everything he was and did, despite the fact that he'd nearly killed Oliver, she wanted to help him. At this moment he was a person in need, in pain, and she turned toward the door, opened it, and headed into the hallway without thinking.

"Man, what is wrong with you?" Abigail was with her again, a wet, cold presence by her side. "You're going to help him up the stairs? Really?"

Holly stopped.

"You know," Abigail said, "you should have gone into nursing. Why didn't you?" She snapped her fingers. "Was it because you're certifiably insane?"

"Oh, for Christ's sake." Holly walked to the stairs and paused, listening. "I was only insane temporarily. Because of you."

A wet movement against her shoulder told her Abigail shrugged.

Now there were footsteps beneath them, and voices, three of them. Holly held her breath and listened. Step's hoarse baritone sawed through the night's quiet, drowning a girl's high-pitched jabbering, and through it Vera's grave tones.

"What's he saying?"

"Shhh!" Holly swatted thin air. Her sister was gone again.

Holly's thoughts came clearer, as if the fear and anxiety coursing through her blood scraped away the fog, taking Abigail with them. The trio moved closer to the stairs and their words gained meaning, and the meaning forced Holly backward into the dark.

"I called Nadezhda," Step said. "The team will be here in two hours."

"How absolutely annoying," Vera said.

Step shambled along the floor, one foot dragging.

"He's really sick," said a young voice, a voice Holly recognized. Who was that?

"He's as strong as an ox," Vera said. "Always was. Don't let his size fool you."

"Don't worry about me," Step said, presumably to the young person.

Other voices started to emerge now, a veritable crowd. What's up, and who's that, and what's going on, and we have to pack, and why, and what's the difference, it will be the same at the new place, what do you care. Within all that Holly heard a set of older, deeper voices calling out instructions.

The house was suddenly fizzing with activity. Lights flicked on everywhere and nimble feet ran up the stairs, forcing Holly to retreat to her cell again. She waited, though she wasn't sure for what. She only grasped that something changed with Step's arrival, and the house and everyone in it was awake and vibrantly active.

From her window she watched a dozen or so people carrying backpacks, bundles, boxes to the lawn. As the night faded to dawn, it became clear that the people were young teenagers, rangy and disproportionate, with legs grown long and torsos still catching up, flat-chested or full but not always sure how to carry the weight. Most seemed resigned to their task, though a couple were sitting on the lawn, their bare feet in the lake and their heads on their knees, and no amount of prodding from their peers budged them.

By the time the sun tipped the treetops a lemony yellow, two vans emerged from the foliage across the lake. Behind them came a truck trailering a long pontoon boat, roughly eight by twenty feet, with a flat deck. Men climbed out of the truck and vans and maneuvered the boat into the lake.

For the next two hours, the men ferried the house's residents across the lake and deposited them into the vans. Half crossed in the motorboat, half on the pontoon, carrying boxes, wheelchairs, stacks of equipment, cases filled with cables. They were loud and chatty at first, laughing when one of them tripped on the dock and dropped her backpack into the glittery water. But with half of them gone, the remainder quieted, their faces washed out by the brilliant morning and their backs slumped. Two girls held hands as they waited for the motorboat to return and didn't let go until they were on the other side and had to separate into different vans.

Holly's stomach rumbled. She rubbed her hand over her belly, wondering if they planned to take her away as well or if they meant her to stay. And what about the really sick kids she'd seen earlier? As far as she knew, they were still in that room, attached to machines and IV bags.

The house had hushed after the vans, the truck, and the once again trailered pontoon rumbled away, as if taking a meditative moment to regroup and plan next moves. Stomach empty and demanding, Holly opened her door and peeked out. Silence. She slid along the dark floorboards and hesitated in front of the room with the hospital beds. The view when she thrust the door open disoriented her, and she stopped, her hand climbing to her throat. Nothing but an empty expanse of dirty floor. No kids, no beeping machines. Had that been yet another hallucination?

"If it helps," said Abigail, once again at her side, "I saw them too."

Holly turned to her and put one hand on hip. "It doesn't help. You're not real."

"*You're* not real," said Abigail.

Holly rolled her eyes. "I'm hungry," she said. "Therefore, I'm real." But, admittedly, that told her nothing about what she'd seen last night. She couldn't stay alone anymore, needed to know what was happening, what they were going to do to her. At the end of the hallway was a bathroom, and she entered it, closed the door, and washed her face with cool water. She had to blink a few times and rub a towel over her eyes, because at first the mirror reflected her twelve-year-old self, cheeks round with baby fat, short hair, untidy eyebrows. After a moment, the vision passed, and she was looking at her proper reflection again, albeit wan with pouched eyes and lips so ashen they had no color at all. She smoothed her hair and bit her lower lip to get some color.

"Who are you trying to impress?" asked Abigail.

"Well, I can't exactly go down there and look like death warmed over. Then they'll know they won."

When Abigail remained uncharacteristically quiet, Holly said, "What?"

"They won, kiddo. Don't fool yourself on that front."

"Oh, what do you know."

"I know the same things you do. I'm you, remember?"

Holly squared her shoulders. "I know no such thing. I'm going downstairs. I'm getting myself some food. And a coffee. And then I'm going to demand they let me go."

Abigail trailed her to the stairs, a musty smell wafting off her. "Or what?"

"Or I don't know. I mean, really, what do they want with me?"

A damp hand gripped her wrist. "They're using you to keep Oliver quiet. Have you forgotten?" Her sister's words were softer now, garbled, and when she looked back, she saw nothing but shadows, rippling with the curtained breezes.

Whatever she'd been dosed with had worn off, mostly anyway, and she could look at the house properly for the first time. As disheveled and abandoned as it looked from the outside, it was crisp and new on the inside. Clean, freshly painted walls, wood flooring urethaned to a high, warm gloss, modern light fixtures. The stairs didn't creak, and the newel posts didn't wobble. The first floor, though littered with the morning's exodus, was spacious, encompassing what at one point had been a parlor and a dining hall. Beyond this, she saw tile and assumed a kitchen.

Nearing it, she heard voices, Step at first, then Vera, and the higher-pitched one belonging to the young girl from last night.

"No." Step, low and decisive. Holly pressed her back against the wall, her head turned toward the open kitchen doorway.

"They're almost dead anyway." Vera, dismissive, but with a note of urgency.

Silence, so charged Holly felt her skin prickle.

Step: "No."

A soft slap on a surface, and Vera again: "Then what was the point of this whole rush-rush-rush this morning? We won't be able to get the rest of them out until tomorrow at the earliest, and according to you, the feds are about to descend on us from helicopters and kill us all or drag us to prison any second."

The young voice butted in. "Alyssa is going to talk. She's alive. I went to the hospital and tried to see her, but they wouldn't let me. She'll tell them where we are, if she hasn't yet. She might have already anyway."

Something about the voice finally slid into place, and Holly recognized her as the girl that used to hang around Vera, a wild-haired urchin with freckles and blue nail polish. Mona. Who were they talking about? Who was Alyssa?

Vera said, "Don't look at me like that! I didn't think she had the strength to get out of bed, much less swim across. She was half-dead already."

Step: "But she wasn't dead, and you weren't watching her. What were you doing, Verochka? Tell me. Who were you fucking over when one of our patients developed an allergic reaction that made her skin peel off and then goddamn walked out of this god-damn house?"

Silence again, and Holly's poor, empty stomach rumbled louder than ever. She pressed her hand into her abdomen, but it was too late. Vera flew out of the kitchen and almost knocked her over.

"Stepan!" Vera called, her narrowed eyes fixed on Holly.

He shuffled out, bracing his arm on the doorframe to support himself. He looked even worse in the morning light than Holly imagined—bruises and cuts discoloring his cheeks and jaw, his hand trembling lightly as it bore his weight. It was not possible to fear someone so hurt.

Holly said, "Let's go sit down, shall we?" Because she couldn't watch pain rolling over him no matter what he had done. Sure, he deserved it, maybe even deserved his own wife shooting him, but there was no need to make him suffer more, not right now. She moved toward him, wanted to offer her arm to support him, but Vera interrupted, her hard fist punching Holly in the sternum.

She stumbled back, the wind knocked out of her.

"I've had enough of you," Vera said. "You just couldn't leave it alone, could you? Couldn't take the money." She advanced and shoved Holly again, herding her toward the stairs. "There's a say-ing in Russian. It goes, *Go mad from excess fat.* It means when you have too much of something, anything, you lose your mind."

"What are you talking about?" Indignation made Holly's voice climb. Her? Have too much of something? What did she have too much of?

As if reading the outraged question in her eyes, Vera said, "House, family, children, brothers, so much food you need two refrigerators and a freezer, so much clothes you give it away after you wear it for a year. And you still want more! More money. Sell your soul for more money."

Holly, who had been manhandled halfway up the second floor, shook the other woman's hands off her. "Are you kidding me? What are *you* selling your soul for? What are you doing here? With those children? You're poisoning them! I saw! And for what? For what? You want to live forever? You . . . you're vampires! All of you!"

Vera slapped her, the smack ringing in the sudden silence.

Quietly, Step asked, "What did you see?"

Holly looked up at the corridor and the room where the gurneys stood last night. "Nothing," she said.

"Nothing," Vera agreed. "You saw nothing. You're crazy. You've been wandering about talking to yourself for days."

A furtive movement drew Holly's attention, and she looked down to see that the girl, Mona, had crept out of the kitchen. Her face shone with tears, her eyes bloodshot.

"What now?" Holly asked. The question was directed at Vera, but her eyes skimmed the others as she spoke.

"Soon our colleagues will return," Step said. "You will come with us."

"What?"

"What?" Vera mimicked. "Think about it for just one second instead of being an idiot."

"Where?"

"It doesn't matter where," Step said. "You understand we can't let you go, right?"

Holly started to object, and Vera interrupted. "You're one of us now. If you leave us, we'll have Oliver and your children killed." She clapped her hands, once. "Easy. Not a problem."

"But—" Holly started, and this time Step interrupted.

"Oliver stays quiet as long as you're with us. You stay quiet as long as you're with us. It's all good."

"But we can both stay quiet together," Holly said, sounding just as weak voiced as she worried she might. "What's the difference? We'll know you'll kill us and our children. We'll stay quiet."

Vera: "Nah. You won't. You'll figure out some way to go into witness protection or some other thing. Not interested. You stay with us."

"I don't know anything about witness protection!"

"Oh, enough already! Whiny little bitch." Vera closed the distance between them and gripped her jaw, painfully, between thumb and forefinger, then forced her mouth open. Holly felt something being slipped between her teeth, tablets, three or four of them, and then Vera pressed Holly's mouth closed and pinched her nose. Trying to gasp for air and failing, Holly swallowed, gagged, swallowed again, and Vera let go.

Holly flailed and crumpled, sitting down heavily. She buried her face in her upper arm, blocking them out—Vera directly in front of her, Step at the bottom of the stairs, Mona behind him. And above her, a corridor of gothic horrors and a thirty-foot drop to the ground from any window. Something was once again bubbling through her bloodstream, promising a chilled sweat and nausea.

She couldn't see how to solve this. Her heart hurt, literally hurt, when she thought of her children. All she'd ever wanted was to help the people around her. How had everything gone so appallingly wrong?

She was no longer hungry or thirsty. She leaned her head against the rail and watched Vera recede, walk in jerks backward down the steps as if a film looped in reverse. The bustle in the house resumed, though since it was just the four of them, it was quieter, and Step knelt on a pillow in the parlor at a small round table while the women lugged bags and packets out to the lawn.

The noon light was kind to him, erasing the bruising with a creamy glow, and though his posture spoke of his discomfort, he was laying down cards, row after row, then scooping them, shuffling, and laying them out again.

"Are you playing solitaire?" Holly asked, though her tongue was thick in her mouth. The light surrounding him appeared to come not from outside but somehow emanated from his head.

"I'm looking into the future," he said.

"What's my future?" she asked.

Without looking at her, he scooped the cards again and reshuffled, then laid out a row.

"You will die," he said. "Your end will be complicated and unpleasant, and I'm tired even thinking about it. So that's that. I can assure you almost everyone ends this way. I wouldn't dwell on it if I were you."

"I'm not afraid to die. What's your future?"

"I will also die. But not for a long while."

She hung her head and remembered the saint around his neck, the medal he'd given her that first time she went to Oliver's lab.

"Do you think your saint will protect you?"

He stopped dealing and glanced at her, the remaining color draining from his face. "My saint will protect me," he said.

"What are you?" Holly asked, realizing even as the words were leaving her mouth that she meant something else. She meant, *Are you also an unreal being, like Abigail?*

He turned to his cards, laid another one down. "I am a man. Seeing the hours of our deaths is not such a difficult thing for the people in my family. I believe now that my parents saw their end but refused to accept it. That is the only explanation for how they left me. Or maybe they had made arrangements and the people who were supposed to handle it didn't comply. I'll never know. I just know that whatever happened was meant to happen exactly as it did." He withdrew another card, studied it. "I understand my parents. The cards showed me that Vera would shoot me." He nodded at Holly. "Yes, I saw it. But I didn't believe the cards. I thought I was misinterpreting them."

Holly wondered if being shot by your wife was worse than having your wife destroy your life's work. Step seemed to hold no hard feelings against Vera.

"Aren't you mad at her?" she asked.

He looked at the window, at the expanse of blue and green beyond. "Do you know that Vera means faith? It also means trust. She has a purity you can't understand. But I do. She is true and single-minded in her needs and her goals. She never lied to me and never cheated. I always knew where I stood with her, and I trust her utterly. Since we were children." He cleared his throat and focused on the cards again. "She took care of me when I was only eleven. In shock over my parents' death. I will never be *mad* at her." He emphasized the word *mad* as if it were a ridiculous conceit, a joke.

Holly passed her palm over her forehead. Her skin felt clammy, her mouth dry.

"What's her future?" she asked.

Step swatted the cards off the table and stared ahead. He shifted his knees, and the hitch in his hips forced a strangled groan from his lips.

After several minutes, he said, "From the first time I saw her, she was already looking ahead to when she'd be old and demented. She talked about her perfect skin wrinkling, then would touch her arms and her thighs and talk about her tight muscles getting flabby and weak. Would you believe she was only fourteen when we met?

"She told me she rejected death. She said she had no use for it."

He shrugged and shifted his knees again, his entire body buckling before he gripped the table and straightened himself.

"I couldn't understand why she worried so much about dying. So, I told her I would look into her future. When I laid the cards out for Vera that first time, they showed me her destiny. They also showed me mine."

Holly frowned. "I don't think you answered my question," she said.

He snorted. "You're an idiot."

She tried to stand, but the room spun, and she plonked back down, holding the railing with a white-knuckled grip.

He turned to glare at her. "A self-absorbed idiot. That's why we chose you. Did she tell you that? After your husband rejected her, we looked you up and we could not believe our luck. You were such a tight ball of crazy it was almost fun to fuck with you."

"Oliver?"

"Yes, Oliver. Who else am I talking about? You got any other husbands?"

"He rejected Vera?" What did this mean? That Oliver knew what was happening even before she did what she did? Why didn't he. . . Was he testing her? She tried to slap her face, but her hand flopped with a spasm and didn't obey.

Step shuffled the cards, no longer looking at her. "Vera didn't like that. Neither did our handlers." He shrugged. "But then we discovered you."

Something moved slowly, darkly inside her mind, bringing nausea. "When I first met Vera—" that cold lake, the woman's half-dressed body.

"Yes?" He still didn't look at her, but a small smile quirked his mouth.

"Did your handlers throw her in the water?"

The smile widened. "What do you think?"

She didn't answer at first, then, in a whisper, "She went into the lake alone?" After all, Holly never heard a boat, nor other voices. It had been animal noises and morning silence until Vera's gasps for air alerted Holly out of her trance.

He stared at the cards' new configuration before him. "Your sister's death was all over the news. The moment we read the reports and saw her picture, we knew a miracle was given to us. I thought it was a miracle. Vera doesn't believe. But that didn't matter. It was still stupendous luck for us." He turned to her. "Don't you think?"

He propped his hands on the table, grunted, and forced himself upright. Then limped out of the room. A minute later Vera swirled in and dashed after him. And a minute after that, Mona followed.

Holly waited and digested Step's revelations. They should have made her feel worse, but ultimately, she couldn't feel worse, so she chose to feel relieved. They had played on her weakest point. She hadn't gone mad all on her own. They spurred it.

After some time alone, she tested her arms, her legs. They moved properly, so she pulled herself upright, albeit on unsteady feet. Muffled voices carried into the room. A scream tore through the walls and she gasped, clutched the railing, listened. A thump, followed by more arguing and a second scream, sharp and short.

Stiff-legged, she descended, then froze. The sound of tires on gravel carried across the water and through the open front door. Those vans had arrived. She was out of time.

Fine. There was no winning now, not with whatever Vera had stuffed down her gullet. She would go outside and face her fate with courage because that's all she had left. Herself.

The door creaked as she nudged it wider, and her bare foot slapped the flagstone.

43

Laney

LANEY TURNED HER head at the same time Oliver walked away, his sneakers sinking into the silt at water's edge.

A figure was edging down the island's sloping lawn. The haze and sun made her outline unclear, and there was something wrong with her movement, a stiffness to her spine. At this distance it was impossible to see her features, but the build was right. Was it Holly?

Until that moment, Laney hadn't really believed they'd find her; had thought they might narrow the distance between them, maybe discover a track. The sight of her stalking stiff-kneed away from a dilapidated mansion was almost too startling, and Laney fumbled for her phone, dropping it into the wet grass at her feet.

"Ollie!" The name carried across the water, Holly's voice unmistakable, shrill.

As Laney dialed 911 and demanded an ambulance (why was Holly walking like that?) and police (if Holly was here, was there a chance the Volkins were as well? the runaway teens?), Oliver dashed forward and jumped off the dock, the water up to his thighs right away.

A motorboat bobbed at a post off the island, but the mainland had no such conveyance.

"Oliver, wait." Laney ran toward him. Once he reached Holly, he'd be alone, without protection, and what if the others were there? What if they were armed? She jumped in after him but lagged, the water to her chest, and she wasn't a strong swimmer anymore, certainly not good enough to make it across.

She fought her way onto shore again, the water tugging at her body, then releasing her with a reluctant plop so that she tripped over a tangle of weeds and fell chin first into a piece of driftwood. A moment of intense pain, the light darkening around her, and she was up, running along the shore, searching for any connection to the island. A rowboat? A bridge? What kind of crazy-ass place was this?

Where was Oliver? The lake steamed and breathed, but nothing broke its surface. On the island, Holly screamed again and dashed forward, stopping within feet of the water. She howled, an indescribable anguish, like an animal, and as if in answer Oliver's head broke the lake's surface and gasped air blindly before sinking once more.

"Oliver!" Laney shouted, scrambled for her phone, and where was the ambulance? What kind of Podunk end-of-the-earth place took this long to send responders? She dialed 911 and got a new dispatcher, had to start from the beginning, but didn't finish because now a figure, a woman, had emerged from the house and was racing toward Holly. Laney yelled out a warning.

Too late.

44

Holly

WHEN VERA SEIZED Holly's wrist and wrenched her arm, pulling her toward the house, Holly's breath stopped from pain. The shoulder muscles damaged at the block party flamed with agony. Her body sagged, her legs moving with Vera's to slacken the tension.

Once she could breathe again, Holly turned, her attention having one point of focus, and that was the spot in the lake where she last saw Oliver's mouth gulping for air. Fear engulfed her, shallowed her breathing, forced sweat from her pores. She tried to walk forward, and Vera jerked her again, pointing at the house.

With a grinding cry, Holly, whose every molecule strained toward that awful, still part of the lake, wrested herself free and ran. Vera followed, stretched for her, and this time Holly pushed her with her good arm, pushed again, a third time, until Vera tripped and tumbled onto the lawn, smashing her head against a rock.

Holly paused at the sight of dark blood marring Vera's perfect skin, then with another groan darted to the lake and dove. She swam, an uneven crawl, one arm dragging while the other did the work. Oliver had foundered at about the halfway point between the shores. The water was warm in the top two inches, gelid underneath; it took her breath away.

"If only you were so motivated when I was drowning." Abigail wasn't swimming so much as floating alongside, all long tawny hair and champagne skin, water droplets beading on her forehead and cheeks.

Holly didn't waste breath answering.

"Did you secretly want me to die? Oh, be quiet. I can hear your thoughts, dummy. I know you were a child. But you were a good swimmer. Look at you go now. With no food in how long? A day? And your shoulder sprained? So what was wrong with me? Why didn't you save me?"

Holly couldn't see a thing, swimming as if by radar, her eyes blinded with tears and murky lake. She heard a splash, not one of her own, and changed direction toward it.

"You're right, you couldn't have saved me. I breathed in water before your feet were even wet. I know that. I know you know that. I'm just joshing you, anyway. He's over there. See? That's right, just a bit more that way. He's alive. I can feel him fighting."

She slowed and listened, then filled her lungs with air and dove, kicking down, down, down, arm sweeping. Weeds, darting fish, something hard and inanimate. She pushed upward, gasped in a lungful, and dove a second time. Fish, fish, fish, something sharp. Upward again, another gasp.

Her eyes open, her own breathing deafening and harsh in her ears, she treaded water. A sickening horror descended upon her.

CHAPTER

45

Laney

LANEY DIALED 911 again, and this time the dispatcher said yes, yes, we know, they're less than five minutes away, the GPS coordinates were off, nobody even knows of that house, they're coming.

"They'll need a boat," Laney said.

"They always have one for calls like this."

In the middle of the lake, Holly's sleek head bobbed on the glossy water, then disappeared again. She'd gone diving three or four times, and each time she surfaced alone, Laney's chest hurt more.

On the island, a man she thought was Step emerged from the house and limped toward Vera, who had gotten to her feet and faced Laney. Another figure—with a start, Laney recognized Mona's unruly hair—sprinted out of the house and together with Step tried to drag Vera away, but she fought them. Only when Step grabbed her and squeezed her to himself, his head against her head, chest to chest, thigh to thigh, as if caught midtango, did she stop struggling.

A tremendous splash drew Laney's attention back to the lake, and there were two heads now, Holly's and Oliver's. They floated for a few seconds, then sank out of view.

And finally, finally! A siren neared and an EMS vehicle materialized on the overgrown dirt road, followed by a patrol car, an ambulance, a fire chief's SUV trailering an inflatable motorboat, and somewhere behind, a second patrol car.

"There!" Laney pointed.

A man and a woman raced out of the EMS vehicle, toeing off their shoes before jumping into the water.

Seconds after this, Holly's head popped up again. By then, the first paramedic had reached her and plunged out of view.

"Did you call this in?" Two cops had approached her, squinting against the haze.

The second paramedic had Holly, was guiding her to shore; and then the first one reappeared, arms wrapped around Oliver.

Once on shore, Holly collapsed to the sand. On her knees, she watched as Oliver was dragged to a patch of grass, the EMS team kneeling over him, shielding him.

"Okay," said cop number one to Laney. "What happened here?"

"Hold on." Laney crouched next to Holly. She put her hands on her friend's arms, tried to look her in the eye. Her pupils were pinpricks, the irises unnatural, like golden glass marbles.

"Holly?"

"They are poisoning children," she said.

The patrolmen exchanged glances.

"Are you okay?" Laney asked, which was a stupid question. Holly was obviously far from okay, even though she nodded, not taking her eyes from the group surrounding Oliver.

Laney straightened but held on to Holly's hand, as if the woman were a child. She then told the cops everything—about the Volkins, last week's shooting, the disappearing teens, the runaway boy she was investigating. Throughout the telling, her thumb swept gently over Holly's palm,

"I believe they kept her against her will," she finished, indicating Holly. "And I believe they are running a trafficking operation from that house."

The paramedics hefted Oliver to a gurney, and Laney felt better once an oxygen mask obscured his face. You don't put an oxygen mask on a dead man. Holly, who had waved off efforts to take her vitals, struggled upright, and the original two patrolmen plus the two from the second car stepped closer.

"The Volkins?" Laney asked her.

But Holly didn't appear to hear, was walking toward the ambulance, asking to get in, to be with Oliver. Before the doors closed, she said to Laney, "They're there now. They were trying to get everyone out but didn't have time." She wiped her forehead, leaving a trail of lake grit behind. "I think they killed people in there."

"You saw this?" First Cop asked. He'd come up behind Laney, listening.

"I saw very sick children there. Very, very sick."

"They are still in the house?"

Holly nodded, the paramedics shut the door, and the ambulance began a tortuous exit backward through the dense vegetation.

Laney, four cops, a firefighter, and one paramedic looked at the house. The house was quiet.

"Aren't you going in there?" the paramedic asked one of the cops. He might have been only a few years older than Alfie.

Laney sighed along with the police officers. Real life wasn't like television, and cops often had to follow the same rules as vampires—they had to be allowed into a residence, either by a resident or a warrant.

Unless . . .

"I hear screaming," Laney said. There was no screaming.

First Cop gave her a confused look, but Second Cop nodded. "Yeah, me too. I hear screaming."

The other two caught on. "Yeah, sounds bad. Let's go."

A few minutes later the fire chief's motorboat was in the water and the cops were puttering toward the island.

"I don't hear a thing," the paramedic said.

"Don't you?" asked Laney, then relented. "Emergency exception. If a police officer hears a crime being committed, the emergency exception can be used to enter the premises."

When the paramedic looked even more confused, she said, "Her telling them of a crime committed is not enough. If it weren't for the screaming, they'd have to get a warrant, and even that might be hard with only one person's testimony."

"But there was no screaming," the young man said.

Laney rolled her eyes. "Wasn't there?"

And only then did understanding flood the man's face, along with a fierce blush.

"Yeah," he said. "Got it."

The men were on the other side now, two beginning a slow reconnaissance of the island's perimeter while the others neared the building. Cautiously, they entered, their forms vanishing into darkness.

CHAPTER

46

Laney

LANEY COULD NO longer see what the cops were doing on the island, so she paced. Twenty steps along the shore, turn, twenty paces back. After three laps, she gave up and got into her car. There was nothing for her to do, and the police wouldn't tell her anything anyway, not even as a courtesy. If only some of what she suspected was true, the entire island and everything on it was a crime scene.

It took some maneuvering to turn around and edge past the other vehicles, but she did, and then she was driving away, the gravel pinging off her tires, the light dim and green underneath the trees. As she neared the fork that would take her toward the paved road, she thought she heard a voice calling out and stopped, listened.

Going right would take her down another dirt lane and then home.

On the left, the gravel path narrowed and twined, curving back toward the lake. All was silence. She was about to put her foot on the gas pedal once more when she heard the voice again. It was a cry, sharp and panicked, with a shading of pain underneath. As if pulled by a string, she spun her wheel left and drove slowly into the viridian dark. Sound seemed muffled here. Creeping along the trail, she peered between the thick pines at the brilliant water, white-bright against the umber trunks. The path meandered, sometimes sloping down, so she drove almost on the shoreline, sometimes snaking into the disordered woods. Whoever had called out earlier was quiet or had moved off, but she now felt committed to this path. Whenever she could see the house, she stopped and used the binoculars she kept in her glove compartment to study it.

What did they do in there? What had Holly seen? She became so absorbed in scrutinizing it she didn't notice the girl running past the car until a spray of gravel shot from under the girl's foot and hit the rear bumper, startling her. Laney glanced toward the sound and saw a flash of flaxen hair, a raw elbow, a sneakered foot before the person they belonged to vanished.

"Hey!" Laney jumped out of her car and ran toward the sound of breaking twigs. Was that Mona? "Hey!" She yelled louder, as if that would stop the girl. Branches flipped at her face, scratching, barely missed her eyes, but she chased the flicker of blue jeans and blond hair. It was definitely Mona Powell.

Something heavy crashed behind her, and she was so jittery she nearly bolted into a tree. A boy sprawled before her, crumpled face-down in the slippery moss and leaves, and behind him another one, thin, shaking, holding onto a vine with both hands to stay upright.

She lifted her hands, palms out. "It's okay," she said. The standing boy was crying, silent tears streaking through the filth covering his face and hair. "What's your name?" she asked.

The boy said nothing, but neither did he try to run away from her, and she slowly approached his fallen friend and lowered herself to one knee, feeling for a pulse. There was a pulse.

"There's help just around the corner," she said, withdrawing her phone, keeping her eyes on the standing boy. "I'm going to call, okay? You stay right here, got it?"

Again, the boy neither acknowledged her words nor moved, but stood, a visible trembling traveling from his knees to his face and down again, like a wave.

"Jesus," Laney muttered, and dialed 911 for the fourth time that day.

"Did you come from that house?" She placed her palm against the forehead of the boy on the ground. He was burning up.

The standing boy nodded.

She asked again, "What's your name?"

"Bubba." His voice was soft, a whisper.

Often, when she found herself on the trail of a missing person or within reach of solving something, her heart doubled its rhythm, sending blood to her face and neck. She peered at him. The pictures his mother had shown were of a lanky teen, spotty, with hair shaved at the sides and back, floppy on top. The kid in front of her was easily twenty pounds lighter, and the haircut had grown out, but the same hazel eyes stared out of bruised sockets, and the mouth, full, with a slightly asymmetrical upper lip, was the same as well.

"I'm Laney. Did you boys swim over? You must be pretty good swimmers." She couldn't imagine the prone kid sitting, much less making his way through a cold body of water.

"We didn't swim," Bubba whispered.

"What?"

But he didn't finish whatever he was about to say, because the young paramedic had pulled up behind Laney's car and was tearing his way through the underbrush, medical bag in hand.

"Ambulance is coming," he said. "But I'll probably have to drive them out to the clearing back a ways. The ambulance won't make it here."

As he knelt by the boy, Laney rose to her feet and walked over to Bubba. From what she could see, the only thing keeping him upright was his death grip on the vine.

"Bubba? How did you get here from the house? Is there a boat?"

He shook his head.

"Bubba? Tell me how you got here."

Another shiver took him so hard she heard his teeth chatter. Even from a foot away, she could feel the fever steaming off his skin. "Did you fly?"

He shook his head.

"That was a rhetorical question." She wrapped her arm around his middle and gently guided his hand away from the vine and over her shoulders. His weight, when he leaned on her, was unwieldy but light. He must be only a few pounds heavier than her. "How old are you, Bubba?"

"Eight-t-t-t . . ."

"Eighteen?"

He nodded.

"How did you get here from the house? Is there anybody still there?"

"Tunnel," he said.

"What?"

"Tunnel."

She halted. Of course. Of course, there would be a tunnel. She fumbled for her phone, dropped it, realized poor Bubba would topple if she bent to retrieve it, and continued to the EMT's car, placing the boy in the back seat. He collapsed sideways, eyes closed, breath shallow.

Retracing her steps, she almost missed her phone, but saw it just as the young EMT stumbled out of a birch copse, the other boy draped over his shoulder.

She called 911 again and asked the dispatcher to tell the cops on the island what she'd just found out, then set out on foot, following the very obvious trail of churned mud the two boys (and Mona?) left behind them.

A heap of fallen trees camouflaged the tunnel, though from a certain angle, access to it was wide and clear. The soil leading up to it was tamped down and hard.

Laney, who still, four years out of the NYPD, carried a flashlight in her pocket and handcuffs in her glove compartment, shined a cone of light into the opening. The tunnel sloped down sharply, with rough steps half-carved into the descent and half nature made of roots and rocks. It looked dark, slippery, and generally like a good way to break a bone.

"Hey!" she called out.

Nothing.

She shouldn't go in alone.

She glanced back at the birches and pines hiding her car from view.

Then she went in alone. Because what if there were other children in there, ones who hadn't had the strength to climb out? Because she could help. Because she was a curious motherfucker, and because when had anyone ever helped or hurt her more than she had hurt herself? She'd be fine alone.

The tunnel was colder than she expected. Raw, with slippery stones for a floor, and an odor of animal waste. She imagined the lake's full weight above her and almost hotfooted it out but pressed on at the thought of more sick kids ahead.

What the hell was wrong with people? Why did they have to torture and maim each other? She didn't so much miss being a cop at that moment as miss the authority it used to give her to set things right.

She tripped and pitched chin first into a boulder, her jaw clacking shut so hard she saw stars. Her chin, already bruised from her earlier fall, now gushed blood, the pain like acid on her skin. A curse died on her lips as the flashlight skittered across the floor, glancing its light off a body huddled against the curved wall. Once the blinding pain in her face calmed to a throb, she felt for her light and stood, illuminating the girl.

It took all of Laney's self-control to keep from yelping. She guessed the girl had been exposed to the same chemicals as the teenager found the other day near Sylvan. Her skin was blistered, peeling and meaty, her breathing labored, her eyes unfocused. She'd been lying on her side—half her clothes were soaked and rank—and it was her flung-out hand that had caused Laney's fall. Now the girl struggled into a seated position, though that seemed to use all her remaining strength.

"Can you stand?" Laney asked.

The girl stared at her, mouth working. A dark bubble formed in the corner of her mouth.

"Shit." Laney checked whether her phone had a charge (it did) and reception (nope), then put her flashlight into the girl's hands. "You hold on, okay? I'll be right back." She knelt and touched the girl's sticky hair. "What's your name?"

Nothing again.

Laney looked up. Ahead was the house and cops, the option to summon help. Maybe more kids stuck in the tunnel. Behind was a long-ass climb, a rough trail, and eventually, help.

"You sit tight, yeah? I won't be long." She hoped.

Laney turned forward and began jogging toward the house, using her phone's light to guide her way. Time fell away. Her sense of space fell away. It was just her breathing and this damp dark all around her, until it was only on three sides of her and she'd nearly walked right into a wall.

A dead end. She turned around. She hadn't noticed any forks or splits in the tunnel. Forcing herself to slow down, she retraced her steps until the girl's shape appeared again out of the shadows. She was lying on the floor, immobile.

Laney cursed and spun on her heels. This time she walked with one hand sliding along the wall and the other pointed at the opposite wall. Within a hundred feet she saw a door and put her ear to it.

She could, of course, simply open this door and walk into whatever waited on the other side. But she was trained better than that. She took a breath and knocked loudly, rapping her knuckles on the wood, then shouted, "Hello! Anybody there?"

Yet again, silence was her answer.

Laney braced herself, took a breath, and shoved her shoulder into the door, which gave, splintered, and swung open. A freshness wafted over her, air from above, not much, but enough so she knew it would lead her out. She stepped over the threshold and immediately had to navigate a tight turn, which opened onto a set of steps leading up.

The wooden staircase, though worn in parts, seemed to have been repaired recently and held her weight without complaint. As she ascended, she became aware of footsteps above her, and soon, voices, which told her she was directly underneath the lake house now. She picked up speed, eager to come out into light, when her foot hit something.

A body.

Oliver strapped down with needles and wires. An orderly had come by some minutes ago, drawing curtains around their condensed square of space, and although this afforded a measure of privacy, it did nothing to block out sound.

Someone was raving in a curtained-off square next to them— unintelligible words that sounded like prayers sometimes and curses other times. It was both ceaseless and variable and therefore impossible to tune out.

She scooted closer to the gurney and leaned against it. She'd refused medical attention of any kind and was now feeling the rest of the poison leave her system. Bouts of shivering gripped her, stopping only for waves of nausea. Her head hurt.

"I guess we're even now," she said quietly, not looking at her husband.

As soon as the words left her mouth, the energy between them changed, as if a vacuum opened. He jerked the mask off his face and turned his head toward her.

"Look at me," he said. His voice was low, thick, as hollow as if he were speaking from inside a cave. "I said, look at me. I only have one question for you, and you must answer with the truth."

She nodded and swallowed back a sick, bitter taste.

"Do you want to stay married to me?"

It was not the question she expected. "Yes."

"No, not like that. Think. I want to see that it's the truth. It doesn't sound like the truth. It sounds like you don't want an argument."

She opened her mouth, but illness shook her, and she had to jump, knocking her chair over, and run to the nearest bathroom (thankfully unoccupied), where she retched until she was empty, cold, and more tired than she'd ever been in her life. After washing her face with watery hospital soap and rinsing her mouth, she returned to their curtained space.

Before she even drew the chair up, she said, "I want to stay married to you."

He'd been sunk into the pillows, and at her words he sagged even more, as if he were a defrosted lump of dough released from a mold. He nodded. "Okay, then."

CHAPTER

47

Holly

Holly sat on a hard plastic chair next to Oliver in gency room. He lay on a gurney, his sopping-we dripping onto her knees and then the floor, an oxyg strapped to his face and his eyes closed. She held his ha in a while, his fingers squeezed hers, and every time they wept.

"Oh, baby, don't cry!" A nurse who must have been (i pushing eighty rubbed Holly's back as if she really were "Your man is gonna be fine! He just had himself a fainti underwater." She checked the monitors over the gurney. more often than you think."

Holly started. "Excuse me?"

"Uh-huh. At least five or six every summer. There wa brought in just last week. Went swimming in a crowded la fainted. It's a good thing someone was right next to him it happened. Sometimes it's a real tragedy. Happens a lo teenagers."

The nurse noted something on the computer and smi Holly. "He'll be fine. You're lucky."

They were waiting for test results or a bed, Holly co remember which. The gurney had been pushed into a co

She sat down again. "Is it what you want?"

"I want you. Only you. Only ever you."

"Not only ever."

He looked at her with his sepia eyes. "Maybe not when you were a tween. That would have been weird. Don't you think?"

"That would have been weird."

"Holly." He'd lowered his voice, and she had to lean close, prop her slight body on his shoulder, her ear near his mouth. "I don't have a job anymore. I know they will sue us. It's possible the FBI will be involved because of who . . . who . . ."

She didn't think she could feel more horrible, but, amazingly, she did.

He continued, "In any case, I'm nearly certain they won't be able to pin anything on you. Or on me. I did what I could."

Sitting back, she covered her eyes with her hands.

"Listen," he said.

The harshness in his tone startled her, and she lowered her arms, forced herself to meet his eyes.

"If you mean this. If you mean that you want to be with me, we will be okay. We can fight this, and we will be all right."

"I mean it. Oliver. I never . . . I didn't . . . I didn't cheat on you."

He looked away. "No."

"But if we have to fight a court case, we will probably lose our house."

"I never liked that house."

"Did you know?"

"About the money? Not until last week."

"And you still . . ."

"Love you? Holly, I know why you did it. Why you did all of it. I hate that you didn't think you could talk to me. I hate that this is where we are because of it. I hate that you didn't trust me or love me enough. But I can't hate you. And I can't not love you." He closed his eyes. "Let's stop for now. Okay?"

She nodded and scooted closer so she could place her head on the gurney again. She was too spent to think anymore, and her mind, though not fully lucid, was at least no longer bristling with panic.

A fitful dream state enveloped her, and she drifted, aware of the gurney's stern metal against her chest, of the emergency room's smells, the ranter behind the curtain. So, when the activity level around them increased, she noticed, but incorporated it into her reveries as a storm with rustling and breaking trees, thunder and lightning. Only when someone began to shout did she jerk awake and twitch the curtain aside.

The ER was crowded. Cops and paramedics, nurses, order-lies, doctors were moving, rushing, oscillating in a choreographed dance around a series of stretchers and gurneys, though Holly could see nothing of who was on them. Two were hurried along a hall, leaking dark blood, smearing it on the linoleum. One was moved to the side and a curtain drawn around it. The fourth was parked in the middle as nurses and doctors bent over it and con-sulted each other. When they stepped aside, she saw a small hand hanging off the edge, grimy with dried blood.

"Who is that?" she asked, doubting herself, recognizing the profile anyway.

"Shooting victim," said a nurse. "We don't get a lot of those here. Apparently, there was a shoot-out in some house in the woods." She shuddered.

"Is she dead?"

The nurse glanced at Holly, as if only now realizing she was speaking to either a patient or a patient's relative.

"I don't know, honey," the nurse said, though the lack of urgency around the gurney told Holly everything she needed.

48

Laney

L ANEY STUMBLED AND grabbed for the railing with one hand and flailed with her other, her phone skittering loose, then fell forward into a man's shoulder.

The man screamed, and she scrambled off, had to descend to retrieve her phone, which was still shining a cone of white light into a wall. When she turned the light upward, Step Volkin's tortured face glared at her.

He hunkered sideways on the stairs, one arm supporting his weight, one leg stretched out, and his skin ghastly white. His jeans were black from hip to knee, a damp, heavy darkness she understood was blood.

"Motherfucker," said Laney. The word bubbled up through her fury at his (probable) attempt on her and her son's life, through her disgust at what he'd done to so many people. And mixed in was a feeling of triumph. She'd found him. She had him. She was not letting him go.

More running and loud voices came from above, his body a barrier between her and the door directly behind him. She cursed herself for not grabbing her handcuffs out of her glove compartment. They'd been in her car for so long, never used, that she hardly thought of them. Well, at least she'd worn a belt today.

Quickly, she unbuckled the canvas belt holding up her jeans and drew it out one-handed, the other hand still aiming the phone into his eyes.

"What are you going to do, whip me?" His mouth was bleeding.

"If I have to," she said.

A gunshot cracked above them, sudden, loud, echoing.

He sat up straight, gasping as he did so, squaring against her. She turned off her phone's light and slid it into her pocket. She'd need both hands now.

With a sharp intake of breath, she launched herself forward and up, hands out, knees bent. Her palms connected with his arms, and she used that to propel her head upward sharply, knocking her forehead into where she figured the middle of his face would be. She miscalculated, crashing into his jaw, but her weight drove him back and he yowled with pain even as his arms rose to shove her away. But she wasn't letting go, kneed him in the chest, belly, anywhere she could reach while he struggled to get enough distance for a punch. He got in a solid blow to her cheek, but she'd been in fights before. She could handle the hurt. She now knew exactly where his nose was, and this time when she headbutted him, it crunched, the connection as gratifying as hitting a goal into the net. He made a strangled, suffocated noise, and his fingers clawed into her arms.

Which was fortunate, since that put his wrists within easy reach. She breathed in, and on the outward breath twisted sideways and threw the looped end of her belt over his left wrist, then wrenched in the other direction and coiled the rest of the belt around his right wrist and cinched. He jerked his arm to release it, but she kneed him in the hip with all her weight behind the move, and this time he screamed—a loud, agonized howl that reverberated in her guts, his distress palpable.

She drew the belt tighter, around and around, finishing with a knot; then felt along the rail until she found the top edge and jerked his weakened arms up, hooking the belt around the edge and yanking it down so he was pinned to the railing.

He wheezed, a distraught whining to his breath he tried to suppress. She shot to her feet and bolted over him before he got his wind back. Her hand reached for the door handle and she opened what she hoped was the last door in this infernal subterranean maze.

It wasn't. She'd exited into a basement, cement floor, stone walls, damp and rot, but with small casement windows along the ceiling allowing a spill of daylight. On the opposite end stood a thick, metal door, and when Laney tried to pull or push it open, it didn't budge. She knocked and yelled, her voice swallowed by the walls around her.

Her phone's battery was at twenty percent, thank God, and she dialed 911 yet again, waiting impatiently as the call struggled to connect and then dropped. She knocked and screamed, tried her phone once more. In the house she heard running and loud voices, though the thick stone walls made it hard to decipher the words. She was standing against the doorframe, eyeing the casement windows, when the footsteps neared and suddenly the metal clanged, a lock snicked, and the door smashed inward.

Laney jumped back just as Vera Volkin rushed into the room and pushed the door closed, drawing the heavy bolt across the threshold and snapping shut the heavy padlock hanging through the bolt.

Vera stared at Laney with wide, blue eyes, her face blank with surprise.

Laney backed up and pressed her body against the tunnel entrance.

"Out," said Vera.

"No."

"Get the *fuck* out of my way." Vera strode forward, and Laney noticed the wet stain under her rib. Blood.

Laney put her hand up, palm out. "No."

On the other side of the steel door, running and a crash into the metal. It shuddered. The bolt held.

Vera ran at Laney, but Laney was ready. They grappled, and Laney tripped the other woman. They slammed to the floor, the fall's force knocking air out of both of them.

More crashing on the other side, organized this time.

Laney gripped Vera's wrists and pinned them against the floor as she writhed and kicked beneath her.

"Stop," Laney said. "It's over. Stop."

But Vera turned her head and bit Laney's forearm. Her surprisingly sharp teeth tore skin and penetrated, provoking a bellow from Laney, her arm a hot, burning flare of misery. She let go and Vera threw her off, clambering to her knees.

One more concerted boom rang out and the steel door burst from its hinges, the bolt lock unbroken and hanging off the rotted frame.

The four cops who had gone into the house over an hour ago barreled into the room, guns up, screaming for them to get to the ground.

Laney threw her hands up and dropped to her knees, just as Vera ran past her to the tunnel door. An officer beat her to it.

She made no sound as he knocked her facedown to the dirt and wrung her arms behind her back, the only sign of his emotion the fact that it took him three tries to handcuff her.

All four cops turned their eyes on Laney, recognition and suspicion twisting their mouths.

"There's a tunnel," Laney said. "Through that door. Step Volkin is on the stairs, and there's a very hurt female in the tunnel itself. Teenage, looks like chemical burns to her skin. She'll need help getting out."

Two of the officers stared at her for a moment, then nodded and carefully opened the door, shining their torches into the dark void.

The third officer said something to the fourth and squeezed past the hanging steel door back toward the rest of the house.

Laney, still on her knees and her arms up, looked at the fourth cop, then at Vera. Vera had turned her face so that one cheek lay in the dirt, her smooth, perfect skin grimy, her breathing heavy. "He's on the stairs?" she asked.

Laney nodded.

Vera's eyes closed and her mouth thinned.

"I told you it was over," Laney said, and lowered her arms, sat back onto her butt, extending her legs in front. Her arm throbbed, and she pressed it against her middle. "You could have saved us some hurt if you listened."

Vera opened her eyes, swollen now, red. "I told him I'd buy him time. I told him to get away."

"Well, if you wanted him to get away, maybe you shouldn't have shot him in the ass. Just sayin'."

Vera's mouth twisted. "He was going to kill that idiot Oliver. How else could I stop him?" She breathed out, color draining from her face. Breathed in. Then, "He'd never killed anyone." She turned her face to the wall. "His soul was clean."

"News flash," Laney said, "not so clean. He tried to kill me and my son, and I saw the kids that escaped from here. Looks to me like he didn't mind if they died."

"All me," Vera said. "Our agreement."

Laney bent forward. "What are you talking about? What agreement?"

Vera was quiet. When she spoke next, her voice was thin, faraway sounding. "It's different. Taking a life versus letting a person choose a path. The kids chose a path."

Laney scoffed. "You've got to be kidding me. That's splitting hairs."

"He has faith." Wheeze. "He believes in God." Wheeze. "Not splitting hairs if you believe in God."

"You're crazy. You're telling me you shot your husband to make sure he gets to heaven? You're insane."

Vera sucked in a long breath, held it. Her back twitched as she exhaled. "It was our agreement."

Laney looked up at the cop standing in the doorway. He was the youngest of the bunch, still fit, his uniform loose under the gear on his belt.

"What happened?" she asked. "Up there?"

He blinked and his cheeks reddened.

"You shot her, didn't you?"

The flush spread to his nose and forehead. "I saw"—he cleared his throat—"she was injecting a girl. She didn't stop when told to stop. She—" He was nearly crying, and she felt a stab of empathy. This was one aspect of law enforcement she didn't miss. "I thought she was going to stick one of us. She ran at me with the—" He stopped again.

Laney nodded. "And the victim?" She meant the girl the cop stopped Vera from injecting. She was losing track of the victims in this mess.

The cop shook his head, his eyes as red as his face now. "I don't know," he said. "Emergency Services is on the way."

"May I?" She gestured at Vera.

He shrugged, uncertain, and she took that as assent. She inched toward her adversary and bent, then touched her neck. Vera's skin was cool and clammy, her pulse faint. Laney felt wetness under her knees, and when she looked down, she saw she was kneeling in Vera's blood. A widening pool of it.

A roar of motors neared the house, and she got to her feet.

"I'm gonna—" She pointed at the broken metal door, and the cop shrugged again.

Yet another set of stairs took her to an airy kitchen, and she walked through it toward a spacious and now filthy parlor, which opened out to a porch and then the sloping lawn she'd last seen from the mainland.

Three emergency boats were nearing the island, and she stood back to let the paramedics rush up the stairs, followed by more police and Crime Scene.

Over the next hour she watched seven stretchers carried out and placed on the boats, then ferried across and deposited into waiting ambulances. At some point, the coroner's white van emerged from the foliage on the mainland's shore.

"He's gone," said a voice behind her, startling her.

She turned to see one of the older officers who'd gone into the tunnel an hour ago. "What?"

"We found the female with the chemical burns, but not the guy."

"You're kidding me."

He narrowed his eyes at her.

"I tied him to the railing."

He looked out at the glittering water. "Well, I guess he untied himself. What did you use?"

She felt the criticism like a burn and didn't answer. The tunnel had at least one misleading passageway she knew of; she'd gotten lost herself. It was hard to imagine Step untangling himself and descending those stairs, then hiding, as hurt as he was. But obviously that was what he'd done.

"He's going to come out one of the exits eventually," she said. She didn't ask if they'd plant patrol to wait for him. It wasn't her place to ask.

The officer grunted and turned on his heel, leaving her to her thoughts.

CHAPTER

49

Laney

LANEY FOLDED SHORTS, polo shirts, a few T-shirts, and a swim-suit into her duffel bag. Then she took a pretty summer dress off its hanger and folded that in too, and a khaki pencil skirt. Then she took them out. Then she shoved them in again and a second dress to boot.

Then she stomped her foot and stormed out of her room and across the hall into Alfie's room.

"Are you done packing?" she asked.

Alfie was lying on his bed, earphones on, iPad propped against his knee. He eyeballed her, took off his headphones, and pointed to his own duffel bag, zippered and neatly stood at the foot of his bed.

"You packed your swim trunks? Sunblock? Deodorant?"

He rolled his eyes and then glared at her. Yes, he was right. They were going for only three days, and she was overthinking the whole thing. And it wasn't like they were going to another planet but only to the Jersey shore, where the Boswell family owned a beach house and the Boswell brothers took turns staying during the summer months.

"Should we not go?" she asked.

He sighed and put his headphones back on.

She sat down next to him, and he sighed again and took them off again. She said, "Do you want to go?"

"Mom."

"I mean, if you think you want to rest up before school starts, I get it."

"Mom."

"I'll text Jack and tell him we can't go."

"I want to go."

She chewed her lip. "Yes, of course. We haven't been on a vacation in years. Never mind me." She headed for the door.

"Mom."

From the hallway, she stopped and looked at him. His expression was strange, and she realized it was because it was so adult. In that moment he wasn't her teenage boy, a week away from his junior year in high school, but someone grown and clever.

He said, "It's okay."

"What's okay?"

"I like Jack."

Well, that was something.

Back in her room, she stuffed a lace-trimmed blouse into her bag, then opened a dresser drawer. Inside was a small perfume box, an exorbitantly expensive one she bought for herself when her divorce came through—on the advice of her lawyer—and never opened. A beat of hesitation, and she unfolded the cardboard, slid out the cut-glass bottle, and tipped a bead of the scent onto her fingers. It smelled expensive.

Oh, what the hell. She put it back in its box and buried it inside her duffel bag.

The invitation to the beach house had come a week ago, two days after the raid at the lake. She'd been at work, writing her final report on Bubba Gardner, her soul feeling light and clear. The boy was undernourished and hospitalized, but he was alive and, according to his mother, on the way to recovery. He and the boy with whom he escaped were talking to detectives, reporters, the FBI. Anybody who asked got an earful. Experiments with calorie restriction, medication, injections. They didn't know what was done to them, had been half out of their minds for two-thirds of the time. But whatever they couldn't name, their bodies told.

The girl, the one Laney had found in the tunnel, was worse, still not speaking. The first one to escape, the one with the blistered skin, Alyssa, had regained consciousness only the day before, and if she had anything to say, Laney didn't know it.

Because the case spanned three separate regions, Sylvan, Havencrest (where Sunny River was even now being dismantled), and the Catskills, getting the full story was taking time. Throw in the backers of Calypso Technologies and that the alleged traffickers might owe allegiance to a different country, and the FBI entered the picture.

What started as a bizarre incident at a block party had onion-skinned itself to expose a dark and far-reaching organization, of which Step and Vera Volkin were only a small unit. Vera had died on the way to the hospital, and her body was still at the coroner's. Five victims had been rescued from the house, though only two of them were in any condition to speak to investigators.

Step, Mona, and at least eighteen young men and women who had lived at the lake house—at least according to Bubba—vanished, spirited away in dark vans on that last day or gone through the tunnel.

Laney wondered if Step had crawled (she couldn't imagine him walking in his state) down the stairs and hidden in one of the tunnel's false passageways. Had he waited and then slithered along its dirt floor until he emerged into the nighttime woods? Or was there another passage? Another exit? She didn't know, and from various silences surrounding the case, she believed none of the agencies handling it knew either.

She finished typing her report, uploaded it and the photographs she'd taken of Bubba in the forest and later at the hospital. She didn't upload the one of Bubba's mother holding him across her chest like a Renaissance Madonna, but she had it printed and taped to the wall of her cubicle.

She was about to open the file for her next case when Jack placed his elbows atop her cube separator and peered at her computer screen.

"Yes?" she asked.

"Do you have plans tonight?"

"For what?"

He stared at her, nonplussed. "Erm . . . I was thinking sushi."

And still she was confused. "You were thinking sushi? About what?"

He lowered his eyes as a flush inched up his cheeks. "Laney, I'm asking you out to dinner."

"Oh." She looked back at her screen. Everything about this was not good. He was a colleague. He was the boss's son. He was god-awfully handsome. And where had dating handsome men gotten her? Divorced and eighty thousand dollars in credit card debt, that's where. Divorced and alone.

"No," she said.

Jack slid around the edge of the cube and sat on a chair, then wheeled himself into her orbit. "Why?"

"We work together."

"I like you."

"You're the boss's kid."

"I know you like me."

"I don't like you."

"I think you do."

He was right. She liked him. She'd liked him from the very beginning, even when she thought she didn't. He was good at his job, and he was honest in a way none of the men she'd been close to had ever been. True, he'd held things back from her, just as she'd from him. But there was an earnestness in him that spoke of a fundamental decency.

"I'm a lot older and I have a teenager."

"It's just sushi."

But then it wasn't just sushi. The dinner turned out fun, a lovely evening by the Hudson, the food fresh and delicious. He had a sense of humor—a droll cleverness that made her guffaw into her beer.

"I like the way you laugh," he said, after they'd both downed two large Sapporos.

They had to Uber to their respective homes, and the next day he asked if she'd like to go to the beach for the weekend.

"I don't like leaving Alfie," she countered, buttoned up again, on alert.

"I wouldn't want you to. Bring him. There are four bedrooms. More than enough. He can bring a friend."

And that was what led to her duffel bag and the two pretty summer dresses plus a pencil skirt and the very expensive perfume on the inside of her wrist.

But really, she was just going for a few days, and only because why not, and not at all because this could lead to anything.

She was fine alone. Better than fine. She didn't need Jack Boswell.

"I'm going to write Jack and tell him we won't be going," she yelled out into the hallway.

"Mom," Alfie said from his room.

50

November: Laney

I N THE DARKENED auditorium, a medley of big-band jazz and
Broadway musicals bopped and thumped against the old walls,
and Laney unbuttoned her sweater. A few hundred parents and
siblings generated a humid heat that hung in a mist above everyone's heads, shimmering to the music's beat.

Laney, who only ever listened to rock and alternative, found
herself enjoying the high school concert more than she expected.
But then, she wasn't there for the songs. Alfie was hard to miss,
towering over the other boys, his thick curls adding at least an
extra five inches to his height. He'd had two sax solos already and,
according to the printed program, was to play a piece on the piano
later (not that he ever shared that information with her ahead of
time). To her, his musical ability seemed like magic, supernatural
in its complete difference from her own skills.

For about three weeks in August, after the raid on the lake
house and Mona's disappearance, he stopped playing his instru-
ments. Laney tried talking to him about it, would ask him to play
for her, but he'd shake his head and close his door. Or leave for a
bike ride and not come back for hours.

One night, over bowls of lo mein and fried wontons, she asked
Alfie point-blank why he stopped playing music.

"I thought you loved it," she said. "What's going on?"

He put down his fork and looked at his noodles, his shoulders hunched. Then he said—slowly, as if figuring out his thoughts as he spoke them—"When I play, I forget about everything. I don't want to forget Mona." He rubbed his eyes. "I'm afraid to forget her."

Laney nodded. "Makes sense."

He raised his eyes at her. "Do you think she forgot about me?"

"Not a chance in hell."

"Do you think I'll ever see her again?"

"Stranger things have happened." She put an extra wonton into his bowl. "Don't deny yourself something you love, okay? Just don't."

He nodded.

Even so, it was another two weeks before he picked up his sax, and not until school started did he turn on his keyboard.

In the auditorium, her phone vibrated. She didn't look at it. Wouldn't look at it. It vibrated again. Then, five minutes later, again.

She looked.

I'm sorry, read the text from Jack. *I got held up at work.*

She turned off the phone. Their weekend at the beach had been nice because she loved the beach and there'd been a preposterous number of cocktails. There was one moment on the boardwalk, when the light had turned cobalt—sky, surf, sand, everything washed in blue—and Jack leaned against the railing next to her, so close their arms touched. A blaze of desire engulfed her and she felt her lips, her skin, her throat melting with it, and right behind came terror.

"What?" Jack asked, softly, uncertain.

Unable to speak, she turned on her heel and ran away. She ran the length of the boardwalk, all three miles of it, in her flip-flops, then veered onto the sand and into the now dark ocean, rooting herself into the sand as the waves crashed against her. The cold strength of it sobered her and cleansed her of both yearning and dread.

At work the week after, and for the next three months, she was polite, friendly. She bought him an occasional lunch, met him for a drink here and there, but more often than not she told him she was busy. Hell, she *was* busy. Made sure she was busy. She had her own cases, worked all hours, then wrote the reports, etc., etc. When she couldn't plead work, she said, oh, Alfie needs me to drive him here or there. Rehearsals. Sleepovers. Boy Scout trips. There was no limit to the blocks she could put between them.

Tonight, though, tonight Jack was meant to be at the school. Had promised he'd be there for her, for her boy.

Despite her best efforts, she had been looking forward to seeing him, even though she'd already seen him at work earlier. She'd dressed up. Daubed on lipstick and a coat of mascara.

The concert ended on a raucous rendition of "Ode to Joy," and Laney made her way outside to wait for Alfie, where the other families also waited, fanning their flushed faces and catching up with the latest gossip.

A light touch on her shoulder startled her—the tension in her muscles ingrained after years on the job—and she spun, only to face Holly, the out-of-context jumpiness making them laugh. She hadn't seen Holly in months, and the sight of her, neat and carefully packaged in a mauve jacket and plum-colored jeans, opened something in her chest, as if allowing her to fully breathe in. She'd missed their easy conversations, the way she never felt she had to try.

"Hey," Laney said. "What are you doing here?"

"Oh, my cousin's kids are in the band." Holly rubbed Laney's shoulder, a light, gentle gesture. "Alfie was great! He's such a sweet boy."

Laney nodded. Somehow, they'd never really sifted through the summer's events. Despite several texts trying to arrange a lunch date or cocktails, their lives continued on separate tracks, diverging further and further from each other.

"How are you doing?" Laney asked.

Holly's face tightened around her eyes and mouth. "Oh, you know," she said.

Laney, never being one for small talk, looked away, as if searching the crowd for her son.

"Hol, we're going!" called out a large man behind them.

Holly smiled at Laney and put her arms around her. "I miss you," she said into Laney's ear, then pulled back and held her hands. "Stay in touch."

Laney nodded again. *Stay in touch.* It was what people said to each other when they had no intention of doing it.

"I mean it," Holly said.

"Okay."

Enveloped within her extended family, Holly Dubois melted away, and Laney remained in front of the school alone as the other families thinned and dispersed.

At last, Alfie loped out of the building, told her he was going to get pizza in town with his friends, and handed her his saxophone case.

"Have fun," she said. "Do you need money?"

"I'm good," he said, already disappearing into a small, churning crowd of boys that locomoted amoeba-style across the parking lot and onto Main Street.

She looked around. She'd lived in Sylvan for almost five years now, and in all those years the only true friend she'd made was Holly Dubois. Oh, Laney knew her neighbors, of course. The other Boy Scout parents, sure. Enough to say hello, how are ya, how's the kid (because even if she remembered the parents' names, she often forgot the children's).

In three years she will be forty, and Alfie will be living away at college. And just like that, she'll be on her own again, the world a vast and troubled danger zone surrounding her.

She walked home along the dark and chilled streets, the saxophone case swinging at her thighs. Behind curtains, other families watched television or sat at dining room tables. One house was having a party, and a group of people had spilled onto the frozen front lawn, laughing.

At home, she turned on her phone and opened a bottle of ale. Three more texts from Jack.

Hey, she typed. *I'm home. What are you doing?*

The answering dots danced for a full ten minutes, long enough for her to finish her first beer and pour a second.

Can I come over? he asked.

She pretended to herself that she was thinking about it, then typed, *Yeah.*

He brought a six-pack and a bag of pretzels, and they sat on opposite ends of the couch with the bowl of pretzels between them. In the dim lighting he was all angles and dark hollows, his spare figure sideways, one ankle under his thigh, his long arm thrown across the backs of the cushions.

Her fourth drink put her over the edge, and she moved the bowl of pretzels to the coffee table and inched toward him. He was warm. It was the first time she'd been that close to him since those minutes on the boardwalk, the first time that close to anyone since her divorce. She lifted her face and his lips were on her, desire sweeping through her, shaking her so that her breath caught in her throat. She couldn't get enough of him, of his skin, had to draw his shirt up so she could press her hands against his sides, his shoulders.

He grabbed her around her waist, tumbling her onto her back, and suddenly she couldn't breathe at all, as if an iron hand squeezed around her throat. She pushed and pushed at him and finally he responded, sitting back with his hair disheveled and his pupils large and dark.

"What?" he asked.

But she sprang from the couch and ran to the bathroom, locking herself in. It took fifteen minutes and a great deal of cold water on her face before she opened the door and came out.

He was sitting in the kitchen, checking his phone. He'd smoothed his hair and rearranged his clothes.

"I'm sorry," she said.

"Laney."

"No, really. I don't know what happened."

"Laney."

She sat down. "What."

"What do you want with me?"

She sighed and put her hands over her eyes.

"Look at me." He sounded hurt.

She lowered her hands. "I never told you about my ex."

"No."

"I loved him. Like crazy loved him. Like I think there was more crazy than love, actually. And turns out he never loved me back. I just kind of wished our marriage into being, but it was a fantasy." She leaned forward. "What I'm saying is that I have no idea how to translate my feelings. The last time I felt this way, it turned out I was really, really wrong about everything."

The corner of his mouth quirked. "So, you're saying you're crazy in love with me?"

She sat back. No, she wasn't saying that at all. God forbid. What was she saying? "I think what I mean is, all the people I've ever trusted betrayed me."

He shrugged. "It happens."

"I don't want it to happen to me."

"I'm not the betraying kind."

"I don't know that."

He sat up straight. "Do you want me to leave you alone? It's okay. It won't be a problem at work."

"No."

He rose to his feet, walked into the living room, and brought back the remaining three bottles, opened two of them, and handed one to Laney.

"Tell you what," he said. "We don't really know each other, right?"

"No."

"And it looks like your one and only BFF has other things on her plate."

"Yes."

"So how about I become your BFF for a while? I could use a BFF myself."

"Stop saying BFF."

"What do BFFs do, anyway? Do you go get your nails done together?"

Laney rolled her eyes.

"Do you go shopping?"

"I hate shopping."

"Well, no wonder you're all alone on a Friday night."

"Hey!"

"All right, pretend I'm Holly. What do we do?"

She took a healthy glug of beer. "We drink and talk about stuff."

"Well, I'm pretty good at drinking and talking about stuff."

"She knew all the town news."

"My brother is a detective, and my cousin is a lawyer. I know all the town news and then some."

She guffawed. "Okay. You got the job. For how long?"

He drank the rest of his beer and opened the last bottle. "I guess until one of us gets bored or the other one decides to give sex a chance."

The word sparked and sizzled between them.

"It's a deal," she said.

51

November: Holly

Holly poured more wine into her glass and topped off Oliver's. The children had scattered for the evening like billiard balls, one to each corner of the carriage house—Freddie and Hannah on their phones and Kiki curled into a sweaty, sleepy ball on the couch, Buster draped over his knees.

The carriage house belonged to one of Holly's cousins, a lawyer who lived in the master house on the same lot. His tenant had moved out at the end of the summer, and since the Dubois family was technically homeless, he'd offered them the cottage. Three months on, they were still there, their house undergoing structural renovation.

It was a tight fit, the five of them squished into two bedrooms and a living room, with Hannah bunking in the tiny attic.

Although the cousin had little experience in corporate espionage law, between him and the rest of Holly's family, a veritable wall of defense erected around her.

"Did you steal the stuff?" her cousin had asked, and before she could answer, said, "Never mind, don't tell me. Haha. In any case, these kinds of things are very hard to prove. What do they have on you? Nothing. One video of a woman with long hair and a baseball cap. Could be anybody. Could be my neighbor across the street. They have even less on Oliver. I'm telling you, you should sue for your job back. No? Too bad. You'd win."

Oliver didn't want to sue for his job back.

"I heard from the contractor," Holly said. The wine wasn't sitting well with her, but she drank it anyway. "They'll be done next week."

"I heard from the people in Vancouver."

Holly tipped the rest of the wine into her glass and downed it like medicine. "Okay," she said. What else could she say? The odor of espionage clung to Oliver even if, as her cousin put it, they had nothing on him. The only company that responded to his job query was headquartered in British Columbia. She had never been away from her family, from this town. The thought filled her with terror.

Oliver reached for her hand. "It won't be forever."

She said nothing.

He said, "You don't have to come with me. I'll pay the bills here if you choose to stay."

She pushed aside her glass, stood, walked around the kitchen table, and straddled him. Then she put her arms around his thick shoulders and leaned her head against his head. "Abigail always said I was too timid. She said I never wanted to do anything."

He pulled her close and ran his hands up her back, down, untucked her sweater, and back up, but this time underneath, on her skin. She said, "I've always thought that if I'd taken that acid tab she offered me, then she wouldn't have had it with her and she wouldn't have gone into the water high."

He stopped rubbing her back, held still, held his breath. They never spoke about Abigail's death. Almost never spoke about her at all.

"Or if I hadn't been afraid to run into the water as soon as I saw her in trouble, I would have saved her. But I felt self-conscious. Can you imagine? I worried someone would think I was inelegant." She pressed her cheek against his neck and breathed him in. "We're going to lose the house, Oliver. After we pay the contractor and the legal fees, there'll be nothing left."

He began stroking her hair again. "Does that mean you'll come with me?"

She snorted into his neck. "Do you really want me to?"

"I'd be pretty sad up there alone."

"Oh, I don't know. I hear there's good fishing."

"I don't fish."

"Hiking."

"Not a fan."

"Craft beers?"

"Okay, there's that."

They sat in silence until he moved her so he could look at her. "You're my family. I want you with me. I want my children with me."

"Well, then we'll all go."

"I'm not going to Vancouver!" came an angst-filled preteen cry from the living room.

Holly turned toward the voice. "You can stay with Uncle Adam."

"I'm not staying with Uncle Adam!"

"Vancouver or Uncle Adam."

"No!"

"Vancouver or Uncle Adam."

An outraged silence followed.

"Oliver," Holly said, keeping her voice so low that he had to tug her nearer. But she had no words for what she felt, so she said nothing.

She didn't know how she would live without her brothers and cousins and aunts and uncles around her. Except for college and right now, she'd never lived in a house other than the one they were about to put on the market. Sylvan was her home. It was where Abigail was buried, where her parents would be laid to rest soon enough.

"It's like I've lived in a castle all my life," she said. "And never left it. It's a beautiful castle, filled with people I love. But in this castle, even the dead don't ever leave. I've walked step in step with my sister for twenty years, keeping her tied to myself when all she ever wanted was to get away. I know every stone, every window, every dungeon. And it's all I know."

"So, you're saying it's time to lower the drawbridge?"

"Something like that."

"There be dragons," Oliver said.

"Plenty dragons here too," Holly said.

After that night, everything moved quickly. Oliver accepted the job in Vancouver and began the visa paperwork for himself and the rest of the family. He left within two weeks, flew home for Thanksgiving at her parents', then back to Vancouver, the rest of them set to follow the day after Christmas.

Holly packed, made last-minute doctor appointments, school appointments, lunch and brunch and dinner appointments with everyone she'd be leaving behind. Her publisher had dropped her, so there was no rush to start writing again, even if her brain had been able to produce. Which it hadn't.

She moved through her days in a blank state, forcing thoughts down and away. She'd have time to think later, after the children were settled, after the apartment they were to rent had curtains. She was neither happy nor unhappy, and whenever the old heaviness rolled over her, she'd tuck Buster under her arm and take him for a walk.

Early mornings often found her at the town lake. Only then, with the air still dark and the birds quiet, did she mourn all over again. In a way she could never explain to herself, much less to anyone else, losing Vera tore her soul almost as much as losing Abigail. True, she didn't go mental the way she did when she was twelve, but the same feelings of guilt, of opportunity lost, of an inability to rescue tormented her. She understood that Vera had researched her history and played to it, played up the similarity in looks. What Vera never knew was how truly similar to Abigail she was, playacting or not.

All thoughts in this direction made Holly want to howl, and she would stand up, walk briskly, report neighborhood and family gossip to Buster. When it was an acceptably polite time, she'd text her friends, her cousins, her aunts and uncles and parents, and so the day would begin for her, with every second of every hour filled to the brim and then some.

A week after Thanksgiving, she visited Adam. His illness had paused, and a hint of color bloomed in his face. She handed him an envelope, a little money she'd squirreled away just for him. For the kids, she said. For Christmas.

He looked at the envelope without taking it, sighed, and drew her in, wrapping his arms around her.

"Please," he said. "Don't. You don't have to do this. We love you."

She held the money awkwardly, but he squeezed her harder and she nodded, stuffed it into her pocket.

Maybe in January, after everything settled, she would find a therapist. She promised herself that this time she'd talk about everything. All of it. Well . . . maybe not the part where she broke the law. She'd probably need to keep that to herself. But everything else—she would pour it all out. That or the loony bin once and for all for her. She felt it in her bones—the need to be done with the grief and the guilt before it ground her to nothing.

As with every motivation in her life, it was the need to save and protect her family that guided her in this decision. Except this time, she knew it was herself she needed to fix. For their sake, she could do it. For them, she could do anything.

ACKNOWLEDGMENTS

Foremost, enormous gratitude to my agent, Paula Munier, who championed this book before it was a book. Your trust in me gave me the necessary fuel to keep going. And thank you for always responding to my questions with speed, knowledge, and humor. I couldn't have asked for a better guardian to shepherd me through publication.

Huge thank you to Terri Bischoff and Matt Martz at Crooked Lane Books for providing such an amazing home for my books. I'm thrilled with the level of attention and care my stories have received from your team.

And speaking of crackerjack teams! Thank you to Melissa Rechter and Rebecca Nelson for your hard work and scrupulous attention to detail. Thank you, Madeline Rathle, for your tireless efforts to get my books and me noticed and reviewed and doing it all with superb professionalism.

Thank you again to Emily Beth Rapoport for a great edit. This novel is much stronger for it. And thank you to Nicole Lecht for a gorgeous cover.

Heartfelt thank you to the wonderful authors who took the time to read my early drafts: Nancy Bilyeau, Jason Allison, Brenda McQueen Neil, Christopher Ryan, and V. S. Kemanis. Your enthusiasm and insights made this whole writing thing feel like a party.

Diane DiGiacomo gave me much-needed medical advice and explained how group homes work. Thank you for accepting that my characters are real people to me and discussing their insanities during our many, many walks.

Boris Klebanov did a stupendous job explaining biomedical research and the path medication takes from lab to pharmacies.

Keith Allison told me what cops can and cannot do and walked me through all sorts of random procedural details. I'm sure I still got a lot wrong, and that is all on me.

I wrote many chapters and character studies with the River Writers Circle at the Patisserie Didier Dumas, and I deeply appreciate the magic that came from this writing group. You will be missed. Donna Miele, thank you for leading it with such warmth and kindness.

I must thank my wonderful neighbors for providing such awesome fodder with our massive block parties. You are NOT in this book! But the party is. If there's any detail about the book that seems improbable, the one that's completely real is the block party. Well, minus the shooting and arson.

At its core, this novel is about family, and I am incredibly lucky to have a deeply loving and supportive one. Keith and Ian, I can't imagine life without you, and for you I would do anything. My cousins on both sides of the Atlantic are my cheerleaders extraordinaire, and I appreciate all your support: Nelly, Galya, Leo, Boris, Toly, and Alex.

My mother, Galina Naymark, passed away during the writing of this novel. Of all people in my life, she has influenced me and my direction the most. She gave me my love of books and encouraged my curiosity about everything. She supported my choices absolutely and made me believe I could succeed at anything. But above all, she believed in putting family first, and that is one ideal I inherited from her. The character of Holly DuBois is not based on my mother, but she has my mother's unshakable devotion to her family. May the earth rest lightly on you.